BEFORE

I LET

YOU

GO

KELLY RIMMER

BEFORE
I LET
YOU
GO

GRAYDON
HOUSE

GRAYDON HOUSE

Recycling programs for this product may not exist in your area.

ISBN-13: 978-1-525-82084-7

Before I Let You Go

Copyright © 2018 by Lantana Management Pty Ltd

For questions and comments about the quality of this book, please contact us at CustomerService@Harlequin.com.

BookClubbish.com

Printed in U.S.A.

In memory of Gregory Prior

BEFORE

I LET

YOU

GO

1

LEXIE

When my landline rings at 2:00 a.m. on a Thursday morning, I know who's at the other end of the line before I pick it up. Only one person in my life would call at that hour; the same person who wouldn't hesitate to ask for something after two years of silence, the same person who wouldn't give a single thought to the fact that I need to be at work by 8:00 a.m.

As I bring the handset to my ear, I brace myself for the one thing that contact with my little sister has brought me in recent years.

Chaos.

"Annie?"

"Lexie," Annie's voice breaks on a sob, "you have to help me—I think I'm dying."

I sit up and push my hair out of my face. My fiancé, Sam, had been asleep on the bed beside me, but he sits up, too. I glance at him and see sleepy confusion cross his face. As a physician, I periodically have late-night calls regarding patient emergencies, but never via the landline. I've moved houses twice since I last spoke to Annie, but I've always made sure the same number followed me, just in case she wanted or needed to reconnect.

Now, here she is—and just like I always feared, she's calling me because she's got an emergency on her hands.

"What's going on?" I ask.

"My head hurts so much and nothing helps the pain. I'm seeing double and my feet are swollen and…"

They are troubling symptoms, but as Annie speaks I recognize the slur that indicates she is high. Frustration floods me, and I sigh impatiently.

You're thirty now, Annie. Are you ever going to grow up?

"Go to the hospital," I say. I feel Sam stiffen on the bed beside me at the hard edge of my tone. He's never heard me speak like that, and I turn toward him again, an apology in my gaze. It hurts me to be cold with Annie, it even hurts to recognize how only seconds into this phone call I'm already boiling up inside with impatience and frustration toward her. This is my baby sister. This is the same kid I shared a room with for our entire childhood, the same sweet nine-year-old who used to beg me to play "mommies and daddies" with her after our dad died.

But I've been dealing with her addiction for years, and even after a two-year break from the drama, the weariness returns as soon as she does. If this was a one-off, I'd probably panic and rush to her aid—but it's not. I have lost count of Annie's desperate 2:00 a.m. phone calls. I couldn't even tally the times she has gotten herself into a hopeless situation and called me to find her a solution.

"Lexie, I can't," Annie chokes now. I wait, expecting some long-winded story about not having health insurance or having a warrant out for her arrest or something simpler like not even having a car, or having woken up from a binge to find herself lost.

When the silence stretches, I know I need to end the call. I try to push the phone call to its inevitable conclusion as I prompt her, "Well?"

"Lexie, I'm pregnant. I can't go to the hospital. I just can't."

I've been a GP for several years—I thought my poker face was pretty good, but I'm not prepared for this. I gasp and feel Sam's gentle arm snake around my waist. He rests his chin on my shoulder, then presses a soft kiss against my cheek.

My first instinct is to assume Annie is lying. It wouldn't be the first time, although she generally lies only for some financial or pharmaceutical payoff. The last vestiges of sleep clear from my brain and I quickly consider the situation. There is something different about this scenario. Annie isn't asking me for money. She is asking for help.

"If you're pregnant then those symptoms are even more troubling. You *need* to get to a hospital."

Annie speaks again, her voice stronger and clearer. She is determined to make me understand, and there's no way I can ignore her plea.

"If I go to the hospital, I'll fail the drug test. I just *can't*."

I slide my legs over the edge of the bed, straighten my posture and take a deep breath. I'm immediately resigned to what this call is going to mean. Annie is back—this peaceful period of my life is over.

"Tell me where you are."

Sam tries to convince me that there are smarter ways to approach this situation than jumping in the car myself.

"Just think about it for a second," he says quietly. "This is the same sister who nearly got you fired two years ago, right?"

I bristle at his pointed tone, and I'm scowling as I reply, "She needs me, Sam."

"She *needs* medical help. And even if we go there right now, the best we can probably do for her is to call an ambulance anyway. So why don't we just do that in the first place?"

"Because her situation is complicated and they won't understand. If I go to her, I can talk sense into her. I *know* I can."

There's a hint of impatience in his eyes as he scans my face in the semidarkness, but then he sighs and throws back the covers on the bed.

"What are you doing?"

I frown at him, and he walks briskly toward the wardrobe as he mutters, "I'm not letting you go to some trailer park by yourself at three o'clock in the morning."

"But you have surgery all day tomorrow, Sam. This isn't your problem."

"Lexie, your problems *are* my problem now. I'll be fine, and if I'm not, I'll postpone the surgeries. If you're going, I'm going, so either call an ambulance and get back into bed or let's go."

So I let him come with me, but even as he drives across the city, I feel anxiety grinding in my gut. Sam knows only the basics about Annie's issues. He's been supportive and understanding, but at the end of the day, he's from one of those "old money" northeastern families; the biggest scandal in his entire lineage is his parents' somewhat amicable divorce. And now, four months after our engagement, here he is looking for an obscure trailer park in the middle of the night, to give medical care to my pregnant, drug-addicted sister.

He hasn't ever met Mom, and I'm not sure he ever will. I haven't seen her myself for almost two decades—not since the day of my sixteenth birthday, when I walked out of the strict religious sect she moved Annie and me into after Dad's death. We speak on the phone from time to time, despite that being against the rules of her community—since Annie and I turned our back on the sect, we're dead to them. I hate calling her because I usually hang up feeling lonely. A call to Mom is like telephoning another planet. She's so disconnected from my world, and I have completely rejected hers.

I try to keep an open mind as we drive. I don't want to think the worst of Annie, but it seems like her situation has gone from bad to worse over the past two years. I think of her every day—

but in my thoughts, she has lived a much healthier life than the one I fear I'm about to see. It was the only way I'd been able to deal with throwing her out of my house two years ago. I imagined that she was working somewhere—maybe writing again—maybe she has a nice little apartment, like the one she had in Chicago after she graduated. I pictured her dating and going out with friends and shopping for clothes at little boutiques. Annie always had such a beautiful sense of style, back when she cared about how she looked.

It's well after 3:00 a.m. when we find the place. It's an older-style trailer, and even in the semidarkness of the trailer park, there is no denying that Annie is somewhere near rock bottom. The trailer is falling to bits—one side is dented, as if it's been in some kind of car accident, and there's black tape holding a panel in place. There is an awning at the front, but the support beneath it is damaged, too, so one corner of the roof leans down toward the ground. Trash cans are stacked against it, each overflowing with waste so that a scattered carpet of filth rests over the ground beneath the awning. There's a narrow path through that trash right to the front door, and inside the trailer, the soft yellow glow of a light beckons. As soon as the car pulls to a stop beside the awning I reach for the door handle, but before I can open it, Sam takes my other hand in his.

"If things are too messed up in there, we're calling an ambulance and going home. Okay?"

"She's harmless, Sam," I promise him. "Annie is only a danger to herself."

"I trust you," he says. "That's why we're here. But there's only so much we are going to be able to do for her without a hospital. If she has preeclampsia, we'll need to force her to go. Right?"

"I know," I say on a sigh. "Let's just play it by ear, okay?"

As we walk toward the trailer, Sam walks so close to me that I can feel his breath on the back of my neck. The door swings slowly open and then Annie is there.

Once upon a time, I was so jealous of her beautiful blond hair and her bright blue eyes, and those delicate, elfin features. The woman who stands before me now is nothing more than a shadow of my beautiful sister. The blond hair is now wiry and thin and hangs around her face in matted tendrils. Her eyes are sunken, her skin sallow; and through her parted lips I see the telltale black marks of rot on the edges of her front teeth. My eyes drift downward, and I take in the jutting ball of her bump—a horrifying contrast to her otherwise skeletal frame.

I'm not seeing my sister—I'm seeing a wasteland after war. If I wasn't so desperate to help her I might turn away and sob.

"Thanks for coming," Annie says. Now that I can actually see her, I identify a quality in her voice that had eluded me over the phone. Yes, she is weary. Yes, she is scared. Yes, she is tired…but more than all that, Annie is broken. She has called me because she had exhausted all other options.

I climb up the stairs and duck to step inside Annie's trailer. I see the unmade bed, the old-style TV, the vinyl-clad table. Every single surface is littered with trash, but there are piles of books haphazardly stacked among the mess. Annie was an English major. She worked for a children's book publisher and she had some short stories published in magazines. At one stage, she was even working on a book of her own. It's heartbreaking to see the books in this place—the one throwback to the life she has lost.

"Who is this?" Annie asks, and she nods toward Sam. He is a big man, a broad man, and he looks so cramped in this tiny trailer. He has to bow his head to stand. As I look between Sam and Annie, I can barely believe that *both* of these people are now technically my family. They couldn't be more different.

"This is Sam," I murmur. "He's my fiancé. He's a doctor, too."

"Of course he is." Annie sinks onto the bed and shoots me a withering look. "Only the best for our Lexie."

"Do you want help, or not?" Sam says, before I can respond. Rather than feeling pleased for his automatic defense of me, I feel instant and bewildering irritation. Annie is startled by his short tone. Her gaze snaps from my face to his, and then color floods her starkly white cheeks until she looks feverish.

She doesn't answer Sam—instead, she rubs her belly gently with her palms and she lifts her legs up onto the bed. My gaze zeros in on her monstrously bloated feet; swollen to nearly double their normal size, the skin pitted around her ankles. I was already nervous for Annie—but my heart sinks at the sight of those feet. I scan my eyes over her body and survey her belly.

"How many months?" I ask. It's difficult to assess how far into the pregnancy she is because her bump is tiny, but then again, so is she. I'm collating a mental catalog of what I know of heroin use in pregnancy, assuming that's the drug she still favors. If she's been using for the whole pregnancy, the baby's growth may have suffered.

"I think I'm due soon," Annie says. "I haven't seen a doctor."

"Not at *all*?" I wince as the judgmental words leave my mouth to hang in the room between us. Annie's eyes plead with me to understand—as if I could, as if there is *any* excuse for what she's just told me. After a fraught pause, she shakes her head, and a tear drains out of the corner of her eye to run over her weathered cheek. She wraps her arms around her bump protectively, but when she looks at me, her guilt is palpable.

I approach the bed and motion toward Sam, indicating that he should pass me the medical kit he's carrying. His hand descends upon my shoulder, and he gently steers me toward the cracked vinyl chair that runs alongside the small dining table.

"I'll assess her," he says. His tone is gentle, but the words are firm. I shake my head, and Sam's gaze sharpens. "She's your sister. You need to let me do this."

I open my mouth to protest, but Sam isn't going to back down, so I sigh and sit slowly. At the last minute, the urge to care for Annie myself surges again and I straighten and shake my head.

"She *is* my sister, Sam," I say. "That's *why* I should be the one to assess her."

Sam doesn't budge, and his gaze doesn't waver.

"You know as well as I do that you're too close. You can't possibly make an impartial assessment here—your judgment will be clouded." Sam's gaze becomes pleading. "Lexie, *please.* Let me do this."

I sit, but as I do, my fingers twitch against my thighs and my foot taps against the floor of the trailer. The urge to take charge is so great that even my body is revolting. I've never been good at sitting back when a problem needed solving—particularly not when it came to my family. The only thing that stops me from pushing him aside and reviewing her condition myself is that he's right— I'm far too close to this situation to remain objective. Besides, this *is* Sam, the person I trust more than anyone else in the world.

He sits on the bed beside Annie and withdraws a digital blood pressure machine from his pack. After he fixes it to her arm, he offers her a reassuring smile.

"Can you tell us a bit about what's going on?"

"I started getting headaches last week, but they're getting worse. Tonight I couldn't see…everything was doubled and blurry."

Sam leans over and palpates Annie's belly, then picks up his stethoscope and listens near her belly button. After a moment or two I see his shoulders relax just a little, and I know he's found a heartbeat. He continues listening, and I'm desperate to know how stable the rhythm is.

"How long have your feet been like that?" I ask Annie.

"Maybe a week? I'm not sure…" The digital machine beeps several times to indicate a problem. I lean forward and am not surprised to see the numbers flash on the screen: 160/120. Annie and the baby are definitely in trouble. I fumble for my phone— do I call an ambulance? Sam doesn't seem to be panicking, and perhaps I wouldn't be either if Annie were a patient who had walked into my office, but right now I'm simply a terrified sister.

"Has the baby been moving, Annie?" Sam asks as he rises away from her belly.

"I think so...?"

Sam turns to stare at me. Our eyes lock.

"Annie," I say gently. "We have to get you to a hospital. Now."

"Lexie, I can't," Annie chokes. "My friend failed a drug test last year and they took her baby. Her son went into foster care, and she never got him back. I *can't* let that happen to my baby. I just can't."

I want to point out the dozens of reasons why she shouldn't be allowed to bring a baby home to this place at all, especially given her current state of mind. The mess of her life could not be more evident, but those shockingly high numbers on the BP machine are burned into the forefront of my thoughts. Annie needs urgent medical attention. This is not the time to lecture her about her addiction or her suitability as a parent. This is the time to persuade her, and I have to tread lightly.

But despite this, I know that Annie is probably right about the drug test. If she fails a narcotics test, it's quite likely she'll be charged with chemically endangering a child—and that's a felony in Alabama. I've never had it happen to a patient personally, but I've heard of several cases in the media.

We'll cross that bridge when we come to it—the immediate need is to get her to a hospital to push anti-hypertension drugs into her system to bring her blood pressure down. Plus, that baby needs urgent monitoring—proper monitoring, not the very limited heart-rate check we can do here—and if we don't move fast, there might not even be a baby to save. I don't want to tell Annie this—in part because I don't want to stress her further and push her blood pressure even higher. But if explaining the immediate threat to her baby's health is off the table, I don't know *what* I'll say to convince her. I'm relieved when Sam rescues me.

"Annie, I know this is hard. But your condition is very poor, and the baby is in serious danger. There is only so much Lexie and I can do for you here. We'll take you to my hospital, and I promise you—you'll get the very best medical care possible."

"But I'll be arrested," Annie says. She wraps her arms around her belly again and shakes her head. "I can't. I just can't."

"I *won't* let that happen," I promise her. I have no idea if that's true, but I'm so desperate that I'll say pretty much anything to get her to the hospital. Annie slowly raises her eyes toward me. There is both fear and hope in her gaze—but suddenly I don't see her haggard appearance or the pitiful trailer.

I just see my baby sister—the little girl who used to see the world as a place of wonder, a child of limitless creativity and potential. I see her sitting frozen under the tree in our front yard, holding my hand with a death grip as we watched the procession of mourners stream into our house after Dad's funeral—trusting me to take care of her, just as I'd always promised Dad I would.

I see the child who faced our childhood with courage, the child with a simple optimism and faith that we'd make it through together. I see the girl with an innate sense of fairness who rallied and fought against the rules of our strict childhood home, and then the determined young woman who marched right on out of there when she could take it no longer.

Creativity, passion, courage, optimism—in this moment, I see only the essence of who Annie *really* is. Suddenly she is not an addict or a potential criminal, not even a somewhat negligent soon-to-be mother—she is simply my Annie, and she is sick, and she needs my support.

Maybe *this* is the moment when it all turns around.

"You promise it will be okay?" she chokes.

I lean over and I take her hand in mine, and I squeeze it hard. Is this going to haunt me? Perhaps—but I can imagine a worse fate.

"I *promise* you."

2

ANNIE

To Luke:

You told me to write the things I can't say, so here I'm sitting in my room with a pen in my hand. I haven't written in years, and I can't believe I'm writing in this *journal. It's the only possession I've ever kept for more than a year or two. This notebook has been sacred to me, right from the day I got it—the best day of my life, May 28, 1993.*

It was the day before summer break and the whole school had shuffled into the auditorium for the end-of-year awards ceremony. I saw Dad as soon as I stepped through the door. He had such a presence about him—he was tall and strong, with thick blond hair and that huge smile he wore whenever he saw us. I knew that he must be there for Lexie—she always won an end-of-year award. Mom taught second grade, so she was always at the presentation, but this was the first year Dad turned up. I figured Lexie must have done something quite extraordinary to warrant him missing a shift, and I was excited to see what it was.

I kept glancing over my shoulder to look for Dad at the back of the room with the other parents, and if I angled my head just right, I could see him beaming toward the stage. Even now, if I close my eyes, I can still picture him like that—the proud, expectant smile on his face—his clean-shaven jaw strong and his blue eyes sparkling. After a while, Dad saw me peeking at him and he gave me a wave and a grin.

Lexie won her usual academic achievement award, and I clapped so hard that my palms stung. When she was on stage accepting it, she looked down at my class and she beamed right at me. I was so proud of her—I don't think it even occurred to me to be jealous.

And then something completely and beautifully unexpected happened. The principal announced that this year there was a new prize that had been arranged for a uniquely gifted student. I assumed it would be an award for Lexie—everyone knew she was the smartest kid in school, and she was going to middle school the following year so it made sense for them to honor her one last time. But then the principal said the right last name, but the wrong first name.

Annie Vidler.

I waited for him to correct himself. My teacher came toward me in a crouch and waved at me to go toward the stage, and I gave her a confused glance. Why would I win a special award? The only unique thing about me was that Lexie Vidler was my sister.

By the time I got to the podium, I was dizzy with confusion and embarrassment, and I thought that any second now the principal would realize his mistake and everyone was going to laugh at me for thinking that I might win a prize. But then he shook my hand and he passed me a certificate and said into the microphone, "This award goes to Annie Vidler for extraordinary achievements in creative writing. Annie's poetry and stories have amazed the teaching staff this year, and we felt it important to recognize such an exceptional talent."

And then I looked out at my whole school, somewhere between spellbound and dumbfounded, and I saw that Lexie was on her feet clapping with her hands over her head, and Mom was standing on the side of the room, still beside her class but wiping a tear from her cheek, and even my dad was standing on his chair at the back of the room cheering and clapping. He pumped his fist in the air and I saw him shout, and the applause felt like thunder rolling over me.

Dad carried me home on his shoulders that day. Lexie told me she was jealous that they made an award just for me—for all of her achievements, that had never happened to her. Mom let me pick the restaurant for dinner; I picked Italian because I knew everyone liked it. While we waited for dessert, Dad and Mom gave me a present wrapped in silver foil with a big pink ribbon around it. It was this journal.

"For my future writer," Dad said. "I can't wait to see where your talent takes you, my little love."

That night, Dad tucked me into my bed with the notepad in my arms cuddled close to me like a teddy bear. I remember thinking that my notepad was too precious to use on ordinary words so I'd have to save it until I could come up with a worthy story. It's telling that I'm thirty years old and I've only just written in it today, and only because you suggested it. Maybe the only thing that makes this story special enough for this journal is that I'm clutching at straws. I have tried everything else to get better—maybe this link back to those happier times with Dad has some magical power that methadone maintenance programs and rapid-detox regimens and inpatient rehab centers do not.

The day I got this journal was the very best day of my life, which is pretty pathetic, isn't it? But I do still remember every aspect of it—from the chalky smell of the auditorium, to the feel of Dad's strong shoulders beneath my legs as he carried me home, to the taste of the Parmesan on my spaghetti at dinner. I remember most of all the way that, although he'd swapped his standard day shift to a night shift so he could make it to the assembly and although he really had *to go to work that night, Dad lingered in the room I shared with Lexie after he put us to bed. For the first time, I could see that he was every bit as proud of me as he was of her.*

"Look after your baby sister, huh?" Dad said to Lexie when he finally rose to leave. He often said that to her, ever since they brought me home as a newborn and she was jealous of all the attention I got. You were so cute, Mom used to tell me. We had to convince her that we actually got you just for her so she wasn't jealous. *Long after my cuteness had worn off, the phrase lingered—meaningless, other than a small reminder to us both that as sisters we belonged, in some small way, to each other.*

But that night, as she did every other time Dad said it, Lexie nodded with utmost seriousness, and even after Dad had left the room and I was drifting off to sleep, I heard her say softly, "I'm proud of you, too, Annie."

Those words meant so much, and the day meant so much, and I closed my eyes that night as the happiest seven-year-old in the world.

But although it was a great day, Luke—I actually remember the exact date not because that was the best day, but because the worst days followed.

3

LEXIE

Annie freaks out when Sam tries to call an ambulance, and I calm her by suggesting that we could maybe just drive her. Soon we are making our way to the car, headed for Sam's hospital—and the panic within me gives way to dread. There are closer hospitals, and certainly more suitable options, but he is adamant that she will get the best care with his colleagues. Annie hesitates again when she realizes that Sam works at one of the more upmarket hospitals in the county. Maybe she's worried about the bill. Well, if she is, that makes two of us.

"Can't we just wait until morning and go to Lexie's clinic?" she asks, and I almost wish we could—at least then I could keep her from his workplace.

"You need to be admitted to a proper hospital. My clinic doesn't have the right facilities."

"My hospital," Sam repeats firmly. "It's the best option."

Still, I catch his arm after he helps her into his car and pushes the door closed.

"But she won't have insurance," I whisper somewhat awkwardly.

"It's fine, Lexie. She's family—we'll take care of it," is all he says. I spend the thirty-five-minute drive worrying about how this is going to play out. Sam's parents covered his tuition—but I have hundreds of thousands of dollars of debt between my student loans and the credit cards I used to put Annie through rehab, plus Sam and I *did* just buy the house, and the bill for Annie's treatment could be immense. Maybe Sam will get a staff discount, and Medicaid will surely cover some of it…but even so…this is likely a huge financial undertaking.

I'd have covered her bills myself, probably without even thinking twice about it. But Sam is involved now, and it feels wrong for him to pay for Annie's care. And then there's the potential for untold drama—the last time I let Annie near my clinic, she was caught breaking in one night raiding the meds cabinet, and I almost lost my job over it.

Annie is in the front seat and I'm in the back, so I can't actually talk to Sam about my concerns. We will just have to sort it out later, once the emergency passes and we're sure the baby is fine.

As he drives, Sam calls the obstetrics ward on the Bluetooth car kit and briefs the consultant obstetrician on the situation. I notice the way that he carefully avoids any reference to Annie's addiction, other than a quiet murmur right toward the end of the call, when he simply says, "There is potential for the infant to suffer NAS."

I doubt Annie knows what "NAS" stands for, but *I* know: neonatal abstinence syndrome. It's a cruel start to life—all of the physical symptoms of opiate withdrawal, crammed and compressed into a tiny newborn's body. I saw a few cases during the obstetrics rotation of residency. I watched those little babies shake and scream for hours on end, until they'd sweated through their clothing and vomited up every drop of milk in their stomachs. We treat NAS in much the same way that we treat heroin withdrawals—with gradually decreasing doses of opiates—but it's a very difficult condition to manage. There's nothing worse in the world than watching a brand-new baby writhe in an agony that could have been avoided.

I'm about to welcome a new niece or nephew who will have one of the worst possible starts to life. There is only one upside to this situation: most NAS babies come through the awful early weeks relatively unscathed. Long-term outcomes are usually good, as long as the baby goes home to a stable environment. I stare at Annie, sitting in the front seat quietly weeping, and wonder if there is *any* chance of that happening in this case. What kind of upbringing can she offer this baby? And who else is there to support this child? Where is the father? Is my sister's entire support network *me*?

When we reach the hospital, Sam parks in his staff parking spot and turns to me.

"I'm going to get Annie a wheelchair. Can you please wait with her?"

When Sam leaves the car, Annie finally speaks.

"I've really fucked things up this time, haven't I?"

"You need to stay calm, Annie."

"I tried, Lexie, I *promise* you."

"Does Mom know about the baby?" I ask. Annie shakes her head. "Can I tell her? Or do you want to? We can call her in the morning."

"No, I don't want to worry her—I'll get clean first, then we can call her... I just need to get my shit together..."

Annie's voice is starting to wobble, and I realize this isn't the time to have this conversation, so I let the subject drop. We sit in silence for a while, other than the lingering echoes of her sporadic sobs.

"Sam seems nice," she says eventually.

"Sam is wonderful." I look out the window to see him approaching us with the wheelchair. "Wait here a second?"

Before she can respond, I slide out and shut the door behind myself. Sam parks the wheelchair beside Annie's door and stares at me over the roof of the car.

"Are you okay?" Sam asks me. His eyes are bloodshot and there are already bags hanging beneath them. He won't be operating today, which means that five or six patients will have to wait for their surgery. Sam is a general surgeon; these were unlikely to be lifesaving or critical surgeries, but it's still a huge inconvenience. The patients will now have to wait weeks or months for their operations to be rescheduled.

This is what happens whenever Annie reenters my life— things fall to bits, and she's always oblivious to how the effects flow on and on beyond her. It's remarkable how one person's presence can disrupt every little thing that is ordinarily secure. I know it's too late to go somewhere else, but I can't hold back my reluctance to proceed.

"We shouldn't have come here, Sam," I say quietly, keeping my voice low so that Annie will not overhear us. "We should have gone over to Montgomery Public. You don't understand what happens when she's around—she's chaos personified. It's just too risky for her to be in your hospital."

"If she's here, she'll be treated well. The nursing staff will give her extra attention, and there's a high-risk obstetrician I trust implicitly—her name is Eliza Rogers, and I'm going to call her in the morning to ask her to care for Annie personally. Trust me, Lexie, this is for the best. Plus, your clinic is only a few blocks away, and our place is only a twenty-minute drive. She's going to need us."

"Annie doesn't just come into your life and pass through it. She takes prisoners and leaves a trail of destruction."

"Well, whatever happens—we'll handle it together, right?" I hesitate again, and Sam raises his eyebrows at me. "Look— we're just going to have to talk about this later. She needs treatment *now*."

He's right, and I know it. I force my thoughts away as I help

Annie into the wheelchair. For better or worse, she's here now. Sam navigates the wheelchair through a maze of brightly lit hallways, and he's nearing the ward when I finally glance at my sister. I find her staring at the floor, her jaw set hard. Guilt rises as I wonder if she'd heard my conversation with Sam over the roof of the car.

"Are you okay?" I ask her quietly, and she slowly raises her eyes to me and says, "Have I *ever* been okay, Lexie?"

I don't know how to answer, but while I'm fumbling for words, we arrive at the maternity ward. Things begin to move quickly; Annie is sent to give a urine sample and then taken to a private room. A monitoring unit is fitted to her belly, and after several failed attempts by a nurse, the consultant manages to fix an IV into Annie's arm. No one mentions her collapsed veins or the pockmarked scars along her inner elbow. No one says aloud what I know they are thinking—what I'm thinking, although I hate myself for it.

Filthy drug addict.

We are medical professionals. We know addiction is a disease. We know how hard it is to beat, and how hard it is to access treatment around here. Between meth and narcotics, there's an epidemic of addiction in this state and there aren't enough rehab centers. Then there's her pregnancy, which would disqualify her from treatment at all but a handful of rehab centers in the entire country. Annie represents an impossible mix of circumstances that the rehab industry just isn't equipped to deal with. I know this, her doctors know it, her nurses know it.

But we aren't just medical professionals—we are also human beings—and Annie is in a truly terrible state. She's lying on the bed now, but she's restless and she's scratching compulsively around the sores and scabs on her arms and mouth. Every now and again she noisily blows her nose, or dissolves into fits of compulsive sneezing—all symptoms of her body craving the next fix. Even I can't stop an instinctive feeling of *disgust* at the sight of her, and an automatic fury on behalf of the baby who's been dragged along for the chemical ride.

I'm ashamed of that as her sister and as a doctor, but the feeling is as natural as my next breath. I see it in the staff treating her, too. I see it in the way they hesitate for just a second before they touch her, in the silent frowns and narrowed gazes, even in the way their glances flick toward the door again and again as they wait for her to stabilize. I know they want to get out of this room, to move their attention onto more worthy, less uncomfortable patients.

The professional thing to do would be to reserve our judgment. The best we can offer is to judge quietly.

Our training tells us that addiction is a disease, too; a disease with no real cure, a disease that's difficult to treat. But human nature wants to ignore that training, and to pretend it's some kind of moral weakness that has brought Annie to where she is now. Maybe we need to believe she's chosen this life, or that she deserves it somehow, because the alternative is unbearable, unfathomable—even if she is completely blameless, we're still going to be repulsed by her. And besides which, if she's a pregnant drug addict because she's a bad person, then she's not like us: we're *good* people. We could never find ourselves in her position. We are comforted by our sense of smug superiority. It's a security blanket, a shield.

The IV is finally seated in Annie's arm. I crane my neck to see what drug has been prescribed, but I can't make out the label.

"What are you treating her with?"

"You're Ms. Vidler's sister?" The consultant frowns at me as he looks up from his chart, and I frown right back at him.

"I am," I say, then I add, "I'm *Dr.* Alexis Vidler."

"Well, *doctor* or not, I'm not sure you should be in here while we're stabilizing her."

"Please, Ron. Let her stay for support?" Sam intervenes, and the consultant sighs but he nods. I open my mouth to ask again about the drugs they have just added to her IV, and Sam shoots me a pointed look and presses his forefinger to his lips. I watch the clear liquid drip through toward her veins—winding its way down into her body.

Would it be nifedipine? Or labetalol? What dose have they got her on? If it's not high enough, they are just wasting time. What if I don't speak up and they don't get the pressure down quickly enough and what if—

"Can you just tell me how you're planning on treating her?" I blurt, and Sam takes my hand and very gently tugs me toward the door. I plant my feet hard against the vinyl floor and he pulls a little harder. When I resist, he gives me an exasperated look.

"But she's my sister, Sam," I protest fiercely.

Tonight is apparently a night for firsts. I met Sam at a physicians networking event, but I've never once seen him speak to a patient. I imagine that he would use the kind of tone he uses on me now—supportive, but also firm. He's never needed to speak to me that way, and I find it both disarming and irritating.

"Exactly. So if you can't leave them to do their work, you'll need to wait in the hall."

I groan in frustration and snatch my arm away from him, then walk to sit in a chair at the corner of the room. Sam follows me and sits beside me, but he doesn't take my hand.

"Annie," the consultant says quietly, "are you on a maintenance program?"

Annie scowls at him.

"Do I look like I'm on a maintenance program?"

The doctor's expression doesn't change.

"Okay. So can you tell me what your usage is like?"

"My *usage*?" she repeats, and she laughs bitterly.

"Annie," I say gently, and she turns her gaze to me. I see the stain on her cheeks; she's embarrassed to be discussing this with them, and maybe it's worse because I'm in the room. Well, I'm not going anywhere, so she's just going to have to get over it. I prompt her gently, "Please, talk to him. It's really important."

Annie swallows, and her gaze falls to the shape of her feet, hidden now by the hospital blanket. After a minute, she says unevenly, "At least half a gram a day. My last bump was about eight o'clock last night."

"Thank you," the doctor says, and he types into the computer then adds, "I'll need to consult with a specialist, but I think the best option is going to be split-dosed methadone."

"I'm not going on a fucking maintenance program," she snaps, and I sigh and run my hand through my hair. Sam reaches across between the chairs and squeezes my knee gently. I grimace silently at him.

"Given how heavy your use is, it's going to be a very uncomfortable stay if you don't agree to something to prevent the withdrawal, Anne," the consultant says, firmer now. Annie glares at him.

"That's why it's not going to be a *long* stay."

"Annie," I interject quietly. "Will you agree to take some methadone just to get you through the next few hours? Until we can get your blood pressure stable?"

Annie's gaze narrows.

"Can I do that?"

"Of course. You can withdraw your consent for it anytime. But taking it now will ease off the withdrawal symptoms for a while…so the hypertension drugs have some time to work."

"Fine," Annie snaps. "Just this once."

It's always like this with her. The big battle for her sobriety has been a marathon series of much smaller battles that each needed my careful, attentive management and focus. I'd almost forgotten how difficult she can be. In the seconds after Annie agrees to the maintenance drug, I close my eyes for a moment and try to gather myself. Sam releases my knee, but he slides his arm around my shoulders and pulls me gently against him. I feel the brush of his lips against my hair.

"I'm okay," I whisper to him.

"I know," he whispers back.

Sam holds me for a while as we sit and watch the staff work. I glean tiny pieces of information as I eavesdrop; there was some protein in Annie's urine but not a lot—which may mean she has preeclampsia, and she will need to be very closely monitored. She has, inevitably, failed the narcotics test. Annie responds quickly to the anti-hypertension medication and her blood pressure finally levels out, then starts to drop.

They give her a sonogram with a portable machine right there in front of us, but Annie is becoming drowsy from the medication and is only half-awake to see her child on the screen. I watch the shadow of a smile pass her lips as the first image swims into focus. I move closer to the monitor, and while I've seen countless sonography scans in my time, there's something different about this one. The baby's body shape appears, and as I identify its form, it's no longer a fetus. It's my sister's baby; my niece or nephew. For all of her faults, Annie already loves it, and in some bizarre way, I already love it, too—just because it's hers.

The sonographer measures the velocity of the blood passing through the placenta and umbilical cord and then in the baby's brain. The measurements are all within safe ranges, at least now that Annie's blood pressure has stabilized. The baby's femur and humerus lengths suggest that Annie is probably about thirty-five weeks into the pregnancy, but the baby's belly is much smaller than it should be. This is a typical pattern for a fetus with a growth restriction, but that's expected given Annie's addiction and her blood pressure issues.

"Yeah, this little one is going to be tiny," the sonographer confirms quietly. "But things look okay, considering."

This is the closest thing to good news that I could have hoped for given the circumstances, and I flash a teary smile toward Sam, who offers an equally weak smile in response. There's a long road ahead of us—but for now, Annie and the baby are safe. I release a long, heavy breath, and I decide I'll shift closer to the bed so I can hold Annie's hand as she sleeps. Sam has other ideas.

"Let's get a coffee?"

"I can't leave her," I say. He offers me a quizzical smile.

"She's sleeping. Let's take a minute while things are calm."

The sonographer is packing up, and the flurry of nurses and doctors is easing. Still, I hesitate—her situation could change in an instant. It's unlikely, though. She's on the right meds now, and even if something *does* change, at least there are monitors fitted so the staff can react.

"Okay," I say with a sigh, and he rises and gently pulls me to my feet.

Sam leads the way to a table in the corner of the cafeteria, and we sit opposite one another. Hospital cafeterias are creepy places in the middle of the night. I've never been to this one before, but I somehow still miss the swarming mass of staff hastily eating between crises, and the overwhelmed fathers trying to inhale coffee between diaper changes, and the teary relatives grieving bad news. The cafeteria is always a place of extremes, but it's never more uncomfortable than when it's empty.

For a while, we sit in silence. I nurse my coffee and stare down into the black liquid while I try to collect my thoughts. There is a swirling mess of ideas and concerns and worries in my mind— and I try to pick one out to speak to Sam about—but then all of a sudden I can think of only thing one thing to say.

"Sorry."

I blurt out the word—almost pleading with him to accept it, as if this were all my fault—as if an apology could make it all better, if only he says *that's all right*. Maybe there is something to my guilt—after all, I *have* buried my head in the sand for the last two years. I have made a dreadful, unforgivable mistake by not checking on my sister at least every now and again. I should have known how bad things were. I should have known how desperate she was.

"Honey." Sam raises an eyebrow at me. "None of this is your fault."

"But this will get worse, you know. It's never *one* thing with Annie."

"Well—at least she's asking for help now. The baby's heart rate was all over the place. Another few days and it would have been too late."

"They'll have to report her."

"I know."

"Do you think she'll be charged?"

"Well, Annie can't really handle any stress at the moment… maybe we can convince them to wait a little bit."

"And then?"

"I don't know, Lexie. We are really going to have to take this as it comes," Sam says, and he sighs and says reluctantly, "You shouldn't have promised her that there would be a way around prosecution."

"I know." Here comes the guilt again. I bite at my lip, then I whisper, "I just wanted to make her come in for treatment. She'll forgive me, won't she?"

"You probably saved her baby's life—maybe hers, too. So, if she doesn't forgive you, that's on her—not you." The conversation stalls again, and I stare at my coffee and try not to cry. After a while, Sam reaches across the table and squeezes my forearm. "You haven't told me much about her, only that you've been estranged and that she has an addiction. How long has it been since you spoke to her?"

"About two years. The last time I saw her was a few months before you and I met."

There is an echoing sadness in Sam's eyes. "What happened?"

"She moved in with me the year after she finished college. We had some rough years—stints in rehab, ups and downs…you can imagine. But then I started my job at the clinic and I really thought she was doing better. She was in a methadone program, and although she absolutely hated it, things seemed stable. But then one night, she broke into the clinic. They caught her in the meds room." Tears threaten again, and this time there is no stopping them. I groan and reach for a napkin to wipe my eyes. "It was my fault—I'd let her get into the habit of coming in to visit me at work occasionally. I thought she was just lonely. I should have known she was trying to figure out how to break in. I'd left my security pass on the hall table—and I'd forgotten my PIN code a few times so I'd been stupid enough to set it to the same one we used at home. It just didn't even occur to me that she'd ever do anything to risk my career."

"I can't imagine Oliver took that very well," Sam says, referring to my boss at the clinic.

"That is the understatement of the century." I sigh. "He would have been pissed if she'd just broken in—but she didn't smash a window. She walked in through the front door and right into the meds room because of my carelessness. I got a formal warning, but the worst thing was that Oliver—and the other directors at the clinic—well, they *looked* at me differently. I should have known better, but I trusted her because she's my sister. It's taken a long time to earn back their faith in me."

"So, after that...you threw her out?" Sam says. His tone is mild, but when I look at him I'm sure I see something dark in his eyes. Judgment? Disapproval? I frown at him.

"I didn't just 'throw her out,'" I say defensively. "I'd only ever made things worse in all of my attempts to help her, and it was only when she nearly ruined *my* life, too, that I finally realized she had to take responsibility. I enrolled her in rehab for the umpteenth time, and when I dropped her off I told her that she wasn't welcome back at my place until she actually finished the program."

I tried to keep tabs on her while she was in the rehab clinic, but per her usual pattern, she didn't last long. Annie was never uglier than when she was detoxing—and never more dangerous than when she was asked to hand control of her life over to someone else.

"I wasn't criticizing you. I'm just trying to understand so I can help. We're going to need a plan. Maybe if we can brainstorm what's gone wrong in the past, we can think of a way to get her some help that actually *helps* in the future."

I hear a clear accusation in Sam's words, but I'm far too tired to tell if it's really there or I'm just being paranoid. I narrow my eyes and I say sharply, "You're going to find an answer that I've somehow missed all of these years, are you? Well, I've tried long- and short-term inpatient programs, at least three outpatient programs, and I even took her off to a luxury program overseas—she lasted a *week*. We've tried Narcotics Anonymous, several secular NA alternatives, a rapid-detox clinic, and she's been on and off methadone and Suboxone for years. No one can make Annie do anything she doesn't want to do—in fact, the fastest way to infuriate her is to try to impose rules on her. What rehabilitation program on earth can deal with someone who is so counterdependent that simply setting boundaries with them is enough to see them—"

I'm aware that my voice is rising and the words are starting to run into one other, but it's only when Sam draws in a sharp breath and pushes his chair back from the table that I realize how hysterical I sound. I break off midword, and Sam raises his hands helplessly. There's sadness and hurt in his eyes. I've been embarrassed about Annie all night, but finally, I'm embarrassed about something that's entirely within my control.

Sam has been amazing tonight. He doesn't deserve to bear the brunt of my frustrations.

"Lex, I'm just trying to help. I'm not insinuating that you've missed the obvious. We're both exhausted. We can talk about this tomorrow when we have clear heads. Let's go back and check in on her, and if her BP is still stable, we can go home for some sleep."

"I can't go home." I shake my head. "I need to stay with her."

"You have to take care of yourself first, Lexie."

"Well, I've tried that too now, and that approach appears to have been the worst failure of all," I snap again, and I rise and throw my half-empty coffee cup into the trash. It splashes up the sides of the bin and to the wall beside it, as Sam watches in silence. When I turn to him, I'm not embarrassed anymore, I'm only angry. How can he not see how impossible this situation is? She *needs* me. "But you should go," I add curtly. "Get some sleep."

"I'm not going without you. Come on."

"No." The word echoes all around us in the otherwise silent cafeteria, and its edges are hard and fierce—it's jarring. Sam's gaze doesn't waver.

"Everything is going to feel better after some sleep, I promise you."

"But I'm supposed to look after Annie—I promised Dad, and I've let her down, and I've let *him* down—and I just can't fix it if I'm not here."

"You haven't let anyone down, Lex. Your sister is sick, and *she* has made some bad decisions." He speaks firmly to me again, and I want to crumble and sink into the comfort of the arms he opens toward me, but I can't. I step away from him, and the backs of my thighs collide with a chair. Sam sighs and exhales then runs his hands through his hair. We stand there in that frustrated silence until I see his expression soften. "If you don't want to leave, we can go sleep in one of the residents' bunk rooms. We'll let the staff know where to find us if anything goes wrong. We could be back in Maternity in two minutes if she needs us."

It's a compromise—a good one and a sensible one. I can see Sam would much rather go home, and I don't blame him—we won't sleep well here, and we're both exhausted. Still, there is no way I'm leaving this hospital until I'm sure Annie and the baby are fine, so Sam's suggestion is the only way either of us are getting any rest tonight.

I nod. Sam steps back toward me and wraps his arms around my shoulders. I move into his embrace and press my face into his neck.

"You're a good sister, Lexie. She's lucky to have you."

"She's a mess. You should have known her before. She was amazing."

"Maybe this is rock bottom. Maybe this baby is the chance she needs to be that person again."

As we walk back toward Maternity, I try to cling to Sam's words as if they are a lifeline. I want to believe he's right, but my hope feels fragile—hollow almost, because we've hit so many rocky bottoms before, and Annie always manages to find further depths.

4

ANNIE

Luke,

You keep telling me I need to connect with my pain, and I do understand the logic of that—although I'm not even sure yet that I'll ever let you read that I wrote that down, and I'd rather die than admit it aloud.

I'm going to start from the day after I got the notebook because that's when it started—the glacial slide from when my life was worth something to the mess I'm in now. I woke up excited that day. I came down the stairs with my notebook in my hands and I was a ball of pure anticipation about the summer break.

Then I saw Mom and Lexie at the kitchen table, and the excitement turned into shock, and the shock turned into dread. They were sitting opposite one another, a pile of crumpled tissues on the table between them. Captain Edwards was at the end of the table. They were all crying.

No one ever told me my dad was dead. They didn't have to. Their tears told me, and their silence told me; even the slump in *my mother's shoulders told me that life was never going to be the same. Later, I'd piece together fragments—he'd been at a fire, and just when they thought the building was clear, someone thought they heard a cry from inside. It was too hot and too dangerous by that stage and Dad wouldn't let his team go back in, so he went in himself to do another sweep, and while he was inside the roof collapsed.*

I never saw his body, and I wasn't allowed to go to the funeral, and so it was a long time before I really believed he was dead. Instead, to me, he was just gone—he had simply left—and I knew that was my fault. Dad had swapped shifts that day so that he could be at the assembly for me. He should never have been at that fire.

It rained the morning of his funeral. Lexie and I had to wait at home with one of Mom's elderly aunts, but we didn't know her at all and she terrified us. She wore strange clothes and wouldn't let us watch TV, so as soon as the drizzle stopped, Lexie and I hid outside away from her. The wake was at our house, so after the service, dozens of people arrived to make their way up the path to the front door.

Lexie and I didn't talk much. We sat in the echoing shock of our grief, watching strangers as they went inside our house to mourn our father, as if we were the onlookers to their tragedy, rather than the other way around. When the procession finally slowed down, Lexie hugged me, and she told me things were going to be okay—but I was sure she was lying and so I finally started to sob. The guilt and the grief and the shock and the pain were just too much to bear.

When her hugs failed to console me, Lexie did the only naughty thing I can ever remember her doing. She walked the length of the path that ran from the street to our front door, and she made a basket with her skirt, and she picked flowers from the agapanthus that bordered the walkway. There were two straight rows of alternating white and purple plants—and Lexie methodically stripped every single petal, until they were overflowing from her skirt and she was struggling to juggle it all.

I finally, reluctantly dragged myself up from the grass beneath the tree and went to ask her what she was doing. She told me to stand on the lawn, and then she waddled over to my side with the flowers still in the skirt of her dress, and she told me to spin. I resisted at first, but she grew insistent and so I awkwardly twirled, but I felt stupid and angry. Soon Lexie dropped the flowers onto the ground and she began to gently toss them over me as I spun. The wind picked up, and my clumsy twirl gradually became more free. I twirled and the flowers rained down around me onto the lawn and the sun came out from behind the clouds, and for just a second, life was something close to beautiful again.

"Smile, Annie!" Lexie shouted, and at first I couldn't, but as I danced and twirled the corners of my mouth lifted just a little and then I did smile and Lexie smiled, too. Soon we were throwing the petals at each other and then we were dancing and laughing as if the world hadn't really ended three days earlier.

Lexie caught my wrist in her hand to stop me, and she thumped her other hand hard against my chest and she said quite forcibly, "Do you feel that? That lightness inside? That's Dad. He's with us still, I promise you. He would never leave us, not ever, Annie."

They really were the worst days, Luke. But even then, my brave big sister made sure there was a silver lining.

5

LEXIE

I wake the next morning to the familiar sounds of hospital foot traffic on the other side of the door. Sam and I are in the residents' bunk room, and sometime while we were asleep he pulled me right onto his chest. I offered to sleep on the top bunk, but it didn't take much convincing for me to join him. Although it was cramped, I needed the comfort of his body against mine. And he was right about my state of mind—even on this taste of sleep, I feel much more rational. I slide from the bed and Sam stirs.

"What time is it?" He sounds like he's in rougher shape than I feel. I glance at my phone and am relieved to find no missed calls.

"Ten."

It was just after five by the time we got back to the bunk room, then I was on my phone for a while—trying to figure out how to word the email I had to send to work. I knew Oliver would check his emails the moment he was out of bed, and I knew he could call in a replacement for the next few days. Taking off work was particularly inconvenient as a GP, but necessary from time to time, so of course the clinic had procedures in place.

The cause of my hesitation was a vigorous internal debate

about whether I needed to reveal that Annie was back on the scene. I just wasn't sure how he'd react, given how close she came to costing me my job last time. So for a good ten minutes I typed and then deleted text, until Sam impatiently took the phone and drafted the email for me.

Oliver, I'm so sorry—I've had a family emergency. I won't be at work for the rest of the week. I'll call you once I know more. Lexie

As soon as I nodded, Sam hit the send button. That was at 5:15 a.m.

"He doesn't need to know any details yet," Sam had murmured, as he pulled me down onto the pillow. "We can deal with it later."

"Things must be going well if the staff on the ward haven't called," Sam surmises now, and I have no doubt about that. He made sure his colleagues in Maternity knew to contact us for any change in Annie's condition. This hospital is his domain, and I can tell he's highly regarded. Sam is a surgeon, a man who works with his hands—but at heart, he is a devoted people person. He has chosen this career for no other reason than that he cares very deeply about his patients.

I smooth my hair into a ponytail and wait for Sam to pull his jeans on before I open the door. We walk hand in hand back to Maternity, and Sam politely responds to countless greetings as we make our way through the halls. At the ward, he goes to speak with the nursing staff and to see if Eliza Rogers can spare him a minute or two, as I head to Annie's room.

She's resting against the pillows watching television, a tray of untouched food in front of her. The color in her face is better, but she still looks drained.

"How are you feeling?"

"Tired, but the headache is gone." Annie hits the remote to turn the television off and struggles to pull herself into a sitting position. I help her, adjusting the bed and then offering my arm for her to drag herself upright.

"Have you seen the obstetrician?"

"Yes, her name's Eliza. She came in a while ago and said things are looking better than when I came in."

I'm going to need much more detail than that—but I know Sam will be able to give me a better picture of Annie's situation after he talks with the staff. My mind races forward to the next challenge, and I say to Annie, "We need to call Mom."

Even though my mother and I are hardly close-knit, I'm sure that she'd *want* to know about this situation. Mom mentioned to me in our last call a few weeks ago that Annie has been calling her, too, and I assume they've rebuilt something of a closer relationship while Annie and I have been apart. So I'm surprised when my sister shakes her head.

"Not yet. Please, Lexie. Give me a few days, okay? It's not like she's going to be angry that we didn't call her straight away. She probably won't even care."

"Don't say that, Annie." It feels strange to defend Mom, but in this case, I'm sure that Annie is wrong. "She does care."

"Maybe. She just has a funny way of showing it sometimes," Annie mutters, and she picks up a piece of toast, breaks off the crust as if she's going to eat it, but then lowers it back to the tray. "I have been speaking to her a bit more lately, but I haven't exactly been honest about my situation. So she doesn't know about the baby or that I'm still using, and she's going to be upset with me for lying and... I just want to be able to tell her I'm on top of this before we call her, okay? I just *need* to be clean first."

Thoughts of Annie's relationship with our mother—clearly as confusing as my own—fade to the background as I focus on her other bewildering statement. *Clean?* Annie is staring out the window, her gaze distant. I lean toward her as I say very gently, "Annie, you *can't* actually detox until the baby is delivered."

"What? Of course I can," Annie says stiffly. "I know I've messed up until now—but with the right help—"

"No, I don't even mean 'you *can't*,' I mean—you shouldn't. It's not safe. Withdrawals would probably start premature labor."

She stares at me. Her blue eyes are clear and I have her full attention, but I can see from the twist in her eyebrows that she still doesn't understand what I'm telling her.

"But... I nearly did it at home—a few times. I was just going to do it alone... I tried..."

"Probably a good thing you didn't." I smile at her gently, and she shakes her head. The lines on her face seem endless, and when she frowns, the hollows in her cheeks grow deeper. Annie looks too frail to be the weapon of mass destruction I've known her to be over the past six years. I take her hand in mine and squeeze it tightly. "There are well-established protocols for dealing with addiction in pregnancy. I'm sure Eliza will have a plan."

"But—*you* said I could take the methadone just once."

"Well, yes... I did but... I mean, you have to be taking something."

"But I can't stay on methadone." Annie is visibly frightened of this possibility. She hates methadone, and she always did seem miserable on it. Then again, she always ended up using while she was on it, and I've never been sure how much of her "misery" was put on to preempt the inevitable relapse. I'm instantly impatient with her—assuming she's going to resist the maintenance treatment so she can go right back to using street opiates. I'm surprised when she whispers desperately, "Lexie, methadone withdrawals are as bad as heroin—if they put me on that, won't the baby still have to detox once it's born?"

Now *I'm* confused. I'd assumed her fear and concern were all about her own dislike of methadone—it hadn't actually occurred to me that she'd be concerned for the baby. I soften a little at her uncharacteristic display of selflessness.

"There are alternatives..." I say gently. "But yes, it doesn't matter what the maintenance drug is. The baby will have to detox, no matter what happens from this point."

"But I was… I was just going to stop, before it comes. I can't let the baby…" She chokes up, and she's getting wound up—this is the very last thing she needs given the situation with her blood pressure. Her naïveté is completely heartbreaking. I want to pull her into my arms and tell her that it's all going to be just fine, but that would be a lie—it's not. There are ugly times ahead for her and her baby…and as soon as that thought strikes me, I feel the pinch in my chest as I acknowledge that this means there are also ugly times ahead for me, and for Sam. I want to protect Annie, and I know we need to keep her stress levels down to help control her BP, but pretending there is anything like an easy solution available to us now is ridiculous.

Now, anger rises within me so suddenly that I'm caught off guard by it. I'm half-inclined to cut this conversation short and storm down the hallway to ask this Eliza what she was thinking by *not* making this clear to Annie in their very first meeting.

"There just *has* to be a way for me to get clean before the baby comes." She's thinking out loud now—digesting the implications, her voice shaky and rough—but determined, as if she could somehow negotiate with me to find a way to change the workings of human biology just for her. "Lexie, you have to *make* them find a way. You don't know what detox is like—it's not something a baby should have to feel."

"Annie, I've watched you go through withdrawals. I *do* know what it's like. And we know how to help infants through it. It's going to be okay."

Annie shakes her head, lips pursed.

"I'm not letting my baby start its life like that."

"It's too late to avoid that now."

"But what if I stay in the hospital and just go cold turkey? They can monitor the baby, right?"

"With your blood pressure the way it is, the last thing you

or the baby needs is severe stress like withdrawal. You could go into labor—or even worse."

There's a slight pause, then Annie whispers hesitantly, "Worse?"

I work to clear the lump of guilt in my throat before I can bring myself to admit, "The baby would probably go into distress—there's a much higher chance of an emergency delivery, and a chance it might not even make it. Do you understand?"

"Fuck..." Annie starts to cry, and I flick my glance toward the monitor. Her BP is rising—very slowly—but the numbers are trending upward, and I need to end this conversation.

I didn't mean to scare her, but Annie is intelligent—she can understand this. If she wasn't so upset, I'd just explain to her about physiological withdrawal, so that she can see that there are complex systems in place here and both she and the baby legiti-mately *need* the opiates for the time being. But she's staring at me as she sobs—and I'm actually starting to wonder if I shouldn't have left this conversation for her doctor. "I know you hate it, love, but staying on maintenance is the only way forward. It's the best thing for the baby."

The door opens and I'm relieved to see Sam, but the relief doesn't last long—it's only a moment or two before I notice the police officers right behind him, and a middle-aged woman wearing a white coat and a scowl close behind them. I widen my eyes at him, and Sam offers me a silent apology with his grimace.

"Anne Vidler?" one of the officers says, as soon as he enters the room. Annie does not respond. Instead, she continues to stare at me, as if I can somehow prevent this from happening. I suppose that's fair enough. After all, I *did* promise that I would. The other officer walks to the end of the bed and checks the nameplate, then nods to his colleague. "Anne, the presence of narcotics has been detected in your urine. Under Alabama law, chemical endangerment of a child is a..."

"Annie has high blood pressure," I say sharply, and I rise to my full height and address the officers as if I'm her lawyer, rather than her sister—although I'm still holding her hand, and I'm holding it so tightly now that my fingers are cramping from the pressure. "It's medically imperative that she avoid stress, so you'll need to leave the room now, please."

"Dr. Rogers said that her blood pressure is stable."

All eyes turn to the woman in the coat, who barely hides her disdain as she points to the monitor and says sharply, "I told you it *was* but that I wasn't sure she was ready for this—and you've proven me right. You need to leave. Now."

The police officers exchange confused glances, until one finally drops some papers onto Annie's bed and they leave the room. I glare until the door closes behind them, and then gasp in disbelief when one remains right in my line of sight, guarding the door. Now when I look out, I watch a woman approach him. Through the small window in the door, I can see only from her shoulders up—but that's more than enough for me to recognize the no-nonsense demeanor of an unsympathetic professional. She stands with the officer, her expression set in a fierce frown. I wonder what her role is.

"Are they going to stay?" I murmur, and Sam says quietly, "There was some concern Annie might try to leave the hospital. They're just here to make sure she remains until tomorrow when there'll be some kind of hearing." He picks up the warrant from where it sits on the end of the bed, and sighs heavily as he folds it up and passes it to me. I take it with my left hand, and stuff it into my pocket without looking at it.

"Don't you worry, Annie," the doctor says very gently. "You're not going anywhere until it's completely safe. We'll probably keep you here until you deliver."

Annie shakes her head frantically.

"I can't stay here that long."

The doctor approaches the bed and takes Annie's other hand in hers.

"I know it's difficult, but it's really important that you stay calm, Annie." She flicks her glance to me. "You must be Alexis. I'm Eliza Rogers. I'll be overseeing Annie's care."

"I need to speak with you," I say tightly, because although I'm impressed with her handling of the officers, it's surely *her* fault they are here in the first place—who else would have called in her failed drug test? Besides which, I'm still frustrated by how little she's explained to Annie so far.

"Certainly." Eliza nods, but her attention is already back to Annie, who is breathing heavily and fidgeting on the bed. "Let's make sure Annie's okay, and then we'll talk."

Sam's hand descends on my shoulder, and I release Annie's hand to turn back toward him. His gesture is one of comfort, but also, somehow, I know it's a warning—a plea for me to watch my tone with his colleague. His gaze locks with mine. Sam is sad and he's worried, and I take his unspoken plea on board—we do *need* Eliza, so I can't really afford to make an enemy of her. I reach up, squeeze his hand against my shoulder in another unspoken communication—*I understand*—then turn back to Annie.

She's staring at the ceiling and there's a thin sheen of sweat over her brow. Annie is white as a ghost now, and the systolic blood pressure reading has increased by seven points since I came into the room. It ticks upward, this time skipping three points higher, and Eliza releases Annie's hand and says quietly, "I'm going to organize some more medication for you, Annie. Something to calm you, okay?"

As soon as the doctor leaves the room, Annie looks to me. Her eyes are wild with fear and desperation.

"What are we going to do?"

We. I know that I told her that I would somehow prevent this very thing from happening—but still, her casual use of the shared pronoun frustrates me. This *is* her problem; this situation is entirely her doing. It's so typical of my sister that she is already assuming that I'm going to create a way out of the mess for her. I can't look at her for a moment, I'm too frustrated, but as I look away, her vitals monitor catches my eye and my resentment evaporates because it *has* to. With every digit that number rises, the baby's health is compromised, and so is Annie's. I take a deep breath and I meet her gaze, then I offer her a calm smile.

"First things first. Let's get that BP back under control, and then we'll make a plan."

6

ANNIE

Luke,

I wonder what you're thinking about that last entry. I know you're looking for the key that unlocks me—did you think that was it? Did you scribble down on that notepad of yours "daddy issues" and then treat yourself to a cookie for being so clever? Did you feel sympathy for me? Did you feel pity—or maybe it was disgust— maybe you're thinking to yourself, Christ, is that all that's behind this life of disaster? That's her pain? Millions of children a year lose their parents—why couldn't Annie cope? She's so weak. Pitiful.

Well, if that's what you're thinking—you're wrong, because I did cope, Luke. Even as a child, I figured out that life would somehow go on. I knew that it would never be the same, but I understood that the days would just keep coming at me...one after the other... an inevitable tide of time that would not stop even though I felt like my world had ended.

Mom, on the other hand, never seemed to grasp this concept.

That peak grief she was caught in during the early days after Dad's death never seemed to ease off. Weeks passed—then months—and Mom never got back to living. I figured that one day she'd go back to work, but even months later, she still could barely drag herself to breakfast most mornings. And even when she did, Lexie made the breakfast, and sometimes she went as far as to feed Mom, spoonful by spoonful, as if Mom was a baby.

Our mother lived in her pajamas, and whenever something good happened—like when Lexie still somehow managed a straight-A report card at the end of the worst school year of her life—Mom would smile for a moment then hug us, but she'd immediately dissolve back into sobs. Over time, her embraces became a source of anxiety for me—if something wonderful happened that I knew Mom would celebrate, I learned to keep it to myself to avoid the inevitable breakdown afterward.

Soon Lexie was doing almost everything Mom and Dad used to do—picking me up from school, doing the laundry and the gardening, and even the groceries on our way home from school. For a while, we did the shopping over two days because we couldn't carry all of the bags home at once. Lexie figured it out—she wrote a grocery list, and then she split it into two shorter lists to divide the weight. She'd stop to pop sweets in my mouth as we walked so I didn't complain about my arms getting tired as I carried my half of the bags. Eventually, one of the guys at the fire station saw us walking home, and from then on, every Tuesday afternoon we were ferried to and from the grocery store by a uniformed fire department officer.

But other than the small kindnesses shown to us by Dad's colleagues and the teachers at school, there were no adults directly involved in the day-to-day workings of our lives—certainly no relatives coming to check in on us. I knew that Mom's and Dad's parents were alive and even lived nearby, but we'd seen them only a handful of times in our lifetimes. I'd wondered about this, particularly when they came to the wake but then immediately disappeared again. In the past, when we'd asked Mom or Dad about their families, their answers had been vague. They said that our grandparents loved us but just couldn't come to see us very often. You don't miss what you've never had, not even when everything else goes to hell. And Lexie was at the helm, and life just went on.

I still believed in Santa Claus then, and so at Christmas that first year, Lexie made me write a letter and then told me she'd mailed it for me. She convinced Mom to get the tree out of the attic, and then we put it up with Christmas carols blaring on the CD player. Mom watched for a while, but Lexie and I finished as she rose and silently took herself back to bed.

I woke up Christmas Day to find a sea of gifts beneath the tree. Santa had come and there were gifts for all of us—Lexie had the set of Roald Dahl books she'd asked for, I had everything I'd asked for, except, of course for Dad's return—but even in that case there was a new photo of Dad framed and sitting on the mantel beside the Christmas tree, smiling down on us as we tore open the gifts. "Santa" had even bought Mom a new nightgown.

Lexie's cooking skills rapidly improved, but she wasn't up to the challenge of a turkey so she made spaghetti Bolognese. Mom came to the table and said grace. She wept afterward, but even so, she stayed until the end of the meal. Lexie and I ate and chattered over the low soundtrack of Mom's sobs. By then we were so good at drowning out that sound that we barely even noticed—it was a good day, and I remember both missing my father's presence at that *table and knowing that if he really was looking down on us, he'd be so proud of the way that Lexie and I were carrying on.*

It wasn't an orthodox way for a family to exist—but it did work. Mom's state of mind was confusing, and from time to time I'd get nervous about it, but I still had Lexie—and she managed to compensate for most of what would otherwise have been lacking in that home. Dad's insurance had paid off the mortgage and we had his pension trickling in, so other than a sign of life from Mom, we wanted for nothing. Lexie kept up with her academic extension classes, and I had a good group of friends at school and my stories to hide in whenever it all got to be a bit too much.

But then, Robert came into our lives. So keep your notepad close, Luke, and wait before you treat yourself to that triumphant cookie, because shit is about to get ugly.

7

LEXIE

As Eliza administers the sedative to Annie, I slip quietly from the room and prepare to confront the woman with the bun. She offers an introduction before I have to ask.

"Mary Rafferty," she says, extending her hand toward mine. I shake it briskly, and she continues in her broad drawl, "I'm a social worker with Child Protective Services. And you are?"

Social worker? I figured CPS might get involved after the birth, but that's still a long way off—why would she visit today?

"Dr. Alexis Vidler," I say stiffly. "I'm Annie's sister."

"Ah," Mary Rafferty says, nodding knowingly. "Well, that explains it."

"Explains what?"

"I wondered how an addict could afford this place."

I bristle at the scorn in her tone, but I push down my irritation. I'm tired and angry, but thankfully at least smart enough to realize that a CPS social worker is the last person on earth I can afford to offend at this point.

"What can I do for you, Ms. Rafferty?"

"Well, CPS will be petitioning the court to strip your sister's parental rights. I'm here to take a brief medical history and get a rundown on her living situation to help the judge with his decision in the case."

She delivers this announcement in such a nonchalant, unguarded way that if I listened to her tone instead of the words, she might have been announcing her plans for the weekend. I gape at her.

"What?"

Mary Rafferty gives me a quizzical frown. She seems perplexed by the outrage in my tone, which only outrages me more.

"Didn't you read the paperwork the police officers brought in? Anne has been charged with chemical endangerment of her child. That's a felony."

"She's been charged—she hasn't been found guilty."

"Well, she failed a drug test and according to her doctor, she's admitted to using heroin. *While pregnant*, Dr. Vidler." Mary gives me an incredulous look. "Surely you as a doctor can understand how serious that is."

I can't help it—I flush. I'm embarrassed by my sister's behavior, even as I start to defend it.

"She has an addiction," I mutter defensively. "It's an illness. She needs help, not—what did you say? To *strip her of her parental rights*? What is that going to achieve at this point, other than to stress the hell out of her? The baby isn't even due for weeks. There's time to sort all of this out."

"Respectfully, Dr. Vidler, that's not how this situation is going to work. Decisions need to be made about that child's welfare, and your sister is not fit to make them."

"The child's welfare? What decisions need to be made *right now* that she's not 'fit to make'?"

"Well, the doctor who reported her to us overnight was concerned that she might discharge herself and attempt to use illicit drugs again. That's obviously not in the child's best interests. Besides which, he said there was some medication she refused. Are you aware of that situation?"

"Medication?" I repeat, and I scan back over the events of the day and can't figure out what she's talking about, until I remember that early-morning discussion about methadone. "Oh—well, yes, she wasn't keen on methadone, but she took it eventually."

"Methadone? Oh, I didn't realize…well, that's a bit different, then. Judges don't generally like to see these addicts go from one drug to another, even if it's a legal alternative…they generally want to see moms in an abstinence-based program."

"Well, she *can't* just go to rehab," I snap. "She's incredibly sick, and she's pregnant. Going into withdrawal now would be a recipe for disaster."

"Oh, I see." Mary Rafferty frowns, and then withdraws a notepad from her handbag. "Could you spare me a few minutes to discuss this some more before I go in to speak with her?"

I laugh incredulously.

"You're *not* speaking to her, Ms. Rafferty. When those officers came in earlier her blood pressure spiked, and her specialist is sedating her as we speak. If you go in there, she's going to panic, and she can't afford to."

"Oh, I'm afraid I'm going to have to insist," Mary says, and she plants her palm flat against her chest and leans forward toward me, offering an apologetic grimace. "I really need to get a history here, and also—well, I just have to understand her living situation. I could come back later today, I guess. But I'll need time to put together a report so I can make a recommendation at the hearing tomorrow."

"You'll have to make do with speaking to me," I say. "She's in no state for an interrogation right now."

"Not an interrogation, Dr. Vidler," Mary gently scolds as if I'm a child. "I just need to understand her situation so we can figure out what to do with this baby."

"I hope by that you mean figure out how to help her care for it."

Mary Rafferty's good-natured smile disappears in an instant, and now she seems confused.

"Dr. Vidler—you can't seriously think she's an appropriate person to care for a newborn."

"You've literally never even *met* her. How dare you make a judgment like that?" I hiss. I'm infuriated. Just then, the door opens gently and Eliza and Sam emerge.

"You might want to take this conversation away from Annie's doorway. She really needs to sleep now," Eliza murmurs.

"Good idea," I mutter, and I use the interruption as an opportunity for a deep breath to try to deal with my *own* blood pressure. We take a few steps farther into the corridor, and Eliza and Sam linger until I offer introductions all around.

"Dr. Rogers, Dr. Vidler here was just telling me that Anne isn't well enough for a chat today. Can you confirm that?" Mary says quietly.

"Yes, I'd much rather you left it," Eliza says, frowning. "What's the rush?"

"I need to prepare a report for Anne's hearing tomorrow—for the judge, you understand," Mary says, then she glances back to me. "I guess you and I could cover the basics, Dr. Vidler. If you don't mind."

"Of course." I sigh. I *do* mind—I just want to go back into Annie, but I know the alternative is Annie having to have this conversation, and I know we can't afford that right now.

"And I'll need to speak to you, too, Dr. Rogers," Mary adds. "Could you spare me a few minutes sometime today?"

"When you're finished with Alexis, find my office and have my secretary call me," Eliza says abruptly. "I've got rounds to do now. I'll come as soon as I can."

She gives us a curt nod and shakes her head a little as she walks briskly away.

"Can I join you?" Sam asks, and I hesitate. I don't even know why. It just doesn't seem right that Sam should have to sit through this—but then again, he heard most of it last night, and I'm frazzled, so the idea of backup is appealing.

"Thanks," I murmur, and I take his hand.

"Let's walk up to the meeting room, shall we?" Mary murmurs. "We can finish this conversation there."

"Actually," Sam says, "would you mind if we go to my consulting room? It was a late night—I suspect both Lexie and I could do with some coffee, and we'll be much more comfortable there."

"You're a doctor, too?" Mary says, and her eyes widen again, as if she just can't make sense of two successful professionals having *any* connection to a failure like my sister. I want to wrap my hands around her skinny neck and throttle her. Instead, I clench Sam's hand tighter, conscious of the sharpness of my gaze but unable to prevent it. "Well, certainly, Dr. Hawke. Lead the way."

Sam's receptionist brings a pot of coffee and some cookies, and we sit around the little conference table in his office. Mary sets her notepad and a clipboard with some printed forms onto the table, and once she's added sugar to her coffee and thanked Sam for his hospitality, she turns her gaze back to me.

"I just want to be very clear, Dr. Vidler," she says quietly. "My role here is to help the court keep that precious little baby in your sister's belly safe. I'm not here to judge, I'm here to help. The state of Alabama has terrible issues with drug-addicted babies—"

"Babies cannot be 'drug-addicted,'" I say tersely. "It doesn't make any sense. There are two components of an addiction, a physiological component and a psychological component. The correct term is *physiologically dependent*. That's not the same as 'drug-addicted.'"

"Well, sounds to me like you're splitting hairs, but it doesn't matter much. You can use whatever term you want, Dr. Vidler. Your sister has been abusing heroin while she's pregnant, so I'm sure you're aware her little one is in for a world of pain once it's born. Her decisions to this point suggest to me that she's not fit to continue making choices that affect the welfare of her child, which is why we are petitioning to remove her parental rights."

"Is that what the hearing is about tomorrow?" Sam asks quietly, and Mary nods.

"Yes, that's correct. Judge Brown will consider my report and make a ruling. If he rules in favor of our petition, well—if her specialist *does* agree with your assessment, Dr. Vidler, and Anne can't go off to rehab or detox just yet, then I'll recommend that she remain in custody either here or via incarceration until the birth. Just to keep the baby safe, you understand."

"We need a lawyer," I say, exhaling, and Sam nods. I glance at him. "Should I go find a lawyer before we discuss her history?"

"Oh, no, Dr. Vidler, that's not necessary." Mary gives a gentle laugh. "No, this is just background about Anne's medical history. I'm a social worker. I'm not making any decisions myself—just gathering the facts to assist the court." She offers me a consoling smile. "So, why don't you start at the beginning and tell me how long your sister has been an addict for?"

I give her as little detail as I can, but still, I'm racked with guilt as I speak to the social worker, as if I'm betraying Annie just by telling the truth. I skim over years of frustration and pain, providing only a reluctant list of points. Mary's expression is grim when we start, and by the time I reach the events of the previous night, she's stopped writing and she's staring at the table. I'm not even sure she's listening to me, until I stop midsentence and Mary looks up. There's sadness in her gaze, and I have an odd spurt of adrenaline pump through my body as I realize that she has already made up her mind.

"Well," she says quietly, "thanks for your time."

"Annie can beat this," I blurt, and Mary hesitates.

"Dr. Vidler, you're clearly a devoted sister, and I respect you for that."

"You didn't even ask about her living situation," I say. This is just not fair; Mary has such a small part of the picture of Annie's life. How can she decide her suitability as a parent based only on her history of rehab attempts?

"Let me guess, Dr. Vidler." Mary sighs, as she packs up her notepad. "She's either living with you, or she's on the streets. Which is it?"

"She has a trailer," I snap. "It's not the Shangri-La, but it's a roof over her head."

"Does she have a job? A way to support herself? A way to buy diapers and formula and pay medical bills?"

"I don't think so, but she—"

"Look. None of this matters, not really—not at this stage. Maybe later, once she's been through rehab and she's clean. But I'm sure you can understand, all that matters for now is making sure your sister can't damage that precious baby any more than she already has." Mary stands and slides her handbag onto her shoulder.

"Annie matters, too," I croak, and I stand. "Surely helping *Annie* is the best way to help her baby."

"That's not my area of responsibility, Dr. Vidler," Mary says quietly. "But I'm sure the judge will do everything in his power to give your sister another opportunity to get herself sorted out."

"You said Annie will probably go to rehab," Sam says quietly, and Mary nods. "Will she get a say which facility?"

"Well, it just depends on what the judge decides…but why do you ask?"

"My employer has opened a new rehab clinic out at Auburn. If Annie has to go into an inpatient program, that might be a good option for her."

"I can certainly make a note of that in my report, Dr. Hawke."

Sam rises and walks Mary to the corridor, and when he returns, he stands behind me and gently massages my shoulders. I slump forward and press my fists against my eyes.

"They're going to take her baby away."

"It sounds like it."

"Is this what we do now? A woman fails a drug test and we *remove her parental rights* just like that?"

"Apparently."

"This is bullshit. Shouldn't we rush in at her with resources to help her get clean and care for the baby?"

"We're going to need to find that lawyer, Lexie."

"I know." I sit up and exhale. Sam's gentle kneading of my shoulders continues. "But first, I really need to speak to Eliza."

"What are you going to tell Annie?"

I shake my head hastily.

"Nothing, yet. Not until I talk to a lawyer." Sam's hands slow, then pause, and I tilt my head back to stare up at him. "I'm not going to worry her until I know just how bad this is. The social worker made it seem bad, the cops make it look bad—but what do I know? Maybe all she needs is a decent lawyer to untangle it."

"Maybe," Sam murmurs, but I can tell he doesn't believe it any more than I do.

"This new rehab place…" I prompt him.

"Maybe it's a long shot, but I thought it might be worth mentioning. They have intensive recovery programs from four to twelve weeks, and since it's owned by the same company we'd get a reasonable discount on the fee. Plus, it's only an hour away, so that's a bonus."

"Okay," I say, and I rise. "I need to get back to her in case she's woken up."

We return to Annie's room to find her still dozing lightly, so we quietly take the visitors' chairs to wait for her to wake. I pretend to play with my phone while Sam reads a newspaper, and the silence is a relief. I'm flicking through my Facebook feed, but I don't see anything that flies past me on the screen. My mind is elsewhere, back in Sam's office, reliving the conversation with Mary Rafferty. Maybe I could have liked Mary, if I'd met her in another professional setting—one where she and I were on equal footing, instead of this messy encounter. Now that I'm calmer, I can recognize that she was almost charming in that polite, friendly way I've grown to appreciate after eight years in the South. I'm still bristling at the way she leaped to judge my sister, but I reluctantly acknowledge that's probably necessary for her job. How many times a day does she have to quickly assess a child welfare situation?

Her intentions are probably good. Surely no one would work for CPS unless they genuinely cared about children. But that doesn't change how completely, bewilderingly messed up all of this is, or how maddening it is that the state's first response is to grab for Annie's parental rights. I'm only hoping that an attorney can make sense of this.

"Lexie." Annie's eyes are still closed when she speaks suddenly, and I startle.

"Yes?"

"You're tapping your feet and it's driving me insane."

I didn't even realize I was doing it. I press my feet hard into the floor and mutter, "Sorry."

Annie wakes properly then, and after toying with the cookies and juice box that someone left on her table while she slept, she asks Sam if he will do her a favor.

"Sure," he says warily.

"Can you get Eliza?" she asks. Her voice is small, and as soon as he leaves the room, I prompt her, "Are you in pain?" She's scratching herself again, and her eyes move quickly around the room, like she's scanning for an escape route. I frown and approach the bed. "What is it, Annie?"

"Eighteen hours," she mutters.

"What's eighteen hours?"

"Since I *scored*, Lexie. Eighteen hours since I scored. Maybe they can give me a little morphine. That's safe in pregnancy, isn't it? Just a little, I won't need much—just to take the edge off."

"You've already had the methadone," I murmur, and Annie scowls at me.

"Fuck methadone. Did you see the dosage he ordered me? Twenty milligrams. You think that's going to keep me out of withdrawal? I *need* something more."

The door opens, and Sam and Eliza interrupt what was probably about to become an ugly sparring match.

"Let's chat," Eliza says, and she helps herself to a seat at the edge of Annie's bed. "Feeling okay?"

"No," Annie says abruptly, but then she sighs. "What's the plan?"

The overall picture Eliza presents to us is murky. Annie and the baby are stable for now, but if there's any change at all in their condition, Eliza will deliver immediately. In preparation for this, she's giving Annie a series of steroid shots to mature the baby's lungs, because there's also no telling how it's going to cope with delivery. It's surely going to be tiny—with an estimated size of only a few pounds.

"The baby is suffering from what we call intrauterine growth restriction," Eliza tells Annie carefully. She then goes to great pains to point out to Annie that this might just be related to the high blood pressure, and perhaps it would have happened anyway, even if narcotics weren't a factor. I know that it isn't as simple as that—perhaps Annie's high blood pressure is just genetic, and the baby's reduced size just bad luck. But heroin abuse in pregnancy tends to restrict the growth of the baby—and then there's Annie's poor lifestyle. And in any case, if Annie had been under proper medical care, she'd likely have been on bed rest and medication to manage all of this before it impacted the baby's development.

"So if things remain stable," I ask Eliza, "when will you deliver?"

"Ideally, we'll keep the baby in utero for another four weeks..." Eliza murmurs, but I can tell from her careful tone that she's not optimistic about this time frame.

"And how are you planning on managing Annie's withdrawal symptoms?" Sam asks quietly.

"I consulted with an addiction specialist this morning, and he agrees that methadone is the best option for you, Annie." My sister gives a frustrated groan, but Eliza's gaze doesn't waver. She presses on patiently. "There are alternatives we might have considered if your condition wasn't so complex—but given that there are a lot of moving parts here, we want you to stick with the methadone. We know it's completely safe."

"It just doesn't work. Not for me. Look at me now, for God's sake."

"Ron ordered you a very low dose last night," Eliza explains. "He thought it best to treat you conservatively given how unstable things were—but seeing how quickly you're experiencing withdrawal symptoms, I'm suggesting a much higher dose."

"It won't work anyway. Methadone has never stopped me from using."

"Okay, tell me about that. Why doesn't it work, Annie?" Eliza asks gently.

"It just *doesn't*," Annie snaps at the doctor. The frustration and impatience in her tone seems inappropriate somehow, perhaps because of how carefully Eliza has prompted the question. But Annie is coming apart before our eyes and all I can think is... *thank goodness we didn't tell her about the social worker.* I'm not sure Annie would be up to dealing with that news just yet—and she's clearly not kidding about the withdrawal symptoms. She's trembling, and the hands that have been resting on her belly press her hair back from her face behind her ears, then again when the hair falls forward immediately, and she groans in frustration and clenches her hands into fists. "You *know* it doesn't work for me, Lexie. I was on methadone when I was at your place last time, and that was a disaster."

"Annie," I say softly, "this time just has to be different. You don't have a choice this time—you *can't* just go cold turkey, and don't you think it's going to look better for the judge tomorrow if you start some treatment before the hearing?"

I don't tell her about Mary's comments about judges "not liking" maintenance programs, and if I'm honest with myself, I'm not sure I understand it. How could judges not like one of the only evidenced-based treatments we have to offer people suffering addictions? I make a mental note to clarify this with the attorney.

"Well, I only came here in the first place because *you* said you wouldn't let them charge me," Annie snaps. I open my mouth to respond, but Sam interrupts flatly,

"And if Lexie hadn't convinced you to come here, your baby might not have made it even this far." I shake my head at Sam furiously, but he persists, and I groan in frustration as he pulls all of the coldness right out of his tone as he adds quite calmly, "Lexie can't fix this for you, Annie." Annie is staring at him through narrowed eyes, but he shrugs, unaffected by her anger. "This is *your* mess, and there's no easy way to fix it—no easy path out of trouble this time. There's simply no painless solution for Lexie to find."

Annie's nostrils flare, and now she and I are both staring at Sam. He has no right to speak to my sister like that, even if he *was* defending me. But nothing he has said is untrue. Every single word was simple, uncomfortable truth. I'm so torn—a jumbled web of contradicting emotions. I'm angry with Sam; I'm angry with Annie. I'm grateful to Sam; I'm worried for Annie.

"I don't *care* if it's painful. We just have to keep the baby safe, and then we have to find a way that I can keep it," Annie croaks. "I don't *care* what happens to me. I just want my baby to be okay. Can't you all see that?"

"I can see it," I whisper, and I fumble to wrap my fingers through hers. Annie looks at me, her gaze desperate, her eyes filled with tears.

"Lexie, I want to do better," she chokes. "I want to keep my baby. I'll do anything, I promise. What you said earlier…are you *absolutely* sure there's no way to stop the baby from experiencing withdrawal?" She's directed the question to me instead of Eliza, and this time I catch myself before I take charge. I look at Annie's obstetrician, who shakes her head sadly.

"I'm so sorry, Annie. There's probably not. Sometimes, babies exposed to narcotics in utero do avoid NAS, but it's rare."

Annie sighs and wipes at her cheeks then rubs her temples. When she speaks again, she's pitiful—her tone is completely flat and she's staring into space.

"So I don't have a choice, then."

Oh God, Annie. You have no idea yet how little choice you're going to have.

"You *have* had a choice," I say suddenly. Annie looks to me in shock and I realize she's assuming I meant about using the drugs in the first place, so I clarify hastily, "You've chosen to come here with us and do the right thing for your baby. You could have kept burying your head in the sand and stayed at the trailer. I know that would have been easier. So don't sell yourself short, okay?"

Annie slumps again.

"So if I stay on the methadone, can I go home?"

"Oh, no." Eliza winces, and she shakes her head. "No, that's absolutely not an option—not given how unwell you were when you came in. You'll need to stay here in the hospital until you deliver."

"But I can't afford this place," Annie whispers. She slumps forward, wraps her arms around her bump again and says flatly, "I can't stay here."

"We're taking care of it, Annie," Sam says quietly.

"I don't even know you. I can't let you do that," she snaps. It's amazing how quickly Annie's miserable desperation morphs back into anger and resentment. As her desperation for a fix mounts, her mood will become increasingly unstable. I know from experience that if she's not sufficiently medicated soon, this easy irritation will grow and grow until her rage is completely out of control.

"Lexie knows me well enough to agree to marry me," Sam points out, then he flashes her his most charming smile. "I *know* that you want what's best for your baby, Annie. I barely know you, but even I can see it, plain as day. This hospital can provide you with the best medical care in the state. Eliza is one of the top high-risk obstetricians in the country, and we have a neonatal intensive care unit on-site. *This* is the place to be, Annie."

"What do you think?" Annie glances at me. "Do you really want me here? At your fancy boyfriend's fancy hospital?"

Not even a little bit.

"I want what's best for you and for the baby. And Sam's right, you're not going to get any better care than you are here."

Annie takes a deep breath, then bursts into noisy sobs.

"I'm sorry, I really am, I'm so sorry. I'm sorry about all of this—sorry that you've all been dragged into it, sorry for the baby…but if they take it away, I just don't know how I'll live with myself—"

The grief on Annie's face is unbearable. I stand and wrap my arms around her, pulling her hard against myself. I press my lips against her stringy hair and guilt washes over me like waves. She smells like her trailer; like poverty, and addiction and a total lack of self-care—and it's wrong. This is not who Annie was supposed to become. I rub my hand up and down her upper arm, and note automatically the sinewy muscle beneath my fingers, and the bone…it's all too close to the skin. It's a miracle that Annie has been able to sustain a pregnancy at all.

"Annie," I say, my voice low and urgent, "all that matters is doing what we can *now* for you and the baby, okay?"

"I'm going to try harder, I really am. I really want to be a good mom."

"And you are *going* to be," I say firmly, but I have to add a silent prayer even as I say it that the court gives her a chance to at least *try*. "But step one has to be staying in the hospital and starting on methadone. A proper course, a decent dosage—enough to really hold those withdrawals at bay."

Annie clears her throat, and she forces out a long, slow breath. Then she wipes her eyes with the back of her wrists, and as she snakes those skinny arms back around her belly, she offers me a single, silent nod.

I'm spellbound by this compliance—this relatively easy agreeability. I try to think of the other times Annie agreed to use a maintenance program, but the years have blurred in my memory, and all I remember for sure is that it has always been difficult to get her on board. She used to complain of bone pain—agonizing, supposedly—right from her first dose. I'd researched this and found that narcotics withdrawals *can* cause pain—but Annie was always on a high enough dose that this should never have been a factor. I'd eventually come to the conclusion that it was just yet another excuse—setting up the scenario so that when she used again, she had something to blame.

But Annie has never had a reason outside of herself to stick with the maintenance programs before—it's always just been her. As I consider this, I'm startled by a burst of optimism. Maybe she can make it work this time. Maybe the baby is reason enough for her to finally, *finally* get her shit together.

"Good." I breathe the word on a sigh of relief, and Eliza rises immediately.

"I'm going to go organize the prescription and we'll increase that methadone right now—before your withdrawal gets any worse, okay? You know how this works—the symptoms will stop almost immediately."

"Thank you," Annie says unevenly.

"Can I speak to you for a minute, please, Alexis?" Eliza asks quietly, but there's an undertone of tension and I realize that I've known Eliza for all of ten minutes and I've already pissed her off.

"You already discussed some of this with her?" Eliza says sharply, as soon as we are safely out of Annie's earshot in the hallway.

"I talked to her about methadone and NAS just before the police came, yes. But why didn't you? Shouldn't that have been the first thing you sorted out with her?"

"I *deliberately* didn't talk to her about how we'll handle that aspect of her treatment—I wanted to speak to the addiction specialist first so that I didn't overwhelm her before I was sure which approach to recommend. I understand that you're her sister, Alexis, and that you're also a GP—but *I'm* her specialist, and if we're going to work together to get your sister through this pregnancy, you're going to have to leave the medicine up to me. Are we clear on that?"

"I need to be involved in these decisions—I need to understand exactly how you're planning on treating her," I say stiffly.

"Even if you were a specialist consulting obstetrician—which as I understand it, you aren't—it's not appropriate for you to treat your own sister. Her case is complex. She's under my care because she needs to be. I'll try to keep you in the loop when it's practical, but this is the last time you tread on my toes. Right?"

Eliza and I lock eyes. She's red-faced and frustrated, and so am I, even as I understand the logic behind what she's saying. Wasn't I just thinking the same thing myself this morning?

But this is Annie—my Annie—*my* sister, *my* responsibility.

Sam clears his throat behind us, and I turn to find that he's followed us into the hallway. My frustration eases when his concerned, pleading face swims into view. I sigh, and then glance back to Eliza as I nod.

"Why don't you concentrate your efforts on finding Annie some legal help?" Eliza suggests.

"Fine." I sigh, and Sam takes my hand.

"Thanks, Eliza. For all of this."

"Thank me when we get that baby safely out into the world and well," Eliza says quietly. "There's a long road ahead for them yet."

It's not as easy as I expect, but two hours and four phone calls later I find myself sitting in the offices of Bernadette Walters, attorney at law. I'm frazzled by then—if not from the multiple calls it took to find the right lawyer to actually help us—then by Sam's determination to hover at my side while I did so.

"I'll come with you," he says, when I tell him the details of my appointment with the lawyer.

"I'll be fine, Sam. Why don't you go check in on your patients?"

"Are you sure? I mean, I'm off today so I figured I'd just tag along with you, see if I can help."

"You really don't need to do that," I say. "Go and check in with your office." He hesitates, and I sigh and pull him close for a hug. "Honestly, Sam, I'm fine. We've put you out enough. You don't need to come with me to the lawyer, too."

"I'm not 'put out,' Lex," he murmurs into my hair. "I'm in this for the long haul—I'm going to do everything I can to help you help her. But I do have some things to check up on, so I'll go to the office now and catch up with you later." He kisses me gently, and stares into my eyes as he adds, "You'll call if you need me?"

"Of course," I promise, and when he finally starts to walk away, I actually feel confused. He's crowding me a little, and given that there's a big part of me that still wants to pretend none of this is happening, I'm relieved for the space. But I've also never had someone support me through a crisis before, and as I watch Sam disappear down the hallway, I miss him so much more than I would on any ordinary day.

I've never needed to contact a criminal lawyer before, but if I had, I didn't imagine I would have opted for one who had a dusty office above a furniture store. But despite Bernadette Walters's disappointing office accommodations, she comes highly recommended by the attorney Sam and I used to manage the purchase of our house. Bernadette has successfully defended a number of patients in a similar situation to Annie. She's tall but extremely thin, and she has a frantic energy about her—she speaks at a million miles an hour and is constantly adjusting the fall of her hair around her shoulders.

I stare at her and try to figure out how old she is. She's wearing a trendy fitted shirt and a pencil skirt, but the jewelry she's paired it with could easily have been snatched from the wardrobe of a senior citizen. Her face is smooth, but her long dark hair is liberally streaked with gray. I average the contradictions out and decide that she's probably in her fifties—but I could easily be twenty years off in either direction.

After polite greetings, Bernadette insists that I call her "Bernie," and she all but snatches the paperwork from my hand before I've even taken a seat. She scoops frameless reading glasses up from her desk and begins scanning the page as she sits.

"This chemical endangerment law was never meant to apply to pregnant women." She sighs, shaking her head. "They enacted it in response to cases where meth labs were found in family homes…baby in the playpen in the kitchen, sucking on their pacifier while Mom and Dad cook meth on the stove right next to them. Unfortunately, about the same time some DAs decided they were going to try to address the so-called epidemic of babies born with neonatal abstinence syndrome, and the wording in the statute was vague enough that it allowed them to push the law to a place it was never supposed to go." Bernie looks up from the warrant and meets my gaze. "In short, Lexie, your sister is in some serious trouble here. There's a criminal charge to deal with, as well as the immediate matter—the hearing tomorrow that could potentially revoke Anne's parental rights over her fetus."

"So, what do we do?"

"Ordinarily, my advice would be to get your sister into a rehab center as quickly as humanly possible—if it *is* humanly possible, which it generally isn't since rehab centers avoid pregnant women like the plague," Bernie tells me, peering at me over the top of her glasses. "But my secretary told me that your sister is quite unwell so that's probably not an option anyway."

"She won't even leave the hospital before the baby comes," I inform her. "Even if she does, she obviously can't detox while she's pregnant, and the social worker said that a pharmacological maintenance program doesn't count."

"Unfortunately not. My experience is that here in Alabama, judges generally don't count an opioid-replacement program as adequate effort toward rehabilitation."

"Well, that's just bullshit," I snap, then I wince and shake my head. "I'm really sorry—I just don't understand. All of the science says that maintenance programs work, particularly if it's in conjunction with therapy. So why wouldn't it *count?*"

"Absurd, isn't it? Look, we're generally dealing with very conservative judges, and there's nothing in the law that says that people need to be referred to *evidence-based* treatment. We see a lot of referrals to abstinence-based programs. Twelve-step programs are particularly popular."

"But that doesn't make any sense." Particularly not in Annie's case. I did drag her to a twelve-step program for a while when we ran out of alternatives, but just the mention of "a higher power" is generally enough to give both of us hives.

"You're preaching to the choir here, honey." Bernie sighs. "I know how frustrating all of this is, believe me. It's like the law was passed by a bunch of men in suits who never even intended to address this scenario," she says, then she snorts, "which, of course, is exactly what happened. But let's take a step back for a second. Give me an idea of what we're dealing with here with your sister, Alexis. Does she have a criminal record?"

"I don't know," I admit. "I don't think so. I mean, she's been charged at least twice before—but I think the charges were dropped both times. She was charged with possession in Chicago, but she got off on a technicality. And then two years ago she was caught trying to steal narcotics from a medical clinic, but the charges were dropped."

But for my groveling and pleading with my boss, that attempted theft of class A drugs charge would have put her away for a long time. There was CCTV footage of her doing it, plus the security guard at work caught her while she was still in the meds room.

"So is this her first attempt to get clean?"

I clear my throat.

"Not by a long shot, unfortunately."

"So, how many previous attempts at rehab?"

"Many," I admit. "But you know, this time might be different, with the baby and all…"

"Has she met with the CPS social worker yet? This…" Bernie looks down at the paperwork in her hand and reads, "Mary Rafferty?"

"No, Annie was too sick to be interviewed, but I spoke with her this morning."

"How did it go?"

"Not well," I murmur. "She seemed to have made up her mind pretty quickly that Annie wasn't going to make a fit mother."

"Are they doing a home visit to review Anne's living conditions?"

"No, she said not at this stage."

"All right, Alexis. Here's the thing." Bernie lowers the paperwork and she sighs. "There's pretty much nothing I can do for your sister tomorrow."

"Oh." I'm confused, and I frown at her. "I don't understand. Why did you agree to take the case if you can't help?"

"There are two courts involved in your sister's situation—the juvenile court, which will hear the petition to strip Annie of her right to parent the baby, and the criminal court, where she may eventually face trial for the chemical endangerment charge. The immediate issue is the parental rights challenge, and there's nothing I can do for her in that regard." She turns the paperwork around so I can see it and she points out, "It will be heard in a juvenile court, which is closed to everyone but court staff. Annie will have to go on her own. She can't even have legal representation. But this hearing is all about the *baby's* best interests, so an attorney will be appointed to make decisions for the baby on a day-to-day basis. We call it a guardian ad litem. In this case, they've nominated a guy named Bill Weston. I've come across him before. He's a nice enough guy, but like a lot of attorneys who opt to do this kind of work, he's a real, old-school conservative. And if tomorrow goes as I expect it will, he'll be the one who gives consent or otherwise to all of your sister's treatment for the duration of her pregnancy."

I blink at her, then I shake my head.

"No! Surely they can't do that!"

"Actually, they *can* do that, and it looks like they're going to."

"But that's not fair."

"No, it's not."

"We have to do something. We can't let them do this."

"I'm so sorry, Alexis. There isn't *anything* we can do. That's just the way this is going to play out, I'm afraid."

I'm slipping into shock. My face feels hot and my mouth is dry. I hear a frantic, rhythmic tapping I can't identify, and then I realize it's the sound of my feet beating against the floor. Bernie leans forward on her elbow and her gaze is sympathetic.

"The judge is going to review the social worker's assessment, and if she's not even going to bother to visit Annie's home at this stage—I'd say it's pretty certain she's going to recommend that Annie lose her rights to the child. The judge will probably make a ruling to appoint Bill as guardian ad litem, and he and the assistant DA will make a deal with Annie. Most likely they'll set some kind of requirement for her to complete a rehabilitation program, parenting classes, attain some minimum living standards and probably get and keep a job…that kind of thing. And if and when she meets those requirements, they'll restore her parental rights and generally the DA will also drop the criminal charges."

I don't want to admit this to Bernie, but the reality is, if they set *those* particular requirements, then Annie is going to have to completely reconfigure her entire existence.

"At least there's hope?" I say, but I sound defeated, and Bernie grimaces.

"I guess so. But you should know that in practice, once parental rights are stripped from a woman like Annie, it can be almost impossible to get them back. CPS really doesn't make it easy on their clients, but Annie does have one advantage that almost none of my other clients in this situation have."

"And what's that?"

Bernie smiles sadly.

"You."

I exhale a shaky breath and tilt my head back to stare at the ceiling. I'm trying to reconfigure my expectations for the next twelve months of my life. Instead of planning a wedding and focusing on my work, I'm going to be once again diving down a rabbit hole with Annie, this time, dragging Sam along behind me.

"So if they do offer her some kind of deal to get herself sorted out tomorrow," I ask reluctantly, "and she fails to meet their requirements—what happens then?"

"Well, if she doesn't satisfy the demands of the court in full, she'll be tried for the chemical endangerment offense. Realistically, if that happens, she's likely to get a prison term."

My gaze snaps back to Bernie.

"Prison?" I gasp.

"They aren't insignificant sentences, either. Let's say the baby is born healthy, but Annie can't satisfy the DA that she's reha-bilitated and the trial proceeds and she's found or pleads guilty. That's a sentence of one to ten years."

"*What?*"

"And let's say the baby *isn't* healthy, but the DA decides its illness or injury is somehow related to her drug use. That's ten to twenty years."

"But—"

"And if—I mean, awful as it is to say…well, if the baby hap-pened to die, and there was *some* way to link the death to her drug use? That's up to ninety-nine years."

"How close does the link have to be?" I whisper. I'm think-ing about Annie's high blood pressure and the baby's restricted growth and all of the things that could still go wrong. And even *I* have wondered whether Annie's health crisis is related to her drug use—so, it's not such a long shot for her prosecutor to draw, if, God forbid, something tragic *did* happen.

"Just off the top of my head, one direct precedent does come to mind—a woman with a history of premature birth went into labor very early, and the child didn't survive. She had tested pos-itive for meth, but she had an expert witness willing to testify this had nothing to do with the stillbirth—but the woman's re-quest to have that specialist testify on her behalf was declined. She pled guilty in return for a reduced jail term—it was too risky to go to trial with the cards so obviously stacked against her."

"A woman lost her baby, and the state *jailed* her for it?"

"Unfortunately, yes. Are you familiar with the Jane Doe chemical endangerment case of 2015, Lexie?"

"Should I be?" I stare at her blankly, but Bernie's sigh speaks of a frustration that's much larger than this god-awful situation with my sister.

"Every woman in America should be familiar with that case," Bernie mutters. "A woman was imprisoned on drug charges—she's known as Jane Doe because the juvenile court case was closed, like your sister's case is. Jane Doe requested leave from the prison to have an abortion she had already booked before she was locked up. Just like your sister here, the DA petitioned a juvenile court to strip Jane Doe of her parental rights, and the fetus was given a guardian ad litem. Keep in mind, we're talking about a first-trimester fetus in an *unwanted* pregnancy. If the law can be applied to overrule Jane Doe's wishes, then it's hardly surprising that it's been applied to intervene in your sister's case."

"Did she have the baby?"

"No one knows what happened to her, actually. We're talking about the juvenile court, just like your sister's hearing tomorrow—so the matter was sealed. The only reason we know about this case at all was that civil rights advocates petitioned a federal court on her behalf to try to get her access to the abortion clinic, but just before the ruling came down, Jane Doe suddenly changed her mind and apparently decided she didn't want the termination after all. And because we don't know her name, we don't know where she ended up."

"Is this common?" I ask Bernie, shaking my head. "These chemical endangerment charges? CPS taking people's kids away like this?"

"Well, that's actually hard to say. Chemical endangerment charges like Annie's are on the increase, but it's impossible to say how often families are losing their children as a result of them. Those juvenile court hearings are closed so...no public records available." She snorts and shakes her head. "Awfully convenient, some might say."

"Why isn't there an uproar?"

"Pregnant drug addicts, Alexis. *Pregnant drug addicts.* How much sympathy do you think the general public has for women who use illicit drugs while they're growing babies?"

I knew Annie was in trouble, but it's slowly sinking in that this situation is even worse than I'd considered. "What the hell are we going to do?"

"All we *can* do about this hearing tomorrow is to coach Annie a little in how to deal with the proceedings, and then make sure she understands that she has to precisely complete whatever is required of her after."

This reminds me of Annie's other crisis, the situation with her blood pressure. I clear my throat and shuffle forward in my chair. "Well, actually, Annie just can't leave the hospital, not even for the hearing. It's not safe."

"Okay. I'll call the judge and request a bedside hearing. We'll need a letter from her obstetrician confirming her condition and quite clearly stating that she can't leave the hospital."

I call the hospital, and I speak to Eliza's secretary, who emails the letter through within minutes, and that's enough to convince the judge to move the hearing to Annie's bedside. Bernie high-fives me when this is confirmed, and after making plans to visit Annie with me in the morning, she walks me to the door of her office.

"I know it's a lot to get your head around, Alexis."

"You're not wrong about that." I laugh weakly, but the sound is hollow and I feel a thundering headache coming on. I press my fingers to my temples and try to calm myself down. Bernie grimaces and pats my shoulder a little awkwardly as she adds, "I know this is frightening, and the custodial sentences for this crime are incredibly tough here in Alabama—but still, there *is* a way to avoid them. Annie just *has* to complete whatever treatment the judge mandates. If your sister really wants to raise her baby, this is her last chance to prove she can do the right thing by it."

8

ANNIE

Dear Luke,
  That year with Mom so unwell—

Luke,
  The year after Dad's death—

To Luke,
  After a while, we—

Luke,
  I can't fucking do this.

Dear Luke,
  This is my fifth attempt at this entry and it's awful and I'm a mess. But I'm going to keep trying until I make it work. It hurts to do this, and when I hurt, I want to get high. Since I'm in rehab, that's pretty much off the table, and so instead I get angry. You

might have noticed that when I stormed out of your office this morning.

But I need to get better. I need to get back to my baby. So here goes nothing.

As we passed the twelve-month anniversary of Dad's death, Mom gradually began emerging from her depression. Lexie had been promising me this would happen eventually, and she was quite triumphant when the improvement started to become obvious. There were little indications at first—coming home from school to find Mom reading a book with the curtains open, or Mom actually eating without Lexie nagging her into it, or spontaneously dressing and doing her hair. I had forgotten how pretty my mom was with her hair freshly washed and hanging loose around her shoulder blades, and the first time I walked in the door to find Mom wearing a dress instead of her pajamas, I was so shocked that I actually dropped my school bag.

It took a long time to realize that there was a pattern to these good days—but finally, we figured out that the good days were Wednesdays. Lexie and I racked our brains to try to figure out what it was about Wednesday that made Mom so happy—was one of us born that day? Was it the day she married Dad? Was it a coincidence— or maybe it took so much out of Mom that it took her a full week to get the energy back to do it all again?

Then school break came. The first Wednesday of the break, the three of us were sitting around the table eating breakfast when Mom told us that she was expecting some guests. This was even more shocking than the sight of Mom in her dress. She had been declining most requests to visit with her for a full year, and as far as Lexie and I knew, she'd lost touch with all her friends.

"I have some friends who visit me on a Wednesday," Mom told

us. "I'm excited for you girls to meet them. They've been helping me find meaning in what happened."

I was curious at first, but as soon as we opened the door that day, I felt my heart sink. I remember staring at the people on our doorstep, and then looking to Lexie to see if she was as confused as I was. I realized immediately that Lexie wasn't confused—she was suspicious.

Even at first glance, Mom's "friends" weren't your average visitors. Robert was there front and center, surrounded by women carrying Bibles. The women were each styled in variations on a theme—they all had very long hair beneath neatly pressed head scarves, and they wore skirts to their ankles. But although Robert was just an average, clean-cut-looking guy, dressed relatively normally, there was something about him that made my skin crawl. It took me years to put my finger on it—all I knew at the beginning was that I didn't like him, and I really didn't trust him.

Lexie and I pretended to read in the living room so we could eavesdrop on the goings-on in the dining room. Robert led a Bible study, and Mom joined in with as much enthusiasm as we'd seen her show toward anything since Dad's death. She'd always been quietly religious, as had Dad, but this entire affair seemed different somehow—much more pointed, much more zealous.

"They're from a sect...it's like a closed church. I think they all live out at that little village near the lake—it's called Winterton."

There was another shock awaiting us when Robert and the women went to leave. At the door, Robert paused, and while he turned his gaze to Lexie and me, he said to Mom, "So, Deborah, we will be seeing you all on Saturday?"

"What's Saturday?" Lexie asked him. I was glad she asked. I

wanted to know, too, but I was too petrified to speak to Robert—his presence was so imposing.

"It's the Lord's day, Alexis. Your mother is bringing you to worship with us."

Sometimes at Christmas, Dad and Mom took us to church services, but religion had been such a small part of our lives.

That Saturday we had our first taste of life in the fundamentalist sect Robert belonged to—which is kind of like someone who'd only ever seen puddles being dumped without a life jacket in the middle of the ocean. Mom made us wear our longest skirts and we had to wear our hair down, and then Robert picked us up in a minivan. Mom rode up front with him while Lexie and I sat in the far back and whispered guesses about what this church was going to be like. We speculated about how weird it was going to be, and we were definitely right about that, but we had no idea what we were in for. Lex and I were still thinking we were headed toward a church like the ones we'd occasionally been to with Mom and Dad.

We weren't prepared for an isolated community in its own little village, five miles out of town. And we certainly weren't prepared when, as we were walking into the long, windowless hall where the services were held, Robert turned to us and passed us head scarves. He stared into my eyes as he fixed it over my head, and my heart started to race and butterflies with razor-sharp wings seemed to appear out of nowhere in my stomach. I felt cold and confused and uncomfortable, and I had no idea what it meant or what to do about it. When he was done, Robert rested a hand on Lexie's shoulder and one on mine, and he said very sternly, "Girls, you are not to speak once we pass through those doors. You may only ask questions and speak when the service is over and we move out of the auditorium. Not so much as a whisper, got it?"

And so for the next three hours we sat in stunned, bored silence as the service dragged on and on. There were hymns and prayers and several sermons—all delivered by men. The women in the congregation sat in total silence—even the female children sat silent, their eyes glazed with boredom, just as mine and Lexie's were. I tried to amuse myself during this enforced silence—looking around at the congregation, wondering who all of these people were. I imagined lives for them. The lady in the blue head scarf was Jill, an expert marksman and martial arts expert, who worked in a shoe store by day and fought crime by night. The young woman next to her was training to be a nurse, and she wanted to work in Africa when she graduated. The plump, elderly woman with the gray shawl had once fallen in love with a king of some far-flung country, but his family did not like her and he sent her away, and she'd never again given her heart to a man.

This game amused me for some time, until I realized with some shock that one of the subjects I was imagining a world for was actually my grandmother, Dad's mother, and she was sitting with a woman whom I recognized as Dad's sister, Aunt Ursula. I had met this aunt exactly twice—once in an awkward exchange at the grocery store when Dad was still alive, and then again as she left his wake. I tried to draw Lexie's attention to this shocking discovery, but she was staring at the preacher, and the more determined my attempts became the more attention they drew from Mom. Eventually Mom shot us a furious glare and I gave up. But having realized that Dad had some tie to this odd church, I began to wonder if Mom did, too. It didn't take me long to locate her mother also, sitting several rows behind us.

I had no idea what to make of all of this, but it unnerved me and I felt myself becoming oddly teary at the realization that this odd, uncomfortable place somehow had links to my family. When the service finally ended and we filed back outside into the too-bright sunshine, Lexie caught my arm and whispered into my ear, "We have to get her away from these people."

When our grandmothers approached a few minutes later, their cordial greetings and awkward small talk did nothing to comfort Lexie or me. We knew—right from the beginning—that something was off about that community.

The challenge with freeing her from these people was that we'd become so isolated over that year since Dad's death. Mom had effectively become a shut-in, and our old network had all but vanished from our lives. Lexie and I talked to some of the teachers at school, colleagues who had also been Mom's friends, but she became very defensive when they tried to talk to her and was then angry with Lex and me for mentioning it. Lexie even walked to the fire station one afternoon to see if Captain Edwards could help, but when he came to the front door, Mom refused to speak to him. So while we were worried about Mom's involvement with the strange church, we didn't know how to stop it, and Mom always reacted violently whenever we questioned her about it.

"They are helping me, girls. Can't you see that? Your dad's family is there, and so is mine—I need the support so that I can be a good mom to you. It's working, isn't it?"

And she was certainly right about that. Mom seemed calmer and more stable, and she cared again about us. She little by little opened up to us about an entire history that we'd never known, explaining that she and Dad had grown up with their families in the village, but that they'd left together in their late teens.

"We just wanted to see what else was out there in the world, and I wanted to go to college but wasn't allowed to while I was there—

girls are only allowed to study up to the end of middle school," she explained to Lexie and me. "And because we left, we weren't allowed to stay in touch with our families much after that. But, girls, I need my family now, and I need my friends there. You need them, too. I know the services are long and it all seems a bit strange, but can you go along with it? For me?"

So of course we said yes, but that didn't mean Lexie or I liked what was happening with Mom. She might have been coming out of her shell, but she was also rapidly adopting the assembly's rules in our home, and our lives began to change. The preachers at the church prohibited television and the radio, and so Lexie and I came home from school one day to find ours on the front curb. We begged her to reconsider this, but Mom became increasingly convinced that TV and the radio were pathways for "worldly ways" to enter our house.

"You can survive without them," she said stiffly, when I threw an Olympic-level tantrum in a last-ditch effort to get her to change her mind. "There are no televisions or radios in Winterton—not even in the cars. No one even misses them."

Then she began to censor the books we were allowed to read. I was right in the middle of a Nancy Drew phase—Nancy was wearing only a bathing suit on one of the covers, so that was the end of that. Soon Mom was compulsively checking the books we were reading and asking us about what we had learned and discussed during the school day. Lexie and I were worried about where her paranoia might end, but we weren't at all prepared when she sat us down after dinner one night to make an announcement.

Mom had decided to marry Robert and she would be selling the house. We would all be moving to Robert's home in Winterton.

"Your dad and I were wrong to start our family out here, and I can see that now. This world has nothing to offer us except pain.

You girls will be so much better off out there, where I can keep you safe. The elders can teach you to live righteous lives."

We cried and we screamed, and we told her we would never go—as if we had a say, as if we had any power at all as eight- and twelve-year-old girls. I was too young to realize it—but for a child, there is protection in stability, and strength to be found in a life that feels controlled.

But when Mom decided to move us into Robert's house, Lexie and I were about to find out just how vulnerable and powerless we actually were.

9

LEXIE

"So, what happened?"

Annie is sitting up in bed when I get back to the hospital from Bernie's office, breathtaking hope and optimism in her eyes.

"It's not good."

"Didn't she take my case?"

I sit on the edge of the bed and take Annie's hand in mine. She's watching me closely.

"Annie," I say carefully, "you're in a lot of trouble."

"I know," she whispers. "Of course I know that. But surely the lawyer can help?"

"She..." Oh God, where do I start? This would be so much easier if Annie didn't have that blazing hopefulness in her gaze. I take another deep breath. "Well, the lawyer—Bernie—she's arranged for the hearing tomorrow to be held here at your bedside, so that's a good start."

"Okay. Great." The fear on Annie's face eases for just a moment, but then she scans my face again and she sighs. "Tell me, Lexie. I can take it."

"There are a few things you need to know." It's like the lump in my throat keeps creeping higher, and it takes a more determined effort to clear my throat this time. My palms are sweaty, as if *I'm* the one in trouble. "The hearing is actually about the best interests of the baby, Annie. It's the juvenile court, so it's a closed session. That means you won't be allowed to have Bernie here with you."

"I can't have a lawyer with me?"

"No, Annie."

"Okay then—can *you* come in?"

I shake my head.

"Only the court staff can be in attendance."

"But...aren't I the one in trouble?"

"Well, yes..."

"But I can't even have my own *lawyer*? Isn't that in the Miranda rights?"

"This hearing tomorrow isn't a criminal trial. It's just about the baby. They..."

I can't say it. I try several times, but the words stubbornly refuse to leave my mouth. I meet Annie's gaze, and her face falls.

"They want to take it away from me already, don't they?"

"The hearing tomorrow is to remove your parental rights."

"They aren't even going to give me a *chance* to try to raise it?" she whispers, and her eyes fill with tears. She squeezes them shut and sinks back onto the pillow. "No, Lexie. Please, no."

I take her hand firmly in mine and press on.

"If the judge agrees with CPS tomorrow...they'll appoint a lawyer to the baby, and he will make the decisions about your treatment from here on in."

Annie's eyes open. Her brow furrows as she digests this. When she speaks, she's uncertain.

"Wait—you're saying *I* don't get a lawyer, but the baby does?"

"That's right."

"And this lawyer is going to make decisions about my treatment now?"

"Until the birth, yes."

"But... I'm already doing everything the doctors have said," Annie says. "Isn't that enough?"

"The court is just going to try to ensure that the baby is safe."

"Safe," Annie repeats, and her voice is no longer in a whisper. Her nostrils flare, and now she's staring at me, the beginnings of rage simmering just below the surface. "What's that supposed to mean?"

"Annie, don't get defensive," I say softly.

"Defensive? You've got to be *kidding* me. You're telling me that some lawyer is going to decide what's best for *my* body and *my* baby—"

I cut her off as her voice begins to rise. There's more she needs to know, and I need to keep the conversation moving forward— I can't afford to get distracted by an argument with her now. Particularly not when I actually agree with pretty much everything she's saying.

"The judge is probably going to send you to rehab and give you a chance to get better set up for the baby...but as long as you do *exactly* what he wants, there's a good chance the DA will drop the chemical endangerment charge."

"Right." Annie sighs, shaking her head. "So it's that easy, is it?"

"Well, at least it's not hopeless, not if you follow through with whatever they ask of you. If you can get and stay clean, this is all going to work out okay—and I know that's what you want, too." Annie doesn't respond. I shake her forearm and say pointedly, "Isn't it?"

"Of course it is."

"The thing is, Annie...*if*...and I'm not saying this is going to happen, but..." The damned lump in my throat is back. Annie seems to refocus and fixes her gaze on me again. I exhale and press on. "If you can't satisfy the judge's requirements, then it might mean prison time."

"I know," she says, and I'm surprised.

"You do?"

"I told you back at the trailer. My friend was charged last year." Annie glances at me, then away. "I don't think you realize what we're dealing with here, Lexie."

"Maybe I don't really understand. Maybe I can't. But I'll tell you one thing, it doesn't really matter whether I understand or not. Whatever is coming, I'll be right beside you every step of the way."

"Even though I've let you down again and again?" she murmurs. She's staring at the roof now, dry-eyed but miserable.

"I've missed you," I say simply, and Annie glances at me.

Her gaze searches mine, then she offers me a sad smile and admits, "I've missed you, too."

"We're going to face this together, okay?"

Annie nods.

"Lexie, all that I want to do is k-keep my baby," she says, and as her voice breaks, she reaches for me and starts to cry. I wrap my arms around her and hold her close against me.

Tomorrow's hearing could bring anything, but I know one thing for sure. Two years' distance from Annie has melted away into nothing in under twenty-four hours—we're instantly close again, in a way that only sisters can understand. Our history—all of it, the good, the bad, the ugly—it's built an intimacy between us that's immune to the ravages of time and distance. This new situation I'm navigating with Annie is stressful and difficult, but on some level, I'm actually relieved that she's returned. I'll pay the price of dealing with this mess if it means I can have my sister back.

What Annie is facing is a nightmare—but she is my sister. I'd never want her to face this alone.

There's nothing I can do to convince my brain to switch off when I try to go to sleep. Even when I do sleep, my dreams are haunted by shadowy scenarios of Annie in a prison cell while her baby lies screaming, out of her reach on the other side of the bars. When the sun rises, I sit at the kitchen table with Sam, and we nurse strong coffees.

"It's not too late. If you need me, I'll take off work today," he offers.

"Oh, Sam." I wince a little, then reach across the table and squeeze his wrist. "I love you for suggesting it, I really do. But people are relying on you."

His gaze is steady on mine.

"You're the only person who matters to me, Lex. And I have a feeling you're going to need me."

"And I'll have you, but that doesn't mean your patients can't, too," I say gently, and Sam tilts his head toward me.

"Are you sure you're going to be okay today?"

"I can't even go *in* to the hearing, so it shouldn't be too difficult for me," I mutter, and Sam offers my feeble attempt at humor a laugh it really doesn't deserve.

"I mean *after*, Lexie. You're going to be dealing with the fallout on your own."

"I've been doing that for my entire life, Sam. I can handle it for one more day."

"Call my office if you need me. I'll let Cathryn know to get me out of surgery if anything drastic happens."

"I will," I promise, and I rise and walk around the table. I stand beside him and rest my hand on his shoulder. Sam turns to stare up at me.

"I mean it, Lexie. I'm here for you, in any way you need me. Okay?"

I bend and kiss him gently. "Thanks, Sam."

"Will you come in my car to the hospital?"

"No." I sigh. "I need to pick up a few things on the way."

I move to walk away, but Sam pulls me gently down onto his lap.

"You look so tired," he murmurs. There's a crease in his brow, and his concern is palpable—an open invitation for me to lean on him. I don't want to burden Sam—but I'm exhausted, and I'm anxious about what the day is going to bring.

"I couldn't sleep... I had awful dreams about it...about her."

"You're a wonderful sister, Lexie."

I don't feel like a wonderful sister. I feel powerless and frustrated, and honestly—I'm terrified. And the worst of it is that today is *not* going to be the end of all of these awful emotions. We're still right at the beginning of this chapter of Annie's life, of my life, and it could be decades before she finds her feet, if she ever does.

"Do you think people can change, Sam?" I whisper. For just a moment, he grimaces as if he really doesn't want to answer my question, and I clarify, "I just mean, do you think there's any chance she's going to overcome this?"

"The legal stuff?"

"The addiction."

Sam's gaze softens.

"People beat addiction every day, Lex. It's hard and messy, but you wouldn't have fought like you have for her over the years if you didn't see glimpses of a person worth saving among all of the chaos. Right?"

That's definitely true. I think of Annie reacting to the news of the legal complexities of her case, and how that beautifully optimistic spirit just kept trying to rise to the surface, even as I delivered the news that pushed it back down again and again.

"Right."

"So it's not a case of needing to change who she is. It's a question of *healing*."

"That's the thing... I'm a doctor. I *get* that. Healing people is what I do for a living. Why haven't I ever been able to help her?" I ask, and my voice sounds small even to my own ears.

"Have you ever had one of those diabetic patients who just

doesn't want to take their biguanides? They constantly insist they're just going to lose some weight, exercise some more..."

I think of two current patients. It's not an uncommon scenario at all.

"Of course I have."

"I get it, too. I get patients referred to me for gastric bypass or even gallbladder surgery. They come for the consult and get all of the information and when I tell them they can book in with Cathryn on the way out, they hesitate and say they'll call instead, and that usually means they won't. All you can do is keep giving the advice, keep educating, keep waiting. All you can do is offer them the treatment and hope they'll reach the point that they can face it. Addiction is the same principle, even if it works in reverse. Annie has been self-medicating for how long? Seven years? And she's getting sicker and sicker, and you've given her the advice and you keep passing her the treatment on a silver platter, but until *she's* ready to own her healing..."

"That's what's so frustrating about this. What if she's still not ready for that? How can they set *healing* as a legal requirement for a person?"

"I really don't know, honey. I guess we just hope we catch a break and this legal stuff just happens to coincide with her being genuinely ready to embrace it."

I sigh and glance at the clock.

"You really need to go, and so do I."

"I love you, Lex."

"I love you, too."

We share a gentle kiss before we part, then I slip into my car and turn toward the hospital. I stop at the mall on the way and race through the corridors to several stores—picking up some clothes and toiletries for Annie. On my way back to the car, I see the children's wear store, and I glance at my watch to check the time before I dart inside. I'm in the store for only a few minutes, but I leave with a huge bag of tiny clothing—once I start dropping white and yellow beanies and booties and jumpsuits into my arms, I find that I just can't stop. Somehow, I feel like I need to keep Annie focused on the baby—on the goal at the end of all of the hard work that lies ahead of her. Maybe the judge is about to ask the impossible of her, but don't parents *do* the impossible for their children? Annie loves this baby already; I can see it. Maybe this is the equivalent of those awful situations where a child's life is in danger and a mother somehow finds the strength to lift a car or run through a fire. Maybe if she just keeps her eyes on the prize of a better life for her child, Annie can find a way to get well.

When I finally make it to Annie's room, I'm carrying several bags from the babywear store, and she raises an eyebrow at me, then says stiffly, "You do realize a judge is coming here in a few hours to tell me I'm not allowed to keep my baby?"

"No, he's coming here in a few hours to probably tell you that there are some hurdles you need to leap before you *can* keep your baby," I correct her. "And you and I *both* need to believe you can clear those hurdles, so we need to start planning for when you do."

Annie hesitates, then offers me a strange little smile.

"Even so, you didn't have to rob the Babies 'R' Us. You've gone a bit overboard there."

"We can sort through it later and anything you don't need, I can return," I say firmly as I place the bags on a table in the corner of the room where I know she'll be able to see them during the court session.

Then I place the other bag onto the end of her bed, and I withdraw the maternity dress. It's corporate wear—a modest, long-sleeved dress, charcoal gray with a pink trim, designed to draw attention away from a pregnant belly in the workplace. Annie would never wear this dress ordinarily—not just because she hasn't held a professional job for seven years, but because she always had such a striking sense of style, and this dress is just about as dull as they come. I wasn't sure at all what Annie should wear for this hearing, but I figured she should probably dress up, to show her respect for the proceedings.

"Thank you," she says as she surveys the dress, but she seems unconvinced.

"It's just for the hearing, Annie. You can burn it after if you want." I pass her another bag, and she peers inside. "Toiletries. Some nice shampoo and some makeup. Take a shower and I'll blow-dry your hair."

Later, she sits in the visitor's chair by the window and I run the brush through her long blond hair. It feels soft now after a wash, but it's thin and patchy in places. I let it fall through my fingers as I work the hair dryer, and I can't help but think back to all of the other times I've done my sister's hair. In the community, we had to wear our hair long—it was considered a terrible sin for a woman to cut her hair. The fashion in the sect was to wear our hair down beneath the inevitable head scarf—but the style wasn't actually enforced, and so Annie and I had one small, shared and tolerable act of rebellion—instead of wearing our hair down, we liked to braid it. It set us apart without forcing us out.

I used to braid Annie's hair before school most days—it was thicker then, and so shiny and soft. I'd twist the hair around itself until the braid was tight and perfect, and then sometimes, just to prolong the peaceful moments when it was just Annie and me before we faced the day, I'd pretend I made a mistake and start all over again.

Before I know it now, I've braided her hair—out of some lingering habit that has resurfaced while I was daydreaming. Annie reaches up to touch her hair, and then we share a sad smile. There are echoes of those days in her eyes, and I know she can see the same in mine.

"I didn't even mean to braid it," I admit. "Muscle memory in my fingers I think."

"Do you think about Winterton, Lexie?" she asks me quietly, and I straighten and shake my head firmly.

"Nope. I don't."

The truth is, I *can't* think about that period of my life. I have put a wall around it in my mind—sometimes I even imagine it like that. If I think back over my life, I remember the great years of Dad's life, and then I hit the wall. It's twenty feet tall and there's barbed wire at the top and there is no gate to get inside it. The wall keeps the detail in. I remember the basics—Mom's depression, we moved into the sect, I left and I left Annie behind—but the wall keeps the rest contained, except in moments of weakness like the one that just passed.

It's a self-preservation thing. Sometimes, when I look at Annie's life and I look at mine and I wonder just how they could have worked out so damned differently, I wonder if that wall is the only thing that's saved me.

"I think about it," she whispers, and her hand falls from her hair to her lap. "And I think about Dad."

"You need to keep your spirits up for this hearing," I say, and I open the makeup I bought her at the drugstore. There's nothing I can do to hide the sores around her mouth, but I can at least add some color to her cheeks with the blush and frame her eyes with some mascara.

When I'm finished, I survey my handiwork, and then I smile.

"You look beautiful."

"I look haggard."

Annie climbs back into bed and I reattach the monitoring leads to her belly and chest, and we sit and wait for Bernie. It's not long before she breezes through the door, and after an introduction and pleasantries, she gives Annie a five-minute boot camp on surviving the hearing.

"The important thing at this hearing is that you show remorse, and that you show them that you're determined to turn things around," Bernie tells her. "No excuses, and no matter what happens—you keep your cool. You need to convince that judge that you know you have a problem but that you're determined to turn it around and you're willing to do whatever it takes. Got it?"

"Okay," Annie says, but she's visibly nervous now, and when I take her hand her gaze locks with mine. We both know that this is *exactly* where it all goes wrong. She has every intention of staying put here in this hospital for the time being—but once a judge tells her she has to? That will change everything for Annie. Assuming the outcome of that hearing is a court order that dictates what Annie can do with her life in the next few weeks, it will be like waving a red flag in front of a bull.

No one tells Annie what to do. Not Robert, not Mom, not me, not rehab clinic directors, not boyfriends. Giving her a directive is the fastest way to make her rebel.

But this time will be different, it has to be. This time, she has the baby, and she's going to make this work.

I saw it in her eyes when she agreed to take the methadone, and I see it even stronger in there now. Brighter than the fear, brighter even than the marked sense of desperation that she wears around herself like a shawl these days, there's a sense of determination in my sister for the first time in years. I see it in the steely way she holds my gaze, and in the stiffness of her shoulders and the steady, tightly controlled rhythm of her deep breaths.

There's movement at the door, and I see a man in a suit through the window. He peers in at us, and even at this first glance, there's no mistaking the clear judgment in his eyes.

Oh God, please don't let that be the judge.

"I'm going to be right outside." I modulate my voice—keeping the words low and steady, and as I rise I keep a firm grip on her hand. "The whole time, I'll be right outside. As soon as it's over, I'll come in and we'll talk about it. Would that be good?"

"Yes. Okay."

"And we'll look at the baby clothes. The *baby*, Annie. What-ever happens in here, just think about the baby. Okay?"

Eliza steps through the door and offers Annie a smile. She closes the door behind her, and she says quietly, "I've asked the judge if I can be present for your hearing so I can keep an eye on your BP, Annie. I hope that's okay."

Eliza and I exchange a glance, and relief hits me like a wave from my head to my toes. She doesn't need to be in the room to monitor Annie's BP—the staff can do it from the ward office, via the electronic monitoring system. The only reason Eliza needs to be in this room is to give Annie some moral support, and I'm so grateful that I could hug her. Maybe I will, later.

Bernie and I wait outside as the officials file into Annie's room. Four men enter, followed closely by another woman, and Mary Rafferty comes in last. She directs a polite smile to me as she enters, and I force myself to return it. Bernie greets each of them, and once they are inside, she explains, "So, Judge Brown is the man with the beard, the assistant DA was the guy with the purple tie and the young guy with him is his paralegal. The fourth man is Bill Weston—the attorney nominated to be the baby's guardian ad litem. The first woman was a stenographer to record the proceedings, and I'm guessing that last one was your CPS social worker?"

I nod, then we fall into a terse silence. It quickly becomes too much, and I need to do something to burn off the nervous energy I feel, so I pace the hallway while the hearing takes place. I walk up and down outside Annie's room, and I stand on my tiptoes as I pass her door, trying to peer through the window. The angles aren't right, and it's hard to see what's going on, but I do manage a glimpse of Annie at one point—and immediately wish I hadn't. In that momentary glimpse I see only her pale, tear-streaked face, and that means I spend the remaining ten minutes of the hearing with my fists clenched, wondering what the hell they are saying to her.

When the door finally opens, the men file out, but the assistant DA stops to speak quietly with Bernie. I'm torn between staying to listen in on that conversation and racing in to comfort my sister. The second impulse wins, and when I enter the room, I find Eliza sitting on Annie's bed holding her hand.

"Are you okay? What happened?"

"The first part went just like Bernie said," Annie whispers, but then she is simply overcome. She looks up at me—her blue eyes swimming in tears, her lips thin and her brow furrowed—and then she shakes her head and closes her eyes. I look to Eliza.

"The judge has appointed the guardian ad litem to make decisions about Annie's care until the birth," Eliza clarifies quietly.

"That fucking judge hates me," Annie chokes. "He said if I want to get the baby back, I have to go into rehab as soon as it's born."

"Not immediately," Eliza corrects her carefully. "You'll have a week to recover."

"A *week*?" I gasp, and Annie starts to cry again. I try to imagine how that will work. Seven days to get to know her newborn. Saying goodbye seven days into her newborn's withdrawal. God, that would mean that Annie would likely be around just long enough to see the baby start to really suffer before she has to drag herself away.

"The judge was concerned that Annie has had so many attempts to get clean," Eliza explains softly. "He ruled that the baby should go into foster or kinship care until Annie has successfully completed a rehabilitation program. If she can graduate from the ninety-day program at the new facility at Auburn, they'll review the situation."

I look to Annie again. She's a mess, completely distraught. We should have prepared her better for this. I just assumed there'd be more time, and there *should* be more time. The baby will probably be in the hospital for weeks after the birth. Surely the judge could give Annie at least that long to find her feet and see her child get well before they tear her away.

"What's the rush?" I say. "Surely they could leave it until the baby has finished withdrawals."

"Annie isn't actually the baby's legal guardian," Eliza murmurs a little awkwardly. "The CPS lady recommended she be allowed access here in the hospital until we discharge her, but to be honest, I think she's lucky the judge even granted her that. He was pretty tough on her."

"Lucky?" I repeat weakly, and I look at Annie again. She's drawing in heaving breaths, trying to calm herself down.

I spin toward the door and move to follow the judge. I'm on autopilot—each step fueled only by mindless rage, and a towering sense of injustice that I can't even begin to make sense of. Annie has made mistakes. Yes, Annie has made monstrously bad decisions over the course of her adult lifetime—but this? What good does that idiot think he's going to do in forcing her away from her baby straight after its birth? Those early weeks are so crucial for bonding. And if the goal is for Annie to be an effective parent, surely allowing her time to bond with her son or daughter should be crucial. I'm cataloging all the points to this argument as I storm toward the door, ready to confront this judge as soon as I catch up to him, but Bernie steps in front of me as I leave Annie's room and she says flatly, "Whatever you're about to do—don't even think about it."

"But if they just give her some more time—"

"However bad this is, speaking out of session to that judge is going to make it worse."

"But this is all bullshit! It's not right. We have to appeal."

"This isn't *Law and Order*, Alexis. There *is* no appeal—I told you, this is a juvenile court hearing. Judge Brown has made his decision and we need to find a way to make it work now."

"Make it *work*?" I repeat, but I'm outraged and my voice is too loud and other staff members are starting to stare at me in the corridor. Bernie pushes me into Annie's room and closes the door behind us. She leans against it, as if I might physically burst past her into the corridor, and I close my arms over my chest and glare at her, and suddenly I'm angry with Bernie, too. She *should* have warned me that this might all happen quickly. I should have known to prepare Annie for this.

"Okay, so they've thrown the book at you, Annie," Bernie concedes. "But rehab is actually a good idea, right? Annie? You want to get clean, don't you? Well, maybe the timing isn't ideal, but this will give you a chance to complete a rehab program and be clean and ready to get your life together before the baby is old enough to notice you're even gone."

"I can't let my one-week-old baby go into fucking foster care," Annie says, and she's snarling at Bernie, who raises her eyebrows and says quite calmly, "Foster care *or* kinship care, Annie."

"What the fuck is *kinship* care?" Annie demands, and suddenly everyone is staring at me. I feel the flush creeping up my face.

I should have thought about *this*, too. I should have run the idea by Sam. I should have been better prepared. I stare at Bernie, and my vision goes blurry, and then I turn back to Annie and I whisper, "It means the baby would go to a family member until you're ready to care for it."

A family member; we both know what that means. Annie would never allow the baby to go to the community, even if Mom wanted it to—and even if Mom *did*, Robert would never allow that.

Which leaves only one possible person if kinship care really is the way to go.

"You?" Annie whispers, and the tears are rolling down her face and she wraps her arms around her belly as she chokes, "Would you do that for me? I can't ask that of you."

"The baby will probably be in the hospital for some time as we manage the NAS symptoms," Eliza points out, but I hear her only from a distance, because I'm staring into my sister's eyes.

She said she couldn't ask this of me, but her gaze is pleading, and without a single word that's exactly what she's doing.

"How long did you say the rehab program will be?" I ask, as the buzzing in my ears grows louder. Maybe…maybe if it's only a month, the baby will be in the NICU the whole time.

"Ninety days."

Three months. There's no way the baby will be in the NICU that long. That means the baby would need to come home with me, probably for several months.

"Could you, Lexie? Would you? Please?"

I should check with Sam. I *know* I should check with Sam. But Annie is breathless with desperate hope, so I rush to the bed and I take her hands in mine and I whisper, "Of course I will."

10

ANNIE

Luke,

You made me cry this morning. That's not easy, so I'll give you credit—what you said gave me a lot to think about. You're right—I do carry a lot of shame. In fact, even writing that made me angry—because for me, shame and anger are always entwined. If I'm angry, you can bet your ass that something made me feel ashamed first. It's just how it works. I'm easily embarrassed, I'm self-conscious—I'm well aware of the catastrophic disaster my life has become. And it's heavy. Shame is heavy on me...it's crushing...suffocating.

That doesn't mean I don't deserve it.

I'm still crying. Fuck, I hate this. Well, while I'm already a mess, I may as well tell you about Robert. I hate writing his name, you know. I hate saying it, too. There was a period of a few years when I was estranged altogether from Mom when I just refused to say that name aloud—it would stick in my throat, and I'd almost gag if I tried.

I digress, so let me pick up where I left off in the last entry.

We learned more about him over the weeks before the wedding. He was a widower; his first wife had died in childbirth along with his infant son. He spoke about his first wife and lost child freely, but with an odd sense of distance from the loss.

"It was the Lord's will, just like your father's passing. Who am I to question it? It was their time."

Lexie and I found this sense of acceptance to be maddening, particularly when he started to expect it from us. Any time we complained about the forthcoming move, he responded with rapidly increasing impatience, as if we were being completely unreasonable. Mom wasn't much better—she was excited about the move and renewed contact with her family, and she couldn't seem to understand why we weren't.

"But you'll see your grandmothers and aunts and uncles every day, girls. It's going to be so much easier on us all."

"So much easier on you, you mean," I snapped at her a few times, and each time, I was promptly punished with time in my room alone. This gave me time to think about all of the ways that this move was going to ruin my life—and time to panic about moving away from the house that contained all of my memories of my father. I'd lie on the floor and sob, but if I thought really hard about Dad, I'd always catch a sense of him in the room with me. It was a tiny glimmer—just a hint of his presence—but it was generally enough to calm me. I'd think about Lexie's words the day of his funeral, and I'd remind myself again and again that Dad would never leave us—he just wouldn't. I took some comfort in the idea that whatever was coming, Dad would somehow be watching over me.

And I was certainly seeing his family—and Mom's—more than I ever had before. Mom kept taking us to Winterton to visit with them, trying to help us adjust, I think. Winterton was a quiet little village, with ordinary-looking houses and a main street with average businesses. I suppose if you looked closely enough, you'd realize something is "off" about it—it's perhaps a little too neat, a little too tidy. All of the residents are sect families, all of the businesses are run by its members, and the church runs the only school in the village.

And so, all of the men you see in Winterton are clean-shaven with very short, neat hair—and almost all of the women look similar, too, with long hair beneath head scarves, and extremely modest clothing. There are no run-down homes, and almost everyone has a new car, and there's virtually no unemployment—the church offers interest-free loans to its members to establish or develop their own businesses, so the main street of Winterton has a surprisingly wide variety of stores and there's even an industrial area.

It's not exactly a closed community. There are no gates at the town entrance, and the regional city of Collinsville, where we'd grown up, was only five miles away. Some Winterton residents run businesses in Collinsville, and I'd eventually realize that Collinsville residents liked to visit Winterton for the stores. It's a nice place, and its residents are for the most part good-hearted, well-meaning people with close ties to their community and a fierce dedication to their faith.

Even so, Winterton is not a welcoming place. Members of the sect are never allowed to eat with nonbelievers, so while there are restaurants, only community members can utilize them. Exclusions like this exist all around. Even if an outsider wanted to move in to the village, they'd find it almost impossible to be employed there or find housing. And while the men took turns participating in "street preaching" over in Collinsville to share their faith, this generally amounted to a group of them standing on the steps of the post office shouting Bible verses at passersby on a Saturday morning. If evangelism was the goal, this activity was an endless failure. I never saw them actually convert to the faith, and visitors were not welcome in the services. The congregation was totally stable, with the periodic exception of new children born or members forced out.

But those on the inside of the sect are cared for in a way that most people in the outside world never experience—it's a restrictive lifestyle, but for those who comply perfectly, Winterton offers a tight-knit community. I'm convinced that's what Mom was seeking—after she lost Dad, she wanted to return to the close embrace of the somewhat sheltered world she'd grown up in.

I can still remember the shock I felt the first time Robert took us to his house. By then, we'd heard him speak from the pulpit quite a few times, so I'd wrapped my head around his seniority in the sect. His uncle had once been the head of the sect for all of its assemblies worldwide, and the closest thing to clergy the church had, because there were no pastors or priests. All ministry was done by the men in the church, and where decisions needed to be made, the board of elders took responsibility collectively.

At some point during Mom and Dad's exile, Robert's once-illustrious uncle had also been withdrawn from. That rejection is considered to be the worst fate that can befall a member of the sect. All ties are cut with a member who is withdrawn from—prohibitive clauses in their "interest-free loans" are called in and access to their own family is restricted, and then intense intimidation is used to drive them from their homes and the village.

But Robert had escaped his uncle's controversy unscathed and was now on the board of elders. All of the women in the assembly seemed to think Mom was quite lucky to be marrying him. His

house was enormous—but it was sterile. Like all other commu-
nity homes, there was no television or radio, but in Robert's house,
there was also no sense at all that this was a home. *Mom had*
decorated our real home so beautifully—with soft furnishings and
photographs and artwork, and throw blankets on the couches and
cushions and knickknacks. The sterile, whitewashed walls of Rob-
ert's home disturbed me almost as much as the idea of living in the
community did.

"It needs a feminine touch," Mom admitted to Lexie and me as
we slowly packed the life we'd shared with Dad into moving boxes.
"But...give me a few months, and I'll make that place feel like home
for you. It's a beautiful house, so much potential..."

But as the wedding day neared, Robert was at our real home
more and more, and he became increasingly involved in our deci-
sions about what to take and what to throw out.

He deemed the most innocent of possessions "worldly"—and
showing any sign of attachment to something was a surefire way to
have him declare it as an idol and insist that it make its way into
the trash. Even Lexie, who was so good at flying under Robert's
radar, got into a few teary arguments with him about what she was
or wasn't to take. In the end, he insisted that we whittle our entire
house of possessions down to only a handful of boxes. By moving
day, all that followed me from my old life to my new one was a box
of clothing, a few teddy bears and a handful of books—including,
thankfully, my precious journal.

When the truck pulled up to his house, one final shock was in
store. When Lexie asked where our room was, Robert shook his
head.

"In my home, you'll have separate rooms."

"*The girls have always shared a room, Robert,*" *Mom said hesitantly.*

"*I'm the head of this house, Deborah. The girls will have their own rooms.*"

"*Maybe they could share just for a while, until they get used to—*"

"*No!*" *Robert said flatly, and then he turned on his heel and went back outside to the truck. Lexie and I looked to Mom, who stared back at us helplessly.*

"*I'm sorry, girls. We need to respect Robert's wishes.*"

I sobbed as I set up my new bedroom. In the house we grew up in, Lexie and I had beds side by side in a big bedroom with pink walls and beautiful lace curtains that Mom had sewn herself. In the new house, our rooms were at separate ends of a long hall. The walls in our rooms were white, and the few belongings I had been allowed to keep did nothing at all to make my room feel mine. *I felt utter disconnection from everything I had ever known, from the very first moments in that place. Like a plant torn from the earth, the roots of my soul were exposed.*

At dinner that night, Robert fired one final prewedding missive.

"*From tomorrow,*" *he said,* "*you'll both call me Father.*"

"*I'm so sorry, Robert, but we can't do that,*" *Lexie said automatically. It was the first time I'd heard her defy Robert—but in typical Lexie fashion, she did it with the utmost respect.*

"*This is my home. Your mother will be* my *wife. You will be my children, and you'll address me appropriately,*" *Robert said.*

Lexie took a careful breath, and she said quietly, "*Dad is, and always will be, my father.*"

"*I can't call you it, either,*" *I said, and I glanced at Mom to find she was pleading with us with her eyes.*

"Well, you won't eat my food unless you give me the respect I deserve," Robert snapped. *"Go to your rooms."*

"Mom?" I whispered, but Mom was staring at her plate. The smile was gone—Mom was back to being fragile, and she withheld herself from us again—just as she had during that awful year of near silence after Dad's death.

"Fine!" Lexie snapped, and she ran from the table, so I followed her. We lay together on her bed, and she wrapped her arms around me.

"We'll find a way to get out of here," she promised me. *"Mom will come to her senses. You'll see."*

"What if she doesn't?"

"I don't know. We'll find a way."

It wasn't long before Robert threw the door open and insisted that I go to my own room. Lexie held on to me, her fingers digging into my waist, her body shaking against mine. I cowered in her arms as he shouted at us.

"This is my *home. You are children—*female *children. You will learn your place here—this filthy, worldly disrespect has no place in this house—"*

Until that night, I'd never really heard an adult scream at a child in fury. Robert's thundering voice was violence to my ears, and I eventually released my hold on Lexie to cover them to block the sound out. As I did so, Robert tried to drag me out of Lexie's arms, and Mom appeared in the doorway.

"Please, Robert," she begged, and we all fell silent. When I looked to her, I was surprised to see Mom was crying, too. *"Please, let them share a room—just until they settle in. This is such a change for them—and they have so much to adjust to. I'm sure*

the girls will agree to call you Father if you let them share a room. Right, girls?"

I looked to Lexie next. We held a conversation with our tear-filled eyes. I simply could not bear the thought of walking down that corridor on my own and climbing into a cold bed without Lexie nearby to comfort me. Everything might be wrong with our lives now, but as long as Lexie and I stuck together, I was sure I'd be okay. And for her part, I could see determination in Lexie's eyes. Either she needed me close, too, or she truly understood just how much I needed her. When the silent conversation came to an end, Lexie nodded toward me, and I echoed the movement with a nod toward Mom. Lexie spoke for both of us. She whispered, "Right. We will."

Robert refused to help us move the bed, so Lexie, Mom and I struggled to get it down the hallway, but it was worth it. We pressed the two twin beds right up close to one another so I could hold her hand as we went to sleep.

He didn't raise the issue of our shared bedroom again. That decision to let us stay together was one of many Robert made over the years that made no sense to me. I loathe him—I hate him—but even I can see that Robert is no one-dimensional villain. Allowing Lexie and me to share a room was a surprising concession on a night that was otherwise full of fear and pain and loss. There would be other times over the years that followed when he would catch me off guard with a completely unexpected kindness—like when he gave Lexie money for my rehab one time, and the fact that he has allowed Mom to speak to us via the phone even though it breaks one of the community's most sacred rules; the separation between those "in" and those of us who are "out" is supposed to be absolute. But from the beginning of our life with Robert, he was not only our evil stepfather—he was also Mom's husband, and regardless of all of the awful things that he's done to me and to Lexie, on some level I do believe that Mom loves him. Her life is not one I could bear myself, but her marriage to Robert seems to have made my mother happy.

I hate him anyway. Small acts of kindness do not cancel out the many ways he damaged me.

11

LEXIE

I know that Sam has a thirty-minute break for lunch between surgeries. I find him in his office, where he's reviewing case notes as he eats a sandwich. As soon as I step into the room, he scans my face, then he rises from his desk to pull me into his embrace. I feel anxious and fidgety, like I'm wound too tight inside. I lean into him, expecting comfort at the warmth of his body against mine, and I'm disappointed when it fails to rise.

"How did the hearing go?" Sam asks me, and he pulls me gently away from him to peer down into my face. I search for words, and when they fail me, I sigh and shake my head.

"Not good. I mean, most of it was as we expected, but the judge came down on her pretty hard. She'll pretty much have to go to that place at Auburn as soon as she's discharged."

Sam's eyes are locked on mine.

"So...what happens to the baby?"

I clear my throat, and shake my head as I disentangle myself from Sam altogether. I press my hands deep into the pockets of my jeans to keep them still, and then I stare away at the wall behind Sam's ear as I admit, "Well, it will stay in the NICU, but once it's discharged—it goes into foster care or..." I clear my throat. "Or it stays with me."

"With *us*," Sam corrects me with a frown. "Lexie, I keep telling you—we're in this together. Do you *want* to care for the baby while Annie gets better?"

"That's the thing, Sam..." I say, but I still can't look at him. I let my gaze fall to the floor. "I don't know if she'll finish that rehab program."

"Well, it sounds like she'll have to if she wants the baby back."

"It's not that simple. It's never that simple. There's no better way to send Annie off the rails than to insist she *do* something."

"And what happens if she doesn't graduate the program?"

"They will arrest her immediately," I whisper, and Sam takes me into his arms again and pulls me hard up against himself. He strokes the back of my hair as he says quietly, "That's a pretty good incentive to play nice while she's in there, honey."

"It's like there's a switch that gets flipped inside her whenever anyone tells her what to do. She automatically does the opposite."

"So...are you worried that if we take the baby for a few weeks, we'll be stuck with it forever?"

"*Stuck* with it?"

Sam winces and shakes his head.

"That came out wrong, but you know what I mean. We are certainly capable of caring for a newborn for a few weeks—we can call it practice." He offers me a smile, but the one I give him in return is forced. "But...if you really think she's not going to give rehab a shot, even with the future of her kid in the pic-ture...well, we need to sit down and talk this out, don't we?"

I hesitate, then I whisper, "I already told her I'll take the baby."

"Lexie..." Sam is shocked, and I'm immediately defensive.

"She was so upset, and I can't let my niece or nephew go into the foster system. God—that kid is already going to have NAS to deal with when it's born—and—"

Sam interrupts—his words are sharp and I can see impatience in the stiffness of his shoulders and the hard set of his jaw.

"Look, we'll make it work. I just wish you'd *talked* to me before you agreed to this. Have you even thought about your job? You can't take indefinite time off. You told Oliver you'd be back on Monday. How are we going to juggle all of this? Especially if it *does* end up being for the longer term."

"I will go back to work on Monday," I say. "And he let Ira take three months off last year when he and his partner adopted that baby from China. I'll look into unpaid parental leave. And if they won't let me do that, we could get a nanny. I'll find a way to make it work."

"Lexie, I know you will. You are the most capable woman I know—but we are going to be in this *together*. That means you don't have to deal with it on your own, but it also means—" Sam draws in a deep breath, then he groans impatiently "—well, frankly, it means that I *do* have to deal with it, too—and you need to talk to me before you make decisions like this. Got it?"

I feel my face flushing, but I nod silently. I hate this, and I'm completely mortified that it's happening. I hate that Sam is inconvenienced by Annie, just as I am—just as I always am. She's *my* problem, she's my burden to bear—my responsibility. Sam is still frustrated. I can see it in the way he's holding himself, and even in the way he's avoiding my gaze now as he processes what I've done. Just as I feel defensiveness rising, he glances at me and his tone is gentler as he says, "We're going to figure all of this out, okay? Let's talk some more over the weekend. The baby's not going to come for weeks. There's plenty of time to make a plan."

I nod and take a step backward away from him.

"You should eat your lunch, and I need to get back to her."

"I'll come by her room when I'm done."

"I'll just meet you at home," I say. "I'm not sure how long I'll be here today."

Sam's brow furrows. As I register the lingering displeasure in his gaze, guilt sweeps over me and I just can't face him any longer. I offer him a weak smile but then leave his office quickly to return to Annie.

Less than forty-eight hours have passed since Annie returned to my life, and even my relationship with Sam already feels off-kilter.

Knowing I'll be back at work on Monday, I decide to spend the weekend with Annie. I rise early and wander quietly through the house—packing a box with things that she and I can do to fill the time over the day, and then I stop off at a diner.

"Hey…" I greet Annie warmly when I finally step into her room. I have the box under one arm, with the milkshake and coffee I ordered at the diner balanced precariously on top, and in my other hand is a paper bag full of sweet treats for her. Annie has always had such a sweet tooth.

"Oh, hi." She stabs at the remote control on her lap and the television she'd been watching powers down. "What are you doing here so early?"

"I'll go back to work on Monday. I thought we could hang out."

"Don't you have a real weekend to look forward to? I'm sure that oh-so-together fiancé of yours has some plans I'm getting in the way of. Golf or polo perhaps, or a day at the country club?"

Her barb hits closer to the truth than she realizes. Sam loves to play golf, and we joined a country club together last year.

"All I'm doing this weekend is catching up with you," I tell her firmly, and I awkwardly angle the box beneath my arm toward her. She removes the milkshake and the coffee and rests them both on the table over her bed. I walk to the corner of the room to dump the box onto the larger table, and as I release it, I immediately pick up the untouched bag of baby clothes I brought the previous morning. My intentions were good, but Annie was simply too upset to look through the clothes with me after the hearing. Maybe today will be a better time.

I return to sit at the end of her bed and watch as Annie's face brightens when she opens the bakery bag, but then she hesitates.

"Is this stuff okay for me to eat? They said low sodium so..."

"It's definitely not low sugar, but it should all be low sodium," I assure her, and once again I'm surprised by the care she's taking. Maybe I shouldn't be—after all, it's natural for a mother to want to do the best by her child. Then again, this particular mother has spent the first eight months of her pregnancy injecting illicit narcotics into her veins on a regular basis. And just like that, I'm judging her again. From admiration to condemnation in two simple thoughts. It never really goes away.

"You're feeling okay?" I ask her, and she shrugs and tears open a cinnamon bun.

"I'm feeling...scared," she murmurs after a while.

"It's okay to be scared."

"I never meant to get pregnant. The baby's father...he's not a great guy. He's in prison now, but he was my dealer," she says, and then she clears her throat. "I didn't realize I was pregnant—not for a long time. I've been such a mess, the days and weeks and months meant nothing until I felt it moving. Then I knew, and I've felt bad in my life—guilty, I mean—but never like that."

"How are the cravings, Annie?" I ask her gently, and she laughs bitterly and shakes her head.

"Which answer do you want, Lexie? The one where I tell you what I'm supposed to tell you, or the honest one?"

"The honest one."

"How many times a minute does my heart beat?"

I glance at the monitor beside her bed, and I say, "At the moment, about eighty-two."

"In that case, I probably only think about getting high five or ten times every heartbeat."

"The methadone should be taking the edge off it."

"Oh, yeah, the *methadone*," she snorts, and then takes a long sip of the milkshake. "They're split-dosing me, so I have it morning and night. I already figured out if I'm going to bust out of here and score, the best time to do it would be in the evening just before the night dose."

"You wouldn't feel it anyway, not like you normally do—the methadone is an antagonist, it stops the high," I tell her, and I feel my face flushing, and I wish I hadn't asked. I don't know why I'm so embarrassed by this discussion—perhaps it's because I wasn't expecting her to answer me. Annie was never this open with me about her addiction—it was always something she juggled in the shadows. I've spent as much time trying to get her to speak openly about it as I have dealing with the fallout of her trying to keep it secret. "And it has a long half-life. Even on a split dose, the methadone would be in your system from the morning dose."

"I know you're a doctor and all, but I know that *much* better than you do," she tells me. "Remember when I was at your place on Wilder Street? You dragged me to the methadone clinic yourself before work each day and you watched me take it—I didn't miss a dose. And then you'd go to work, and I'd score. It gave me no rush, no buzz... I did it out of pure, unbreakable habit. I *need* the rush, so even if I know I'm physically incapable of feeling it, I'll still chase it as long as there's breath in my body. Remember that job I had doing web content for the accountants near our house? And I quit after a week? I didn't *quit*. I got fired because I took money from the pretty cash for a hit. The best you can hope for from me is that I'll hide the cravings, because I'll never beat them."

"Why are you telling me this, Annie? Is it to shock me, or because you want help?"

"Neither," she says, and her shoulders slump and she seems to shrink away to nothing in an instant. She gives a heavy, lengthy sigh, then she looks at me and her eyes are glistening with tears. "I guess I just want you to understand. They can chain me to this bed, they can give me methadone, God—they could sedate me out cold. And on some level, I'll still be thinking of scoring. Before anything else—life or death for me or even my baby—I'll always be thinking of scoring. That's who I am now."

"That is *not* who you are," I say flatly. "I don't ever want to hear you say that again. You *can* get well—I know you can. You love this baby, Annie. I've seen it in your eyes. It's the only reason you called me at all."

"I do. I love it so much, it terrifies me," she admits, and her voice cracks and her face contorts. "I'm so scared I'm going to fuck all of this up."

"You are not," I tell her firmly, and I reach into the bag of baby clothes and I withdraw a handful. "Enough of this talk—we're going to fix this, all of it, bit by bit, piece by piece, we're going to put your life back together. But this weekend, you and I are going to reconnect—we're going to put the past two years behind us, and we're going to have some fun. Starting right now. Look at these booties, Annie. *Look* at them." I thrust them toward her, and when she doesn't reach for them, I toss them onto her belly. They are tiny—I got the premature baby size in everything because we know her baby is very small—and these booties look like they were made for a doll. Annie reaches down with shaking fingers and slips her forefinger under the tie that holds the shoes together. She gives a teary laugh.

"They're so small."

"In a few weeks, we're going to slip those onto the feet of a baby. A *baby*. Can you imagine its little toes, all snug and warm in there? God, it's going to be so adorable..."

I dump the handful of clothes onto the bed beside Annie's thighs, and she hesitantly begins to riffle through them. All of the clothes I bought are white or yellow or green, except a single pink-and-blue outfit.

"Do you remember the doll we had at Winterton?" she asks me, and I frown at her and shake my head.

"Doll?"

"Never mind," she says, and she leans forward suddenly and places her hand over mine. I look at her in surprise, and she squeezes hard and whispers, "Thank you, Lexie."

Our eyes lock. This mess of a woman is what's left of my baby sister. She looks twenty years older than she is, and I've never understood how it came to this, and maybe I never will.

I love her anyway. Near or far, broken or whole, I love my sister more than anything else in the world, and somehow, no matter what she does or what comes between us, I always will. There is no off switch to the love between sisters; no way to pause it, no way to destroy it. Even when I pushed her away two years ago, I did it only because I thought it was the best thing I could do for *her* at the time.

Oh, what I wouldn't give to make her life whole. What I wouldn't give to see her thriving and healthy and functional. What I wouldn't give to see her at peace.

If only there was a way to free up all of that beautiful mental energy that she expends thinking constantly about that fucking high. She could change the world with the potential wasting away in that mind—that wild imagination, that crisp creativity. Annie Vidler was never meant to become this disaster. She should have been a poet or a novelist or a philosopher or a journalist, and instead of sitting by her bedside now lamenting the world she inhabits, I should have been watching her win awards and enjoy a life of space to create.

It's too much and it's too heartbreaking. I wrestle my thoughts back to the present, and I point to the cinnamon bun that Annie is holding.

"Eat it," I tell her after I clear my throat. "We're going to play Monopoly."

★ ★ ★

We weren't allowed to play board games in the community—someone had decreed them as worldly at some point—but in the years before, Annie and I played all of the time. I usually threw the game for Annie because if I didn't, she didn't stand a chance of winning. She had this terrible habit of buying every property she landed on—no strategy, always relied on luck.

Typical Annie.

I had a strategy for Monopoly, one honed over years of games with Dad after Annie went to bed. Dad played an ad hoc game much like Annie—and I never got tired of the way he would throw his hands up in surrender and grumble about losing, but there was a gleam in his eye, as if he secretly loved losing to me.

That's exactly how I felt about playing with Annie. I wanted her to win, so every move of the game was the opposite to my winning strategy: I'd buy single properties and pass up opportunities to get the whole color; I'd never buy the railroads or the more expensive properties; I'd go to jail and sit there trying to roll double figures and I'd tell her it was because I wanted to save the fifty dollars.

Annie still approaches the game as if she's six years old. She squeals with delight when she gets a chance card, and she grins mischievously when she enforces the rent charges.

But the game doesn't matter. It's just a vehicle—something to focus our attention on. The important part of the morning is our conversation between turns.

"So, tell me about Sam," Annie asks at one point.

"What do you want to know?"

"Where'd you meet him?"

"At a lecture on keyhole surgery. I held back after to ask him a question about a particular patient, and we started chatting…" I smile at the memory. I had no ulterior motive when I approached Sam, but it was only moments into our chat that I started to wonder if there was something there. "He asked if

I wanted to meet up with him for coffee later that day. Things kind of fell into place from there."

"Do you think it's a coincidence that you found your first long-term partner as soon as you threw me out?" It takes a moment for me to recognize the guilt in her voice, and when I do, I glance at her in surprise.

"Of course it is, Annie," I say gently.

"Hmm. Not so sure." Annie shrugs, and she rolls the dice in silence as I ponder her simple statement. She lands on yet another random property and immediately reaches for her cash. Annie now owns a good portion of the board, but still no complete color sets, and she's still excited to be adding still another color to her collection.

"How could it be anything *other* than a coincidence?"

"I've taken a lot of your energy over the years, Lex."

"So has my training," I point out.

"Yeah," Annie concedes, then she passes me the dice.

"Plus…you know, there's something about Sam…" I say softly. "I'd never met anyone who fit me the way Sam does. He gets me. We have the same tastes, the same interests, the same patterns and routines and habits and… I mean—we have plenty of differences, too, trust me, but—we fit perfectly on all of the key things, you know? I never really believed in 'the one,' but… Sam makes me happy, and I think I make him happy, too. I dated a bit when I was studying, but no one ever checked the boxes the way Sam does."

"That's nice, Lex. That's really nice."

I can hear her jealousy, and it feels awkward to acknowledge it to myself. When we argued over the years, she'd always accused me of thinking I'm perfect, but she's wrong about that—I don't. I'm achingly aware of my flaws—my need to control my own life was a huge barrier to my relationship with Sam in the early days. I felt like he was too perfect for someone like me— like my baggage was immense enough to be an insurmountable wall between us. It has taken two years of very hard work to get my relationship with Sam to the place it is now, and two long years to convince myself that I do deserve happiness. The guilt I feel at having failed to help Annie until now has been like a creeping vine, winding its way through my entire life at times.

I roll the dice and buy the electric company I land on, then pass the dice back to Annie as I ask hesitantly, "And...you said the baby's father was in prison...?"

"His name is Dale. And yes, there was a sting...just after I became pregnant I guess. He was with a bunch of guys we know... they had a shitload of gear on them, splitting it up to sell. I don't think he was actually the kingpin the DEA said he was, but he got twenty years."

"Does he know? About the baby?"

"I did send him a letter...he didn't write back. But the thing is... Dale has a bunch of kids he pretty much ignores already, and we weren't exactly in love, so I think I can say with reasonable confidence that his interest level in this baby is bound to be low." Annie snorts as if she's angry, but her eyes fill with tears. "I should have had an abortion, maybe. But I knew it was probably too late anyway and... I don't know. I was kind of excited. I just thought everything would work itself out better than it has. I've gotten off the smack before, you know. I thought this time I could *stay* off if I was doing it for the baby. I tried a bunch of times to get clean, but the sickness seemed to come earlier and it was more intense than I'd remembered. I tried again last week, that's when my feet swelled up—I thought it was just the withdrawals, but then I took a hit and it didn't get better...that's when I called you."

"And...about the baby...were you imagining that you'd raise it alone, then?" I ask her, then add hesitantly, "In the...in that trailer?"

Annie raises her eyebrows at me.

"Like this would be the only kid in Alabama raised in a trailer."

"It's not ideal."

"Nothing in life is ideal, Lexie. I thought if I could get my shit together, I could get a job and we'd be okay."

I decide to drop the subject, although the urge to point out to her how unprepared she seems is almost overwhelming. What I've just gleaned from this conversation is that Annie does not have a plan—that she is just assuming things are going to magically get better—and she's probably expecting that I'll be the magic bean that solves all of her problems. I clamp down the resentment I feel. I want to connect with her today—I can't let my indignation get in the way of that.

"Do you hear from Mom much?" Annie asks me now, and I shake my head.

"No. I call her every few months." We both ponder this quietly for a moment, then I ask her, "So, given everything, have you thought more about when you might want to call her to talk to her about the baby?"

"Maybe soon. Next week, maybe, once the dust settles."

"Okay."

"You know this hospital has its own entertainment system in the TV...like a fancy hotel."

"Yeah?"

"Yeah. Last night I was flicking through it and I saw they have *Back to the Future*. Remember when we watched that with Dad?"

I laugh softly.

"I remember we had an argument over which one of us was going to marry Michael J. Fox when we grew up."

"Oh, yeah." She laughs. "I forgot about that. Let's watch it again when we finish this game. For old times' sake."

The TV is mounted to the ceiling above Annie's bed and hangs at an angle, so that someone lying close to flat could still see the screen. It's hard to see the TV from the visitor's chair.

About ten minutes into the movie, Annie glances at me and notices the awkward way I'm sitting, and she shuffles awkwardly to the edge of her bed and pats the mattress.

"Sit up here," she says.

"I can see fine," I assure her.

"Suit yourself." She shrugs, then adds a little bitterly, "I'm sure you can afford a fancy chiropractor to fix it if you fuck your neck up sitting like that. You'd probably rather hurt yourself than actually share a mattress with a filthy junkie like me."

"Annie," I groan, and I stand and slide onto the bed. I lean into the pillows and stretch my legs out, then I slide my arm around her shoulders, pulling her close. She sits stiffly, still offended. "*Don't* do that. Don't assume I think those things about you. You're my sister."

"Those things are true, though," she mutters, and I contract my arm around her.

"Would you stop jabbering for five minutes so I can relive my childhood fantasies about Marty McFly?"

"Hands off, bitch," she says lightly. "You've got Sam. Marty McFly is all mine."

We both chuckle, and then she drops her head, resting it against my shoulder. Eventually she falls asleep like that, and as her breathing deepens, I feel myself start to relax, too. I press my cheek against her hair, and I rest, too—somehow complete again, as if a part of myself has been missing for all of this time.

12

ANNIE

So, Luke:

There were few saving graces in Winterton, but chief among them once again was Lexie. She was so much smarter than I, and she quickly figured out how to roll with the punches in that place. I was still fighting to go back to our old school even months after we arrived, but Lexie quietly agreed to attend the community school and set about getting through the curriculum as quickly as she could. Mom kept reminding her as a girl in the community, she could study only until she turned sixteen.

"What's she going to do after that?" I asked one day. "She's already doing some high school curriculum, isn't she? Will she finish it by then?"

"It doesn't matter whether she finishes or not. The day she turns sixteen, she'll have to leave."

"That's so stupid, Mom."

"Women should care for their homes and the men. They don't need to study more than that."

"Even you went to college."

"That was a mistake. Lexie will finish school on her birthday, and she'll get a job with one of the village businesses until she finds a husband."

When I asked Lexie what she thought about all of this, she'd shrug and change the subject. I figured that she had a plan, because there was no way someone as smart as my sister was going to just agree to stop school because she didn't happen to be a boy.

Every good thing in that place had a downside. Mom finally went back to work, but now she was my teacher, and when we were at school I was supposed to call her Mrs. Herbert. Every time I called her Mom, she sent me out of class. Then I found the library— which was vast and right near our house—but even as I explored it, I realized that most of the books were theological textbooks, and the handful of novels in the collection were classics for adults.

"Why aren't there any books here?" I asked Lexie.

"The elders think said novels are worldly." She rolled her eyes.

"What are we supposed to read?" I asked, bewildered. Lexie picked up one of the ever-present Bibles and pressed it toward me. When I frowned at her, she laughed and withdrew it. "But…"

"Just write your own stories," she suggested. "Your stories are better than anything you'll find in this stupid cult."

For a while, that's what I did. I had little notepads full of stories hidden in our bedroom and in my schoolbag. I'd slide them inside workbooks so when I was bored in class I could get right back to them. I was writing a series of tales about two orphaned sisters, Tara and Ellen, who were detectives just like Nancy Drew. Day and night, I was thinking about Tara and Ellen. They were all alone in the world, but they were doing okay.

One Saturday afternoon, Lexie and I were in our bedroom talking when Robert threw the door open.

"What is this?" he asked, and he threw one of my notepads onto the desk beside me. I looked to Lexie.

"It's mine," she said. "It's just some stories I made up. No harm done."

"Yours?" he repeated scornfully. "Alexis, your handwriting would be neater than this even if you wrote it with your left hand. No, there's only one person in this family with the letter formation of a preschooler and an overactive imagination."

"They are just stories, Father," Lexie protested. "It's harmless."

Robert turned his attention from Lexie to me, and he crouched beside me and held the notebook right in front of my face. I recognized it then; it was the book that contained the story of how Tara and Ellen escaped from an icy prison cell after being captured by an evil horse rustler.

As an adult, I can see that the symbolism wasn't exactly subtle, but at the time, I couldn't actually understand Robert's fury.

"There must be something very wicked about you indeed for you to need to make up nonsense like this," he whispered fiercely, and he held the notebook right in front of my face. I raised my chin, stubbornly holding his gaze, and he tore the notepad into two even pieces. I didn't even let myself blink. "Focus your energies on the Lord and learning your Bible. If I catch you doing this again, there'll be consequences. Do you hear me?"

"Yes, Robert," I said, and his gaze narrowed. He left the room, but returned quickly with the leather strap from the dining room. I was already well aware by that stage that my disobedience inevitably resulted in serious consequences. The leather belt hung on the wall near the dining room table, and during our first few weeks in

his house, Robert had taken it down to fling it against my thighs when I didn't say "Amen" after grace. That day, he lashed me for forgetting to say "Father," and then he lashed me again for hiding the notebooks, and then for extra-good measure he hit Lexie, too, for her insolence. Neither one of us cried until he left the room, and then nursing our stinging thighs, we lay on our stomachs on our beds and we offered each other empty consolations.

"I'll still keep my notebooks," I said. "I'll just be more careful to hide them."

"Maybe a better idea would be to keep making up your stories... but don't leave any evidence lying around," Lexie muttered. "Just tell them to me instead."

"It's going to get better, isn't it, Lex?"

"Sure it is. He's still getting used to us. He'll back off soon."

"Sorry he hit you."

"I'm really sorry he hit you."

Mom wasn't kidding when she told us we had dozens of cousins within the community. We met a seemingly endless series of relatives we had no clue existed before the move. But we had almost nothing in common with them, not even with the kids our own age. The children who grew up in the community were compliant and quiet, well accustomed to the strict discipline and dogmatic rules. As outsiders, Lexie and I were also excluded—I overheard an aunt explaining our "odd" ways to her ten-year-old son.

"They can't help it, son. They were raised in a world of sin."

I had no idea what this meant as an eight-year-old, only that it wasn't a nice thing to say, and that it somehow explained why even the friends I made at the schoolhouse kept their distance. It seemed the more familiar I became with the community, the more I realized just how much there was to hate.

But there was a window of time each day when no one really seemed to care what Lexie and I did. Without TV and with limited reading material available, we were supposed to stay in our rooms after school to study the Bible or pray—but we quickly figured out that as long as we weren't bothering the adults, kids were left to do whatever they pleased in the afternoons. Most stayed at the schoolyard to play, but as outcasts, Lexie and I attempted that only a few times before we realized we weren't welcome, so instead, we took to exploring.

The woods had been cleared when the village was established, but a small patch of wilderness had been left untouched behind the worship hall. Robert's house was only a few hundred yards away, so Lexie and I would quietly disappear into the trees.

The first few times we tried it, we weren't sure if we were breaking some unspoken rule and we were so nervous about being caught that we just sat on rocks and waited for the ax to fall. But as the days passed, and our trips to the woods went undetected, Lexie and I began to relax. She was far too old by then for make-believe, but I needed it. I needed to escape, and there were no books for me to lose myself in and no TV shows to zone out into, and even the boisterous, fun play I'd always enjoyed with my school friends had disappeared from my life. One day sitting there in the woods, I turned to my sister and I blurted, "Can we play 'mommies and daddies'?"

And Lexie—the smartest kid I'd ever met, well into puberty by that stage and more mature in so many ways even than our mother—stared at me. After a while, she nodded thoughtfully, and then she said, "Deal. But only if I can be the mom."

13

LEXIE

'm onto my fourth consult Monday morning when the phone on my desk rings.

"Please excuse me," I say to my patient, and I pick up the handset. "Yep?"

"Hi, Lexie—we've had a call from the hospital. Your sister's condition has changed. They suggested you come right in." The receptionist is hesitant and apologetic.

"What happened? What did they say?"

"That's all. But it sounded urgent."

I hang up, and I turn to the patient. I've forgotten her name. I know she's here to get her antidepressant script refilled. Where were we up to? I try to flash her a calm smile, but I know I've failed to hide my state of mind when she says hesitantly, "Dr. Vidler? Are you okay?"

I look to the screen. Kerrie Nichols. Have I already asked her about side effects? How long has she been taking these meds? Is it time to review her dosage? What other medication is she on? Is she still depressed?

Your sister's condition has changed. They suggested you come right in.

It sounded urgent.

I've forgotten my patient's name again. I look at the screen. *Kerrie Nichols.*

I can't make a decision about her medication now; panic has wrecked my concentration.

"I'm really sorry, Nicole," I say. "There's been an emergency."

"It's *Kerrie*," she corrects me, and she's confused and annoyed as I rise.

"I'm really sorry," I say again. "I have to go. Please reschedule your appointment—there'll be no fee for these consultations."

I can't leave her alone in my office, so I have to stand at the door while I hurry her out, then I run to the staff room. I unlock it with my swipe key and think of Annie and the time she used this very swipe key to try to rob this place, and how that almost ruined my career, and here I am using it two years later to run out to her—but what if she's really sick, and what if the baby is in trouble?

It must be bad for them to ask me to come right in. Or does the staff at the hospital not realize I'm working, and how many people will be inconvenienced by this?

"What do you want us to do with your patients, Lexie?" the receptionist asks at the door as I'm pulling my jacket on.

I look at her blankly then say, "I'm going to have to reschedule all of them. All of them. I'm so sorry—I don't think I'll be back today. Please tell the patients I'll do all of their consults for free when they return and please tell Oliver he can take it out of my salary and please—"

"Lexie, it's going to be okay. I'll squeeze your emergency patients in with someone else, and I'll talk to Oliver and tell him what happened, okay? Just go to the hospital," the receptionist interrupts me, apparently having had enough of my anxious ramblings.

I speed all the way to the hospital, and I double-park behind Sam's dedicated parking space when I finally arrive. I run through the halls to Maternity, but her room is empty, so I run straight back to slam my palms down on the reception desk and ask the nurse behind it, "Where is Annie? Annie Vidler?"

"Are you Lexie?"

"Yes. What's going on?"

Another nurse appears. She's carrying a set of surgical scrubs, and my stomach drops all the way to my toes.

"She's being prepped for surgery," the nurse murmurs as she passes me the scrubs. "They're going to do a C-section—Dr. Rogers is just securing consent."

"Consent?" I repeat, and the nurse nods.

"She's on the phone with the baby's guardian ad litem. As soon as he gives the go-ahead, she's going to start, so we need to hurry."

I can hear my pulse in my ears. Annie wasn't even allowed to consent to her own C-section, and that is *maddening*—but that's not even the issue that matters most. Something has obviously changed with Annie's condition, and for these drastic measures, it must be serious.

"What happened?" I ask as I follow the nurse to a bathroom.

"The baby went into distress. I'm not sure of the details."

I pull the scrubs on in record time and run through the corridor after the nurse to the operating room. Annie is on the table—the epidural is already administered—and Eliza is behind a curtain, preparing for the surgery.

I have made it just in time, and I can't believe that the peaceful weekend I spent with my sister has given way to this rush of chaos. Annie is sobbing, and I'm desperate to know why this C-section is being done, but I don't want to ask until I calm her down. I take my place beside her face and perch upon the stool that a nurse hastily presses in my direction.

"Everything is going to be absolutely fine, Annie—just try to stay calm."

"But they said the baby was in distress." Annie is panicking, and I can hear the too-fast rhythm of her heart on the monitor. I squeeze her shoulder and force an entirely artificial smile.

"Let's take some deep breaths, okay? I'll take them with you. Let's breathe in…"

Annie locks her eyes onto mine and inhales deeply, then exhales with me. After a few breaths, she closes her eyes and then nods to herself.

"I'm okay. I'm okay, Lexie."

"Of course you are," I whisper to her, and then I stand briefly to glance over the curtain. Eliza is moving very quickly, and I scan the faces of the other staff assisting her. It's some seconds before anyone even notices me standing there—but when a surgical nurse does, she points downward and gives me a firm look. I fix a smile onto my face as I sit and focus my attention on my sister. "What do you think…girl or boy?" Annie's teeth suddenly start to chatter and she shoots me an alarmed look. I squeeze her shoulder. "It's just the epidural. It's okay."

"Girl," she whispers, and she shoots me a watery, terrified smile. "I hope it's a girl. I won't be disappointed if it's a boy either, but I kind of pictured a girl."

I hear movement on the other side of the curtain, and move to rise again, but this time a nurse gently presses my shoulder to hold me in place. I frown up at her, and her gaze is stern. I hear more movement—and urgent whispers—and someone is saying the word *meconium* and I know what that means so I struggle to get back to my feet, then I open my mouth to argue with the nurse. She shoots a pointed look at Annie. I pull my jaw shut and force my attention back to my sister.

"Remember when we used to play 'mommies and daddies' in the woods behind the worship hall?" she asks me unsteadily. I pause and focus because I have to really search my memory, but after a moment it comes back to me. I smile sadly at her.

"I was way too old to play that game."

"You did it for me. I loved it when you let me be the mom."

"I was a bit of a control freak, wasn't I?"

"Was?" she stammers through her chattering teeth, and we both laugh nervously, then she asks, "Will you and Sam have kids?"

"One day. We're not in any rush."

"You'll be a great mom. You've already had a lot of practice."

"You will be, too, Annie." She all but rolls her eyes at me, and I shake my head at her fiercely. "You *will*. You need to start believing in yourself."

"God, even when I'm giving birth and scared shitless you can't help but lecture me," Annie says, but she smiles with some fragility as she says the words. "I think I'm going to shake my way off this bed. And it feels really weird down there." Her voice rises, and I hear her mounting panic as she says, "I can feel pressure—a lot of pressure."

"Are you in any pain, Annie?" the anesthesiologist asks urgently. Annie stares into my eyes, but she shakes her head.

"No, but I can feel them moving inside me I think."

"That's quite normal," I tell her gently.

"I don't like it," Annie says, then there's more movement on the other side of the curtain and urgent whispering, and Annie winces and groans. "No, I really don't like it. Please—can you stop?"

"Almost done, Annie," Eliza calls over the curtain, and then there is another rush of movement and I see a nurse carry something tiny away from the bed. I lean back to peer around the curtain as several doctors and nurses crowd around a table on the other side of the room. No one chastises me now. Every single person in the room is frozen, waiting for the cry.

"What is it? What's going on?" Annie asks me frantically. I look back to her, and tears are rolling down her face. Helpless, I rub her cheek with the back of my finger.

"The baby is out, Annie. The doctors are working on it now."

"Working on it? What's wrong with it?"

"It's a little girl, Annie," one of the nurses calls, and Annie gasps in delight and gives me a shaky grin.

"Told you," she whispers. I can't even smile at her—I'm holding my breath, trying desperately to eavesdrop on the staff, straining to hear some sound from the baby. The tension grows and grows, until I can hardly stop myself from walking right on over there to see what is happening.

But then I do hear it—a tiny, fragile growl, and then a cough and an equally tiny cry. I exhale heavily, as does every other medical professional in the room. Annie's eyes widen.

"That's her? The baby?"

"Give us a few more minutes and you can see for yourself," one of the doctors calls. It's only a moment or two later that a nurse walks toward Annie holding a tiny, blanket-wrapped bundle. She leans low and rests the baby right up against Annie's shoulder.

"Hey there, Annie. Meet your little girl. Isn't she beautiful?"

And the baby is beautiful—purple and *tiny* and scrawny, her face is all scrunched up in protest at the cold air, but regardless of all of that, Annie's daughter takes my breath away. Annie lifts one hand, and awkwardly holding the BP monitor on her forefinger away, she gently strokes the baby's cheek with her middle finger, too overcome with emotion to do anything but stare at her.

"Now, we have to take her through to the NICU for some tests. If she's doing well, someone will bring her to you in recovery later."

"I don't want her to leave me," Annie whispers, and the nurse shakes her head.

"Sorry, Annie."

Annie glances at me.

"Can my sister go? She's a doctor."

"Ah…" The nurse glances around the room to the team, and at their nods, she turns to me. "Come on then, doctor-sister."

"Don't let her out of your sight, okay?" Annie whispers, and I hesitate.

"Are you sure you want me to leave, Annie? You're going to be here for a while."

"No, please go with her. I'm scared she's going to start withdrawal and there'll be no one there to comfort her."

"That will take a while, Annie. Maybe a day or so. And she's going to be okay with the NICU staff."

"She should be with someone who loves her."

I can tell from the determination in my sister's voice that she's not going to change her mind, so I follow my niece and her medical entourage from the operating room into the NICU. As we walk, a registered nurse pushes the humidicrib with the baby, and every now and again I peer down at my niece. She is covered in patches of vernix, but in between, I can see her skin has that strange, translucent, purple-red tone that premature newborns tend to have. Still, I'm surprised by how well she's doing—she's much healthier so far than I had feared she would be given the rush of the C-section. She is breathing on her own, for a start, and she is active—pressing her fists around her face, and stretching her legs uncertainly as she adjusts to the realities of life outside the womb.

"Why did they deliver?" I ask the nurse.

"Mom's BP was unstable overnight, then Bubba here had a few strange trace results during monitoring this morning. They did an ultrasound, and the blood flow had deteriorated over the weekend. Dr. Rogers decided it was too risky to wait. A good call, too, I'd say, given that meconium. She's a teeny thing, but she's breathing so well—maybe she was a bit closer to term than we expected."

In the NICU, the staff performs a number of tests on the baby. There's a series of criteria hospital staff use to evaluate a newborn's physical condition in the moments immediately after birth, a scale of health known as the Apgar tests. The baby's results on this scale are better than I expect—she scores a five on the first check, and then seven points out of ten on the second five minutes later. Annie's nameless baby is crying now, a weak, warbling sound, and a nurse shushes her gently as she rocks her in her arms. Even the cry is a good sign, though, and the nurses and neonatologists are cheerful as the tests conclude.

"This is much more pleasant than what I feared we might be doing with this one today," one of the NICU nurses remarks as she pulls a tiny knitted beanie onto the baby's head.

"What does she weigh?" I ask.

"A little under five pounds—but she's doing very well, considering. You ready for a hold, Aunt?"

I've held hundreds of newborns during my training and the three years I've spent in general practice. Something about this one seems different, though, and I hesitate a moment or two before I nod. The nurse glances toward my shirt and says, "Skin-to-skin is best, if you're comfortable with it."

"With me? But..."

"Baby doesn't care whose skin she's cuddled up to, Aunt. She just wants to be held—she wants to feel the warmth of your skin and hear your heartbeat against her ear. We do kangaroo care here with some of our preemies. It makes a huge difference for the stability of their vitals. And if this baby develops NAS, she's likely to need all the help she can get—but if you aren't comfortable with it..."

I shake my head hastily as I unbutton my shirt. I open it all the way, but leave it hanging over my shoulders, and I leave my bra on. Once I've taken a seat in the recliner beside the humidicrib, the nurse unwraps the baby and passes her to me. It's awkward—the baby has monitoring leads attached to her chest and an oxygen cannula in her nose. She's cool to the touch so I reach to take the blanket she'd been wrapped in and I pull it around both of us.

"Hi there, I'm your aunt," I whisper. The baby's tiny skull

rests against my breast. I see the shape of Annie's features in my niece, and I feel an odd contraction in my chest. The baby squirms a little, but then her tiny eyes fall closed, and she relaxes into me—apparently unfazed by all of the frantic activity surrounding her birth. I laugh weakly and look up to the nurse, who gives me a knowing nod.

"I'll be right over here if you need anything."

The staff all shift around to other activities, but left in this corner of the NICU, I'm effectively alone with my niece. I catch her little wrist in my forefinger and thumb, and I stroke my hand along her tiny little fingers. Her skin is soft, and I'm suddenly startled to remember that this fragile, innocent child has already been exposed to heroin for its entire existence.

I know from my previous experience of newborns with NAS that this baby is likely to be fine for a day or so. There's yet another assessment scale the nurses and doctors will use to rate her symptoms hourly, maybe even more frequently if she's suffering. Once her symptoms reach a threshold, she'll start opiate treatments—morphine, most likely. I ponder this for a moment, and immediately begin to imagine this fragile infant in the throes of withdrawal. My throat constricts. Watching Annie withdraw had been one of the most difficult things I'd ever seen, including *all* of the difficult things I've dealt with in my medical career.

I don't even want to think about what this baby is going to go through—I want to pretend everything is going to stay peaceful, but now that the thought has crossed my mind, it's all I can think about. The NAS babies that I saw during my rotations through the hospital where I trained screamed and shook and turned purple, suffering pain that no mother or doctor could completely take from them. All the medical staff can really do is keep their morphine up regularly, and step it down as slowly as possible over the early weeks of their lives.

Suddenly I'm livid—full of rage toward Annie—and hot tears of fury fill my eyes. I *know* addiction is a disease—as a doctor,

I'm well aware of that. But the disease has now spread its ugly roots into the most vulnerable stage of another life, and for all of the times Annie has hurt me and I've forgiven her, I wonder if this is just one selfish act too many. She *could* have called me earlier. She *could* have found a way into treatment, if she'd called me. Instead, she'd buried her head in the sand, held tight to her pride and her habit, and now this tiny baby has to deal with the consequences.

Maybe I've let your momma down over the years, kiddo, and maybe she's already let you down herself—but I promise, I'll find a way to make all of this right so you two can have a life together.

14

ANNIE

Dear Luke,

Imagination can be a refuge, and soon Lexie and I had created an elaborate world all our own. Somehow, the life I lived in the woods with my sister became more real to me than the rest of my existence. The trees were my home—boulders my furniture, sticks my utensils, the dirt was my carpet and the birdsong was my background music.

Lexie would "tuck me in." My mattress was the cold dirt, my sheets a carpet of rotting leaves, and my pillow was a rock—but I didn't feel any of that, because in my mind, I was back in my real home. My fantasy was so vivid to me that I could breathe in the familiar smells of the old house...the lingering scent of the cakes Mom always baked back then, the citrusy cleaning products she'd used, even Dad's aftershave. I could almost see the pink walls of the bedroom Lexie and I used to share. If I strained my ear, I could hear Dad climbing the stairs to say good-night, and I could almost *convince myself that if I rolled over the other way, I'd see Lexie tucked in beside me.*

"What song do you want tonight, sweetheart?" Lexie would ask as she stroked the hair back from my face.

"Sing me 'Twinkle, Twinkle, Little Star.'"

"Twinkle, twinkle, little star, do you know how loved you are? In the morning, in the night, I'll love you with all my might... Twinkle, twinkle, little star, do you know how loved you are?"

The first time she sung the verse, I protested.

"That's not how it goes!"

"Mom used to sing it that way when you were little. I remember standing at the door and listening when you were a baby." Lexie smiled at me, and from that day on, she'd sing that funny little lullaby to me, and the tune and the lyrics would wrap their way around me until I felt safe and happy.

"I don't remember that."

"You were a baby, silly. But I can remember for the both of us."

One afternoon, as we walked to the woods, Lexie bent to pluck a seeded dandelion from a random patch of grass. She offered it to me.

"Make a wish?"

I took the dandelion but just before I was about to blow it, I paused. I looked at her, so wise beyond her years, and she was everything to me—because without Lexie, I knew that I was lost. I wanted to use the dandelion to wish that Mom would come to her senses and that we could go home somehow, that we could be a real family again. Life had been difficult since we lost Dad, but it had been only awful since Robert came along. I was sure that if Robert and the community were out of the picture, I'd be happy again.

But it seemed selfish to use the wish for myself. If anyone de-

served to be happy, it was Lexie—she was all that had saved me from utter misery over the years since Dad's death. I passed the dandelion back.

"No, you can have it."

"Why?" she asked, and she flashed me a quizzical smile as she accepted the stem back into her palm.

"It's your turn, Lex."

She raised the dandelion to her lips, then hesitated.

"Actually, let's do it together. Okay?"

I smiled at her as I nodded, and we each took in a big breath, then at the same time we blew gently against the seeds of the dandelion. They scattered as the wind caught them and pulled them away from us. I glanced at the stem and every last seed was gone.

"What did you wish for?" Lexie asked me.

"Isn't it supposed to be secret?"

"Well, we shared that dandelion so...we have different rules," she decided.

"I wished that we could be a normal family again."

"See... I wished the same thing," Lexie said, and she tossed the dandelion stem away and pulled me in for a tight hug. "It's bound to come true now!"

After that, we always searched for dandelions on our way to and from the woods. It became a ritual that we did not need to discuss or negotiate; we both knew exactly how it would run. When one of us found a dandelion, she would offer it to the other and we'd blow the seeds together to silently make the same wish.

Shortly after we started our dandelion-hunting ritual, Lexie found a doll behind the cupboard at the schoolhouse, and she managed to sneak it out in the folds of her skirt. The next afternoon, we stole a tea towel from the kitchen to make a blanket, and from that day on we had a baby to fuss over during those games in the woods. Given that Lexie always wanted to be Mom, this meant I now had to play the role of Dad, but I didn't mind that one bit.

"What should we call her?" I asked Lexie as she made a little crib for the doll between two moss-covered boulders. Lexie paused, and then she grinned at me.

"Dandelion," she announced, and I giggled.

"That's perfect."

I was quite sure that our wishes would come true one day, and that the miracle doll was some kind of hint from the universe that it was working things out for us. We just needed to be patient.

15

LEXIE

An hour passes before a nurse tells me Annie is ready to see her daughter. This time, as I walk the long hallway, I get to push the humidicrib myself. The baby opens her eyes as I'm walking, and she stares up with that vacant, unfocused stare newborns have. I smile at her anyway. I know it's pointless, but I just can't help it.

Annie is in the first bed in the recovery ward, flat on her back staring at the ceiling. Her gaze is as unfocused as her daughter's seems to be, but as soon as I near the bed, she perks up. She stretches her head up from the pillow to catch a view of her daughter.

"How is she?" Annie asks me. Her speech is a little slurred, and her words are rushed—she's anxious, and I wonder how they are handling her pain relief. Is the epidural still active? Or is she on morphine? Annie will be seriously resistant to opiates after so many years of abuse. Her dosage is going to be difficult to calculate, and I hope the staff is accounting for this.

"She's great, Annie," I say gently. I push the crib up close to Annie's bed, and I carefully lift the baby out and hold it toward my sister's face. She's still on a little oxygen, but mainly as a precaution given she's breathing pretty well on her own. Annie starts to cry, and she reaches to stroke the baby's cheek with her forefinger.

"Oh, she's so perfect," Annie croaks.

"She is. She's doing well. Really well."

Annie leans carefully to very gently kiss the end of her daughter's nose. "Hello there, little one."

"Are you thinking about breast-feeding her?"

"I'm only going to be here for a week. Doesn't seem much point." Annie sighs, and I shift the baby a little closer to her on the pillow.

"A week is still a great start, Annie. She'd at least get your colostrum."

"The nurse told me that, too. But if I start feeding her, I'm scared it will be even harder to leave."

"It's totally up to you. Either way, I think they want to give her something to drink soon."

"Okay," Annie murmurs, and she sinks back into the pillow, but turns her head to stare at the baby. "She's just so beautiful. I can't believe something so perfect came out of me."

"What are you going to call her?" I ask my sister softly.

"Dandelion," Annie whispers, and I lean closer to her and frown to concentrate. Surely I misheard her.

"Sorry? What did you say?"

"Dandelion." Annie says the word firmer now, but there is a quiet determination in her voice, as if she had anticipated my resistance.

I drag myself to my full height and frown down at my sister as I say carefully, "I don't think 'Dandelion' is actually a name."

"It *is*," Annie murmurs simply, then she stops and stares at me, issuing a challenge with her slightly glazed eyes. I fall silent as I try to figure out how to play this.

"Well, it's not a very well-known name," I say eventually.

"Listen, Lexie," Annie says flatly, "I *know* what I want to call my daughter. I've had a lot of time to think about this, and Dandelion is the name that I have chosen. I realize it's not the most common name, but I think it's beautiful. So, that's my decision."

"It's selfish to give a child a name like that," I mutter, and I glance at the baby again. *Dandelion.* What middle name is she going to choose—Cactus? Banana?

"Well, it doesn't actually matter what you think," Annie whispers. "This is my daughter, and I'll call her what I want to. Her name will be Dandelion. I'll call her Dani for short."

"This little baby is already having a very tough start because of you. Do you really want to lump her with a name that's going to haunt her for her entire life?" I say, and my tone is sharp—much sharper than I have ever used in polite conversation with Annie. We're both a bit taken aback. I usually reserve that tone for our arguments—the screaming matches that come after she's done something self-destructive. But this is *worse* than self-destructive—the stakes have been raised. Now there's another life in the mix. Annie frowns at me, and I can see she's annoyed with my interference, but damn it—I can't sit back and let her name the child after a *weed.*

"How dare you?" Annie says, and now her tone is sharp, too, but she's still weak and although she forces the words out, there's no power behind them. I take this as a sign that Annie is also unsure of her choice, and so I go for the knockout punch. I know I'll be glad I did this later, when the baby has a sensible name. A real name. A name she can proudly claim when she's on the Supreme Court one day.

The problem is, I'm just so angry with Annie. When I speak, I'm not just sharp with her, I'm positively bitter.

"I dare because someone has to speak up for that little girl. She's got enough hurdles to overcome because of you without being burdened by a silly name."

Annie stares at me. I should feel guilty, but I don't, because although I'm embarrassed by my awful tone, I'm actually relieved I didn't vent *all* of my frustration and anger toward her. There's still plenty bottled up, and there's still a chance it might explode, depending on what she says next.

"But…" Annie swallows, and she looks at the baby again. She is visibly uncertain, and I exhale a breath I didn't realize I'd been holding.

"Daisy," I suggest. "Daisy—it's still floral, still unusual, but it's an actual name. What do you think?"

"Yes, Daisy is nice," Annie says weakly, then she clears her throat. "I'm awfully groggy, Lexie. Do you think you could take her away for a while so I can sleep?"

"Don't you want to try to feed her first?"

"Maybe later," Annie whispers, and she kisses her baby's cheek and closes her eyes. I lift the baby carefully into my arms, and once I've rested her in the crib, I hesitate.

"Annie?"

"Hmm?"

"You can decide on the name later, okay?"

"Hmm…"

She's either already asleep, or maybe she's pretending to be. I sigh and start to push the baby back to the NICU, but I'm only a few feet down the hallway when I'm stopped in my tracks by a memory surging to the front of my mind.

I'm back in the woods. Annie is walking along beside me, her long braids over her shoulders, holding the stupid doll I stole for her, wearing a broad beam on her face. Robert had taken away every single thing that gave my sister joy over the first few weeks in the community. It was as if he had set out to break her spirit, and I was starting to think it was working.

Annie had stopped smiling. I hadn't realized what a difference a smile makes to a person's face until hers disappeared. I'd always been jealous that Annie got Dad's big blue eyes, but they were no longer so appealing when their sparkle disappeared. Looking at my sister and watching her fade away was like losing my father all over again; maybe even worse because it was slowly happening before my eyes.

So I stole the doll. I told Annie I found it behind a cupboard at school, but I actually took it from one of the kids who lived next door—I sneaked into her bedroom one afternoon when everyone else was playing at the schoolhouse. I just wanted to make Annie smile again, and it worked. The doll was a tool, just like the games I used to play to distract her during those long afternoons—simple ways to try to keep her connected to the childhood the sect and our new stepfather seemed determined to take away from her. From *us*. I can barely believe Annie remembers that doll at all—it was nothing, a pathetic straw that I clutched at when I didn't know how else to help her.

But now, two decades later, Annie wants to name her baby after that doll, and my first reaction was to dismiss the suggestion as if it were meaningless.

I turn to stare at the door to the recovery room, but I can't bring myself to go back. I tell myself she's asleep and I can talk to her about it later, but the reality is, my throat feels tight and I know I'm going to cry. I avoid the gazes of hospital staff as I return the baby to the NICU, and then I go to my car and I finally start to sob.

I cry for the Annie who went into that community, I cry for the broken creature who escaped six years later, and I cry for the baby who one way or another is going to pay a price for her mother's pain.

16

ANNIE

Luke,

Even as a nine-year-old, I knew I should have been figuring out ways to stay under the radar. Unlike Lexie, I just couldn't bring myself to blend in. Her instinct was to survive long enough to escape, mine was always to fight.

I was never malicious or spiteful. I just wanted to go home, and so I fought constantly against any sign that I might be assimilating into that place. In the first few years, they were relatively small rebellions—skipping lessons at the schoolhouse, talking during the worship services, refusing to say "amen." The punishments started small, too—those spankings with the leather strap barely penetrated the fierceness of my rebellion. And initially, they really were just light strikes against my skin—and Mom sat silently as he administered them over his lap, right there at the dinner table. I'd stare at Lexie while he hit me, and she'd stare right back—her eyes wet with tears, her nostrils flared. One night, when she tried to intervene, he hit her, too, and we both ended up in bed hungry.

"Just leave it, Lexie," I told her. "I don't even care if he hits me."

"Can't you just say it? Just say 'amen' and be done with it. It's just a stupid word," she whispered to me in the darkness.

"I can't let him win."

And even when the beatings grew fiercer, the pain didn't bother me—I actually found a measure of satisfaction in the frustration I could see on Robert's face as he reached for the belt night after night. But I hated that he'd hit Lexie, too, and so eventually I did learn to say the word at the end of the blessing, just to keep the peace for her.

Robert won that battle, but I still felt like we were at war, and the conflict soon shifted to my clothing. All women in the community were required to wear long skirts year-round, but in the summer, I tripped on one of my outings to the woods with Lexie and ripped my skirt. Inspired, I tore the bottom half of the skirt off, and I came to breakfast the next morning with it falling only as far as my knees.

Robert rose silently, lifted the belt from the hook beside the table and dragged me by the neck of my shirt back to the bedroom I shared with Lexie. He threw me onto the bed, and for the first time ever, he lifted the skirt and pulled away my underwear and he brought the belt down onto my bare skin.

"Keep your mouth shut," he hissed, when I cried out. I heard a hesitant knock at the door. I knew it was Lexie, and so did Robert—he turned toward the door and he thundered, "Leave us, Alexis!"

Her footsteps did not retreat as I bit the insides of my cheeks to stop myself from crying out. Robert brought the belt onto my bare skin again and again. For the first time, he hit me until his rage subsided—and when he was finished, I was bruised and barely able to move. I crawled stiffly along the bed to press my face into my pillow as Robert hissed, "You are a filthy, sinful little girl, Anne, and I swear to you that I'll beat the sin out of you if I have to."

Robert told Mom and Lexie that I was not allowed to go to school that day, and he prohibited Lexie from seeing me. From the bedroom I heard Lexie's wild protests.

"Mom, you can't let him do this to her!" Lexie had wept, and my mother spoke firmly to her.

"Robert is the head of this household, Lexie. We have to trust him to discipline Annie as he needs to. You'll see. Sooner or later, she'll respect him for his correction."

When her lessons finished, Lexie ran home from school and she burst into the room.

"What did he do to you?" she asked me, her face red with rage. "I'll get the police. He can't hit you like that. It's not right."

"I don't even care," I said to her, and I went back to staring at the ceiling, as I'd been doing all morning since they left. I'd been in some kind of shocked trance, more numb than stoic—I hadn't shed a single tear. "He can hit me, but he can't hurt me."

"Annie, you have *to stop provoking him.* Please.*"*

"I'm just getting started."

I had all morning to think about the incident with the skirt, and I'd come up with a plan. It was against the rules for girls in the community to cut their hair—the sect adhered strictly to a biblical teaching that long hair was a woman's crowning glory. *But the girls at school were encouraged to do "feminine activities" like cross-stitch and other crafts, so I had easy access to scissors.*

When the bruising on my thighs had gone down enough for me to go back to school, I slipped a pair of scissors into the pocket of my skirt. I waited until everyone else was asleep, then I went to the bathroom and gave myself a jagged bob and even a fringe.

When I arrived at breakfast the next day, Robert was so angry that I thought he was going to kill me. As he dragged me back to the bedroom, I could hear the way his breathing caught in his throat and I started to worry—what would happen if he did actually kill me? Would anyone even care, other than Lexie? I wasn't sure, but I didn't want to die, and for a few moments I really wondered if I'd gone too far. The belt against the still-fresh bruises on my thighs was agonizing that day, and I couldn't help but cry. I heard Mom and Lexie arguing on the other side of the door, and Robert must have, too—because after only a moment or two he stopped. He lifted me with two tight fists against my upper arms, until I was dangling in front of him at eye level. His breath on my face was hot, and I wanted to cower away from him—but I wouldn't. Instead, I stared right back and I clenched my teeth so that they couldn't chatter.

"Filthy, sinful little whore," he hissed, then he threw me onto the bed. When he left the bedroom, he slammed the door so hard that the hinge broke.

Robert made Mom drag me before the entire women's assembly that week to apologize for dishonoring the community and the Lord. Lexie begged me to do as they asked—just so that the fuss would die down. I was all set to, until I found myself sitting on a stool on the stage of the worship hall, staring out at that sea of judgmental faces.

Two hundred women and girls stared back at me. Their gazes were sharp, and in pockets all around the room, women and girls whispered to one another. I could feel their condemnation and the odd hum of excitement in the air. I was a living, breathing scandal, and the drama of my haircut was the most exciting thing that had happened in Winterton in forever. This was as close to a frenzy as the women were generally allowed to experience, and all of that energy was focused on me. *The butterflies in my stomach disappeared and all I felt was sick and terrified. My skin was clammy, my heart was racing and the expansive hall seemed to sway before me.*

They were enjoying this. *They all thought I was a monster—a child of the devil.*

Over a haircut.

The absurdity of the moment struck me, and I started to laugh. It was a nervous response, nothing more than anxiety manifesting itself physically, but to the crowd, it seemed a further rebellion, and I heard the audible gasp that rippled through the assembly. This was fuel to the fire of my nerves, and the laughter grew louder.

Mom was on the stage, too, wringing her hands and pacing around me as she waited for me to say the magic words that would make all of this go away, but my laughter confused and then infuriated her—the pleading in her eyes faded, until she was simply staring at me with that same disgusted look in her eyes that the crowd wore.

"Stop it, Annie! You need to say sorry," *she pleaded, but I could only shake my head. I was petrified—in physical shock at the public shaming—and although I'd had the best of intentions to apologize and put the whole thing to rest, I couldn't* stop the giggles.

And when she realized I wasn't going to apologize, my mom burst into tears and for the very first time *during all of this, I actually felt a little guilty. When Mom ran away, one of her sisters stormed up the stairs onto the stage and took over the process of facilitating my confession.*

"Admit your sin to the congregation!" my aunt roared. My nervous laughter faded and finally disappeared. I stared up at her, at the sharpness of her stare and the red that stained her cheeks. Even

now, twenty-one years later, I can still remember how small I felt under that scornful gaze.

That's when I decided that I wouldn't apologize. Until that moment, I had the best of intentions, and the only reason I hadn't said the words they wanted to hear was that my nerves had gotten the better of me. I was still nervous and still terrified, but suddenly I was also determined. That same sense of indignation that saw me defy Robert almost daily in our house rose within me, and I met my aunt's gaze and I said, "No."

I barely croaked the word because my throat felt so tight. I'm not even sure if she heard me, because my aunt circled around me and then bent close to hiss right in my face.

"Tell them about the darkness in your heart, Anne. Confess your sin and repent."

"No," I said again. My voice was just a little louder this time—more steel within the word. Another woman joined us on the stage, and she pressed an accusing forefinger into my face and thundered, "Elder Robert told us you cut your skirt last week and tried to go to school with your knees exposed. And now this—cutting your crowning glory, dishonoring the Lord. These are the lustful acts of a slut, Anne Herbert. You are trying to distract the men of this community with your appearance, aren't you? You want their desire, don't you? Whore!"

I was nine years old. I had no idea what any of that meant, only that the other women in the room were still staring at me, nodding their approval at the accusations. I wasn't even sure what I was supposed to do or say—so I stood and tried to run away. The aunts cornered me and pushed me back onto the chair and the questions continued. I have no idea how long it went on—only that eventually,

I slipped away from them altogether. Maybe my body was still there on the stage, but my mind was somewhere else—somewhere safe.

But still... I didn't apologize.

Later that night, Robert sat me on the couch and lectured me— pacing the length of the room as if he was too charged up to sit still.

"The devil is in you, Anne Herbert," he thundered, and I snapped out of the strange half sleep I'd been in since the women's meeting as I shot to my feet and hissed back at him,

"My name *is Annie* Vidler."

Mom burst into tears, and I froze. Robert raised his hand and slapped me. I slammed my eyes shut instinctively, and when I opened them, I saw that Mom was holding her hand over her mouth, her knuckles white. She watched in silence as Robert dragged me into the bedroom for another beating.

"You just have to stop, Annie," Lexie whispered to me in the woods in the days after the incident. "I know you're trying to make a point, but this isn't the way to go about it."

"I have to," I said stubbornly. "I'm not like you. I can't just make myself fit in here. I hate these people."

"I do, too. But we have to survive until we can leave, and you're just making things harder for yourself."

"I'm going to convince Mom to take me home."

"Home? Annie—this is home now. There's nowhere else for us to go—she sold the house, and her family is all here. She couldn't take us away even if she wanted to."

"But she could work at the old school, she could—"

"Annie!" Lexie grew impatient with me, and she raised her voice—something she'd do a lot in the years that followed, but it was rare enough then that I fell silent. "You're making life even more awful than it already is, not just for yourself, but for all of us—for

me and Mom, too. Please—can you please try a little harder to just go along with all of their nonsense?"

"But Lexie..." I started to protest again, but I fell silent when Lexie's expression softened and she pulled me into her arms for a hug. Her arms were the safest place in the world, and when she embraced me, the sick tension in my belly unfurled...at least for a little while. Her arms were a fortress, confining my anger and keeping the demons away. Just for a few moments while she hugged me, I was actually just fine.

"I know it's hard, Annie," she whispered against my hair. "I hate it here, too. But we have each other, don't we?"

"Yeah."

"And as long as we have each other, we can get through anything, right?"

"Okay," I said, and when she released me I looked right into her eyes and I promised, "I'll try harder, Lexie. I'll try to fit in."

And I did try for a while, but I'd gotten into such a habit of being the bad girl, it seemed I couldn't stop even when I wanted to. I tried to make friends in school, but everyone knew who I was by then—if not by reputation, then certainly by my haircut. Lexie and I had never fit into the community, but now we were completely ostracized, and I found myself acting out to simply deal with the intense loneliness I felt.

No one smiled at me. No one was kind to me. When I walked down the street, the other kids crossed the road to get away from me. If I tried to hug Mom, she'd pull away. I craved contact and acceptance—and I started to wonder if there wasn't something more to the way the community rejected me after all.

Maybe I really was the bad girl.

I argued with my teachers and the elders, and I antagonized Rob-

ert, and I smashed a window in the kitchen just because, and I tore Robert's precious family Bible then refused to admit it was me— even after he beat me until I bled. If there was a way to anger him, I found it. It became a game to me—a form of entertainment—but it was a game that increased the isolation that made me miserable in the first place and a game I couldn't seem to stop.

Three and a half years after we arrived at the community, Lexie turned sixteen. She had a farewell party at the school the day before her birthday, and Mom lined a job up for her at the general store. The smartest kid in the community was going to be doing the filing for a purchasing clerk.

I woke up before dawn on her birthday and found Lexie sitting on the edge of my bed.

"What's going on?" I asked her. I was groggy, and while I noticed immediately that she looked different, it took me a while to realize why. "Where did you get pants from?"

"I stole them from Robert," she whispered, and she lifted her shirt to reveal a belt fashioned out of twine. "You have no idea how amazing it feels."

I was amused by this odd turn of events, until I realized how serious Lexie's behavior actually was. Robert would lose his mind when he saw her—this was the kind of stunt I'd pull, not Lexie. I sat up and stared at her. The pace of my thoughts slowed to a standstill.

Something bad was about to happen.

"Have you lost your mind?"

"Annie... I'm leaving today."

"Leaving?"

"I'm going to go. Now."

"You can't leave me, Lexie. You can't leave me alone here." I started to cry, and she took my hands in hers and she squeezed hard.

"I can't stay here, Annie—I have to get out and find a way to go to college. It's for you, too. By the time you're sixteen and you can leave, I'll have a house and a job, and I'll be able to take care of you."

I begged her not to, but Lexie left that day.

I was never sure why she didn't warn me...maybe she assumed that I already knew she was planning to leave. If she did, she might have overestimated my intelligence, because I never saw it coming.

17

LEXIE

"You can't just bail midway through the morning. Do you have any idea how much disruption that caused?"

I figured Oliver was going to be annoyed, but I didn't expect him to be angry. When I arrive at the clinic, he all but drags me into his office and lets loose.

"My sister was taken into emergency surgery—" I try to explain, but he cuts me off.

"Were you *performing* the surgery?"

I know I need to tread lightly, but Oliver's sarcasm leaves me defensive, and I scowl at him.

"It was a C-section. She needed someone with her."

"This is the sister who broke into the meds room two years ago, right?" I look away, and Oliver sighs. "So what you're saying is, two years later, your boundaries with her are no better than they were."

This hits a sore spot, and I wince but then I blurt, "I need to take some time off. She's going into rehab and she has a newborn. She needs me to help care for it, or it'll go into the foster system."

Oliver stares at me incredulously for a moment, then he sighs heavily and rubs his forehead.

"Jesus, Lexie. Are you seriously going to ask for time *off* after you pulled that shit this morning?"

"There's no one else, Olly." I'm pleading now, and I should be embarrassed, but all I can think of is Annie and the baby and that awful moment this morning when I dismissed her chosen name. I can't let my sister down again. I *won't*. "I have to do this."

"I'm not going to grant the leave, and I'm doing it for your own good."

"But—"

"Don't *but* me, Lexie. If you really need time off to babysit your sister, resign."

That last word hangs in the air between us—a threat that I'm not sure Oliver is entirely serious about. The look I give him is half pleading, half incredulous.

"Don't do this, Olly."

He shakes his head—he's warming to the idea himself, I can tell by the gleam in his eyes when he leans back in his chair and surveys me. Oliver Winton is actually the best boss I've ever had—and I've learned so much from him in the last three years. But I'm well aware that I need him more than he needs me. I'm sure he likes me, though, and we do work well together. Surely he won't make me leave.

Surely.

Hopefully.

"I can't have an unreliable physician on the team," he says. "Your patients *need* to be your priority. If they aren't, then you should leave."

"I haven't taken a sick or a personal day in two years." I'm getting defensive again, and my words are sharp. "These are exceptional circumstances. I'm asking for just a few weeks to figure all of this out—the baby will be in the NICU for some time. After that, I need to get her settled in at my place. Then it will be business as usual, I give you my word."

"No, then your sister will come out of rehab and you'll be taking every second day off to go searching under all of the bridges in town to see if she's overdosed."

"How dare you—" I gasp, but he cuts me off with an impatient wave of his hand.

"I'm trying to *help* you. You know what codependency is, right? You and your sister are a textbook case. You'll let her waltz in and out of your life and blow it up whenever it suits her forever if someone doesn't force you to reevaluate things. I don't want you to go, Lexie—the patients love you, and you're an excellent physician. But… I can hire another excellent physician within a few hours of interviews. And I'd be damned unlucky to get another one with a family life that's as much of a disaster as yours."

I stare at him. Tears cloud my vision, but I blink them away.

"Give me four weeks," I whisper.

"Did you hear *anything* I just said?" It's Oliver's turn to be incredulous.

"Four weeks, Olly. Four weeks, and I promise it will all be sorted out, and I'll be back and the most loyal staff member you've ever had on your team. It'd take you at least a few weeks to recruit a replacement for me anyway, right? So you have nothing to lose."

"Fucking hell, Lexie."

"Please?"

"*Unpaid* leave."

"Of course." The relief crashes over me, and I freeze—debating whether or not I should hug him.

"Christ," Oliver groans, then he stares at his desk as he points a stiff finger toward his office door. "Get out of here before I change my mind."

★ ★ ★

I'm sitting in Annie's room several hours later, holding the baby while the nurse tends to Annie's dressing. She is still groggy and in pain.

"I'll talk to the doctor again," the nurse murmurs, but she's impatient, because Annie has been complaining for hours now. Within minutes of her last shot of morphine, Annie wanted more, and the nurses have already discussed it with the registrar on duty and confirmed the dose is correct. I can't tell if Annie is genuinely in pain or just wants more drugs, so I feel for the doctors.

When we are alone again, I approach the bed with the baby, and Annie brightens just a little.

"It's difficult to get the dose right," I tell her quietly. "Your tolerance to the opioids would be pretty high, and the methadone…"

"I know," Annie interrupts me, but she speaks weakly. She looks exhausted. "But I have seven days with her, and right now I'm in so much pain I can't even think straight. They need to give me something more so I can function a bit more, because I won't get these hours back."

I sit on the edge of the bed so Annie can see the baby, who's wide-awake but content. Annie raises her hand to touch the baby's arm, and she smiles gently at her.

"Hello, little one. You look happy."

"The baby looks like Dad," I tell Annie, and she looks at me in surprise.

"You think so?"

"Well, she looks like you, and you do, so…"

"I thought I might give her Nell for a middle name. It's not exactly Neil, but it's close."

"And her first name?" I say hesitantly. I glance at Annie. "I'm really sorry about before. I shouldn't have…"

Annie looks at me blankly.

"Before?"

"Don't you remember? In recovery?"

Annie shifts her gaze from me back to the baby, but I know she's lying when she says, "I was too out of it. I don't remember anything of recovery. And anyway, her name will be Daisy. Daisy Nell Vidler. It's beautiful, isn't it?"

I hesitate, because I *do* still think Daisy is a much more sensible name, but I don't want to overturn my sister's wishes. There's a soft knock at the door, and when I turn around, Sam is there. He's carrying a huge bunch of flowers and a pink It's a Girl balloon. He offers me a smile.

"Hey," he says, "can I come in?"

"Of course," Annie says. He approaches us at the bed and stares down at the baby.

"Well, Annie. Your daughter is beautiful. Congratulations."

"You didn't have to buy me flowers," she tells him a little stiffly. "You've done enough, Sam. You really have."

"Ah, nonsense." He waves a hand toward her dismissively. "You're family, and she's family. By the way, does 'she' have a name?"

"Daisy," Annie tells him.

"That's a beautiful name, Annie. Congratulations."

He makes room for the flowers on her bedside table and sticks the balloon a little awkwardly into the bunch, then opens his arms and nods toward the baby.

"Can I?" he asks, and I pass him my niece.

"Sorry I didn't call you," I say as I adjust the baby's blanket around her in his arms. I'm momentarily distracted by how natural Sam looks as he holds the newborn. He'll hold our babies one day, if we're lucky enough to have them. If he sticks around after all of this chaos... "It's been a whirlwind."

"It's fine. I had my spies keeping an eye on you two," he assures us. "I wanted to come by earlier but I had a patient emergency myself. I've only just finished now."

"What time is it?" Annie asks, and I turn to the clock on the wall.

"God, it's nearly seven o'clock."

"Have you taken some time off work?" Sam asks me carefully, and I nod. "In that case, I thought we could drive home together tonight and travel back in together tomorrow. If you're ready now."

"I don't think I should leave Annie yet—" I glance at her, and she shakes her head.

"I'm exhausted, Lexie. I'm just waiting for something stronger for the pain, then I'm going to sleep."

"Are you in much pain, Annie?" Sam frowns, and I try to shoot him a message with my eyes—*danger, don't get involved.* He also seems to be trying to send me a message right back—*trust me.* I do—I'm sure Sam is very well versed in the complexities of this pain-management scenario—but as much as I trust him, I also know Annie, and how manipulative she can be.

"I've asked for something more," she mutters, but she seems embarrassed, and that's pretty much confirmation that she is playing us.

"I'll stop past the office on the way out and ask them to review your dosage, okay? You need to sleep well tonight so you can make the most of your time with this little one tomorrow."

Annie's eyes fill with tears, and she nods.

"Thank you, Sam, that's all I'm worried about," she whispers unevenly, then she glances at me. "He's a keeper, Lexie."

"I know," I murmur. I glance at Sam again, but he's staring down at the baby. "We should go, then." I bend to kiss her forehead. "I'll see you in the morning."

We walk Daisy back to the NICU—Annie can't lift her yet, and the baby will need close monitoring over the next few days. Once she's safely back with the staff we walk through the corridor alone. Sam takes my hand in his and glances at me. "Tough day, honey?"

"It could have been a lot worse," I say, but suddenly, I feel tired all the way down to my bones—and I still need to call Mom. "I just can't wait to get home."

"I'll quickly speak with the consultant about her meds. They're probably being conservative with the dosage."

"Or the dose is perfect and she just wants a harder hit."

"No, I could see it in her eyes," Sam says. He says it with complete confidence, but I hear the arrogance in his tone, and it irritates the hell out of me.

"They're dosing her high enough, Sam. She's playing you."

"Lex, trust me, okay?" He says this dismissively, and my hackles rise. "I deal with post-op pain all day, every day. I know the signs, and your sister was in genuine discomfort."

"But she—"

"Let me talk to the staff. It will be obvious from the dosage if you're right."

It takes all of thirty seconds with the nursing staff to discover that I'm *not* right—the consultant has ordered a standard post-caesar morphine dose for Annie. All of this leaves me completely confused. I'm angry for Annie, and I regret that I didn't believe her and advocate for her—and I'm embarrassed to have doubted Sam.

But I'm also fatigued, and part of me thinks it's *her* fault that I'm so suspicious of her. I've fallen for her tricks before.

"I'll go back and tell her," I murmur to Sam, when he reaches for the phone to call Eliza. He nods at me, and I walk back down the corridor to Annie's room. She startles when I open the door, and I see that she's been crying.

"Are you okay?"

"It hurts," she whispers, but she avoids my gaze and stares at the ceiling instead.

"The dosage is wrong. Sam is calling Eliza to get the order fixed." She nods once, so I know she's heard me. "I forgot to tell you, I'll call Mom to let her know," I add hesitantly. When Annie shakes her head, I say softly, "Annie, she needs to know."

I'm insistent even though I know the conversation is not going to be a fun one. *Surprise! Annie just had a baby. Oh, and she's been charged with child endangerment, and she's going into court-ordered rehab in seven days. If that doesn't work, she's probably off to jail for a decade. So that's our news—how's the weather over there?*

"She's going to be so pissed."

"I'll deal with her."

"Do you think she will come?"

"I honestly don't know. Do you want her to come?"

Annie thinks about it for a while before she shakes her head.

"I don't want her to see me like this."

"Well, if it's any consolation, she'll only come if Robert lets her."

Annie finally looks at me, and we share a sad smile. I turn back to the doorway, then ask, "Is there anyone else I should call?"

"You think I'm pathetic, don't you?"

Her sharp tone seems to come from out of nowhere. I look to Annie, confused.

"Don't, Annie… I'm just trying to help."

"I have a feeling that seeing me like this is probably satisfying to you," Annie says bitterly. "Did you just *know* that one day I'd come begging you for help again? It's probably killed you that it's taken two years."

She can be so mean, so condescending—and I'm so tired. The day has been emotionally exhausting—a roller coaster that seemed to be winding its way toward a peaceful rest—until now. I want to get out of the room before things deteriorate further, so I take a hasty step toward the door. "I'll be back in the morning. I'll bring you some things—some breakfast again?"

"Don't fucking bother. I don't need your charity."

I open the door but I hesitate before I step out, and the impulse to bite back is too strong. I ignore the weariness on her face and the pain in her eyes as I whisper bitterly, "If you really don't need my charity, I'll have the hospital send you the bill for your care then, shall I? And the lawyer? And the rehab clinic?"

I step out of her room before she can reply, although I know it's unfair of me. I don't understand why she does that—why she has to push me away. What more could I possibly do for her than I've already done in the last few days? What more can she possibly expect from me?

"Ready to go?" Sam approaches me, and I nod. "Are you okay? You're flushed."

"Just ready to get out of here," I mutter, reluctant to tell him about Annie's little mood swing. I'm concerned about how he'll react. He'll either storm into her room and tell her off, or justify her behavior by pointing out that she's *just* had a baby, her hormones are all over the place, she's in significant pain and she's probably terrified. I'm not sure which would annoy me more, so I keep my mouth shut.

As soon as we get home, I walk right into our bedroom to make the call to Mom. Robert answers, his voice gruff and abrupt.

"Hello."

"Hello, Robert. This is Alexis. Please can I speak with my mother?"

Ever since I had to call them to beg for money the first time Annie needed to go to private rehab, he's allowed us relatively easy access to Mom over the phone. I have no idea why. I'll never know for sure, but I suspect his surprise lenience with the rules is because he feels guilty for how hard he was on Annie when she was a kid.

Robert doesn't respond to my request, but this is pretty typical—on the rare occasions that I call, he doesn't waste time with small talk. Instead, I hear muffled sounds and then my mother's voice comes through the line.

"Oh, hello, Lexie," she greets me, and she sounds delighted, as she always does when I call. "It's so nice to hear from you."

I'm startled by the nervous butterflies in my stomach. For a moment, I actually think I'm going to lose my nerve. I clear my throat and pick up Sam's pillow, then cuddle it close against my chest.

"Hi, Mom," I say. "Listen…something has happened with Annie. She's okay, but I—well, I don't know how…"

"Is everything okay?" Mom asks, and I hear the mounting concern in her voice. Mom loves us—I know Annie has her doubts, but I don't. The decisions Mom has made, even the questionable ones, have all been because she thought she was doing the right thing at the time.

"Annie had a baby today, Mom."

"A *what*?"

"It's a girl. Her name is Daisy Nell." I let Mom digest this, but she's silent for a long time. I press my face into Sam's pillow and inhale deeply, but the moment stretches, and eventually I prompt, "Mom? Are you okay?"

"I'm fine," Mom says stiffly. "I'm confused, but I'm fine. I spoke to her two weeks ago and she didn't mention a baby. She said she was busy with work."

"Work?" I repeat blankly. "I'm not really sure about that, Mom. She thought she could clean up her act before she told you, but she got sick and the baby had to come early. Annie has still been using drugs, so Daisy will probably have to go through withdrawals over the next few weeks." I know I'm giving Mom a lot of shocking news all at once, so I try to soften it a little as I add, "But she should be fine eventually, too."

"Oh…oh, no. Annie, no," Mom whispers—her voice is thickening. She's near tears, and suddenly I am, too. "How has it come to this, Lexie?"

"She has a problem, Mom."

"She needs to get herself right with the Lord."

"She needs to get herself right with *herself*, Mom." I sigh impatiently. "Look, I just wanted to let you know. The thing is… the police and Child Protective Services are involved, because she had a positive drug test at the hospital. She's been charged because she used drugs while she was pregnant, so now she has to go to rehab next week."

"Rehab is good. You just have to help her stop now, Lexie. She's got a child now," Mom says. This is simple to her. I just need to sort Annie out so she can be a good mom. To my mother, this is a moral failure, not an illness, and it's one that Mom sees as transferable—I'm more responsible than Annie, so I can solve this if I just apply myself.

It's nothing new, but it's maddening.

"She can't just *stop*. If she could stop, she would have stopped years ago. She's an addict, for God's sake."

"Please don't speak like that, Alexis. You know it upsets me."

"What upsets *me* is watching my sister waste her life to this addiction, Mom. I'm frustrated and I'm tired and I just want you to understand what a complete mess this is. Annie is going to rehab next week *without her baby*. The baby will stay with me until she's released—in three months' time. Do you understand that?"

"So what do you want me to do? You *know* I can't come." Mom is whispering now. I imagine Robert has come closer again, and I know she's going to wrap the call up even before she does. "Well, thank you for letting me know. We will have the church family pray for her."

"Mom. Please at least talk to Robert about coming over. To support Annie. Please."

"You know that Robert and I believe Annie needs to resolve her issues on her own. She has made the decision to walk away from her faith and—"

"Don't you even want to *see* your granddaughter?"

"I would really appreciate it if you could find a way to send a photo to me, Alexis. Truly, it would mean the world," Mom says stiffly. "And, of course, please keep me informed if anything changes."

"I'm going to go before I say something I regret," I choke, as tears fill my eyes. It still stings that my mother would choose Robert and the church over Annie and me, time and time again.

"How did it go?" Sam asks me, as I come down the stairs into our living area. He offers me a very full glass of wine, and I accept it gratefully.

"It went exactly as I knew it would," I mutter blithely as I curl up on the couch. "She'd probably jump on a plane and come down to see the baby if Robert would let her, but he won't, so she's happy to leave all of the mess to me." Sam sits beside me, then pulls me gently against him and wraps his arm around my shoulders. I lean into him and release a frustrated sigh. "God, you're going to run screaming away from me when you realize how messed up my family is."

"You *did* warn me it's all a bit messy," he says.

"A bit?"

"It is what it is, Lex. We'll manage."

I close my eyes and let myself sink into the moment. It's peaceful in our house, even more so in Sam's arms, and I gradually start to relax.

"She's beautiful, isn't she?" Sam murmurs, sometime later.

"Daisy?"

"Yeah."

I smile softly and nod.

"Yeah, she really is."

18

ANNIE

Luke,

I almost brought this journal with me to our session yesterday, but then I lost my nerve. I'm a coward. I don't want you to ask me about Robert. I'm scared that if I hear you say his name, I'll lose my mind.

Let's see if I can write this down. I've never said it aloud. No one knows—no one in the world, except for Robert and me. It's a secret we share that binds us—that's part of the problem. I'm bound to the only person on earth whom I hate more than I hate myself.

At least when Lexie was around, I had someone around me who wasn't completely sold on the extremism in the community. She and I could giggle over the ludicrousness of some of the rules, or point out the imbalance between the way the men behaved and were treated, and the way us lesser mortals—the women—were expected to behave.

But once Lexie was gone I was on my own. People were constantly reminding me of my own sinfulness, of my disgrace and my moral failure for not managing to fit in—those voices took up resi-dence in my mind. And so the acts of rebellion—the pull toward self-expression that I'd always felt—the stubborn insistence that I needed to find a way to be different...those things became less about asserting myself, and more about being who I was gradually com-ing to believe I was.

Bad.

Different.

Sinful.

Tainted.

The louder those voices grew inside my mind, the worse my be-havior became. And the harder Robert clamped down on me, the more determined I was to find a way to break free. As my behavior escalated, Robert's punishments morphed from strict to sadistic—and then Lexie left, and the loss of control seemed to send him a little mad. In the days after her birthday, he locked me in my room for four days without food so that I could "fast" to atone for my sins, and when that didn't work, he told me I wasn't even allowed to go to school until I sought the Lord's forgiveness.

I didn't enjoy going to school, but it was, at least, an escape from our house. When Robert banned me from going, the consequence was complete and utter isolation. And because I was alone, I was more vulnerable than I had ever been before.

The first time it happened, I woke up the next day and convinced myself that it had been a nightmare. I was furious with myself for imagining such a disgusting thing—wasn't this still more evidence of my sinfulness? It was difficult to convince myself to ignore the physical signs that my nightmare had been real, but I was twelve years old—denial was a much safer option than facing the reality of what he'd done.

But after that first night, I found it so hard to fall asleep, and I was wide-awake the next time he came—awake enough to fight; awake enough to hear his threats and justifications.

You deserve this, you filthy little slut. This is all that you are good for. If you tell your mother, I'll throw you both out—do you understand that? Where would you even go?

If I had already started to fall victim to the voices that said I was bad, once Robert started coming to my room at night, I believed wholeheartedly in every self-deprecating cry that crossed my mind. Now I had evidence—he was strict, but everyone in the community revered him as a good, God-fearing man. Why would he hurt me like that if I wasn't already damaged in some way?

I blamed myself. I had been causing him grief for years. Clearly I deserved what he was doing to me. And then there was Mom. She had already lost one husband, and if I told her, she'd surely leave Robert immediately and then she'd sink back into that shell. Her smile would disappear again. There were practical considerations, too—Lexie used to remind me that Mom had sold the house and signed Dad's pension over to Robert—so we'd be cast out, and we'd have nothing.

So for my final two years in the community, I became a model citizen. I grew my hair and I even stopped braiding it—I wore it long down my back, just the way all of the other women did. I wore the head scarf and I went to services and I did my schoolwork and I read the Bible in the afternoons like I was supposed to.

If he had set out to break my spirit, Robert finally found a way to do it. It didn't stop his visits at night—but conforming meant that at least Mom was proud of me again.

And I hated him—and I hate him—and every second that I was there and I saw the triumph in his eyes as I finally, finally gave in and complied with the stupid rules of that place, I hated him more, until that hate became part of who I am. People who have never had cause to hate do not understand how it stains you. Hating for the very first time is black dye seeping into white fabric—you can scrub and scrub and scrub and wash and wash and wash, but there will always be a stain—the fabric forever changed.

And if it has long enough to fester, hate stops feeling like anger or rage and it feels only like pain.

If you had asked me, before we moved to the community, when we were at that big house in the suburbs with the beautiful flowing agapanthus on the path, who are you, Annie? I would have said that I was the daughter of Neil and Deborah Vidler, and that my father was a hero, and that my mother nurtured as easily as she breathed. I'd have told you about my brilliantly clever big sister, and I'd have told you that one day, I was going to write a book, and until then I was going to read and read and read and live every adventure that life offered me.

I left the community when I was fourteen, right at dawn so I didn't cause a fuss—just like Lexie did. I didn't leave because I was old enough to leave. I left because my period had started, and I was terrified I would become pregnant if I stayed. I left because I had to, and I left because I figured that no one would bother to follow me. They all knew that I wasn't worth saving.

I left with a broken spirit and an irrevocably damaged soul. And as I walked away from those gates that day, if you had asked me who I was, I'd have told you that I was a sinner—a girl who been used because that was what she deserved. Someone who cost her family its happiness, someone who cost herself her soul.

19

LEXIE

When I arrive at the hospital the next day, I find my sister sitting up in the chair by the window with her daughter in her arms. She barely moves when I open the door. Her gaze is fixed on Daisy, and I'm anxious that I might be interrupting a private moment between my sister and her daughter. I hesitate and almost leave the room to give her privacy, but as I take my first step back she looks up. Annie smiles at me, a serene, proud smile—she's a completely different person today.

"Hey," she whispers. "Come on in."

Despite the rough farewell we had the night before, I asked Sam to stop on the way into the hospital so I could pick up coffees and more sweet treats for Annie. I set all the gifts on the bed and approach the chair.

"She's so perfect," Annie whispers, awestruck. "I can't believe how much I love her. There's nothing I wouldn't do for her. No one told me it would feel like this."

"I'm amazed you're already out of bed. Are you feeling okay?" I ask gently, and I sit very carefully on the arm of her chair. I still feel like I'm interrupting—but then Annie angles the baby toward me and very gently slides her into my arms. Suddenly, this isn't their moment—it's *ours*. As I nestle Daisy against myself, an involuntary smile crosses my face. "Hi there, Daisy."

"I'm actually feeling okay," Annie says. "I thought I was going to die when they made me get out of bed, but I took a shower, so I'm feeling even better now. And I slept like a log last night, but the nurses woke me up a few times so I could try to give her the colostrum."

"So you decided to breastfeed her after all?"

"For the next few days, yeah. That hurts, too, but they said it'll help her with sucking and stuff so… I'll make it work." She clears her throat and says, "I'm going to be okay, you know."

"Of course you are," I say. "And this little one…well, I think she might be the most beautiful baby I've ever seen."

"I thought that, too…" Annie says. "I thought the hormones had made me blind. She could have two heads and I don't think I'd notice this morning."

We both laugh softly, and then I press my forefinger against Daisy's palm. Her fingers contract too stiffly around mine, and I wonder about her muscle tone.

"Do you know what her NAS scores have been?" I ask Annie.

"They were great yesterday, three and four, I think they said. But this morning was seven, and a while ago it was nine. They said if her score is over eight for three checks in a row they'll medicate her. I know it's pretty much inevitable."

"Some babies skip it. But it's pretty unlikely."

"I know. And I know I've already asked a lot, but I'm really going to need your help, Lexie."

"Anything, Annie," I promise her, and she bites her lip.

"I need to go to rehab, and I need to make it work this time."

"I know."

"I tried, all of the other times. I really did. But this time, *she* needs me. I think that will make a difference. I've never loved anything in this life as much as I love that baby. I'm going to make this work. I'm going to give her a better life—I have to."

I can see the determination in Annie's eyes again, and I'm comforted by it. It's funny, because I've *always* seen the potential in her. It was there all along, buried under a pile of chaos, hidden from the world—but I caught just enough glimpses of it to keep on believing in her, at least on some level. This is another peek at a future that I have always seen in my mind, another glimpse of the woman whom I have always believed in. I haven't put up with Annie's shenanigans for all these years because I'm an idiot, I have put up with them because I just couldn't give up on the person I knew she could be.

We stare down at the baby together for a moment, and then, I glance at my sister again and I whisper, "Whatever you need, Annie. Anything you need."

Tuesday is a nice day—a peaceful day. Annie is content, and Daisy is well. But that brief glimpse of peacefulness is gone by the time I arrive at the hospital the next morning. A nurse directs me to the NICU, where I find Annie in a silent, dark room off the main nursery. She's rocking in a rocking chair, and Daisy is in her arms. The baby's cry is weak, but high-pitched—the kind of cry that hurts to hear.

"Hi, Annie," I whisper as I enter the room. I notice the tray of breakfast that sits untouched beside her. Annie looks up at me, and her face is streaked with tears.

"Her NAS scores were too high. They started her on morphine last night, but she's still unsettled this morning." I lift a piece of toast and bring it near Annie's face. She looks at me incredulously. "I'll eat when she settles," she whispers, and she stares down at her daughter again. "Yesterday I kind of thought that she was going to be okay. But last night…her whole body was shaking and she broke out in a rash and she wouldn't drink. And then she wouldn't stop crying… She went all floppy, and then she was too stiff, and it was just…" Annie shudders, then pulls the baby right up against her cheek. "I can't even explain to you how much withdrawal hurts. To know that I have put my own baby through this, I don't know how I can live with myself."

"You're going to live with yourself by doing better," I say firmly. "You are going to focus on being the best mom you can be from now on."

"Is Mom coming down?" Annie asks. Her voice is tiny—like she's a child again.

We didn't talk about Mom yesterday—I didn't bring it up, and Annie didn't ask. I hesitate before I admit, "I don't think so. She wants me to send her a photo."

"Don't you fucking hate her sometimes, Lexie?" Annie sighs.

"Of course I do," I snort, and Annie releases a surprised giggle.

"Is it any wonder the mess that I am?"

"You've got some problems, but everyone has problems."

"*You* don't," Annie says pointedly, and I grimace.

"Of course I have problems. I just deal with mine in a different way."

"A healthy way," Annie surmises, and I shake my head.

"I don't know about that. I mean—yes, I have a career and there's Sam…and we have a house now…my life looks good. It *is* good but—I make stupid decisions. God, I'm so used to controlling things that even when someone else is doing a caesarean on my sister I want to take over."

Annie laughs weakly.

"Tell me about this house."

And so I tell her. I tell her about the rambling house that Sam and I have purchased, and the minor renovation that we are midway through—even the address that seemed so auspicious—*Seven Neil Lane*, like Dad himself had blessed it for us. I tell her how I'm getting the colors just right because we're going to repaint it. And how one day our kids will have bedrooms there—*big* bedrooms that they can share if they want to. I tell her about the agapanthus we are planting along the front path, and the new weatherboard that we just had fixed to the exterior—dark gray, with a bright white trim. I tell her about the huge attic, and the office with the bay windows, and the big bifold windows in the kitchen and the adorable guesthouse. I tell her about the parties Sam and I threw over the summer last year. The whole neighborhood came, and our block is teeming with kids—they climbed the trees and ate Sam's "famous" barbecue. Annie has always been the storyteller of the two of us, but today, telling her this story seems to be energizing her.

Maybe I shouldn't paint this glowing picture of my life while hers is in ruins. But I can see the joy in her eyes from the distraction, and as Annie relaxes into our chat, Daisy seems to relax, too. Eventually, she falls asleep. We sit in the dark room and talk until the nurse comes to do another NAS assessment.

"Come on," I tell Annie, when the nurse takes the baby. "Let's go get you some breakfast."

"I can eat this," she protests, but I shake my head.

"It's cold now. Daisy will be okay for a few minutes. We'll get something fresh. A muffin and some proper coffee from the cafeteria. Okay?"

Annie shuffles out of the NICU, casting glances over her shoulder toward Daisy as we go. At the door to the main ward, she winces in pain, and I fetch her a wheelchair. As I push her along the hall, she reaches up to squeeze my hand against the chair handle and she croaks unevenly, "Lexie, will she be okay? After all this?"

"I know this is awful for us to watch, for the medical staff, too. But studies show that long-term outcomes for NAS babies tend to be positive—when all other factors are equalized."

"Translate that into English for me, instead of doctor-speak?" Annie asks. "I just want to know if I've ruined her for life."

"It means that once she's withdrawn, if she has a stable home and a healthy mother, she's going to be just fine."

Annie nods, and releases my hand. She raises her chin and I see her straighten her spine.

"I'm not going to fuck up this time."

"I know, love," I reassure her, and it's less than half a lie. "I know."

"Hang on a second, Lexie," she murmurs, and I stop the chair cautiously, watching to see what she does. She pulls herself out of it with a wince, then walks around the chair to throw herself at me—wrapping her arms around my neck. I'm not expecting the embrace and I startle a little, but she only tightens her grip.

"Thank you, Lexie," she whispers, and I wrap my arms around her skinny little frame and blink against the tears that have sprung into my eyes. She draws in a deep breath and relaxes the hug, then leans back to stare into my eyes. I think she's about to say something else profound, but a twinkle rises in her gaze and for just a split second, I can see a mischievous, childlike quality in her again.

"What was that you were saying about coffee and doughnuts at the cafeteria for breakfast?" she asks me.

"I think I said 'coffee and muffins.'" I laugh softly.

"I'm pretty sure a doughnut is just a muffin with a hole in the middle."

"Got a hankering for doughnuts this morning, huh?"

"Every morning. Always."

"Return to your chariot, then, madam, and we'll see what we can do," I tease her gently, and I help her back into the chair, then start the long walk down the hallway.

20

ANNIE

Luke,

I had no idea where to find Lexie. If she'd been writing to me, Robert had intercepted the letters, and if she'd called, no one had ever told me. But that was just as we expected when she left—by walking away, she was rejecting the church, and that meant those left behind were supposed to behave as if she'd died.

But I knew my sister wouldn't have forgotten about me, just as certainly as I knew she'd have fallen on her feet when she got out into the real world. So I walked out of Winterton and toward Collinsville, and there wasn't a doubt in my mind that I'd find refuge with her.

I had a small backpack with my most prized possessions—a photo of Dad and my journal. I had only the clothes I wore—I hadn't taken any others because I never wanted to wear them again. Every article in my wardrobe was a clear signal to anyone in the area around Winterton that I came from the village. I never wanted to be associated with the sect again. I wanted only to be free, and as I walked those first few miles, that's exactly how I felt. The air tasted different, and breathing felt easier—like my chest had been compressed and suddenly released. I laughed a few times, just because I was out of the house and just because I was never going back.

It was only as I reached the outskirts of Collinsville that the magnitude of my situation really hit me. I had no idea what Mom and Robert would even do—maybe they would follow me? No one had gone after Lexie, but she'd been older—almost an adult. I'd never heard of a fourteen-year-old leaving Winterton before—the other children my age were different, almost robotic in their obedience.

And if Robert did come for me, what would he do? The thought was terrifying—what punishment could he possibly inflict on me that was worse than the ones I'd suffered already?

I'd been brave and excited, but soon, I was shaking and sobbing, running along the road toward an unknown destination. I hid behind bushes when cars came from the direction of Winterton, and a sweeping paranoia came over me—I startled a flock of birds in a tree and when they flew away, I heard the sound of footsteps in the flapping of their wings.

Collinsville is a small place, and a distraught, half-crazed fourteen-year-old walking along the highway wasn't going to go unnoticed for long. A police car soon pulled up alongside me. Convinced Robert had sent them for me, I tried to run away. The officers caught me, and when they pinned me to the ground, I panicked all over again.

"Hey! Kid! Settle down!" one of the officers shouted, after the wild thrashing of my wrists almost caught his jaw. "We don't want to hurt you. What happened? Where are you going?"

"My sister," I sobbed. "I need to find my sister."

"You're from Winterton?" the other office said, leaning over me *warily. I shook my head—irrational in my fear. Of course they knew I was from Winterton. My clothes would have left them no doubt.*

"Where is your sister?"

"I don't know," I admitted, and then I started to sob again. "Please don't make me go back. I can't go back. Please help me."

"If I release you, will you stop hitting me?" the first officer asked. When I nodded, he slid off me and took my hand to help me up. "Let's go to the station and figure something out."

"You're not going to take me back?" I asked. I let him pull me to my feet, but I planted them hard. I was ready to run—I wasn't going anywhere near that car until they promised me.

"Right now, we're going to the station so you can tell us what's going on. Then we'll make a plan, okay?"

At the station I met a sympathetic female officer, who made me hot cocoa and casually chatted with me about my situation. I gave her a heavily sanitized account of my issues at home—I focused only on what I figured would seem serious enough for them to let me stay away, but not bad enough to get anyone into any real trouble. I was also pretty sure I'd asked for the worst of it—would they arrest me if I told them? I didn't want them to ask Robert about it, then come back and tell me in disgust that it was all my fault anyway. But mostly, I didn't want Mom to ever know, and so I kept my mouth shut. I felt I might be a terrible, wicked person, but at least I was good at keeping secrets.

At the end of a very long, teary chat, the female officer agreed that she thought it was best for me to find Lexie. That just left the problem of how exactly to do that. All I had was Lexie's name, and the belief that she might have found her way to a university somewhere. The officer asked if I knew anyone else in Collinsville whom we could call. I racked my brain and came up blank—until it suddenly occurred to me that I did know someone. Someone I could walk across the road to speak with, actually—the fire station was there.

Captain Edwards knew exactly where to find Lexie, because she lived in his basement for twelve months after she left Winterton. He and his wife had taken her in while she studied for the GED and then started at community college and saved some money. She was now in her second year of a four-year course at Chicago State, living in a dorm on campus, and Captain Edwards had her cell number.

A cell phone. *I'd never even seen one, and when Captain Winters first passed his phone to me, I had no idea what it was. I sobbed while I tried to explain to Lexie that I couldn't go back to the community, and once she got over the shock of the call, she was resolute.*

"Ask Captain Edwards if he can bring you here," she said firmly. "I'll take care of you."

It wasn't as simple as that—there were legalities to sort out because of my age. The police officer had to call Robert and Mom, and while she never told me the details of the conversation, she told me that if I wanted to go to Lexie, I wouldn't be forced to return to Winterton.

And so, two days after I walked away from Robert's home, Captain Edwards delivered me to Lexie. I was fragile, confused and still scared. Every now and again I'd start shaking for no reason, as if I were in shock.

I kept expecting someone to tell me that Robert changed his mind and was coming to get me, and every time Captain Edwards's phone rang I'd feel adrenaline surge all the way through my body. But there were no last-minute disasters, no more drama to contend with, and when I finally walked into Lexie's room, she was sob-

bing. We held each other and cried until we were both exhausted from the intensity of the moment.

"It's over, Annie. You're with me now. It's over."

She had a bed already set up for me—an air mattress on the floor. She'd amassed a small collection of Nancy Drew books over the years since we parted, and they were waiting on my pillow.

"I know you're too old for them now." She shrugged. "But every time I saw one, I thought of you. I thought you might want to catch up."

That night, I was too wired to sleep or even to lie still on the little bed she'd prepared for me. I tossed and turned, and every time I even tried to close my eyes, I heard the door opening or the sound of his footsteps in the hall outside. I'd startle awake and begin the agitated cycle of fidgeting in my bed again. Late in the night, I heard a sound from Lexie's bed, and then she reached down and fumbled for my hand. I let her take it. Then the soft sound of her slightly out-of-tone singing filled the dorm room.

Twinkle, twinkle, little star.

Do you know how loved you are?

In the morning, in the night.

I'll love you with all my might.

I was asleep before she even made it through the verse.

I never told her about Robert—although I thought about it. I'd get all psyched up to confess what had really happened back at Winterton—but the words would stall and then die in my throat. She was so happy, positively thriving at college…and I was half-terrified she'd blame herself for leaving me, and half-terrified she'd blame me for letting him do it.

Unlike Lexie, I left the community without a plan, and also unlike Lexie, I immediately began to flounder. She had lived with

Captain Edwards and his wife until she found her feet, all the while finishing high school and charting a course to med school. To support herself at college, she worked nights as a nursing assistant at a nursing home, she was a dorm leader on campus and she was tutoring. All of this was necessary to make ends meet without the added burden of her little sister in tow. Luckily, she managed to convince the dorm administrators to let me live with her for at least a few months while we figured out what to do.

I'd been in the community for six years. I'd never been a teenager without the structure of the church. I didn't even know where to start. Lexie figured out the details and enrolled me at a high school, but I struggled from the very first class. I had no idea about basic science—or how to structure an essay. Even my math skills were patchy because the church school paid lip service to state requirements for the girls' curriculum. After all, women were never allowed to work outside the home, or even to manage their own finances, so why learn algebra?

"It was hard for me, too, at first," Lexie reassured me when I came home in tears the first day. "I'll help you study. You're smart, Annie. You can catch up."

"But you at least got to do that accelerated science and math program," I sniffed. "And I don't have your wonder-brain. I'm not a genius like you."

"You just need to work a little bit harder till you catch up. You can do this, Annie."

While academics were a struggle, they were nothing compared with the battle I faced socially. I had no idea how to interact with the other students, and just dealing with the crowds at the enormous high school was enough to leave me feeling a constant sense of panic. Whenever I was out of the classroom and on the busy grounds, or even in the cafeteria or school assemblies, I felt singled out. It was as though every person in the crowd knew my secret—that I was different and broken—and at any moment, someone was going to point it out. Sometimes when I felt that panic, I'd find myself confused about where I was. Was I in the cafeteria, or in the worship hall? Was it an ordinary lunch day, or was I being brought before the congregation to confess?

I was on edge all of the time, and it was exhausting.

During this adjustment period, Lexie had limitless energy for me, but her time was scarce—she was working so hard. I was just one of the many complicated balls she had to juggle. I was grateful to her—but I was feeling increasingly depressed, although I barely had the words to express the darkening storm clouds in my mind.

I remained determined to make it work, though, and did my best to cope. I went to class as late as possible to avoid the crush in the halls, and ate lunch in an empty classroom alone. I read voraciously and figured out the essay thing, and was soon doing well again in English—but math and science were foreign languages that no one ever taught me to speak.

By the second semester, I was skipping the classes I didn't enjoy. The upside was that one day while I was hiding from my teachers, I found an unlikely group of friends. They were also outcasts— a small, ragtag band of exceedingly dramatic kids with too much eyeliner and attitude. I didn't exactly join their group, but became friendly enough with one or two of them to learn some tips on how to blend in.

Unsurprisingly, when the school year ended, I didn't have nearly enough credits to progress to sophomore year. Lexie was absolutely livid. Up until that point, I'd rarely seen her angry.

"Don't you understand, Annie? School is everything! How could

you hide this from me? You need *to go back to school next year and sort this out—you'll redo your freshman year and make more of an effort this time!"*

I'm smart—not Lexie *smart, but smart enough to have a level of self-awareness. Smart enough to understand that since I left the community there have been two distinct parts to Annie Vidler. There is the regular, everyday me—and there is the Bad Me. The regular me runs on regular things and likes sappy movies and good books and golden sunsets. The regular me is a good friend and loves her sister and has quite a way with words.*

Then there is the Bad Me. It's the blackness—it's the darkness—and under it all is the pain. The bad Annie can be dormant for months at a time, but she is easily aroused—all it takes is an authoritative tone or demanding voice or an accusation or a dismissive glance. It doesn't take a genius to figure out that Bad Me is fueled by my hatred for Robert.

Understanding my pain does not mean I can control it.

*Lexie didn't even know about the Bad Me until she unwittingly unleashed her. All it took were those words and that tone—*don't you understand, Annie? You have to make this work*—and I was completely out of control. The rage rose from somewhere deep and dark within me, and once it was unleashed, its appetite for destruction wouldn't rest.*

We had a huge argument and someone from an adjoining dorm room called campus security. When they came to check on us, I completely lost my mind. I don't remember doing it—but later Lexie told me that I smashed a hole in her door.

That argument was the first time a tide of rage washed away my common sense. I was not going to be told what to do. I simply wasn't—not even by Lexie. She wasn't going to control me. No

BEFORE I LET YOU GO

one was ever going to have the power to tell me how to live my life, not ever again.

I was still blind with fury when they dragged me out of the dorm room, a seething ball of anger—kicking and screaming and cursing the guards and Lexie and the world. She followed, still trying to calm me, still trying to intervene—until a group of her friends pulled her away.

I started to sober then, noticing at last the fear and the confusion in her eyes, but I didn't really snap out of my fit of rage until the campus police dumped me at the school gates and told me not to come back. Their dismissal was like a fire hose turned upon the heat of my anger. It was a shock to return to earth only to realize that one mindless temper tantrum, and I had cost myself everything.

I slept under a bridge that night, and the next day, one of those sort-of-friends from school took me in. By the time I had cooled down enough to try to go back to the dorm, Lexie had been told I wasn't allowed to stay with her anymore.

She still had twelve months to go on her undergrad degree, and now, because of me, we had nowhere to live.

That was the first time I messed up Lexie's life.

21

LEXIE

I've heard new parents say that the days go by too fast, but I'd never really understood what that meant before. The days between Daisy's birth and Annie's departure blur and blend and I'm quickly confused about what day it is.

We live extremes through every minute in that NICU. Within a few days of her birth, Daisy is caught in the full grip of withdrawal, and it's heart-wrenching to watch. She breaks out in a rash from head to toe and she can't keep her milk down, then she develops terrible diarrhea. She was born tiny on Monday morning, but by Thursday, she's lost 20 percent of her body weight and there's talk about inserting an IV to maintain her hydration. Daisy has tremors—her arms and legs and jaw vibrate furiously—and when it's at its worst, she gets a startled, petrified look in her eyes as if she's pleading with us to help her.

Possibly worst of all, between her three hourly doses of morphine, Daisy cries that terrible cry—that distinct, agonized sound that NAS babies make, a sound so high-pitched it makes my ears ache. I can still hear it for hours after I leave the hospital each day.

But because these things are all so intense—the peaceful moments, when they do come, are all the more blessed. Annie and

I have long, quiet chats in that darkroom in the NICU—and we talk about everything, and nothing much at all. We dissect every aspect of Daisy's face, looking for familiarities with Mom and Dad and trying to find ourselves in her features. Sometimes, we just sit in silence, and every now and again we look away from the baby and smile at one another. Those moments of silent togetherness are precious to me, and I know they are to Annie, too.

And when Daisy is resting, swaddled and held tight in Annie's arms or mine as we rock in the rocking chair—the easy rhythm of her breathing is like music to my ears. In those moments, I'm reminded that although this is a traumatic and dramatic way to start life—it *will* pass. The NICU doctors are playing with her morphine dosage, trying to keep it high enough to stave off the symptoms but low enough that she's alert. The process takes time, but it's a well-established protocol and Daisy's prognosis is excellent.

I do try not to think much beyond the looming moment when I'll deliver my sister to the rehab center. I try not to think about how it will soon be me alone in the rocking chair, all day and as much of the night as I can manage. If I let myself think about it too much, it terrifies me. I've held human lives in my hands throughout my career, and when I cared for Annie.

But this is the first time I feel the weight of that responsibility.

This is the first time I wonder if I'm up to the challenge.

On Friday morning, I take a drive to the brand-new rehab center in Auburn. This will be Annie's fourth stint in an inpatient rehab clinic, and I've brought the folder that has a record of all of my previous efforts to get her help.

I shake hands with Luke French, the director of the center. He is tall and strong, with piercing green eyes and a receding hairline. Luke seems fatherly, and I can't tell if it's because of his gentle mannerisms or because he's a fiftysomething-year-old male who is entirely responsible for the lives of forty addicts.

"We have tried everything," I tell him, "but if she doesn't get clean this time, she *will* go to prison—she *will* lose her baby. She has to make this work."

Luke links the fingers of his hands together on his desk as he stares at me. There is sadness and acceptance in his eyes; he is clearly someone who has been doing this for a long time. I'm not the first desperate family member to sit at his desk and plead with him for help, nor will I be the last.

"I suspect that you know as well as I do that Annie 'needing' to be sober will not guarantee her success here," he says softly. "Rock bottom is not something you can predict or prescribe. My experience is that addiction is always related to some disconnection—perceived or real—often rooted deep in some historical trauma. It takes an almost superhuman strength to overcome a narcotics addiction, because it takes an almost superhuman strength to look honestly at your past and yourself and ask—how can I heal?"

"Our childhood was less than ideal," I say. "I've tried to care for her in every way I knew how, but I don't think it was enough. We lost our dad very young, and we grew up in a strict religious sect. She has so many issues with authority."

"Many addicts do, and every patient who comes through those doors has a complex story to unpack—we are well equipped to help her. We have a good success rate here, Alexis. I'm confident that if Annie *wants* to do the work, we can help her."

We review the folder together, and nothing he finds seems to shock Luke. He is steadfast and calm, and I'm reassured by that—right up until the time comes for me to walk out of his office and return to the hospital. We shake hands, and then I realize that the next time I see him, I'll be handing Annie over into his care.

I don't want her to be a number to this man. I want him to understand how special she is...how worthy she is of his best efforts. It's silly, because I'm a professional, too, and I'm sure he's going to do his best but… I stop in his doorway and I blurt, "Luke… I…she's a *good* person. She deserves a better life."

Luke offers me a weak smile.

"I honestly believe that about every single person who comes through the doors of my clinic, Alexis. I promise you, I'll do everything I can for Annie."

22

ANNIE

Dear Luke,

Lexie found us a rental a few blocks from her campus. It was a one-bedroom apartment—marginally larger than her dorm room but somehow much less comfortable. The taps leaked, the heat rarely worked and it was on the top floor of a four-floor walk-up, but it was all we could afford since I had cost Lexie both her dorm job and the subsidized room that came with it.

We moved into the new place a week before I started at community college. Lexie thought I might learn better in a more adult learning environment, so I was going to try to get a GED.

Community college was my first foray into the adult world, and it was not at all like I expected. No one seemed to care if I wasn't doing the work, it was all up to me—but I found this motivating. My first semester's results were better than I expected, but at the same time, Lexie's ordinarily sky-high grades dipped a little. One night she came home from her second shift of the day at the nursing home, sat down at the dining room table where we both studied, and cleared her throat a few times.

"What's wrong?" I asked her hesitantly. I could see that Lexie needed to give me bad news, which I dreaded—but worse still was the way that she looked at me.

She was scared of my reaction, and that made me scared, too. I was sure she was going to throw me out. I pictured her whispering miserably to me that she could no longer put up with me and my problems. Where would I go? Lexie was my whole world, but I could hardly blame her. I was the poison that tainted every good thing in her life.

"I'm so sorry," she said eventually, "but you just have to get a job."

I stared at her blankly.

"A job?"

"Just part-time, around school. I can't keep working like this, but if you can bring in just a little income..."

It had never even occurred to me that I should be trying to help Lexie financially. I was almost sixteen, though, definitely old enough to take on a part-time job between my classes, and I was happy to pull my weight. I managed to find a job serving fast food at the mall.

I wasn't quite happy or settled during those years at community college—but I was no longer sad and lost. I was somewhere in the middle, in a state of perpetual okay-ness. What separated me from crossing over to a place where I actually felt content was the sense that it was all superficial—like the structure of my life was built on an empty foundation, and it would all crumble to dust at any second.

Something was still missing, and when I started to think about my future and what I might like to do if I ever managed to get myself into a university, I'd feel a rush of fear from the thought that I *might try and fail. Lexie was constantly encouraging me to make a plan—charging toward a goal had always been her approach.*

I suppose that's why I was so shocked when she casually mentioned one evening that she'd been offered a spot at Johns Hopkins medical school the following year, but she'd decided to defer.

"I just need some downtime before I jump into it," she told me. "I'll take a gap year—work as much as I can, and try to save up some money."

"Is this because I'm not done with my GED yet?" I asked her, and she smiled at me.

"Don't be silly, Annie. It just makes sense for me to get some money saved first. Plus, I can help you study a bit now, and we can hang out some more. That'll be good, right?"

And it was good. We hung out all the time during the rest of that school year—mixing fun with sheer hard work. In between movie nights and chatting until the small hours about boys we knew or clothes or books, Lexie helped me study and pushed me to think about trying to get an undergrad degree after I finished my GED. We'd spend hours brainstorming the possibilities, and then later in the year, Lexie drove me all over the place to check out campuses and go for admissions interviews. The idea of moving away from her was actually quite terrifying, but her optimism was addictive.

Lexie screamed when I got the acceptance letter from Chicago State, and then she caught my wrists in hers, and she danced me around the tiny living area of our apartment, shrieking and laughing. She spun me around the room, and I felt that lightness that she'd drawn out of me that day on the lawn the day of Dad's funeral. I started to laugh, and then I started to cry, and then I pulled away from her and reread the letter in case we'd both misread it somehow.

"You did it, Annie!" Lexie was ready for another round of ju-

bilant dancing, but I was rapidly unraveling from a confused sense of fear and relief. My leaky tears turned to sobs, and I pulled away from her and curled up in the corner of the couch. It was too much—I didn't deserve any of it, I was just taking the place of someone who did deserve to be at that school. I'd just mess it up. I'd fooled Lexie and I'd fooled the admissions staff and I'd somehow even fooled the graders on the GED—didn't they realize I wasn't good enough for any of these opportunities?

Lexie wrapped her arms around me, and she whispered into my ear, "I'm so proud of you, Annie. I'm so excited for you—the world is your oyster."

She seemed to assume that my tears were caused by relief, and I didn't have the words to explain how wrong she was, so I played along. I let her splurge on sparkling wine and pizza to celebrate, and all the while, the sense of dread grew inside me. Even at eighteen years old, I had already figured out that the more you win at life, the more you have to lose.

23

LEXIE

I'm shaking and nauseous when I arrive at the hospital to take Annie away from her baby. I know it's going to be ugly, but I also know it needs to be done. The court order states that she needs to be admitted to the inpatient program within seven days of the baby's birth. Bernie tells me as long as she's at the rehab clinic and the paperwork is completed by 5:00 p.m., she'll have met the requirement.

Sam has taken the day off. He didn't ask before he did, he simply announced his plans at dinner last night.

"I'm going to drive you two up to Auburn," he said, and I couldn't even convince myself to protest. I don't need a chauffeur or a bodyguard—I'm plenty capable of handling this all by myself. But it's over an hour back to our place, and I can't bear the thought of saying goodbye to Annie and making that drive back home alone. So I thanked Sam quietly, and now I feel compelled to thank him again before we step inside the NICU.

"I'm so glad you're going to be here," I tell him.

"Good," he says simply. "I have to admit, it was worrying me a bit...the way you kept trying to deal with all of this on your own. We need to be a team in times like this. Right?"

"Right," I say resolutely, and then Sam links his hand through mine, and we walk through the door into the hospital.

We spend the day wandering in and out of the NICU and Annie's room. We give her several hours alone with the baby, and then Sam and I sit with her for several more. Annie cries a lot—and I cry, too, because all of it's unfair. It's unfair that Daisy is still so sick, it's unfair that Annie hasn't been here long enough to see her improve, it's unfair that Annie has put the baby through all of this in the first place.

And then it's incredibly unfair when 3:00 p.m. ticks around.

"Come on, love. We need to get going."

Annie holds Daisy close to her face, and her tears rise again—quickly escalating into heartbreaking sobs that rack her entire body. She shudders and she wails and she weeps so hard that the NICU nurse asks us if we need a doctor to order a sedative.

"She can't go into rehab *sedated*," Sam whispers pointedly to the nurse, who grimaces and shrugs.

"I don't know how you're going to get her away from that kid otherwise."

"Come on, Annie…" I say again, this time with rising urgency. I'm no longer whispering, because Annie is making a racket anyway. I pull on her shoulder, and she shakes me off, so I clutch it again. We *have* to go. I don't even know what would happen if we miss that 5:00 p.m. deadline—will police just turn up and drag her there? Will she go straight to prison? "I know it's hard, Annie. I *know*. But you have to do this for *her*."

Annie's spine stiffens, and after a long pause, she draws onto some reserve of strength and passes her baby to the nurse. She snatches a handful of Kleenex from a box beside the crib, and she wipes her eyes and blows her nose, and then she stares right at me. Her eyes are bloodshot, and there is such desperation in them…it's the same look she wears when she is craving a fix.

I can't even begin to imagine how much she is craving that

high right now. I doubt I've ever wanted anything in my whole life as much as Annie would like to escape from this moment.

"Let's go," she croaks.

She keeps glancing back at Daisy as we walk down the hallway toward the parking lot, even long after we have left the room where Daisy lies, even after we have turned a dozen corners and she can't possibly see the NICU.

Every now and again, a fresh sob leaves Annie's mouth. Every now and again, she hesitates just a little—her steps faltering, as if…maybe she can't do this after all. Every time this happens, I touch her gently—on her upper arm, or her waist, or the small of her back…and then when she finally stops altogether I wrap my arms around her, and I hope that I can somehow transfer some of my strength to her. Annie cries, but then, once again, she straightens and keeps on walking.

Sam follows close behind us. I keep glancing back at him. He wears a constant, guarded expression until I meet his gaze, and then he offers me the same reassuring smile. I'm glad I don't have to find out what he would do if she turned and tried to run back. I have a feeling he chose that position so he could block her way if he needed to.

By the time we reach the car, Annie seems to have run out of tears. I sit in the back with her, our hands linked on the seat between us. As Sam pulls the car away from the hospital, she clears her throat and says, "Thanks for making me leave, guys."

"We know it was hard," Sam says when I stay silent. "We're proud of you, Annie."

We drive in silence until we are miles down the road, and Annie turns to me and whispers, "Lexie, you will look after her, won't you?"

My eyes have been fixed on my lap, but I drag them away long enough to look at her in surprise.

"Of *course* I will. She'll be my priority until you can come back and take over."

Annie nods, then she looks out the window at the passing scenery. We pass stores, homes, parks. This is such a nice area... the kind of area Daisy deserves to grow up in. Will Annie be able to achieve that for her daughter? And if she doesn't, what will my role be? I can't consider it, especially not now. It's too frightening.

"I know she's on the morphine and they'll step her down slowly, but...withdrawal is actually terrifying, Lexie. It's more *painful* than anything you can imagine, and to think that she's going to suffer through without me..."

Annie is rambling, and it's all for nothing, because I do understand *exactly* what she's saying. I rub my thumb over the thin skin that lies across the knuckles on the back of her hand, and I murmur, "Remember that time when you asked me to help you detox?"

Annie snorts derisively.

"Which time are you talking about? I've done that to you twice." The self-loathing in her tone is hard to hear.

"Annie, *this* time is going to be different. And I was talking about the first time, when you first came to live with me in Montgomery but you didn't make it through the rehab program we found."

"I remember the first day or so."

"I *actually* thought you were going to die," I admit weakly. "You were so out of it, and you were so, so sick... I didn't think you'd make it, and I thought I'd killed you."

We drive in silence for a moment, before Annie turns to me again.

"It feels like the life is being pulled out of you. It feels like whatever it is that makes us more than stone, whatever it is that makes us conscious, whatever it is that makes us human— detoxing feels like that's being pulled out of your body. My baby is seven days old, and she's feeling like that today. I know that the nurses are looking after her, and I know that they understand it as well as anybody, but Daisy needs *me* and because I've fucked this all up so badly, I can't be there for her. I know that I've asked a lot of you, Lexie, and that I have messed up your life more times than we can both count. But I have never needed anything from you like I need you to be there for Daisy in the next few weeks. So firstly, thank you. And secondly, I'll never forget this—I'll always be grateful to you for this. And I'll make sure that I find a way to make this right."

Something warm opens in my chest, like the first rays of the sunrise are hitting my face or like the moment you're rousing from sleep and realize that you're in bed with someone that you really, truly love. I suddenly feel lighter—like maybe it's all going to be okay after all. Annie has never expressed herself so well to me before. In spite of all of her skill with words, she's never managed to thank me like this. I feel the smile on my face—really feel it—because I'm feeling hopeful, and it feels *amazing.*

"You have made a perfect little girl, Annie. You're right—she *does* need you—and I can't be Daisy's mother, but I'm going to be the best temporary substitute I can. I promise you. If she has a rough night, I'll sleep over at the hospital. If she has a good day, I'll take her outside for fresh air. If she needs new clothes, I'll find them, and if she needs formula, I'll give it to her. Until you are back, she'll want for nothing. I *promise* you. Okay?"

"I know, Lex," Annie whispers. "I don't even know why I had to say it." We travel in silence again for a while, until she clears her throat. "There's one more thing."

"Yes?"

"It's just…it's just that if Mom comes, and if…if she tries to bring… I mean, if for some reason Robert comes… I—" Annie is struggling so hard that I begin to worry, and as we reach the highway toward the rehab center, Sam meets my gaze in the rearview mirror. I shrug at him, because I have no idea where Annie is going with this or why it's so hard for her to say. When

I look back at her, she's pale again; even her lips are pale, and she's picking at her fingernails with visible anxiety.

"What is it, Annie?"

"If he comes, don't let him near my baby."

The plea is impassioned and desperate. I feel an odd, uncomfortable shiver run down my spine—and I'm confused.

"I don't think he'd come here—but even if he did, I could try to keep him away, but it would be a bit strange—" I break off, and I try to picture what that would look like. In the unlikely event that Mom did come, and if Robert somehow came with her, how could I possibly explain why I didn't want him near the baby? *"Why, Annie?"*

Annie is fidgeting frantically now, and her uncertainty is completely bewildering. Robert is a horrible man, but he's not a bad man—much like Mom, he's just stuck within the narrow mind-set of his ideology.

"Lex, I can't tell you why, but please promise me—if for some reason he comes here, you have to promise me he won't ever be alone with her—*no.*" She shudders, and then from the corner of my eye I see that she waves her fist in frustration. "Promise me that you'd never let him in the room with her. You *have* to protect her."

I stare at Annie—wishing fervently that I could read her mind. I *need* to understand where this is coming from. And then it hits me.

"Annie...did..." I draw in a sharp breath, and then force the words out, "Did something happen with Robert? After I left?"

This thought is so startling that it's like a punch to my gut. Is she hinting at something? Is it more drama—*everything* about Annie is always wrapped up in layers of drama—is this just some new game I can't see through yet? Is she trying to hurt Mom?

Annie exhales in a rush and says hastily, "You don't need to worry, Lexie, he won't come anyway. I just don't trust him, and I never have. Please, it will help me relax so much if I know that you'll protect her from him. I'm probably being silly, but I don't want to get distracted by worrying about this."

"Okay," I breathe, and I'm so relieved. I know Robert hurt her—he hurt her by dragging her to that place, he hurt her by constantly targeting her, trying to break her spirit, by inflicting the soul-crushing physical abuse when she broke the rules— and that was all horrible, but for a moment I wondered if she was suggesting something even worse. I'm weak with relief that this is not the case. I flash a smile toward Annie and I squeeze her hand. "I promise, Annie. I'll take care of her like she's my own daughter."

"Or like she's your sister," Annie whispers, and I smile at her sadly.

"Exactly. I'll care for her like she's my sister."

24

ANNIE

Luke,

Sometimes, I wonder if everything would have been fine if I'd just gone to Chicago State and kept to myself. That was my plan at first—studying was going to be my priority. Who needs friends anyway? My roommate was a cheerleader and she was completely obsessed with sports, so she seemed to fall immediately into a vast social network and was hardly ever in our room. There were dorm parties, but I found the crowds and the noise to be overwhelming. I found a job waitressing at a diner near the campus, and so I started taking night shifts on the weekends just to avoid the partying.

That's how I met Todd. He was a customer at the diner, and for months he visited regularly, but it never occurred to me that he might be coming in to see me. Since my disastrous attempt at high school, I hadn't really spent much time around boys my own age. So when Todd asked me out on a date, I was actually annoyed with him.

"I don't think it's appropriate to ask a woman out when she's trying to work," I snapped at him, and he shrugged and went back to his pancakes. But he was there again the next night, and the next, and then every night for several weeks. He'd come in very late when it was quiet, and we started to talk a little bit, and then we talked a lot.

The next time he asked me out, I agreed to have dinner with him, and before I knew it I was falling into something like love. Todd was an IT student in his sophomore year, and in the first few weeks we were together, we spent a ridiculous amount of time walking hand in hand and sharing increasingly intense make-out sessions in my dorm room while my roommate was out.

I was scared of intimacy with Todd, but not so scared that I wanted to avoid it. I told him only that it would be my first time, and he was sensitive and patient. When I finally decided I was ready, I downed a few bottles of beer and the whole thing went pretty well, considering. I called Lexie to tell her about Todd, since my relationship with him suddenly seemed more serious and adult, and ironically Lexie and I sat up late on the phone giggling about it like we were thirteen-year-olds.

Todd introduced me to his friends, and my world began to expand, little by little. No one in Chicago knew about my history with the sect, not even Todd, and so to everyone I knew there, I was just a normal—if somewhat antisocial—freshman adjusting to my new life at the university.

But soon I was thrust into uncomfortable social situations with Todd. He'd encourage me to go to parties, although I hated them with a passion. Sometimes, I'd be standing talking to people and for no reason at all, I'd feel panic bubbling up—a wheel racing in my chest, a wave of sweat over my skin, sweeping moments of pure dizziness and adrenaline that would dissipate only when I left.

I was more content alone in my comfort zone—plugging away

on my own schedule and avoiding other people's expectations of me. But I was happier *with Todd, and I wanted to be with him although I could never understand what he thought he saw in me. I assumed he thought I was someone I wasn't—someone good and clever and worthy of his attention.*

I didn't want Todd to see who I was really was, and I really *didn't want him to think I was a freak, so I learned quickly to play along. I developed coping techniques—I'd arrive a bit late, so that I could slip into a party only once it was really loud and busy, and no one would pay attention to me. I'd greet Todd, tell him I needed to talk to someone I'd seen on my way in, then I'd find the quietest corner and I'd try to hide.*

Those things helped—but the biggest key to becoming more comfortable was a few medicinal beers before I left my dorm. It was amazing what alcohol did to my anxiety—those few drinks at the start of the night were the difference between spending the whole night feeling like I was going to suffocate, or me mingling with ease and sometimes even making new friends.

You are a filthy little girl, Anne.

This is all that you're good for, you know.

It was my regular mental soundtrack when I was sober—the voice of impending doom that repelled any possibility of happiness. It was amazing how the thoughts were always right there just below the surface, waiting to rise up to the front of my mind. But alcohol silenced the voices, and let a more confident and calm version of myself break free.

And at first, I thought that maybe I liked Drunken Annie better anyway.

25

LEXIE

Just as I promised Annie I would, I spend most of the first week at the hospital.

It's hard to find the words to describe the agony of watching a newborn baby suffer like that for hours and days on end. I study Daisy closely and I learn to read the signs, but it's easy to tell when the morphine is wearing off. First, the muscles of her legs and her arms go rigid, then her little lips tremble, and sometimes the rash sweeps over her skin like a tide coming in. Eventually, jerky squirms progress until she's writhing and screaming inconsolably.

Sometimes, she cries so hard that her tears all dry up, and that's often when I cry, too. It is as if she gets fatigued from the endless suffering—just as I grow fatigued from watching her suffer. Sometimes, I'm almost crippled by the pain of watching this baby's pain and it leaves me quite weak—as if all I can find the strength to do is hold her and cry. Then, in a heartbeat, I'm furious—I grow livid, and anger burns in me so hot and bright that I feel like it might make me explode. I'm angry with the entire system. It has failed this baby. It has failed my sister.

And then, although I know it is pointless, I let myself be

angry with Annie. This is all *Annie's* fault. I'm off work—I'm trapped in this gray hospital room, I'm watching her daughter go through something horrendous—all because of the choices *she* has made. I'm angry that Annie has made this endless series of terrible decisions that have led us all to this point…angry that she could be so careless as to fall pregnant while in the throes of a very serious, very heavy heroin addiction.

Annie is better than that.

And smarter than that.

Annie is *stronger* than that.

And even as I think these things, I know they are ridiculous—because addiction has nothing to do with being better, or stronger or smarter. I know this in my mind, but my heart is still angry. My mind understands that Daisy will probably be okay, in spite of these difficult few weeks—but my heart thinks if I hear that high-pitched, warbling cry one more time, I might just break into a million pieces, and then it will be my turn to be too broken to ever be put back together. I *know* that we will taper her morphine dosage down over the coming weeks once she stabilizes, but during these gray, endless days, I feel like this will go on forever.

I stay from early in the morning until late at night each day, just as I promised Annie I would. I see Sam on his lunch break when we meet in the cafeteria, or on the really bad days, he brings food to me in the NICU. Sometimes, when I finally get home, I crawl into bed beside him and he wraps his arms around me and I'm too tired and drained to even cry.

There is a fourteen-day period at the rehab clinic where Annie is not supposed to have any contact with the outside world. Given how young Daisy is, Luke has agreed that she can call the NICU once a day to get a status on her daughter—but in keeping with the rehab clinic's policy of an initial period without family contact, she can't speak to me directly. When a week passes, I ask the NICU's ward clerk if she's been calling.

"Well, no. I mean, Bill Weston calls morning and night, and the CPS lady has called a few times, too. And Luke French has called a few times, as well. But there've been no calls from Annie herself. Should there have been?"

I leave the NICU and call Luke on my cell phone. I know that Annie has given him permission to discuss her treatment with me.

"Annie refused to take Suboxone from her second morning here," he tells me cautiously. "She's trying to do a straight detox, and she's been pretty sick."

"That's insane. She was on a huge dose of methadone! Stopping like that—"

"It's difficult—yes." He interrupts me impatiently. "We did advise her against it, but she was adamant this was how she wanted to go about it. So she's still in our detox unit—I visited her this morning and she's still quite unwell. I'm not sure she can cope with any negative updates on Daisy at this stage, but she's been asking after her every day, so I decided to call myself so I can filter what she's told."

"Why didn't you call me?"

"Why would I call *you*?" Luke asks me. He is calm, but the question is pointed—and I'm not sure what he's getting at until he adds, "This was Annie's decision. There's nothing for you to be concerned about. Some might call this progress."

"*Progress?*" I gasp, and I'm spitting with outrage and suddenly terrified that I have left my sister in the hands of a crackpot. "She's still so sick after a week that she can't even pick up a phone to see how her newborn baby is, and you're calling that *progress*?"

"Alexis, you're looking at this the wrong way—your sister has opted to take her recovery into her own hands. She's taken full responsibility for this decision and for the consequences of it. It's not pleasant—but getting to sobriety never is. Annie has chosen to walk a difficult but shorter path for her withdrawal, but she's sticking to it. If that changes, *then* I'll call you. You need to trust me, and you need to trust her."

"Are you kidding me, Luke? *Trust her?* Look where *trusting* her has got me."

"Alexis, I'm going to say something to you now, and it's going to be very hard for you to hear. Okay?"

I scowl and groan, "I'm *not* the patient, you know."

"I know. But you are a part of Annie's problem, Alexis." I gasp, and I'm completely outraged—but before I even have a chance to come up with a retort, Luke slays me with calm, quiet logic. "She has relied on you to bail her out again and again and again…and if she wants to get better, she needs to stand on her own two feet. That means *you* need to stop propping her up—and frankly, I think you've developed a habit of propping her up even before she starts to fall sometimes. You need to trust her, and you need to let her deal with the consequences when she messes up. I know she's hurt you, and I know she's made a mess of both her life and yours several times over. I'm not telling you to stop loving your sister—you're the most important thing in her life other than the baby. I'm telling you that she's an adult now, and if she opts for a more difficult path to sobriety, you need to let her take it because *her* suffering is not *your* problem. Focus your energies on that baby for now—Annie is fine."

By the time he finishes, I'm a mess—silently sobbing in the hall of the hospital, and I can barely manage to squeak out a farewell before I hang up the phone. I rush into a bathroom and splash my face with cold water and then I stare into the mirror. I'm mortified at Luke's take on the situation.

You are a part of Annie's problem, Alexis.

It's not the first time someone has accused me of enabling Annie, and I've worried about that possibility myself. But this is definitely the first time someone has spelled it out for me in such brutally honest terms, and the first time that I've followed that thought all the way to its logical conclusion.

Perhaps by "propping Annie up," I've made things worse for her.

The thought is simply unbearable. I've taken such pride in my role in her life. I've had such a deep satisfaction that I have followed Dad's instructions to me *to the letter*, that he would be proud of me for taking care of my baby sister, just as he always wanted me to.

You are a part of Annie's problem, Alexis.

No. I splash my face again, and my nostrils flare. I have simply tried to help her. I tell myself that Luke is arrogant, and that I have a right to be angry. What would he know, anyway? He's been working with Annie for one week—does he really think he can psychoanalyze us both and untangle the web of our thoughts and emotions, just like that?

I try to ignore the little voice in the back of my mind that points out that I'd be much angrier and far less embarrassed if everything he said wasn't absolutely accurate.

I'm still worried about Annie, and the urge to intervene and to rescue her is so strong that I feel it physically pulling on my chest. It's like she's calling me from the rehab clinic to get myself all the way out there and talk some sense into her. I could convince her to take a maintenance drug. I've done it before, haven't I? Just recently, in fact.

But it wasn't what she wanted then, and it's obviously not what she wants now.

So I dry my face, straighten my spine and walk back into Daisy's room. Luke is right about something, at least. I need to focus my energies on the baby for now, and for once, leave Annie to take care of herself.

26

ANNIE

Luke,

You asked me today when I became an addict, and the question surprised me, because you should know better than to ask. With all of your vast experience and the degrees on the wall of your office, surely you understand that you don't become an addict on a date or in a moment. It's a process that happens degree by imperceptible degree—the frog in the proverbial pot of boiling water. It's not a case of beer that makes you drunk, but the thousand easy sips that it represents. Addiction is, in that way, just like love—in the early moments, you don't see the potential for it to bring you pain—it's just something you slide into between laughs and smiles and moments of bliss. It's something that feels like a shield, until you realize it's actually a warhead, and it's pointed right at you.

I told myself I was just having fun, and sometimes, I really was. I told myself I was being a normal young adult, spreading my wings—learning how to manage myself—even if I was increasingly learning the hard way when enough was enough. I was anxious *the first time I went out to a party and woke up to find I'd drunk so much that I couldn't remember how the night ended or how I got home. This became a regular occurrence during the beginning of my second year at college. I left the dorm over summer break and moved in with some of the other English majors, and it immediately became part of the routine for us all to go out partying every weekend.*

Perhaps there was a single point in my life when I could have stopped the chaos—a fork in the road when I made a choice, and the result is the mess that's happened since. That moment floated past me on a Sunday morning in a park near my apartment. Todd and I had been together for about six months. We had been at a party the night before, and when I woke up, he was in my room— but I couldn't remember us getting back there. He suggested we go for a walk, which was irritating because I was feeling so hungover. Eventually, he lured me from the dark confines of my room with the promise of coffee, and I walked begrudgingly beside him to the diner, our hands entwined, my head throbbing.

Todd bought me the coffee and then we sat on a park bench.

"We need to talk," he said, and I offered him a confused smile. "So, talk."

He stared at me, and my smile seemed to concern him. I watched the way his face contorted, as he was struggling to find the right words. Then he ran his hand through his hair with a frustrated exhalation and said uneasily, "This isn't good news, Annie. I need to tell you something, and it's really difficult for me to say."

"What's wrong? What happened?"

"Maybe we need to think about taking some time out. Just for a little while."

The quiet words hit with the force of a freight train. I leaned away—but continued to stare at him—feeling panicked and bewildered.

"What—but why? Things are going so well. Aren't they?"

Todd looked away.

"Things were going well, but they aren't now."

"What's changed?"

"You have*, Annie!" Todd exclaimed suddenly, and I heard the frustration in his voice as anger. I cast my eyes down. "You're just out of control the last few months—you really embarrassed me last night. And last weekend. And the one before it. How much of that shit did you think I'd put up with? I had to carry you to your room again last night. People were staring at me like I was some kind of predator."*

"You didn't have *to carry me home," I said flatly.*

"Oh, I should have left you at the party then, should I? You were unconscious and you'd been flirting with half the guys on campus before you passed out. God knows what would have happened to you."

"I can handle myself, Todd."

"If that was true, you wouldn't be getting blackout drunk every weekend. I can't keep babysitting you. You just need to sort your shit out—go dry for a few weeks."

"Who the fuck do you think you are, Todd? My father*?"*

I heard the words but I didn't decide to say them. They involuntarily burst from my mouth and in seconds I was on my feet—adrenaline pumping through me. I threw the coffee onto the ground between us, and the steaming-hot liquid splashed all over me. Later, I'd find the drops scalded the bare skin of my calves—but I didn't feel it at the time. I didn't feel anything but shame and anger.

"Annie, come on—I'm not saying we have to break up, I just

need you to think about—" Todd rose, too, and he glanced around the park nervously as he reached for my hand, but I slapped it away and I cut him off.

"Fuck off, Todd."

"Whoa—" He was confused—bewildered by my overreaction, I suppose. I couldn't look at him anymore, so I turned and started walking away. I could hear him calling after me, but I didn't stop. I wanted to go back, but I was mortified. I wanted to turn back to him and apologize and admit that I was struggling and admit that I couldn't deal with the crowds at the parties and ask him to help me figure it all out. I wanted *to open up to him—to give him a little more of myself—because although he'd known my body, he still knew nothing of my soul or my past.*

Sometimes when I'm low, I wonder what my life would have looked like if I'd stopped that day. Oh, we were still relatively new to each other after only a few months—but you know, I like to think that I might have married Todd one day. He probably runs some big IT department now, and he's probably got some nice house in the suburbs and a couple of adorable, healthy kids.

Todd was so gentle and so smart—maybe almost as smart as Lexie—far too good for me anyway. Our relationship was young and fragile—and so it should have been, because that's who we *each were at that stage of our lives. You love like that only once in a lifetime—you can love from a place of innocence only once. It always leads to the deepest hurt, and after that, you're changed and hardened by it.*

So I walked away from Todd, and I went back to my apartment and I cursed him loudly to my roommates. I told myself it was inevitable—hadn't I doubted Todd's feelings for me anyway? But my relationship with Todd had brought me out of my shell and I'd had a taste of how good it felt to connect with people, so I didn't fall back to keeping to myself.

Although he obviously didn't think so, I had been using a degree of restraint with my drinking when we were together, and then he was gone and I was hurting and terrified that it wasn't the partying that scared him away, but that he'd seen too much of who I really was.

So suddenly, I had a whole lot more to escape—because now I was convinced that anyone I loved would flee as soon they got to know the real me. It was just as Robert had said.

This is all you are good for.

Once Todd was gone—all bets were off, and my foundation began to slip.

27

LEXIE

Another week goes by with no word from Annie. I don't
want to call Luke again—he unsettled me so much with
that last conversation. But I do want to know how she's
doing, so I email him early one morning as I'm dressing to go
to the hospital.

Luke, could you please let me know how Annie is doing? I don't
need details, just want to know that she's okay.

Later that day I hear my cell vibrating in my handbag, but
Daisy is unsettled, so I ignore it until I manage to convince her
to sleep. It is almost an hour later that I rest the baby in the crib,
and after I breathe a sigh of relief and stretch my tired arms, I
check the phone.

One missed call—Mom and Robert.

I stiffen and my heart starts to race. In the seven years since
Mom and I reconnected, she has never once called me—it's always been me calling her.

Something must be wrong.

I fly out of the NICU and into the corridor as I return the call. My mind is racing—*What now? What else can possibly go wrong? What if Mom is sick?*

Mom answers with a light, "Hello?"

"Mom? It's Lexie. What's wrong?"

"Wrong? Nothing's wrong. Why? Why did you think something was wrong?"

"You *called* me, Mom! Why did you *call* me?"

"You said you'd send a photo of the baby," she says, then she adds weakly, "I just thought you might have forgotten. I was really looking forward to seeing her."

I'd laugh if the situation weren't so maddening. With all that I'm dealing with here, Mom thinks to call only because she hasn't received her photo? I clench the phone in my fist and my jaw tightens. I close my eyes and try to suppress the rage.

"Do you know what I've been doing today, Mom?"

"No," she says warily.

"I have spent the whole damned day trying to soothe your granddaughter. I've been rocking her, and pacing the halls with her, and singing to her—and nothing has worked. And Annie is too sick to get on the phone and ask how she's doing, and then you think you can just call me and instead of asking how we all are over here, you ask me for a fucking *photo*?"

"Don't speak like that, Lexie," Mom gasps. "You know I can't tolerate profanity!"

"Mom. You should *be* here. You shouldn't be calling me asking for photos, you should be on a goddamned plane, coming to do your part. Annie needs you and the baby needs you and—"

"Alexis, I'm going to hang this phone up right now. You're just lucky Robert isn't home to see how upset you've made me."

"I'll send you a fucking photo when the day comes that I get more than six hours of sleep and I don't spend every waking hour trying to help your granddaughter get better. Until then, you can damn well *wait*."

Mom hangs up, and I growl and press my fist to my forehead.

"Tough day, huh?"

Sam is there behind me, and it's like he has radar for the exact moment I need to see him—but it's also a moment when I don't *want* to see him. I can't bring myself to explain that call, and the worst thing is, I'm not exactly sure why. Sam would empathize—he'd say all the right things, and he'd be angry with Mom, just as he should be.

In all of this, Sam has never once judged me. Maybe that's why I can't tell him. He's been so perfect in all of this. What's going to be the straw that breaks his back? When am I going to see the moment when it's all just too much?

"I have a spare hour today," Sam murmurs as he pulls me close for a hug. "Want to get some lunch out of this shithole?"

"Daisy has been really irritable today—I need to stay with her."

Sam raises his eyebrows and smiles at me softly. It's the smile that enrages me, because it shows me that he doesn't understand at all how much she needs me.

"She'll be okay for an hour, Lexie."

"No, she *won't*," I snap at him, and I pull away from his embrace. "Should I just let her lie in there and cry while we go off for a latte and a sandwich?"

"Is she crying now, Lexie?"

"She just went to sleep—but she's been crying all day."

"And if she does cry now, while you're out here on the phone, what will happen?"

"A nurse will try to console her, but they don't have the time—"

"If she cries for the whole hour we're away, will she be harmed by that?"

"She'll be *miserable*."

"Well, won't she be miserable even if you're there? When did they give the morphine?"

"Just a while ago, but—"

"I'm not taking no for an answer. You've spent every waking moment here for fourteen days in a row—we're going *out*, into the sunshine." When I stare at him stubbornly, he gives me a pleading look. "Think of it this way, honey. If you don't look after yourself, you'll get sick or you'll burn out, and *then* who is going to look after Daisy? Don't come with me to lunch because you want to—come with me because *she* needs you to. I promise, you'll be glad you did." I ponder this for a moment, and Sam pulls me back into his arms and brushes a kiss over my forehead. "Okay?"

We get burgers at a diner down the block, and Sam bans me from saying the words *Annie* and *Daisy* for the duration of the lunch. Instead, we talk about his day, and then we discuss the garden we were clearing in the backyard over the weekends before Annie's issues cropped up, and Sam offers to get right back to the yard work on the weekend.

"Or I could come into the hospital for a few hours and you could stay home and do the gardening," he offers, and in an instant, I'm scowling at him again.

"You spend all week at the hospital. Why would you spend the weekend there for *my* niece?"

"*Our* niece, Lexie. And I kind of want to. She'll be living in our house soon, and I think it'd be good if she bonds with me."

I pause. I feel like I need to be at the hospital myself—that's what Annie is expecting, that's what I feel most comfortable with. But I can understand Sam's logic—and its generous of him to offer. I hazard a smile.

"Okay," I say. "Let's play it by ear but...thanks, Sam."

"Hey, that's what I'm here for."

We go back to our burgers and chat a bit about the weather. As we're walking back to the hospital, a sudden thought strikes me.

"I might just go for a walk before I go back," I say, and Sam glances at me in surprise.

"Great idea, Lex. I'd join you, but I have a patient—"

"No, no—it's fine. I... I might just walk to the Walmart and print a photo of Daisy for Mom."

"Ah, okay." Sam nods, and brushes his lips against mine. "Can we do this again soon, honey?"

I nod, then pull him close for a more lingering kiss. Oh, I do love Sam—I love the way he smells, and the feel of his thick hair through my fingers, and the way that the world feels brighter when he's near.

"I'll see you tonight," I murmur when we break apart.

"Let's get takeout and watch a movie."

"Okay," I agree, and then I make my way to the Walmart. I have taken daily photos of Daisy to show Annie when I'm allowed to visit her so I print out all of these, then I add duplicates of the best ones for Mom. Daisy isn't smiling yet, far from it, but she's still beautiful and I know that Mom will see Dad in her, just as I do.

I scrawl a note on the back of a photo I took of Annie staring down at Daisy, the day before she left for rehab.

Mom, I hope you enjoy these. It would be so great to see you if you can find a way to get here. Daisy would love to meet her Grandma. Love, Lexie.

I write the note, but I know Mom isn't going to come.

Daisy is still asleep when I get back to the NICU.

"We didn't hear a peep from her the whole time you were gone," a nurse assures me. I sit beside my niece and take the phone out from my handbag. There's an email from Luke.

Hi, Alexis,

I'm happy to report that Annie is doing a little better—she has left the detox unit and is now getting settled in her own room in the main facility. This is where the real work begins— because now that she is physically detoxed, we need to start to work on the psychological side of her addiction. I rarely take patients directly under my care. However, Annie and I have built a good rapport, and I'll be conducting her therapy myself.

As you know, at the clinic we have a mandatory two-week period where patients are not allowed visits or calls. However, in Annie's case, she needs some time to adjust to the main facility before she has contact with home. However, you may like to plan for a visit next weekend.

Annie has had a difficult few weeks, but she is still headed in the right direction. You can be very proud of your sister. I believe she has learned a lot about herself even in the last two weeks.

I *am* proud of my sister. I put the phone away and I smile at Daisy.

"Well, well," I whisper. "Your momma might just surprise us all."

28

ANNIE

Luke,

I loved Todd, but I didn't love any of the boyfriends who came after him. Todd was a different breed from the type I was eventually drawn to. He was quiet and considerate and intellectual.

And he hurt me. A lot. So I suppose it made sense that I stayed well away from men like Todd after that.

Lincoln was a football player with a terrible attitude toward women and a fairly heavy weed habit. I didn't feel much of anything for Lincoln, but the sex was pretty good, and he was always invited to great parties. When Lincoln moved on to a cheerleader he met at an away game, I moved quickly on to Owen, who was a moody, angsty philosophy student who was crazy-obsessed with existentialism.

By the time I was in my third year, I'd burned through housemates as quickly as I burned through boyfriends. I came to the conclusion that my apartment-sharing attempts were doomed if other, inevitably bitchy women were involved, so I moved into Owen's studio. He was on a mission to find meaning in experience—and so every day seemed to bring some new quest for novelty. First it was bio-hacking his body to experience "health," then it was starving himself to understand "true hunger," and then finally he decided he would give in to any impulse to drink or get high and see what that felt like, too.

I'd been smoking a lot of weed that year, but Owen was into some darker shit—a little bit of coke every now and again, MDMA before parties sometimes, a low dose of speed when he was studying for exams. Then, just so he could say he'd done it, he snorted heroin one night when we were home alone. There was no reason for it—he just liked to try things. And I'd already had quite a bit to drink and I thought to myself, well, why the hell not?

It burned when it went into my nostrils. I was dizzy—I stumbled and then fell into the couch. Owen had gone just before me, and he was sitting at the table, his eyes wide.

"What do you think?" he asked me, and I stared at him. There was no rush and no euphoria—there never has been for me when I snort. Instead, I felt myself sinking into a simple, blissful sense of contentment and well-being. I felt no less sober than I had before I took it—my mind was actually clearer somehow, as if all of the roadblocks had been dissolved by the drug and suddenly I could see that everything really was right with the world after all. I liked it, and I figured I'd probably do it again one day—but I was certainly not clamoring for more after that first bump. Instead, I felt like Owen and I had a pleasant but somewhat wasted evening on heroin—and truthfully, I wondered what all of the fuss was about.

Owen must have wondered, too, because he came home with some friends from class a few days later with more and told me that they'd decided to inject it. Just once, he told me, so they could compare the high with the one they'd had from snorting. Even after everything else I'd been playing around with that year, the idea of IV heroin disgusted me.

"It's for junkies," I scoffed at him. "You're a fucking idiot, Owen."

What do you make of that, Luke? I was horrified the first time my boyfriend told me he was going to try smack. Me, with all of these self-esteem issues you keep telling me I have, I thought I was too good to shoot dope. Actually, I was so furious with him for taking his stupid experiments one step too far that I went out of the apartment while they did it. I didn't even want to watch.

When I came home, Owen's friends were gone. He had fallen asleep in a puddle of his own vomit on the couch. I checked his pulse, satisfied myself that he was fine and went to bed.

The next day, all Owen could talk about was the rush.

"Annie, you have to try it with me."

"Fuck off, Owen."

"Come on, babe. It was incredible. The high was everything they say it is—the most intense euphoria—bliss that you can't even imagine. You're a million fucking miles away from your problems. It's what life would be like if you weren't already fucked up by it, you know? It will blow your fucking mind. I'll get some more and we'll shoot it tonight, okay?"

I rolled my eyes at him and went to class. One thing he'd said fascinated me. What I hated about being sober—what I still hate about it—is the way that your pain and your confusion are right at your nose all of the time. Being drunk or stoned is like taking a holiday from all of the shit and the pain—and what Owen described sounded like a holiday to another planet. So, that night, I watched as he clumsily cooked the smack. He insisted I sit on the couch, which I thought was a revolting idea. It still smelled of his vomit.

"I'll just do it at the table," I protested, and he shook his head.

"You're going to want to lie down, babe."

So I sat on the couch, and I was careful to place myself in just the right spot to avoid the still-damp vomit stain, and then I let him stick a needle into my arm. I was holding my breath—excited and terrified—and then Owen pulled the plunger back, and I watched my blood draw up into the barrel.

"What are you doing?" I gasped.

"I'm making sure it's in the vein. Don't want to waste it," Owen said, then his face set in a fierce scowl as he pushed the plunger down.

The rush wasn't instant—there was a pause when the needle left my arm—just long enough for me to smell and taste something odd; something alien but not unpleasant. The taste rose in the back of my throat and then raced along my tongue and into my nose—it was blood and chemicals and salt and metal and then...

The rush hit me.

I've heard some stupid analogies for the heroin rush over the years, and I get why—it's impossible to avoid being enthused over it once you've felt it, but it's also impossible to cram the feeling into words given the limitations of the English language. It's like you'd need some other, higher language to describe it.

It was like I was pressed down into the couch by an exceedingly pleasant weight that dissolved me somehow. And Owen was right—every negative thing in the world disappeared in an instant—and all there was to know and to be was bliss. The euphoria lasted for ages that first time—I remember thinking that it might last forever, and that just one single injection might have made life perfect for all time. It was like a lucid dream—I lived in another reality during the high, a much better one—one I could control.

I vomited for hours once the rush finally faded. I woke up the next day and every time I moved, I gagged. And it wasn't like the movies—I didn't rush out and start robbing elderly people to feed an instant habit.

No, when I first started using, heroin was actually just like a new boyfriend. I did want to spend all of my time with him, but I couldn't because I had school and shifts at the diner, and besides, I didn't want to get too reliant on him—so I paced myself.

I used only occasionally during the rest of my time at college. My grades were okay—although if you graphed them from my first semester to my last, you'd see a definitive curve downward. During the first two years, I'd entertained ideas of staying on at school to complete a master of fine arts in creative writing, but by the end of that third year, my GPA was too low to get in and I'd lost the drive to keep studying anyway. But I graduated with a degree, and then I even got a proper job—a foot in the door to a career in book publishing. I was an assistant's assistant essentially, for a small children's book press, but it was a start.

I moved out of Owen's apartment. He was using constantly by then—he'd reached the stage where he even sold his TV to buy drugs and was close to being evicted by his landlord. We didn't ever really break up; I just never went back to him. I set myself up in a little studio, just a half-hour walk from my new office in Chicago. I bought a laptop and started writing. I had it all planned out in my mind—one day, I was going to have a career as a literary novelist. I wanted to write sweeping works of brilliance that critics would rave about and college students would puzzle over for hours on end.

But that was a fairly lofty goal, and I knew I needed to start *somewhere, so I started writing essays and short stories and submitting them to literary magazines. I had a few published, and earned a little money, too—but that little bit of cash felt like so much more because of the way I'd earned it.*

All this time, I was talking to Lexie every Sunday night. She was so busy at med school and always sounded tired—but every minor victory I had, she celebrated as if I'd just won a lottery. She framed the first short story I published and she sent me a photo of it up on the wall of her room. It was actually Lexie's idea that I write a collection of essays and try to publish them as a book. I mentioned this to an editor I met at the ofice, and he asked me to send him some of my work.

It all sounds pretty good at this point, doesn't it, Luke? I'll bet you're on the edge of your seat, waiting to hear how I fucked it all up. Well, by then, I'd been using casually for two years. I'd crave it, but only after a bad day—or sometimes on weekends when I wanted to write and I felt blocked. I couldn't write straight after I shot up—I'd be way too fucked up for that. Instead, I'd use the rush as a brainstorming session. When I came down, I'd sit at the computer and the words would pour out of me.

Heroin was my muse, Luke. The love of your life usually is.

29

LEXIE

Another week passes before Luke calls to tell me that Annie is ready for a visit.

Daisy is now four weeks old. She is finally tapering down on the morphine. The first few times her doctors tried, she got sick again, and had to step back up to a higher dose. But she's making steady progress at last, and she's finally gaining weight. Her face has filled out, and the agonized cry is softening—now, when she's due a dose of her opiates, she cries as if she's a normal newborn.

Daisy changes a little every single day. Her wellness seems to be approaching in slow motion, but then other times I look at the clock and realize how many days have passed and how much Annie has already missed, and I wonder how on earth she will ever catch up. I take hundreds of photos. My phone is never far from my hand, ready to record any positive moment, no matter how small. When I look back at my camera roll some nights with Sam, he teases me for being overzealous.

"It's like you're doing one of those time-lapse films," he says with a laugh.

But I'm achingly aware that I'm not just standing in for Annie's arms and warmth, but also her eyes and ears. At first, I observe Daisy with just a little clinical detachment. But then I start to sink under her spell, and soon I'm riding the waves of it all, so invested in her progress that her every achievement becomes mine.

I wake in the morning and Annie is the first thing I think of, but thoughts of Daisy follow close behind. Will I feel the curl of her fingers around mine? Or will today be all about her distress, and will my only reward be the way she nestles into me for comfort?

When Luke calls to arrange my visit, he tells me that I can't bring Daisy. He's worried that her presence at this early stage would be too destabilizing. It's a moot point anyway—she hasn't been discharged from the NICU. So I make the drive out to the clinic alone. A nurse takes my handbag, jewelry and mobile phone and secures them in a locker. Then I'm taken through the living space—a large, open area with a big-screen TV at the front and a variety of couches, and past it, to the dining room.

Annie is waiting at a table far away from the other residents. She shoots to her feet when she sees me. I walk faster—then I jog until I reach her, and then when she's within arm's reach, I clasp her shoulders and stare at her. Her eyes are puffy and bloodshot, but her pupils are a normal size, and I realize that she's simply been crying.

"Are you okay?" I whisper. Annie's expression crumples and she shakes her head.

"No, I'm not okay. I *hate* it here." Her voice breaks as she speaks, and the sound reminds me so much of that agonized cry that I've been listening to Daisy make for all of these weeks. I clamp my arms around my sister and I pull her close against me, just as I've been doing with Daisy.

"You're over the worst of it, Annie."

She is shaking within the circle of my arms, her frail body trembling against mine. I pull her toward the plastic chairs and position us side by side. She complies, but doesn't remove her face from my shoulder—she's still sobbing quietly into my neck. I hold her for a while as I try to think of something wise to say.

The thing is, I'm all out of wisdom, if I ever had any to offer her in the first place. Nothing I've ever said to her has helped, not one bit.

"How is Daisy?" she croaks after a while.

I drop the package of photos onto the table and she reaches for it greedily. As she opens the envelope, noisy sobs burst from her mouth. She spreads the photos all over the table and presses her hands over her mouth.

"She's so much better, isn't she? Her little cheeks…those gorgeous little cheeks…"

"She's weaning now, and it's going really well."

"I'm only here for her. I'd have left a dozen times already but for her."

"She's a good enough reason to stay, Annie."

"She really is."

After the initial burst of emotion, the photos seem to calm Annie, and I steal a few glances to assess her. She's still skin and bones, still incredibly pale, and quite teary—but although she might not realize it yet, she's definitely in better shape than she was a few weeks ago.

"So you went cold turkey, huh?" I ask her after a while. She shrugs.

"I needed to prove to myself that I could do it."

"And you did."

"I did, but the work is only just beginning."

"Surely after what that detox felt like, everything else will seem manageable?"

"You'd think so, huh?" She laughs, but it's a biting sound— bitterness and anger are right below the surface. "But now I'm doing this intensive therapy with Luke. I really liked him for the first few days—we did the usual sobriety stuff, debriefed the detox… I've heard it all before. But now, he wants to talk about every fucking moment of my life between birth and right now and he's such a hard-ass—he gets pissed off when I don't want to talk about things, and shuts the session down like he's having a fucking tantrum."

"What things are you talking about?" I ask gently, and she frowns at me.

"He's my therapist, Lexie. If I can't talk to *him* about it, why would I talk to you?"

"I…" I'm startled, and I pause before I shrug. "I don't know. I just want to help, I guess."

"You're doing enough. I can't keep relying on you to fix me every time I fuck up. If I'm going to be a good mom, I have to learn to face my problems myself."

"And so… Luke is pressuring you to talk about things you don't want to talk about, but you know you need to if you're going to get on top of this—is that what you're saying?"

Tears fill her eyes, and she shakes her head and admits in a whisper, "I don't even know what I'm saying. I'm so tired and so confused. I just know that I hate it here and I should be with my baby."

I stay for almost two hours. I try to fill her in on the days of Daisy's life that she's missed—but it's difficult to keep the conversation positive when so many of those days have just been hard. I wish I had some tangible milestone to report that doesn't involve her morphine dosage—but Daisy isn't even smiling yet, so I can only talk about the improvement in her symptoms.

When the time comes for me to leave, Annie cries some more, and thanks me for coming.

"Hang in there?" I ask her tentatively.

She looks at me helplessly. "Do I have a choice?"

★ ★ ★

Four days later, I'm driving home from the hospital when my phone rings. It's the rehab clinic, and I answer it anxiously.

"It's me," Annie croaks down the line. I can tell immediately that she's been crying. I clutch the steering wheel harder, until my knuckles turn white.

"What happened?"

"How is Daisy?"

I notice that she's deflected my question. But it must be a good sign, if she's been granted access to the phone?

"She had a good day today—one of the best she's had yet." I take a deep breath, and ask again, "So—what's going on?"

"I can't stay here, Lexie."

I pull to the side of the road. My stomach lurches and I think for a minute I'm going to be sick. I close my eyes and breathe carefully—purposefully, trying to calm myself.

It's like I'm living a flashback to the last time this happened, and the time before that—and those earlier times, I really thought that Annie completing rehab was the most important thing in the world. I couldn't even imagine back then how much higher the stakes could actually be.

"Annie," I say, very slowly and very carefully. "You have to stay. You have to complete the program. For *Daisy*, remember?"

"You don't understand, Lexie. They are *picking* on me. Luke is such an asshole, and *no one* here likes me, and it's just not working. The scar still hurts from her birth all of the time, and I can't forget even for a second of the day that I'm here and not with her where I belong." Her voice increases in pitch and volume. I let her speak, waiting patiently for the rush of energy to fade. As I sit in my car by the side of the highway, my hand is pressed over my mouth to hold in the sobs. It is too hard to talk to her when she's like this. I know from experience that there is nothing I can say to calm her. "Would you just *say* something?" she exclaims eventually.

234

I bite my lip, and I admit in a hoarse whisper, "Annie, I don't know *what* to say."

"You have to *help* me, Lexie! Get me out of here, for fuck's sake! Are you really going to leave me in here to rot like this while the early days of my baby's life slip away?"

She hangs up then, and I open my eyes and stare at the screen on my dash. The call lasted less than a minute.

I go home and I ignore Sam's repeated insistence that I come to bed. Instead, I sit at the computer and I Google for hours, trying to figure out a way to keep her out of jail if she *did* walk out of the clinic. There's no guard at the gate to stop her, no one to save her from herself. Even as midnight passes, I'm still staring blindly at legislation that may as well be written in Greek, and I'm no closer to finding a loophole. And of course I'm not, because if a loophole existed, Bernie would have told me about it.

I wake up at the desk in the office. My neck is stiff and my eyes are gritty. I pour several cups of black coffee down my throat and call Luke at 9:00 a.m. the next morning.

"What the hell is going on? She's obviously not handling the process well at all—why haven't you called me?"

"Alexis, I have explained this to you. Your sister is here to get help and treatment. You don't need to be involved on a day-to-day level. If anything of significant concern happens, I *will* call you."

His nonchalant attitude is irritating, and I can suddenly see why Annie is finding this man's treatment so difficult to deal with.

"Last night she was threatening to walk out of there. So I'd say that's a *significant concern*."

"Annie is well aware that if she leaves the clinic, I have to call the police and they *will* arrest her. She won't risk that," Luke says calmly, and the easy modulation of his tone infuriates me more.

"Maybe you're not the right person to treat Annie," I snap. "She said you're making things very difficult for her, and you said yourself you rarely treat patients directly—maybe someone with more recent experience—"

"Don't you see what she's doing, Lexie?" Luke interrupts me, still speaking very gently. "Can you really not recognize when she's playing you against me?"

I falter, my mouth still hanging open. I try to reframe this whole situation in my mind—to take myself out of the panic of her call and turn off my automatic reaction to the pleading in her voice.

And then I can see, as clear as day, that once again Luke is absolutely correct.

"Shit," I whisper, and then I sigh. "I'm sorry."

"I'm asking her to walk me back over her history, and she's refusing to participate in the therapy. She's not *engaging*—and I don't believe she will make any progress at all until she starts to unpack the things in her life that have led her to this point. So yes, I'm pushing her, and yes, I'm asking a lot of her. But I'm doing it because she can't leave this place until she really makes herself vulnerable. Otherwise she'll wind up right back where she started."

"Okay." My face feels hot as the embarrassment of the moment dawns on me. I'm a doctor, for God's sakes. I should have seen this myself. "I'm really sorry."

"Annie is a woman of incredible potential—she's articulate and intelligent, but that also makes her dangerous because she's just clever enough to know how to manipulate. And as I'm sure you're aware, addiction can make even the sincerest people expert manipulators. Listen, since we're chatting anyway—I'm trying to convince her to join in some of the group sessions to bring her out of her shell a little. Even just occupational therapy would be a good start. A lot of our patients like to do crafts or sports, but Annie's refused everything we've invited her to. Any ideas what might draw her out?"

"She loves to read and write... I mean, Annie *was* an English major. If there's a book club or a poetry group or something like that..."

"No...not really," Luke says, but I hear him shuffling papers. "Hmm. Interesting. When Annie was admitted and we asked her about her education, she just listed a GED."

"No, she has an English degree. Her career kind of died in the mud when the addiction spun out of control, but she's quite a gifted writer," I say. "I have no idea why she wouldn't list the degree on the paperwork."

"I treated a neurologist once who had listed his occupation on admission as janitor," Luke says quietly. "He'd been fired from his job and was embarrassed that his career had failed. Sometimes it's easier to pretend you've never achieved anything than to admit you've had success and failed."

"I think I've got an idea," I say, and I walk up the stairs from the kitchen. I open the door to the spare bedroom down the hall from mine, a room that is used only for storage, and I stare inside. There are boxes everywhere, but only a few are labeled *Annie*. "She has this journal our Dad gave her just before he died...it was incredibly special to her. I don't think she's ever written in it. I still have it in storage here somewhere. Maybe I could bring it next weekend—if she doesn't want to talk to you, maybe she can write her feelings down instead."

I'm due to visit Annie on Saturday, but Friday afternoon, Luke emails me to ask me not to come.

I've had to withdraw Annie's visitation and phone privileges. I know you'll be very concerned by this, but Annie has continued to refuse to participate in her treatments this week and went as far as to refuse to leave her room for our appointment yesterday. I hope that you understand that I'm suggesting we put a pause on contact for both your sake and Annie's—I'm concerned that she would continue to try to draw you in to rescue her. But I've also been thinking about that journal you mentioned—do you think you could mail it over to us?

Right beneath that email is one from Oliver. I groan and glance at the date. The four weeks' leave he agreed to is up, and I haven't even called in to let him know I won't be back next week. I hesitate before I open the email. The subject line is only the word *leave*.

This can't be good. I click the screen on my phone fiercely.

Lexie, Sam tells me that you are immersed in things with the baby. I've changed your leave to adoptive leave so that will give you another two months to figure things out. Come have a chat with me if you're ready before then, otherwise, let me know what you're up to in the new year.

"You called Oliver on my behalf?" I greet Sam at the door that afternoon, a glass of wine in one hand, a scowl on my face. I left Daisy early and have been sitting at home stewing over the email ever since.

Sam looks at me in surprise.

"I know how stressed you are—I just wanted to lighten the load."

"You didn't even *ask me*."

"What was your plan, honey?" Sam asks me pointedly. "Your leave runs out on Monday. It's Friday and you hadn't given it a thought until Oliver called you, right?"

"He didn't *call* me," I snap. I know I'm being an idiot and his method of communication is completely irrelevant but I'm too frustrated and angry to stop myself. "He emailed me. And you had no right."

"So were you going back to work on Monday?" Sam drops his bag near the door and closes it, then shrugs at me, prompting an answer.

"You know I wasn't," I mutter.

"And…"

"Sam!" I exclaim. "It's *my* career. My problem. I dropped the ball, yes—but—"

"And what was I supposed to do? Let you get fired?"

"I wouldn't have—"

"I saw Oliver *last week*, Lexie. He was pissed, but understood. If I hadn't gone in, and you really had forgotten all about your job and just not showed up next week, he would have fired you."

I spin on my heel away from Sam, then storm into the kitchen to stir the spaghetti sauce I made. He follows me and sits at the island watching me huffing and puffing around. After a while, he stands and, ignoring my protests, takes the wooden spoon from my hand and turns me to face him.

"I love you. I get that you have to deal with *some* of this on your own, but you can't deal with *all* of it on your own. You've rejected every offer of help I've made, and I knew that if I asked you if you wanted me to talk to him, you'd have said no. *I* need to be doing something, Lexie. You can't just shut me out because it's messy. This isn't a short-term crisis anymore—this is all going to be a part of our lives for months, maybe years."

"But it's my problem, Sam," I whisper, and my bravado disappears and my eyes fill with tears. Sam brushes the hair back from my face.

"It's *Annie's* problem, Lexie, and she's *my* soon-to-be sister-in-law."

I nod, and Sam cups my face in his hands. He stares down at me, and I clench my jaw to stop the tears.

"I'm sorry," I whisper. "It's just really hard for me to share these problems with you."

"*Why*, Lexie?"

"Habit? Pride? Stubbornness?"

"Please let me help," he says, and then he punctuates his sentences with kisses all over my face. "Please let me support you. Please let me carry you. Please let me *care* for you."

"I'll try. I'll try *harder.*"

He presses his forehead against mine and draws in a slow breath.

"I'm sorry," I say again.

"Okay." Then he adds in a whisper, "So we're okay?"

"We're okay."

"Good," Sam says softly. "Then that's all that matters."

30

ANNIE

Luke,

Everything is darker from here. My story up until now has had shades of light, but we've reached the part where it starts to spiral.

It was such an ordinary night. I had finished the first draft of my manuscript and was working through refining it. I actually had the first few chapters ready to send off to my editor friend. I'd been procrastinating about sending them for weeks, though, and the longer I prolonged it the more nervous I became about how it would be received. I was so worried about the email that I couldn't sleep, so I went out for a walk.

Then I called my dealer and I bought a bag.

I didn't see the police officer—I only realized he'd been watching the deal when he crash-tackled me as I turned to walk away. I was arrested for possession of a controlled substance. The judge granted bail, but there was no one in Chicago I could call to get me out except for my boss and colleagues—and there was no way I could call them. I sat in the cell for half the night before I finally found the courage to call Lexie.

I told her some bullshit story about how it was all a mix-up and I was scared work would find out and I'd lose my job. She called my boss first thing the next morning and told him I was really sick, and she got on a plane. She was in Chicago by lunchtime to post bail.

In the cab on the way back to my apartment, she was silent—staring out the window, her expression completely blank. I kept glancing at her, waiting for her to say something. When we got to my apartment, I made us both coffees, and we sat at my little dining room table.

"The cop told me that you were buying heroin, Annie," she whispered. "You said on the phone it was a mix-up. Can you explain that to me?"

"I was buying weed," I lied, and I said it so convincingly that even I nearly believed it. "I use it occasionally to de-stress when I'm busy at work. I think the dealer panicked when he saw the cop and he passed me the wrong bag. Such bad luck."

Lexie thought about this for a while, and then she nodded.

"And...the weed...are you using much?"

"Hardly ever, Lex, I promise you," I said. "Every now and again—but obviously after last night, that'll stop."

Lexie went home that same day—she couldn't miss any more work. She made me promise to tell her my court date, but I didn't—instead, I called her after it was over and I pretended I'd forgotten she wanted to be there.

I was actually lucky that time. I had been buying from the same dealer for years and trusted him, so I'd accepted the paper bag he'd offered me without checking the ziplock bag inside. The cop had seen me give a hundred dollars to the dealer, which would have been *quite a lot of weed, but the paper bag contained only a few grams of powder. The prosecution argued that if I really did just ask for weed, I must have known I wasn't getting what I asked for purely by the weight of the bag, but the judge felt they'd failed to prove my guilt beyond reasonable doubt.*

"You and I both know what really went on that night, Ms. Vidler," he said to me as he delivered his verdict. "But the prosecution has failed to prove their case sufficiently, so I have no choice but to find you not guilty. Take this as a free pass from the universe and sort your life out, because there won't be a second one."

My lawyer told me afterward that if the cop had seen me check the bag, it would have meant a felony and likely jail time—up to four years. That scared the shit out of me, and I stayed stone-cold sober for weeks.

But I missed the rush and I missed the high. I don't think I was physically addicted yet—there was no withdrawal; instead, I missed it like I missed Lexie...like I missed Mom...like I missed Dad. For better or worse, heroin was part of my family now.

I was more careful when I bought it the next time—I found a new dealer, covered my tracks better, got a bit smarter about hiding it. But then I felt smart, and superior—and more confident that I'd been caught once and I knew how to stop it from happening again.

And I still hadn't sent the chapters, but now I was starting to worry that I'd taken too long. So instead of sitting up worrying about whether the editor was going to like what I'd written, I sat up and worried that I'd missed my one shot to make it.

I started using a little more regularly—every week, instead of every second week—then every few days, and then it snowballed. The more I used it, the less sick I felt after, but the harder it was to hit the rush—so I was using more and more. Soon, I was bumping the minute I walked in the door from work, and then the day came when I couldn't get myself out the door without a hit, and then I was sneaking my kit into my bag so I could bump at lunchtime just to get through the day.

And then I couldn't afford to pay my rent and to buy enough smack to last me the whole week, and so I started selling off things in my apartment. First it was the meager jewelry I'd amassed, then furniture. Soon, my apartment contained only my computer, stacks of books and a mattress.

I got a warning at work for missing days I hadn't even realized I'd missed.

And then one of my colleagues caught me shooting in the disabled toilet and I lost my job.

31

LEXIE

Daisy's pediatrician tells me that she's probably going to be ready for discharge in a few days. This is great news, but it's also terrifying news.

Forty days have passed since the birth. Forty days that I have not worked, I've barely kept up with my laundry and cleaning the house has become a distant memory. Forty days over which Sam has gradually become a stranger I pass in the hallway and share lunch with every now and again. Forty days and my life has shifted from predictable and organized and functional to chaos that I cannot seem to unscramble. I have bonded deeply with Daisy, of course I have; she is tiny and fragile, and she's been in pain for so much of that time. I've wept for her almost as much over this month as I have wept for Annie in the last decade. But now she's coming into my home. No longer can I just clock out and leave the responsibility behind with nurses overnight—no, once Daisy is discharged, it is entirely up to me to keep her safe and well.

And I have to get it right. I can't afford to take a wrong step—Daisy has already been through hell, and there's more to come. If Annie gets herself together in rehab somehow, and we can convince CPS she's up to the task of parenting Daisy, then Daisy will go home with her mother eventually. But where is home? Is it in my house—further extending the chaos? Or is it in the trailer? I don't even know who *owns* that trailer, or how Annie paid the rent…if she has at all. And what if Annie doesn't make it through rehab, as seems increasingly likely? I don't have a clue what I'd do then, and I can't bear to think about it.

Mary Rafferty calls and asks if she and Bill Weston can visit the house.

"There are some formalities we need to attend to before Daisy formally comes into your care," she says. "Bill and I could come by this evening? Maybe after your fiancé finishes at the hospital?"

"Ah…" I fumble to think of a reason to decline or at least postpone her request. "Of course you can, but…"

I trail off, thinking of the dishes in the sink and the piles of laundry waiting for our attention. Then I think of the room where Daisy will sleep, which is full of boxes—some of which I've torn open and tipped onto the floor when I was looking for Annie's diary.

"I know you've been busy with the baby at the hospital, Dr. Vidler. I won't be expecting a clean house, if that's what you're worried about," Mary says gently.

"It's just…we haven't even got the nursery in order yet," I say hesitantly. "We'll do it on the weekend but…"

"Oh, that's not what I'm looking for, either. It's a safety check—a procedural thing, you understand. There's a checklist I need to follow. I mainly need to see that Daisy is going to a home where she will be *safe*. And if there's a thing or two that still needs doing before she comes home, it's no big deal, truly."

I agree to meet Mary and Bill at our place just after 5:00 p.m., and then I sprint to my car and call Sam as I drive home. I spend the afternoon frantically cleaning and trying to restore some order to the house. I hide baskets of laundry and scrub the kitchen, focusing so hard my vision almost tunnels. I

spend ten minutes trying to polish out a tiny stain on the countertop that was there when we bought the house, and when I
can't lift it, I sob. When Sam comes home, he finds me in the im-
maculate bathroom trying to hide my blotchy skin with makeup.

"Uh…" he says, looking at me with visible panic. "What
happened?"

"There's a stain on the countertop," I say, and I burst into tears
again. "What if they say we can't have her? What if they want
to send her to some foster carer who has clean countertops?"

Sam looks at me blankly.

"Can't we just cover the stain with the fruit bowl?"

But by the time we open the front door, the house is sparkling clean and Sam and I are both wearing our brightest smiles.

"It's so lovely to see you again, Dr. Vidler," Mary greets me
with a beam.

"You, too," I say politely, and I step aside to allow them to
enter the hallway.

Sam leads the way around our house, giving a laid-back tour,
mentioning the layout and the renovations as we walk. Mary
scrawls notes, and I twist my neck this way and that, trying un-
successfully to read what she's written. We finish at the room
we're planning to set up for Daisy, right across the hall from ours.

"It's been our storage room," Sam says wryly. "We're going
shopping for baby things on the weekend." I hastily glance at
Mary and Bill, but neither seems bothered by our lack of preparation. Mary catches my eye and offers me a quiet smile.

"Can we take a seat downstairs and have a little chat?"

My knees are stiff as we walk down to the living room. Bill
and Mary sit on the sofa opposite Sam and me, and Sam takes
my hand, then glances at me. He must correctly read in my face
how terrified I am, because he releases my hand and instead
slides his arm around my shoulders.

"The house is fine. There are just a few specifics we need to
discuss," Bill murmurs, then he glances at Mary and at her nod,

he turns back to Sam and me. "Firstly, I'd like to hear whether either of you has any experience with young children, particularly newborns—" He stops midsentence, then cringes. "Wait, that's a bit of a silly question—sorry, I don't usually conduct these interviews with doctors!"

Sam laughs quietly.

"Yes, we're both well versed in the needs of caring for a newborn baby."

"Of course, my apologies. Perhaps you can tell me about your support networks?" Bill asks next.

"We have a good network of friends around Montgomery," I say. "Plus colleagues from our workplaces, and the neighbors are all good people, too."

"Do you have people you could call on if you needed emotional or practical support? Or say if there was an emergency with Daisy and you weren't sure what to do?"

Sam and I exchange a glance. I'm finally starting to relax, because if *this* is the standard we need to meet, we really are going to be fine. "Again, we're both doctors but...if a situation were to arise where we needed more expert help, I play golf with Daisy's pediatrician on weekends, so I guess we'd just call him."

Mary laughs softly.

"We have a set of questions we generally ask in these circumstances. It's a *good* problem to have that most of those questions seem a bit absurd in your situation, trust me."

Bill nods, but then he fixes his gaze right on me, and he says quietly, "I did a background check on you, Alexis—all was in order, of course but... I was surprised by how high your debt burden is. You've still got student loans and several large credit cards—it's an unusually extensive debt, even for someone who's been through med school, isn't it?"

This catches me off guard, and I'm instantly defensive again.

"Annie was in my care from the time she was fourteen, Bill, so I didn't exactly have a lot of time for saving a nest egg to cover my tuition," I say, and Sam very gently contracts his arm along my shoulders. I take a deep breath. "Yes, there was undergrad tuition and then med school tuition—but then Annie needed to go to rehab and she didn't have insurance so I borrowed for that, too. I've been paying it down as quickly as I can, but you're right—my finances could be healthier. I'm working on it, but it's under control."

Bill and Mary don't need to know this—but when we first tried to buy the house, the mortgage was declined because of my outstanding debt. Sam cashed in some stocks so we had a larger deposit and that got us over the line, but at one stage, we thought we were going to have to get the mortgage in his name only.

"Well, yes, but then now there's also the mortgage on this house—and of course you'll be responsible for both Annie's and Daisy's hospital care bills *and* the rehab facility fee. Are you *sure* you can afford to take another eight weeks off?" Bill asks. He's still pleasant, but I can't help but feel like we're finally moving into a make-or-break discussion, and now my anxiety about this meeting seems justified.

"You did a background check on me, too, right?" Sam asks. Bill nods and Sam continues calmly, "So you know that the only debt I have is the mortgage on this house, and I do have reasonable assets."

"So you'll be supporting Alexis and Daisy financially, then?" Bill asks.

"No," Sam says abruptly. "I'm not 'supporting' them like they're some kind of burden. Lexie and I are a team—*she* doesn't have a backlog of debt to cover, *we* do, and when you split it between the two of us and our collective salaries now, it's entirely manageable. And regarding the medical bills, we'll get a substantial staff and family discount off what's left after Medicaid. As Lexie said, it's all under control. Okay?"

"I wasn't accusing you two of poor financial management," Bill says quietly. "I just need to be absolutely sure that I know what the care arrangement for the baby is going to be until Annie is cleared to resume responsibility for her. I would hate to approve this kinship care and then find in a few weeks that Alexis has returned to work full-time and you're leaving Daisy with a nanny or at a day care."

"That's not going to happen." I frown at him. "Although I don't see why it would be a problem if I did. Are you saying working mothers can't be foster parents?"

"Well, obviously a better situation is to have an infant with a stay-at-home carer as much as possible. And in this case, Daisy's NAS is a complication that needs very careful attention. I'd much rather see Daisy at home with you full-time, at least for now."

"And we've just assured you she will be," Sam says.

"We've talked a lot today about this period while Annie is at rehab," Mary says, changing the subject. "Have you two discussed what happens afterward? Or if…heaven forbid…Annie doesn't complete the program?"

Sam and I exchange a glance. We haven't discussed this— partly because when Sam has tried to broach it, I've changed the subject. It's too frightening, and I have too much to deal with day to day to risk a conversation that might not go well. I just don't know how he would feel about us taking permanent care of my sister's kid, and I'm too scared to find out.

I'm not even sure how I feel about it—my thoughts on the possibility of longer-term care for Daisy change all the time. Some days, I'm resigned to its inevitability, and perhaps that's why I'm too afraid to discuss it with Sam. On those days, all that matters is that the gentle love I had for Daisy has grown into something extraordinary and powerful. That devotion is already becoming a force to be reckoned with—my beautiful, innocent niece is relying on me, and I'll do *whatever* it takes to ensure she has a stable upbringing.

And occasionally, I have fleeting moments of clarity when I *know* somehow that I'll be raising Daisy, and I'm petrified of what that means for Sam and me. He's not accustomed to a family that throws curveballs like this. Longer-term care of Daisy may mean assuming responsibility for Daisy while Annie pops in and out of our lives, probably bringing drama with every new encounter. What if Sam decides it's just too much? What do I do then? I don't know. I won't let my niece or my sister down, but Sam is the best thing that ever happened to me. What if he asked me to choose? I couldn't, and I can't even begin to process how I might, and so I don't let myself go there.

Besides which, sometimes I genuinely believe that Annie is going to be fine. All she has to do is stay at rehab, then I can help her set up and resume responsibility for her daughter. When I frame this situation like that in my mind, I can convince myself that I don't even *need* to talk to Sam about a longer-term future with Daisy because everything is going to be just fine.

And as for right now, I'm exactly on the fence. Longer-term care of Daisy might be required, but equally it might not, and Sam and I haven't discussed it so I can't really give Mary a definitive answer.

"We would have to really give that some thought if it happened," I tell her quietly.

"Are you saying you wouldn't consider longer-term care of Daisy?" Bill seems to latch on to this, and his gaze narrows a little.

"No, that's not what we're saying," Sam murmurs. "We're saying we haven't talked about it."

"I think it would be wise if you did." Bill starts to pack up his paperwork.

"What's that supposed to mean?" I can't help it; I'm defensive of Annie. I might doubt her ability to overcome these challenges with every second heartbeat, but I can't bear the thought of someone *else* doing it.

"Dr. Vidler, I'm praying that in eight weeks' time, I'm getting ready to tell the judge that Annie is clean, she has somewhere suitable to live and the means to support herself. I—" Mary pauses, then nods toward Bill "—*we* would love nothing more than to be able to recommend to Judge Brown that the responsibilities for Daisy's care be transferred back to her mother."

There's a *but* hanging in the air. I hold my breath as I wait for it, and I'm fighting the urge to put my hands over my ears like a toddler and shout *don't say it, don't say it, don't say it.* Mary's gaze becomes almost pleading. She offers me a very sad smile and she murmurs, "But I think you and I both know that's an unlikely prospect at best, given Annie's history."

"Annie is going to beat this," I say stiffly.

"I really do hope that you're right about that." Bill sighs. "It's curious, isn't it? How one family can produce someone like yourself, and someone like your sister. It really makes you wonder sometimes."

The way Bill's lip curls whenever he refers to Annie sets my teeth on edge. I rise abruptly and say, "Is that all?"

I show Mary and Bill to the door, and we shake hands and exchange farewells with an artificial level of politeness. Once I close the door behind them, Sam and I stare at one another.

"Did that go well?" he asks, his face set in a confused frown. "I thought it did, but there were some moments there..."

I keep seeing Bill's curled lip in my mind, and my anger simmers.

"They don't know her," I mutter. "How dare they presume to know her?"

I run my hand through my hair and exhale. I need a glass of wine, or a bath, maybe a walk to clear my mind. Sam is standing in the center of the hallway, almost blocking my way back to the living area, and when I take a step, he doesn't move. I frown at him.

"Lex," he says cautiously. "We really do need to talk about what happens if—"

"Don't *you* do it, too," I cut him off sharply, and Sam falls silent, but still, he doesn't shift out of my way.

"You keep postponing this discussion, Lexie, and I don't know what that means. Can't we just talk about?"

"Just *talking* about it is a betrayal of Annie," I say flatly. "If I don't believe in her, who will? So no, I don't want to 'just talk about it' because I want to focus my energies on believing that she can do this."

"But do you?" Sam says, and I scowl at him.

"Do I *what?*"

"Do you believe that she can do this?"

That's the million-dollar question, isn't it? Perhaps if I were a braver person, I'd be vulnerable with Sam right now and admit my doubts. I really could do with a good, soul-fortifying cry in his arms. I could admit to him how scared I am that tossing Annie out of my life two years ago was a colossal mistake that we can't come back from. I could confess to him how out of control my life feels right now and how crazy that makes me feel. I could give voice to the way that the thought that I might not be able to help Annie shakes me to the very core of who I understand myself to be, and how frightened I am that I'll over-compensate for all of that turmoil and doubt by clinging to Daisy too tightly and make an even bigger mess.

I could tell Sam that I'm a fixer—that I'm *The Fixer* in my family. I was the girl who could hold things together when they began to crumble. I was the girl who could, overnight, become an adult if it meant keeping my family together. I'm the woman who stops at nothing to restore order when it's lost, not just in my life, but in my sister's life.

That is *who I am*, in a way that's somehow truer than any other aspect of my identity. And that's why my failure to help Annie makes me question every single thing I know about myself. Her addiction has been a swirling abyss of risk in my life for six years now. If she succumbs to it, then somehow, I'm lost to it, too, because since Dad died, she and I have been linked in a way that I can't separate or even fully understand.

But I'm not brave enough to give voice to any of that yet, and so instead of my vulnerability, Sam gets my defense mechanisms.

"How can you even ask me that?" I snap. He makes a sound that's half groan, half sigh, and I push past him. I walk by the sofas and toward the stairs, and his pleading voice follows me— an open invitation to stop right now before I use the mess of my relationship with Annie to cause damage to my relationship with him.

"Honey, please don't shut me out—"

"I'm going for a walk," I say abruptly over my shoulder. "I just need some time to myself."

I pull on workout clothes and I fix all of my thoughts on the cool air waiting outside. I'll walk around the block a few times. I'll soak up the atmosphere of our comfortable, affluent neighborhood in the early evening, until I can believe again that I belong here. I'll look through windows, into the lamplit glow of the homes of normal families all around us, and I'll tell myself that everything is going to be okay for Sam and me, too, eventually.

But when I come back downstairs, he is waiting for me at the front door. His arms are crossed over his chest, and his jaw is set—and when I look into his eyes I see not anger, but determination.

"Well?" I say, and he opens his arms and turns his palms upward, as if he's surrendering. I look at his hands; strong hands, hands that hold life every single day. They are trustworthy and capable hands, and they belong to a man who shares those qualities.

A man who does not deserve to be shut out. I just wish that I knew how to let him in.

"I'll drop it for now, okay? We don't even have to talk."

"I told you, I need a walk," I say, and when Sam doesn't react, I add pointedly, "by *myself*."

"And I don't want you walking around out there on your own in the dark. So I'll forget about the conversation you obviously aren't ready to have, but *please* let me walk with you. Okay?"

It's my turn for a frustrated sigh, but I let him follow me around as I stomp my way through the neighborhood. When we finally walk back through the door forty-five minutes later, Sam speaks for the first time since we left. "I think I'll cook pasta for dinner tonight. Does that sound okay?"

"Yes," I say softly. "That sounds good. Thanks."

"We haven't watched a movie together in a while. Let's open a bottle of wine and try to relax tonight, huh?"

He's already on his way to the kitchen when I catch his hand. Sam turns back to me, eyebrows raised.

"Thanks," I say a little reluctantly—because although I'm grateful for his patient support, I want to make sure that he understands that word is *not* an open invitation to resume a more in-depth discussion. Sam nods, then twists his wrist around and slides it back so that he can take my hand and pull me toward himself. Once I'm stiffly pressed against his chest, he wraps his arms around my body and just holds me. We stand in silence for a moment. Then Sam kisses the side of my head and murmurs, "I *love* you, Lexie."

The terse walk didn't relax me much, but somehow, that hug and those words reground me. I inhale deeply, and when I exhale, I feel the knotted muscles of my shoulders start to give, and I melt against him a little.

"I love you, too," I whisper back.

"Tonight," Sam tells me, "we relax. Together. Okay?"

"Okay."

The next morning, Bill calls Sam to let him know that we've been appointed as Daisy's legal guardian at his recommendation, with a review planned for the week before Annie is due to graduate from rehab.

"Why did he call *you?*" I frown when Sam tells me the good news.

"Does it matter?"

"No." I sigh. "Not really."

"Have they given you a more definite timeline for Daisy's discharge?"

"Last I heard, they were thinking it would be toward the end of next week."

"We better get some diapers this weekend, then."

"I think diapers are the least of our worries. We better get some *sleep.*"

I'm caught off guard that afternoon when the pediatrician announces that they're going to drop Daisy's last few MLs of morphine quicker than they'd planned—her NAS scores have been stable enough to complete the final part of the weaning process.

"So, when do you think she'll be discharged?" I ask hesitantly.

"Well, if she's stable on this dose today, we'll try her without anything for tomorrow. I'd like to observe her for a day, maybe two—but then we can discharge her."

I head straight to the store to look at supplies. I intend to just browse and return with Sam on the weekend as we have planned, but while I'm there, I decide that I'll go ahead and buy the things that we need. I'm so overwhelmed by the options that I find myself just nodding mutely as the clerk throws products at me. I get a change table with a built-in bath, and the most expensive cot, and organic sheet sets, and the best diapers, and I know that Daisy is quite dependent on her pacifier so I buy a number of those, and then I buy the premium formula in bulk, and I buy bottles, and toys that she won't use for months or years. I tell myself Daisy can use the toys even after she goes home with Annie, and that succumbing to the appeal of a stuffed teddy bear or a set of stacking cups is definitely not a sign that I'm expecting Daisy to stay long-term.

It is only as I get into my car that I realize how much money

I have just wasted—I don't need the formula, for a start. I have no idea what I was thinking—maybe I wasn't. Daisy has some gastro difficulties, which is typical for children with NAS, so she'll stay on prescription formula for months. I console myself that Annie will take the store formula and use it later on, when Daisy is older. And as I leave the store, depleted savings account aside, I now feel more prepared for Daisy's arrival.

When I get home, Sam's car is in the driveway. I reverse into the garage and he opens the internal door and stares at the overloaded car.

"I thought we were doing this together on the weekend?"

"Daisy might be *here* by the weekend," I tell him lightly. "They're going to drop her last morphine dose tomorrow and see how she handles it."

"You didn't think to call me? I wanted to help you with this." Sam is frowning, and I frown, too.

"I just… I didn't think you'd have time…"

"I'll *make* time for these things." And then, patient Sam disappears in the blink of an eye and I meet a new Sam—exasperated Sam. "Jesus, Lexie—I'm getting so frustrated with you cutting me out of this shit. I feel like I'm *constantly* chasing you down these days."

Sam rarely snaps—but when he does—it packs a punch. I'm speechless for a moment.

"I don't mean to," I whisper. Sam sighs and steps out of the doorway, letting me through into the hall. When I join him inside, he catches my shoulders in his palms and forces me to stare at him. I'm stinging at his tone—but I don't doubt that he's hurt. "I'm sorry, Sam." And then I know I have to say something—I know I have to explain myself better, but all I can offer him is a weak, "I just don't know how to deal with this with you."

"I don't know what that means, Lexie," Sam says. There's a desperate confusion in his gaze as he looks down at me. "Isn't it easier to deal with this with me? If it *isn't*, something is really wrong between us."

"I've just always dealt with this kind of thing on my own."

"That's because you've always *been* on your own. I keep telling you, Lexie—we're a team in all of this, okay? I want to know. I *need* to know. You haven't even told me how Annie is doing this week."

"That's because I don't know." I try to think about when I last updated Sam on Annie's progress. When was the last time I actually had a proper chat with him—not one in a hallway or as we're drifting off to sleep—a proper, sit-down discussion? I can't remember. "Luke has taken away her phone privileges. She wasn't doing so well."

Sam scowls at me, and his palms on my shoulders release suddenly so I step back. Now the slightly increased distance between our bodies is starting to feel vast, and I know it's my fault. I sigh and rub my forehead as he says, "You didn't think to mention that?"

"Am I supposed to tell you every little thing that happens with her? Neither one of us has time for that. And do you *really* want to know, anyway? It's *exhausting* keeping up with her drama, trust me."

Sam's face falls, and I feel mine fall right along with it. I have insulted him again, and I didn't mean to. Doesn't he see that I'm trying to protect him from the stress of it all? He crosses his arms over his chest.

"Sometimes, I think you don't know me at all, Lexie."

He said the words quietly, which somehow hurts more than if he'd shouted them. He leaves the room, and I note the downward curve of his shoulders, and the way that his head sits low. I'm alone in the hallway now, and I'm frustrated and embarrassed and angry.

Sam has three perfectly intelligent, handsome brothers who never cause any drama and go about their professional careers like normal people. We know nothing of their day-to-day lives because we don't need to—they're healthy, happy and, just like we are, *busy*. I've met them a few times, but I'm sure that Sam doesn't update *me* every time he talks to them—I don't expect him to. So now I'm supposed to give him a status update every single time I hear something about Annie or Daisy? I'd rather shield him from it—as much as I can, anyway—and just let him focus on his work and continue to enjoy his life. This is my problem—Annie is my problem—and by extension of that, Daisy is my problem. Yes, she is coming into our home, but that doesn't mean *he* needs to be burdened by every aspect of this saga. He should be grateful that I'm saving him from the burden.

I rise and start unpacking the car—my movements forceful. I spend the next few hours setting up the spare room as a nursery, and it's only as I go to fall into bed some hours later that I realize Sam is in the study. I walk along the hallway and see the light coming from under the door.

I raise my hand to knock to ask if he is going to come to bed, but the light flicks off. "Sam?" I call hesitantly.

"I just need some space, Lexie," he calls back.

This is a small thing—he's just sleeping two doors down from me—it's not like he's walked out on me. But it's also a huge thing—because this is the first time that Sam has ever opted to sleep away from me—the first time he's ever told me he needs *space*. Sam loves to cuddle me in the night—it actually took some getting used to at first.

It suddenly strikes me how much "space" we *have* actually had—in all of the weeks since Annie's late-night call, Sam and I have not made love once.

I look back now and realize this is not for lack of trying on Sam's part—I have been pulling away. Maybe I even pulled away in one single and sharp moment the night Annie called. I'm stricken with guilt as I consider this, but the defensiveness remains, and I'm frustrated that Sam does not give me at least a little more leeway.

Maybe I actually *need* him to make himself invisible for a time, while I deal with the magnitude of Annie's situation.

This thought is like ice water on my anger. Over the past two years, Sam has accepted me as I am, warts and all, and he wants to build a future with me. He adores me—I can *see* that when he looks at me—and what do I reward him with? I take him for granted, and I automatically begin cutting him out, right when I need him most. I retreat to our bedroom, but I spend hours lying awake, my racing mind working overtime as I try to outrun my guilt.

I sleep in the next morning, and Sam is gone by the time I wake up. When I finally arrive at the hospital I'm immediately taken to the meeting room with Daisy's neonatologist. He tells me that she is doing amazingly well without any morphine, and that provided she remains stable, he's going to prepare her discharge paperwork.

"But doesn't she still have some issues?" I blurt. "Are you sure this is safe?"

He raises an eyebrow at me, confused—and fair enough, I guess, since he's giving me the best news ever and I'm trying to talk him out of it.

"She's obviously still small, and the rigidity in her muscles might take some time to resolve—and you'll need to keep her on the prescription formula. I'd like to see her back here every couple of days, but I really do think it will be good for her to be in a more relaxed home environment now. She *is* six weeks old, you know. It's time."

I swallow hard.

"Okay, then."

I go in to see Daisy, and find her lying wide-awake, staring up at a mobile someone has moved over her crib. I glance at her chart and see that it's been well over twelve hours since she had any morphine, and she's settled and content.

I text Sam.

I'm so sorry. Can you spare me some time today?

I meet Sam in his office just after lunch. He was in surgery this morning, and he already looks tired. I extend a coffee toward him as a peace offering. He takes it, but he doesn't smile.

I sit in the patient's chair opposite his large oak desk. Sam initially moves to sit behind the desk, then stops himself and walks back around to sit beside me. I watch as he toys with the lid of the coffee.

"I've been dealing with my family's problems on my own for a long time," I say without preamble. "Annie makes a mess, she dumps it on my lap and I clean it up—I've been doing this with her since she was a kid. And Mom was never really engaged, not after Dad died—so I've always just had to be... I've always had to be the adult—the *only* adult. But I've had a nice hiatus for the last two years, and I wasn't prepared for this and I certainly haven't been prepared to share the burden. I'm really sorry, Sam. I didn't mean to leave you out. I didn't mean to hurt you."

I'm babbling, and Sam's watching me expressionlessly. Is all of this too late? I want so much for him to react and to tell me I haven't ruined what we have. Just when I start to panic, he rests his hand on mine. I feel the warmth of his body radiating through to mine. I have been so terrified since my late-night revelation last night. And now with a single touch, I feel capable—confident, supported—*strong*.

"The thing is, Alexis Vidler, I love you more than anything," he says slowly. "Yes, this is a messy situation. But you need to give Daisy a home now, and I want that to be *our* home. I don't want it to be *your* home."

"I'll do better. I promise."

"No, Lexie. I want you to do *worse*," Sam says gently. "I want you to stumble and let me pick you up. I want you to tell me the load is too heavy and let me carry some of it. I *don't* want you to superwoman me out of our life."

When I nod, Sam squeezes my hand gently, and at last we share a smile.

"She hasn't had morphine since last night," I tell him, and his eyes widen.

"How is she?"

"Content."

"So do I need to organize a day off to bring her home with you?"

"No," I say, and when he frowns at me, I add hastily, "I just know how hard it is for you to do that, so I want you to wait for the days when I really need you. There are going to be days when…maybe she's sick or we have specialist appointments or CPS visits or… God, I don't even know, Sam." And I haven't really been planning my words as I spoke, but *that* sentence leads to a thought that just falls out of my mouth and suddenly my eyes are full of tears. "I don't know what's ahead of us. And I'm scared."

"I'm scared, too," he admits.

"You are?"

"Of course I am."

A tear spills over onto my cheek and I press it away impatiently.

"Sorry," I whisper, and Sam shakes his head.

"That's exactly what I'm talking about. *Don't* apologize, Lexie. You're allowed to cry in front of me, for God's sake. I *want* you to."

I nod, and he pulls me close to rest his chin on the top of my head as we hear a hesitant knock at the door.

"Sorry, Sam," Cathryn calls. "You're due in surgery in a few minutes."

Sam's arms remain locked around me.

"Let them know I'm running late—I need ten more minutes."

"You can go," I whisper, and he shakes his head.

"Nope. Not until I finish this."

"I'm okay, I promise." I start to pull away, but his arms don't budge.

"*I* need this hug, Lexie."

At that, I nestle back into his embrace and I close my eyes and listen to the steady beat of his heart against my ear. We stay like that for several minutes, until I gently pull away and brush a kiss against his lips.

"Better?" he murmurs, and I smile.

"Much."

Annie calls me later that evening.

"You have phone privileges back?" I say in surprise when she identifies herself.

"Time off solitary confinement for good behavior," she says wryly. She sounds good, and I'm surprised by my own optimism as I realize this. It's been a good day after all.

"So—things are going better?"

"I don't know," Annie says after a pause. "I no longer think about running away every time Luke speaks to me, so I'm going to take that as an improvement. Whose idea was Dad's journal?"

"Mine."

"Sometimes I think that maybe it's going to help, so thanks," she whispers, her voice suddenly uneven. She clears her throat, then says with artificial brightness, "Enough of this—tell me about my girl. How is she doing?"

"She has also become a star patient since we last spoke. She's completely off the morphine."

"Wow." Annie's voice breaks, and I hear her voice catch on a sob. "That's amazing."

"Yep. She's coming home to my place tomorrow or the next day."

"Oh, Lexie. Oh, thank you." Annie is overcome as she laughs through tears. "This is the best news I could have hoped for. So she's well? She's…normal?"

"For the most part she's doing brilliantly. There are a few areas we need to work on but…yes, Annie, she's an absolute fighter."

"Does this mean you can bring her for a visit soon?"

"I hope so. I'll talk to her doctors." *And yours*, I think, but I don't tell her that Luke has specifically advised me against it.

"I'm so grateful to you, Lexie. I'm going to make all of this up to you. I swear."

"Well," I say, and I'm surprised and pleased by this gratitude, "I look forward to that."

I forgot to buy a car seat.

I got everything else a baby could possibly need; an expensive stroller, all the equipment for the nursery, formula we *can* actually use, diapers in multiple sizes that will probably not fit her until she's two, clothes and a mobile and pacifiers and blankets.

So when the doctor tells me that her discharge paperwork is done, and a nurse asks me to bring the car seat in for a test run, I'm mortified to admit that I don't have one.

I want to cry as I drive myself all the way back to the baby store. It's not a big deal in the scheme of things—an inconvenience—but it's an ominous sign. If I can't remember something like a car seat, what else will I forget? Diaper changes? Bottles? Baths?

I buy the highest-safety-rated car seat, and I drive back to the NICU. I fuss over it in the parking lot, even though the guide at the store installed it, and it's no doubt set up perfectly. I adjust the straps and play with the seat belt needlessly over and over again for twenty-five minutes, until my phone rings.

"Are you ever coming back?" the nurse asks, and there is laughter in her tone, as if this is a joke. I tighten a strap, and then I loosen it again, and then I realize that all this is for *nothing* because I have to take the car seat inside so the staff can monitor Daisy while she sits in it. I groan.

"See you in two minutes."

I head back into the hospital and gather up Daisy. As I lower her into the car seat, I'm almost hoping that she fails the test. It's all about respiration and body positioning—the car seat keeps the baby upright, and some babies who have been delivered early or have been ill struggle to breathe when lying in that position. Daisy will be monitored for thirty minutes. If at any point her oxygen levels drop, her discharge will be canceled.

Which would mean more days that she's safely in the hospital.

The nurse leaves me with Daisy, and I stare at her. She is asleep, her translucent eyelids resting over her eyes, eyelashes hanging down low on her cheeks. I lift my hand, and I very gently touch her face. There is so much of Annie in this baby... so much of my father in her. The light hair, the shape of her eyes. I've seen Daisy mostly cry and sleep over these weeks, but she'll soon adapt to a more typical schedule and begin to hit normal newborn milestones. The rigidity in her muscles should fade and she'll become floppy—the way newborns should be. Soon she will smile. Soon she will laugh.

She is my responsibility. She is my problem. For the time being, she is also my privilege. I need to love Daisy, because somehow newborns know if they are loved. I've read studies of infants raised in orphanages and the difficulties they face with attachment later in life—Daisy literally *needs* me to love her. Daisy has had a very rough start to life, but she's not out of the woods yet. Somehow, we need to get Annie well quickly and in a position to provide Daisy with a stable upbringing.

If we don't, there's every chance that I'll spend the next twenty years repeating what I've been doing for the last twenty—caring for Daisy, caring for her mother. And if Daisy is damaged, she will damage others—just as Annie has. She will damage herself, just as Annie has.

I haven't trained for this. Unlike clinical practice, there's no supervision of stand-in parents—I'm on my own. There's no textbook or reference charts for when I feel out of my depth. This is real life. This is an innocent, fragile and somewhat blank canvas—and I need to start the painting of her life, then hand her over to her mother.

It is all too much, and yet, once again there is no one else but me. I take a deep breath, a sharp breath, and I add mentally with some force—no one else but me *and Sam.*

Quite suddenly I find that I need him. There are still ten minutes left on this car seat test, and now I'm shaking because I'm terrified. I dial Sam's cell and the call is picked up on the second ring. But the voice that comes down the line doesn't belong to Sam. It's Cathryn.

"Hi, Lexie—Sam had to go back into surgery. Can I get a message to him?"

I feel hot tears running over my cheek. I take a deep breath, and ask only for him to call when he gets a chance. I set the cell down on the table beside the car seat, and I look at Daisy again.

My head is full of information on how to care for a baby. I'm more than up to this challenge. Maybe if I tell myself that enough times, I'll start to believe it.

32

ANNIE

Luke,

Let's talk about my sister, shall we? I can tell by the way that you keep asking that you're dying to dig into that fucked-up mess of a relationship.

I'd lived away from Lexie for almost six years by the time things started to fall apart for me. She'd finished med school and was half-way through a residency at a hospital in Montgomery. We were far too busy to visit each other often, so we generally saw each other only for Thanksgiving or Christmas, but we still spoke on the phone every week—in fact, we hadn't missed a Sunday night call in the entire time we'd been apart.

But after I lost my job, my phone got cut off. I was in such bad shape by then—on the tail end of a weeklong binge—I didn't even realize it was Sunday and that she'd be calling. Monday morning, Lexie rang my office looking for me. They told her that I'd been fired, and she was on the next flight back to Chicago.

I had no idea who was thumping on my door that day. I ignored it at first—assuming it was probably my landlord, who was surely starting to wonder where my rent was. But the thumping continued, and then I heard someone yelling, so I eventually realized I had to answer it. I rolled over and sat up, and saw my kit on the floor beside the mattress. I dropped a pillow onto it, pulled a sweater on and stumbled to the peephole.

My stomach dropped when I saw Lexie. She was wild-eyed and panicked, and I turned to look at my apartment. The living area was completely empty—just books and garbage, and a tattered rug left in the middle of the floor. Of course I was aware of the space emptying out as I sold my possessions, but it was only in that moment that I really realized how little was left.

"Lexie! What are you doing here?" I asked, feigning delight to see her. I pulled her close for a hug and hoped I didn't smell too bad—when did I last shower? I had no idea.

She stared at me, and I felt like a specimen in a laboratory right up until the moment she said, "What the hell is going on, Annie?"

"What do you mean?" I asked her mildly, and then I followed her gaze to the empty apartment. "Oh, this? I'm moving."

"You're moving?" Her incredulity was palpable, but I shrugged easily.

"Yeah, I'm moving in with some friends. My furniture is already there."

"And your job? I called and they said you had been fired. I spoke to you last week and you didn't mention moving or being fired."

"I'm—" My mind was so foggy. I couldn't keep up with having to produce convincing lies on the fly. "I have a new job."

"It's three o'clock. You're at home, and you've been asleep. What kind of job do you have that lets you sleep in until three o'clock?"

"I work nights—"

Lexie wasn't buying it. She pulled away from me and started walking through the apartment, and I watched the slow dawn of horror on her face as she surveyed the garbage and the vast emptiness. She walked toward the bedroom and I caught her arm as she approached the door. I glanced inside and saw the pillow had only half covered the kit. The tourniquet was in plain sight beside it.

"Lexie, no—"

She shook me off and walked straight to the pillow. She pushed it out of the way with her foot, then raised her eyes and stared at me.

I know you counseling types like to talk about rock bottom, but I don't actually believe in it—because if it was actually a thing, that moment with Lexie would have been it, and we wouldn't be in this situation seven years later. That moment was worse than anything Robert had done to me, or even the ground falling out from under my world when I lost Dad. Lexie was staring at me with such terror and disgust that my skin was crawling with shame.

I ran into the room, picked up the kit and stuffed it back under the pillow as if that would somehow make her unsee it. Lexie walked right out of the room, and I stood alone for a moment, adrenaline pumping through me. I might have stayed there forever to avoid the looming confrontation, except that Lexie was now alone in my living area, and I couldn't remember where I'd hidden my stash. So I ran back out and found her standing in the middle of the empty space with her arms over her chest.

"You're going to rehab," she said flatly.

I opened my mouth to argue, but only the monster came out.

"Who do you think you are, you controlling bitch. You think you can come in here and fucking fix me? Really?" I laughed at the shock on her face, and then I took a step toward her. Lexie stepped back, away from me, and I saw the fear in her eyes and I

fed *off it.* "*You think you're so fucking perfect, don't you? Clever little Lexie, with her fucked-up-sister project. Well, Dr. Perfect, you can take your good intentions and your perfect life and you can get the fuck out of mine.*"

"*Annie, please—*"

Lexie's eyes were swimming in tears, but through the veil of moisture—they pleaded with me.

"*Fuck off, Lexie! You stupid, meddling bitch—*"

She'd backed all the way to the front door, and then I saw her turn and fumble for the handle. She was scared that I was going to hurt her, and she was right to be. As the door opened, I raised my hands and I pushed her. She stumbled into the hallway and landed against the wall—her face colliding hard as she fell to the floor. I didn't care—I didn't even check that she was okay. I slammed the door and then I turned what was left of my apartment upside down until I remembered that there was no stash left to find—I'd already used it. I needed a fix so bad that the inside of my brain felt like it was going to burn right through my skull, but there was only one thing left to hock.

I sold my computer that day.

I didn't even think to make a backup of the manuscript I'd written, or any of the dozens of stories and essays I'd finished.

I should have known it would take more than a physical assault to scare my sister away; she came right back the next morning. When I opened the door and saw her there, her face marked with ugly purple bruises, I burst into tears.

"*I need help,*" *I choked.*

"*I know,*" *she whispered, and she rushed to embrace me.* "*I know you do, love. But I'm here now, and we're going to sort this out. Okay?*"

It was months before Lexie told me Mom and Robert gave her the money for me to go to a private rehab clinic. Lexie hadn't spoken to them for almost nine years—but when she found out how long the wait list was for the public rehab centers, she felt she had no choice. I don't know if I would have gone if I'd known who was paying, but in the end, it didn't matter. I managed four days of the thirty-day inpatient program. On the fifth day, I got into an argument with a counselor who wanted me to sing at a group therapy session. I refused, she tried to make me and I inadvertently elbowed her in the face.

They escorted me to the door two hours later. When Lexie picked me up, she asked me how I was feeling, and then she casually asked me if I wanted to move to Montgomery to live with her for a while. She didn't yell or cry, or tell me she was disappointed. She simply offered an olive branch, and I grabbed at it with both hands.

If anything was ever going to work, it might have been that approach. Lexie's no-strings-attached love has been one of the only good things that has persisted in my lifetime. She put up with five years of my addiction before it got to be too much and she cut me off altogether—and even then, she reached that point only when I nearly got her fired.

I lived with her for most of that time—I rarely paid rent, hardly contributed around the house, regularly stole from her, went on and off methadone and Suboxone, got and lost countless jobs—I alienated her friends and scared away her boyfriends. I overdosed three times—twice in my bedroom, and for some reason I can't remember, once on the floor of her en suite bathroom. Lexie found and revived me three times. She kept syringes of Narcan in her handbag, and in her car, and in her cosmetics bag.

She found so many kinds of rehabs for me to try—I've done

271

them all. I'd always go when and where she asked—but honestly, I've never understood why she bothered. How many thousands of dollars do you sink into a person before it stops being selfless, and starts being ridiculous? How many times do you bother to revive someone who is nothing but a drain on you and society?

Do you know what impact I've had on her career? Not only did I nearly get her fired from her job at the clinic two years ago, but so much of the energy she should have been devoting to others has been wasted entirely on me.

So whenever you say to me "let's get Lexie in for family therapy" or "let's ask Lexie to write you an impact letter," it pisses me off—because you seem to fail to understand that I already know how much I've hurt her. I'm not oblivious to it—I've seen it first-hand. It's not that I don't care about how much pain I've caused my sister; I do. I'd give anything to undo what I've done to her. She is everything to me.

Sometimes I get high purely to escape the guilt of how much I've hurt her...and of course, I hurt her by using, so then I feel even worse, and I use again, and it just goes on and on. Now do you see why I told you that you didn't need to explain guilt spirals? I've been in one for seven fucking years.

I have been constantly shocked by the depths I've tumbled to—right from that morning after Lexie learned of my addiction, when the miserable look on her face was momentarily the most motivating factor on earth. But the impact of that moment would fade, just like every other "come to Jesus moment" I've skipped past over the years. Every time I decide to get clean, I seem to have the strength to decide it only once.

And you and I both know that sobriety is deciding to be clean—again, and again, and again—making a momentous, exhausting decision every second for the rest of your life. As I'm writing this, I've been here in the clinic for well over a month. The shit should be well and truly gone from my system, but every cell in my body still craves a fix. I have to ask myself a dozen times a minute if it's all worth it—can I even stand to stay here in this clinic for one more minute? Do I even have the strength to face one more minute of asking myself if I want to stay?

Because at the deepest levels of my soul, I don't want to stay here, Luke. I don't want to stay sober. I hate feeling like this—I hate how close I am to my pain. I hate how vivid the shame is. I need something between me and the rage, something to blur down its razor-sharp edges so I can stand to look at it.

But now there's Daisy and I want to see her and I don't want the edges of her world to be blurred to me. I want to know her. I want to be enough for her. And I just don't know how I can do it—with or without the smack.

33

LEXIE

When I get home, I lift Daisy's car seat out of the car, and I carry it carefully up the front steps to my front door.

I rest the seat on the ground, unlock the door, and then I pause. I turn around and stare at my front yard and into the street. I suddenly wish I'd let Sam take the day off to be here to welcome her. It doesn't feel right that I'm here alone for this moment.

This remarkable little girl, who at six weeks old has already been through something so difficult that most adults who attempt it fail, well—she deserves a whole community to embrace her and to celebrate her. Daisy Vidler is a triumph. She is a living, breathing miracle.

I look out across my street. Across the road, Mrs. Winters is tending her garden, and she sees me standing there staring out, and offers me a vaguely disinterested wave. A delivery truck rumbles past. In the distance a dog is barking. The world does not stop to celebrate this—the world doesn't even stop to contemplate it. I bend down and slip the car seat handle up onto my arm, and I see that she is awake. She has the pacifier in her mouth, but she is looking around, a gradually sharpening curiosity in her eyes.

"Come on, sweetheart," I say gently. "Come and see your home—your home for now, anyway."

So I take Daisy into our house, and I gently lift her from the car seat to keep her close as I walk around showing her each room. "This will be your room. This one is mine and Sam's. Here is a kitchen. Here is the backyard."

I feel like an idiot speaking to a baby, but I know that it needs to be done—how often have I told mothers and newborns that they should speak to their child to help their language development? I watched the nurses do this very thing all day at the hospital, and I have always felt too self-conscious to attempt it myself. But now she has *only* me. I could become overwhelmed again by the very thought of this, but I refuse to go there. And so I chat with Daisy. I chat as I set up her diapers and the new formula from the hospital pharmacy. And then, oddly, I keep chatting even after she is sleeping in her cot for the very first time.

When Sam comes home, I greet him with surprising enthusiasm. My mood has lifted. Some strange optimism has risen in me again now that Daisy is safe and well in our house.

"Well." Sam looks at me in surprise when I pull back from our kiss. "So, your first few hours alone with her are going well, then?"

I grin at him, then kiss him again. His skin is rough with stubble, and I rub my palm against his cheek.

"Takeout and beers tonight, to celebrate Daisy's release?" I murmur against his lips.

Sam smiles at me, but says gently, "Let's go easy on the beers. She *is* going to wake up for a feed every few hours."

I grimace, and then giggle, "What was that about you saying you are going to help me out with her?"

The landline rings, and I skip away from Sam to lift it to my ear.

"Hello?"

"Lex?" Of course it's Annie, and I squeal with excitement.

"Guess what? Guess who's here, in my house?"

"She's out of the hospital?" Annie gasps.

"Oh, yes, she is, Annie." I grin, and Sam winks at me as he walks into the house. I breathe deeply and say into the phone, "Don't worry. I've got photos of everything."

I hear Annie sniffle, and my smile fades just a little.

"Are you okay?"

"Of course I'm okay," she says, and there's a weak laugh. "Enough about me. Tell me more about Daisy. Where is she now?"

"She's sleeping in the cot in the room we set up for her. Don't worry, there's a baby monitor right next to her..."

It's an odd conversation, not because of what Annie and I talk about—but what we don't talk about. For ten entire minutes I fill her in on every single aspect of Daisy's care arrangements in my home, and it's only when we go to say goodbye that I ask again, "Why did you call, love? Is everything okay?"

"It was a tough day. But...hearing about Daisy has helped. I'm going to go now, okay? Take care of her for me."

"Of course," I say. "Always."

34

ANNIE

Luke,

I know you are pissed off at me (again), and I know that you're disappointed in me (again?). But I did try to warn you—I don't do singing or big groups of people, and I sure as hell don't do happy-clappy ceremonies. What about this is so difficult for you people to understand?

I can't *stand* it, okay? I'm not being difficult—*you* are being difficult. I'm doing what you asked—I'm trying to work with you. But you have to meet me halfway—what possible good will come from forcing me into a stupid group ceremony? Will I come out of it more sober? Will it cure my addiction? Will it bring me closer to getting Daisy back?

Unless the answer to these questions is "yes," then I'm not going.

Seriously, what are you going to do about it, drag me there?

35

LEXIE

The first time Daisy cries in the middle of the night, I think I'm dreaming. It escalates, but I ignore it for as long as I can, until eventually I shake Sam awake and ask, "Do you hear a baby crying?"

"Lex, it's *Daisy*," he mumbles, and I fly out of bed so fast I stumble over my own feet as I cross the hall. The next morning, I buy a bassinet so she can sleep in our room overnight.

It's strange gaining a baby so suddenly. There's an adjustment that needs to happen—and I spend that first weekend trying to figure out what it is because Sam and I don't quite know what to do with ourselves.

We divide up the backlog of half-done housework—he takes the laundry, I tackle the vacuuming and sweeping—but Daisy starts bellowing as soon as I start the vacuum so I pick her up to soothe her. It then feels like only five minutes later that the whole day has disappeared and Sam is talking about what to have for dinner.

"But what did we *do* today?" I ask him blankly. "How can it be dinnertime?"

"There were diapers…and bottles…" Sam looks at me, equally confused.

"I think this is what they call the 'newborn fog.'"

"I'm sure it'll pass," he says, and I laugh.

"Yeah, when she moves out."

Sam helps a lot over the weekend, but Monday looms, and I'll have a whole week alone with Daisy. I start to wonder when I should take Daisy to the rehab clinic—Annie hasn't seen her daughter for six weeks. As I'm thinking about this, it occurs to me that I haven't heard from Annie since I told her that Daisy was home with me, so I call Luke.

"Rehabilitation is sometimes about ups and downs," he says, and I groan at the ominous declaration.

"What happened?"

"First, the good news. She's really taken to that journal you sent up to us, so thanks for that."

"Excellent…and?"

"Well, we started the journaling project with the goal that she'd let me read it, and we're not quite there yet. Even so—it's helping her to open up—she's spoken to me about a few things already that were off-limits during our earlier chats."

"There's a *but* after all of this positive stuff, and the longer you prolong telling me what it is, the worse I'm expecting it to be."

"I've given your sister a lot of leeway since she arrived. We don't often get patients who are in the immediate post-partum period, and then of course, Annie chose to detox so quickly and that was very hard on her. So, she's been keeping to herself a lot and I've let her as she settled in—but she's a third of the way through her treatment now, and she's still not engaging with the other patients and staff. I can't let that persist—the community-building stuff we do is really very important for recovery. She told me she was going to come to this morning's group therapy session, then she didn't show up. So I had a discussion with her about it and she had some issues controlling her emotions around that."

"She lost her temper, right?" I sigh, and I shake my head. "She always does this…"

"It was fairly ugly."

"So, what happens now?"

"I had to issue her a caution. I'm hoping that will encourage her to comply with the basic community rules here."

"And if it doesn't?"

"I'll give her a day to think about it. If she's not at the community meeting on Wednesday, I'll issue her another caution."

"How many 'cautions' can she get?"

"Three. Then we ask her to leave."

I've been calm up until now, but as Luke says those words, my heart starts to race.

"Oh, shit."

"This isn't a disaster. It's just a minor stumbling block."

"So I was actually calling to see if I could visit…maybe with Daisy," I whisper, and I think he's going to laugh at the very idea, but Luke surprises me.

"You know what, Alexis? I think we might just dangle that carrot in front of her nose and see if it encourages her to move in the right direction. I've got a session with her this afternoon— I'll let you know how it goes."

36

ANNIE

Luke,

When I realized I was pregnant, I thought I'd found The Answer. You've probably heard other patients talk about the same idea—every addict knows about The Answer. It's the silver bullet that you think you need to fix your life—usually something that will cure the addiction—or even better, some way to solve your problems but allow you to keep right on using, which is what you really want to do.

I've sometimes thought the right rehab would be The Answer, or the right boyfriend, or for Lexie to be more supportive in some magical way or for Dad to come back somehow or for Mom to stop being so...disinterested. When I found out about Daisy I was both terrified and delighted—because if anything was going to fix me, surely it would be a baby.

All that I knew of getting high and being pregnant was that the two things did not go together, and so I decided I'd detox at home. I tried and failed a few times, and that made me despise myself even more. I'd be cursing aloud as I put the needle into my arm, then sobbing with guilt until the drug kicked in and I no longer cared.

Later, I'd promise her that was the very last time.

I hadn't spoken to Mom much over the years since she reconnected with Lexie...only on occasions where Lexie had called her and Mom was on the line when I took the phone so I knew I wouldn't have to speak to Robert. But when I realized I was pregnant, I needed Mom. It's crazy because since Dad died, she's hardly been mother-of-the-year material, but I thought somehow she could offer me some wisdom that would help me to be a good mom. I'd brace myself—I'd shoot up in the morning, and while I was still high enough to feel at peace, I'd dial her number on my cell. That way, even if Robert answered, the sound of his voice wouldn't send me into a tailspin that persisted for days.

To help survive those calls with Mom, I imagined that I was living a different life. I was living in a beautiful apartment in Montgomery and working at a small, independent literary magazine. My boss's name was Hector, and his secretary was Irma, and I was mostly reviewing and editing submissions. The money wasn't great, but I was getting by and doing well. I had a wide circle of friends but no boyfriend—I was concentrating on my writing on the side.

In reality, I was living in the baby's father's trailer, which was empty because he was in jail. Dale told me that he'd prepaid the rent for twelve months because he kept blowing his money and at least this way he knew he had somewhere to live for a year, and once he got locked up, it seemed a shame to let a comfortable, warm space like that go to waste. I'd been in a few god-awful crack dens since I left Lexie, and for a while I stayed with another dealer I knew— but then he started expecting sex every time he hooked me up with a fix, and that got old pretty quick. So Dale's shitty trailer was a marked improvement, but it was still a far cry from the beautiful home I lived in when I spoke with Mom.

Mom was also telling me lies of her own every time we talked because whenever I chatted with her, she was about to do something she was excited about. But I knew that in reality, Mom's role was to keep Robert happy and cared for. She wasn't there to live a full life. She was there to facilitate one for Robert.

And so, during those semifrequent conversations between Mom and me, we simply swapped lies—but at least we were connecting. I was hopeful that one day one of us would say something vulnerable or true and when we did, all of the walls would come down around us. But in those few months between my initiating those calls and my realizing I was just desperate enough to call Lexie, neither Mom nor I ever had the courage to be ourselves—and so, at the end of the day, all of the effort I'd put into trying to rebuild that bridge was wasted.

I still wound up alone, and I'm still a failure as a mom.

I know exactly what I was looking for by trying to connect with her again. It was her method of parenting. She'd been an amazing mother before Dad died—the perfect role model for who I know I need to be. One day, I'm going to get Daisy a beautiful big house like we used to have. I'm going to have a job—a career—maybe I'll get back on my feet and start writing again, maybe I'll even marry someone who can be a proper father to her. We'll have enough money for her to have opportunities and go to a good school and get a decent education.

Daisy deserves it. She deserves so much better than what I've given her so far. I have to promise myself and her that by the time she is old enough to understand any of this, I'll have my life sorted out.

I already know what you would say if I let you read this, Luke. You'd tell me that dream for Daisy is just a series of small, manageable steps—steps I don't need my mother for, particularly given where she's ended up. You'd tell me that the first step is simply to get myself to that community meeting tomorrow.

I don't know if that's true, but I'm out of other options, since you issued me that fucking caution last time. So I'm going to put that photo of Daisy in my pocket and I'm going to try to make myself go in the morning.

37

LEXIE

Luke asks me to come in for a family therapy session with Annie. I pack my SUV, loading it with diapers and wipes and bottles and formula and pacifiers and every other thing I can think of, then Daisy and I set off on the journey toward her mother.

She's unsettled on the way, and I stop four times before we even reach the highway. I give her a pacifier. I adjust her seat belt in case it's uncomfortable. I even dangle a brightly colored toy from the straps above her, thinking it might distract her. Nothing works. And a squawking infant in the back seat is much more unsettling than I had anticipated, so I quickly become frustrated.

"Come on, Daisy Nell," I groan, when she starts grizzling for a fifth time. "I thought babies were supposed to sleep in cars! Don't you want to see your momma?"

The sound of my voice—frustrated though the tone may be—seems to console her a little, and a thought strikes me. I start to sing, and she falls silent.

Twinkle, twinkle, little star.
Do you know how loved you are?
In the morning.

In the night.
I'll love you with all my might.
Twinkle, twinkle, little star…

It's amazing how that song takes me all the way back to when Annie came home from the hospital as a baby. It's one of my very first memories—standing in the doorway to her bedroom, watching as Mom fed her and then sung that song as she laid her onto the cot. I remember the soft lamplight and the look of sheer adoration on Mom's face, and how jealous I felt of Annie. I also know that I used to sing that very song to Annie once we moved to the community, and so I try to take myself back to *those* memories. On a scientific level, I find it fascinating that it is so much harder for me to recollect details from that period than it is to remember my happier, early childhood memories.

My voice trails off, and Daisy stirs and then bellows, so I start again. And then again, and again, until I've sung the same damned, maddening verse the entire hour it takes me to get to the rehab clinic. Even once she's fallen silent, I don't want to stop in case she cries again, so I just keep singing.

When we pull into the parking lot at the rehab clinic, I finally stop the song. Daisy doesn't stir, and I breathe a sigh of relief. I clip her car seat into the stroller and push it carefully into the rehab center.

Last time I came, I ran to Annie. This time she runs toward me, but she ignores me altogether. Instead, she crowds over the car seat and reaches to touch her sleeping daughter's face with visibly trembling hands. Annie doesn't say a word. She doesn't even cry—she simply stares, as if she's completely awed by her daughter. I let her stand there until the minutes start to stretch, and then I touch her back gently and ask, "Are we meeting Luke somewhere?"

Annie shakes herself as if I've startled her, but then she takes the handles of the stroller from me. I'm delighted to see her take the initiative, but I'm somehow offended at the same time. Suddenly I start to worry that perhaps I'm getting a bit too caught up in this whole playing-Daisy's-mother game, and does that mean I'm getting too attached? I follow Annie to a table, where she sets the stroller close to her and rocks it gently as she raises her gaze to mine. I smile at her, but she simply stares at me. I can't read her either—is she upset?

"Annie?" I prompt gently, and she looks back to the baby. "Luke said he wanted to speak to us together. Are we supposed to meet him somewhere?"

"Not yet," Annie says. She leans down and rests her head against the stroller's sun visor, staring at the baby. "Let's just take a few minutes alone. You need to bring her here more often. I need to be reminded why I have to make this work."

"Annie, I thought we agreed you'd meet with Lexie and Daisy in my office." Luke approaches us, and I rise and shake his hand.

"Hello, Luke."

"Welcome back, Alexis. There's been some confusion. Annie? Weren't you coming straight in to see me?"

"I just want to see *my* baby for a minute without supervision," Annie says flatly. She tries to stare him down, and I feel a shiver of fear run through me. I know that look on her face, the narrowing of her eyes and the pinch of her lips as she presses them together. That look has never preceded anything good.

"Maybe we can come in to you in a few minutes?" I suggest to Luke hesitantly, but he ignores me—his gaze is on Annie.

"I agreed to this visit on the condition that we conduct a family therapy session at the same time. Annie, you simply cannot change our agreement now. I'll give you some time alone with Lexie and the baby at the end, *after* we talk. Okay?"

Annie's hands are balled in fists. I can see the part of her that just wants to be with her baby, battling against the part that wants to counter Luke's authority. She stares at the baby, motionless, and I don't know what to do. I want to help her. I *need* to help her. Just as I open my mouth to suggest again that Luke give us a few minutes, Annie rises sharply and walks off, pushing the stroller in front of her. I stand, too, but Luke gently touches my upper arm.

"Let me handle this. She *needs* you to let me handle this. Got it?"

It's my turn to stare down an internal battle. I keep glancing at Annie and the rapidly disappearing stroller, then at Luke, who is determined—staring at me with the question lingering in his eyes.

"Okay," I say eventually, and then I walk quickly after my sister into his office.

"I like to start these sessions by touching base with our feelings," Luke says. "I'll go first. Today, I'm feeling frustrated because I had an agreement with you, Annie. I thought I'd been generous in allowing this visit in order to win your trust, but the first thing you did was to go against the terms we'd discussed. Your turn."

"I'm feeling pissed off because I'm an adult woman and a mother and I shouldn't have to give in to your blackmail in order to see my daughter," Annie says flatly.

They both look at me. I stare between them blankly.

"Uh—I don't know?"

"There's no right answer," Luke says patiently, and I adjust my skirt and glance around the room while I try to think of something to say.

"Just say what you're feeling so we can get this over and done with," Annie says sharply. She's looking at the floor, but I can see from the way she's holding herself that she's a tinderbox of anger just waiting to explode. Her arms are crossed over her chest, her eyebrows are knitted and her lips are still in that tight, furious line.

"I'm feeling scared," I whisper. Annie's eyebrows momentarily dip as she ponders this, and then she looks at me.

"Go on," Luke prompts, and I clear my throat and admit, "I can see that Annie is on edge. I know how much she has to lose. I'm scared."

"Are you scared for Annie, or for yourself?" Luke asks.

"Or for Daisy?" Annie says, and I look at the sleeping baby, then back to her mother.

"For you. Only for you."

"I can handle myself," Annie whispers to me, and Luke leans forward in his chair and rests his elbows on his knees as he prompts me, "How does that make you feel, Lexie? When Annie says she can handle herself?"

"It's not a 'how' I feel, it's a 'what' I feel. I want to argue with her, and point out to her how wrong she is. If she could handle herself, we wouldn't be *in* this situation."

"Put some emotions to it, Lexie. We want to talk about the feelings now, not the action they inspire."

"Can I take this one?" Annie interrupts, and I look at her in surprise. Luke nods silently, and Annie stares at me as she says, "You're feeling frustrated. Because you think that I need you to baby me, and I don't want to let you right now."

"I'm frustrated," I concede. "But not because you won't let me 'baby you.' I'm frustrated because we might end up in a situation where I'll *have* to baby you."

"How would *you* feel, Lexie? If you had a newborn and you had to agree to humiliating therapy sessions just to get five minutes alone with her?"

"If I was in your situation, I'd be embarrassed and angry," I agree. "But I'd be angry at myself, not the people who were trying to help me."

"He isn't trying to help me right now," Annie hisses, and her face reddens. "He's trying to control me. Don't you see that?"

"He's trying to get you to a place where you can give yourself over to the process and get *clean*."

"We don't use the word *clean* in here, Lexie," Luke interrupts me. "We use the word *sober*." When I frown at him, he explains gently, "What's the opposite of *clean*?"

"*Dirty*," Annie snaps, and she stands. "Which is what I am—a dirty, filthy junkie. Fuck this and fuck both of you."

She's raised her voice, and Daisy stirs. I watch as Annie's expression shifts from fury to horror in an instant. I see the guilt as it rises in her eyes, and then she glances helplessly toward me. I rise, too, and extend a hand toward her hesitantly.

"You *aren't* dirty," I say desperately. "Please don't say that, Annie. I shouldn't have said *clean*—it's just a throwaway word— I won't use it anymore. Please sit down and let's do this. *Please*. Then I'll stay and you can have some time with Daisy. She's going to need a bottle soon and a diaper change and then she *loves* to cuddle and play. So, *please*, Annie—please—I know it's hard but I promise it will be worth it."

By the time I finish speaking, my voice is breaking and there are tears in my eyes. Annie looks back to the baby, then she slowly, carefully lowers herself back into her seat and looks to Luke.

"Go on then," she prompts him pointedly. "Shrink me."

In the next hour, I see firsthand what Luke is up against. He asks a question, Annie deflects it. He tries again, she responds with sarcasm. He tries again, she shuts down. It's not just the big, deep questions that she responds to this way—it's even the simple ones, like how she's feeling about her progress at the center, or what her plans are for the next week, or how she felt at the whole-community meeting that she dragged herself to this morning.

I'm not sure what he hoped to achieve by having me here. I'm only making things worse, because as I watch Annie block all of Luke's attempts to get her to open up, I interject again and again, imploring her to drop the attitude or to just *try*—and every time I do, Luke patiently asks me to save my comments for engaging in the session myself, rather than trying to facilitate it. Right on cue when the hour is up, Daisy starts to cry. Luke asks for a few minutes alone with Annie, so I take the baby to a small kitchenette and prepare her formula.

Then I take the bottle back to Luke's office so that Annie can feed her daughter.

"If you're comfortable with this, Lexie, perhaps Annie could take Daisy into the dining hall to feed her, so you and I can chat alone?" Luke asks. Annie immediately stiffens.

"Why wouldn't she be *comfortable* with it?" she snaps, and Luke shrugs.

"Lexie *is* Daisy's legal guardian at the moment."

"I'm her *mother*."

"Of course I'm comfortable," I say hastily, and I push the stroller toward Annie and point to the bottle. "She will probably only drink half of that, and then if you sit her up for a while so she can burp..."

"Fine."

Annie pushes Daisy from the room, and Luke quietly closes the door behind her.

"That was actually a very productive session," he says as he returns to his desk. I stare at him in disbelief.

"You've got to be kidding me."

"Let me tell you what some of our other therapy sessions have looked like. Annie sits and stares out the window. Annie writes in her journal but refuses to look at me. Annie throws insults at me and tries to hook me personally. Annie just doesn't show up. Annie shows up, but turns her chair to face the other way."

My heart sinks.

"So, we're doomed, then?" I whisper, and he shakes his head.

"None of this is atypical with court-mandated patients. Sobriety isn't actually something a court can force onto a person."

"What's the plan from here?"

"I didn't ask you to stay back to talk about the plan. I wanted to ask you how *you* felt about what just happened, and to check in with how you're coping."

"I found that session to be frustrating and bewildering, but I'm coping just fine."

"You and your sister have a very special bond, don't you?"

"We do."

"What's the best outcome from all of this for you, Alexis?"

"Annie graduates your program and is well again."

"Be more specific. What does that look like?"

"She…" I hesitate. "She can resume life the way it was before the addiction. She can write, get a job, have a healthy relationship. Get a house. Care for Daisy."

"What about *your* relationship with her, Lexie? What would *that* look like?"

"We'd be friends again," I whisper, then out of nowhere, I'm crying and I can't stop myself.

"How long has it been since you and Annie were *friends*? Your relationship seems almost parental to me."

"Well—yes. It has been, but not always. When she lived with me, I got glimpses of friendship all the time. My best memories of her were when she'd write some brilliant little vignette and she'd let me read it, and then we could talk about it like two scholars… I'd comment on how great the premise was, she'd tell me about something she was trying to achieve…or she'd write a poem, and there'd be this incredible depth to it, and she'd explain it to me and I'd be in awe of her mind and the way she could just *see* something magnificent in the ordinariness of life. Or we'd go out for coffee on a Saturday morning and we'd talk about politics, or the weather—or some cute guy sitting near us or what boots we wanted to buy for the winter. She probably doesn't even remember those moments, but…" I choke on a sob and admit, "I'm living for them. I grieve them. I *miss* the Annie that I shared those things with. She's still in there—behind the

wall the substance abuse has put between us. And I'd give anything to get her back."

"Sometimes to draw something out of a person, we have to
approach them differently. Do you know how you were approaching Annie in those moments of friendship, Lexie?"

"I don't know what you mean."

"Our parents see a very different side of us than our friends
do." Luke shrugs. "I know you've needed to parent Annie, and
after watching you two interact today and speaking to you over
the last few weeks, I think it's become a habit to you. Do you
know what I'd like to suggest? Try being her *friend*."

I stare at Luke, and I try to figure out how I could implement
his advice. *What* is the difference between my parenting Annie,
and being her friend?

Then it hits me: the difference is responsibility. A friend can
offer support, even advice...but a friendship is a two-way street,
and friends hold none of the responsibility for each other's actions. Being Annie's friend means letting go of my ownership
of her outcomes.

"I'll try," I whisper, and Luke gives me a satisfied nod.

I find Annie in the dining hall, sitting in a corner. She's angled
the stroller in front of herself, so that it creates a barrier from the
rest of the room. She has Daisy resting on the table, but she's
supporting her head and shoulders with her palms.

Annie is talking to her daughter quietly. She's smiling, but her
face is wet with tears. I don't want to intrude, so I hang back,
standing in the doorway of the office wing. After a while, Annie
notices me and motions for me to join them.

"See what I'm up against with him?" she says as soon as I sit
down, and the bubble of joy I've floated on as I watched her
with her baby deflates in an instant.

"Have you written any poetry since you came here?" I ask
Annie, and her stare is incredulous.

"I've been kind of busy."

"I miss your poetry. I miss those stories you used to write."

She looks back to Daisy.

"Maybe I could write something for her," she says after a while.

"Did you love writing, Annie?"

"You know I did."

"Why did you stop?"

"It seemed pointless. No one wants to hear what someone like me has to say."

"I do."

Annie swallows.

"I'm writing this journal for Luke. It has…it has *everything* in it. All about me." She glances at me. "Maybe you could read it someday."

"Are you going to let Luke read it, too?"

"I don't know. I'm scared to."

"What are you afraid of?"

"I'm afraid that…loads of things. I'm afraid that he'll pity me. I'm afraid that he'll use it to control me. At the moment, all of the things in that journal are *mine*. They are my secrets, my perspective on the world—I have nothing left but that."

Daisy burps suddenly—the sound surprisingly loud for such a tiny person. Annie and I laugh together, our gazes locking, our faces fixed in smiles. The moment is perfect, and I'm still smiling when I say, "I need to buy some new boots. When you're out of here, do you want to come shopping with me? I have no idea what kind to get. We could go get lunch or a coffee after and talk, like we used to."

Annie looks at me as if I've lost my mind, then she starts to laugh again.

"Sure, Lexie. In two months' time, at the start of spring when I finally get out of this shithole, we'll go buy you some nice warm boots that you won't wear until next winter."

★ ★ ★

I'm feeling positive after the visit to rehab, and Annie calls every night over the next week. They are brief calls, but they are also calm and uneventful—she calls only to inquire about Daisy's welfare. I ring Mom to update her, and when she asks me if I think Annie is going to make it this time, I'm not lying when I say yes.

All of this makes it a complete shock when Luke calls a week later to tell me that Annie has walked out. He tells me that right at dawn, she packed up all of her belongings and she walked out the front doors.

He called when I was dressing Daisy, but I answered anyway because I saw it was him. Now I'm standing frozen in my bedroom, with Daisy wearing only a diaper and the bottom half of her romper. Everything within me grinds to a halt, and I'm holding the phone with one hand and Daisy with the other, and I can't form a single coherent thought.

It's funny how every single thing in your life can shatter with a single decision; and not a decision I had any control over. Everything is suddenly broken, and there is nothing I can do to fix it.

I unfreeze, and then I'm racing—my thoughts and my heart rate and my emotions. I'm panicking and terrified, and I'm sick from the news—nauseous, literally—waves of rolling anxiety that start at my head and work their way down to my toes and it's all I can do to hold on to Daisy and the phone and stay upright. I'm violently shaking by the time I steer myself to the bed and sit on the edge.

"The staff tried to stop her," Luke says now. "She was determined to go." I'm listening to him, but although the phone is at my ear and the volume is fine, it feels like he's calling me from very far away. Still, I hear the apology and the regret in his tone. It is no consolation that Daisy's rehabilitation counselor sounds upset about this, no salve to my wound that he obviously had high hopes for her, too, because I understand what this means. This is the end of Luke's journey with Annie, and once again, the entirety of her mess is about to fall on me.

This feels a lot like the time I tried to call Annie and realized her phone had been disconnected, and then I called her office and was shocked to find out she lost her job. It feels a lot like having the ground giving way beneath my feet yet again. I should be used to this sinking sensation. I shake myself and bring Daisy down from my shoulder into the crook of my elbow, and I pull a blanket out of her bassinet and cover her with it so she doesn't get cold. And then, once I'm sure Daisy is completely fine, I press through the shock and find the cognizance to ask, "Did something happen?"

"She went to a group therapy session yesterday for the first time. I thought that was a positive step. I honestly have no idea, Alexis. But as you'll understand, I've had to report her absence to the courts."

"Do you know what happens now?" I croak.

"I think you'd better ask a lawyer that question. I'm so sorry," Luke says. The conversation is wrapping up, but I don't want to get off the phone. Once I hang up, I'll have to figure out what to do next, and I'm still too shocked to make plans. Still, I can't think of a way to prolong the call and Luke closes the conversation with platitudes. "I really thought we could help her. I hope that somehow, this is the start of a new chapter for your sister."

When I hang up, I walk around the house in some kind of shocked daze, carrying my half-dressed niece beneath her blanket. I stare out the window, over the guesthouse and the backyard. I straighten the cushions on the sofa and I turn the television on and off several times before I realize that I'm caught in a loop.

Annie has left the rehab clinic. Annie is going to be arrested.

At this thought, I finally shake myself out of my daze and call Bernie. After I explain the situation, her take on things is grim.

"They'll issue a warrant for her arrest. Like I told you in the hospital, if she'd gone through with the mandated treatment she might have been able to avoid the chemical endangerment charge—but there's no chance of that now. If and when she surfaces—they'll probably take her straight into custody and I doubt she'd get bail."

"Surely there's something we can do. Surely." I guess I'm up to the bargaining step of the grief process, because I'm already talking money. "I don't care what it costs. Are there other lawyers we could bring in? Specialists, maybe." At Bernie's silence, I up the volume on my plea. "Bernie, there has to be *something we can do.*"

"We've done what we can do Alexis, I'm so sorry." Bernie sighs gently. "Annie had a second chance, and when she walked out of that rehab clinic, she blew it."

She blew it. I'm sick again as I let myself consider what this means. There are no loopholes, no more second chances to make good. Annie is at the end of the road, and the next step in her journey is inevitably jail.

I'm still holding Daisy, but she starts to cry, and I realize I'm crushing her against my chest. I force my locked muscles to soften around her, and stare down at her perfect little face. What does this mean for Daisy? Nothing, in a practical sense today—I'll still finish dressing her eventually, give her the bottle when she cries for it, change her diapers.

But this means everything for this little girl longer term. Her entire world has just been rocked, and she doesn't even know it yet.

"Lexie, I have court soon, so I have to go. Is there anything else I can do for you at this point?" Bernie says very carefully.

"What do I tell her? If she contacts me?"

"If she contacts you, tell her to turn herself in immediately. And the second you hang up the phone, call me. There's probably not a lot we can do, but if she does it quickly, we can say that it was a wild impulse and she's very regretful and desperate to try again."

Now I'm on autopilot—pretending I'm functioning because I can't yet think through all of the implications of this development. When I try to cast myself forward, to make a plan for how I'll deal with all of the ways this can play out, my mind just… stops. It's too much. It's too final. So I don't think, and I don't plan—instead, I tend to Daisy and I put a roast on for dinner for Sam and I don't even call him to tell him what's happened because I'm not yet ready to hear his sympathy or face his questions about *what next?*

This means that when he walks in the door at 6:00 p.m., Sam is smiling and he's chatting about his day. I nod and sometimes I smile but now I've avoided it for so long and I don't know how to tell him. It's only when we sit down to dinner that he says, "Honey, you look so pale. Are you okay?"

I tilt my head at him, and I feel like I'm trying to reach him through a pea-soup-thick fog of shock. How do I say the words?

"Lex?" Sam is on his feet, and he approaches me and crouches beside me. His gaze searches mine. "Did something happen?"

"Annie," I say, and I turn to him and I say through numb lips, "Annie left."

And the walls all crash down around me, and if I really ever was a "fixer" and a "coper," then maybe I'm not anything at all now, because things are broken so badly that I can't do a single thing to sort out this mess.

38

ANNIE

This entry is not for Luke. I don't even know who I'm writing to anymore. I'm just writing out of habit now.

I left the rehab clinic. I'm sitting under a bus stop halfway back to Montgomery. I hitchhiked here, but the truck driver had to turn off. I was going to flag down another car, but then I thought that maybe I should go back and now I just don't know what to do so I'm sitting here, and I'm lost in the truest sense of the word.

I know that all I had to do was tell Luke that the thought of sitting in the big group therapy sessions made me so anxious that I couldn't sleep at night. Those words would be liberating, like so many of the others that I've never managed to say. Luke would have given me that kindly, patronizing look and proposed some overtly simple solution. Medication, perhaps, or maybe just some compromise where we could talk about my anxiety before he forced me to go.

But instead, I did what I always do. I was ashamed of my failure, and the shame spawned the monster, and I let it loose. Now I'm in the deepest hole of my life.

I'm going to jail. I keep saying those words to myself, trying to wrap my mind around what it means. I gather all of the facts I know about prison and try to piece together a picture of what my future looks like. I'm not actually scared of losing my freedom. I mean...maybe I would be, if my life wasn't already such a disaster zone. No, I'm only scared of the distance from Daisy, and the permanence of a conviction. One day my sentence will end, but I'll be a felon. For all of the mess of my existence until now, I've managed to avoid labels that would hinder me from rebuilding a life worth keeping. How will I get a house for Daisy? How will I get a job? Those problems are far in my future, I know, but they loom large in my mind now because a conviction is almost like the final straw for me. Things are already awful, but once I'm convicted, the hope is fading that things would someday, somehow be better.

I've met Judge Brown only once. He spent twenty minutes with me, he dropped a bomb on me and then he walked away. He had no understanding of where I've come from, or where I want to go. I tell myself he was trying to protect Daisy—and isn't that what I want, too?

But I'm more than a mother, and although I barely feel it right now, I'm more than an addict, too. I'm a person and I have a history and fears and flaws and strengths, and I deserved for the court to understand me before they made a ruling that tried to shoehorn me into a box. Rehab has never worked for me—the social pressures are simply too demanding.

And now, as expected, I've lost my temper and I've walked out of the rehab facility and they'll arrest me. And all because of one more bad decision, *it might be years before I get Daisy back, if I ever can at all.*

What do I do now? What I want is to go to Daisy—to take her in my arms and remind myself why I have to do better. I want for Lexie to make me a cup of tea and to calmly talk all of this through and help me figure out a solution.

But I know that I can't do that. The last place in the world I can go today is to Lexie's house. She told me the address, but if I go there, I can only imagine that she'd have to call the police.

So what alternative is there?

It's calling to me even now—the sweet bliss of relief and release. All I need to do is flag down a car, find some cash and get in touch with my old network. I could have a bag of powder in my hands in an hour. I'm already telling myself that if I get high, I'll be able to think clearer and I'll find a solution to this tangled mess. If I get high, I'll feel brave again and I'll be able to do the right thing, whatever that is. This will not be the first time I've convinced myself that heroin will give me courage instead of rob me of my dignity.

But I've been sober for weeks—if I use now, I lose the ground I've gained. Unlike just about everything else in life, sobriety absolutely is a black-and-white issue—you are actively using, or you aren't. And the call of the high is so strong that it seems inevitable, but so much of my life has seemed inevitable—and where has that got me? Why do I rail only against the things that could help me, and never against my habit toward self-destruction?

I don't have any of the answers. I don't know which way to turn to find a light at the end of the tunnel. I just know that I'm blocked in on all sides, but it's my own fault, and no matter what I do now, I'll probably be taken away from my daughter and put in jail.

The thing is…there's not much about this life I have left that's worth staying sober for. Not without Daisy.

Oh, Daisy.

I remember watching the pregnancy test while the second line became visible. I knew by then. I'd felt you moving...gentle butterflies, unmistakably new sensations that spoke to a monumental shift in the purpose of my body. These skin and bones have had little purpose over the past thirty years other than as a magnet for abuse; by others and even myself. But then suddenly, a miracle happened within this body, and everything should have changed, and everything did change.

When I saw that second line, I stopped floating through my days. Oh, you might doubt that now, since I'm still a walking disaster but... I haven't had purpose since I let go of my dreams all of those years ago. But then I had you, and I had something to live for. I still stumbled. I still failed. But I kept trying, because when you were under my heart, I felt like my optimism had returned.

I feel so desperate now, Daisy. That word just isn't big enough for this feeling, but it's the closest I can use to describe it. I feel like I'm struggling for air, struggling for hope, and it's all my fault and I've ruined everything for the both of us.

Well. Not the both of us. You're in Aunt Lexie's house right now, and if it's half the home she described to me, then you're in a very nice place indeed...certainly a better place than I could have offered you.

Maybe a better place than I can ever offer you now.

I don't know what to do now. I don't know where to go or who to call.

And I can sit here all day and all night and I can fill all of these pages with this despair, but at the end of the day, I'm going to have to take a step in some direction.

Or curl up and die here.

I actually wish it were that simple.

39

LEXIE

Sam insists that we at least try to find her, although we both know it's pointless. We drive all the way across the city to the trailer. It's the only place I can think to look, but I know as soon as we turn into her street that she's not there— the lights are off. I bang on the door anyway and think seriously about smashing my way in. Sam leaves the car eventually and he takes my hand.

"We'll try again tomorrow," he promises. I scrawl a note on the back of a receipt and jam it in her door, but even as we drive away I keep glancing over my shoulder, hoping to see some sign of movement in the trailer. I don't even know if she's come back to Montgomery. The clinic is all the way up in Auburn, and she has no money at all. How would she even get here?

The ride home feels much longer than the drive to the trailer, because at least there was a small piece of hope that we'd find her. Now Sam and I sit in a silence that is punctuated only occasionally by a gurgle or coo from the back seat. Daisy is an unspoken question between us. At some point, I'm going to have to ask it aloud.

What do we do with Daisy?

"It's going to be okay," Sam says, and I know his intentions are good, but the throwaway phrase irritates me.

"Really? *How?*"

"She'll turn up, Lexie."

"Sure, Sam. Sure she'll turn up. In a fucking body bag or a jail cell."

I hear his sharp intake of breath and I know that he's hurt by my sharp tone, and I squeeze my eyes shut and try to bring my emotions back under control. Everything feels so confused. Sam is my refuge, but Sam is irritating me. Annie is the cause of all of this pain, but she's the one I'm most concerned for.

And then there's Daisy. Beautiful, innocent Daisy. She's safe and well, but she's actually the victim here.

"Sorry," I whisper, and my eyes are still closed but Sam's hand lands gently on my knee.

"It's okay," he murmurs. "I just wish there was something more I could say. But there isn't."

"No," I whisper. "There really isn't."

I finally open my eyes so that I can stare out at the road as Sam steers the car toward home. There's a cacophony of questions bouncing around in my mind—endless "what-ifs" and "why didn't I's?" and even a few "if only she…" But it's just so hopeless, and now I'm thinking back on my optimism over the last few weeks and realizing just how much harder this hurts because I finally let myself hope that Annie might be getting better.

There is nothing to do but wait. Other than Daisy's still-regular hospital visits, my days now revolve around which of two terrible phone calls is going to come.

Will it be the police letting me know she's been picked up?

Or will it be Annie—inevitably high and in a panic about what she's done?

Several days crawl past me. I phone Mom, just in case Annie reaches out to her.

"She left," I say.

"But...didn't she have to stay? For the judge?"

"Yes."

"Why did they let her leave?"

"It wasn't a prison, Mom. Annie had to stay to avoid being charged, but she could leave anytime she wanted."

"But...you said it was going well." Mom is confused and disappointed, and I completely understand.

"Mom, you know what she's like."

"I *don't* know what she's like anymore. Until you called me and told me she'd had the baby, I thought she was thriving."

"Well, maybe if you left your cult every now and again to come and be with us you'd know our lives a bit better."

"Alexis, that is so unfair."

Everything about this situation feels unfair, but I know I shouldn't have said that to Mom. I sigh and look down at Daisy, who is resting on my thighs, watching me.

"I'm sorry, Mom. She's in so much trouble this time, I don't think there's anything we can do for her."

"Robert says that she will come back to the Lord in time," Mom whispers, but even she doesn't sound convinced anymore.

There's a knock at the door four days after Annie walked out of rehab, and when I answer it, Mary Walters is standing there. Her hair is in a bun, and she's wearing the same cheap suit. She holds her clipboard up against her body like it's part of her uniform.

I'm wearing pajamas and I can't remember the last time I brushed my hair, and I flush because I know this is not a friendly visit—it's surely an unannounced welfare check. Maybe she's even here to gloat, because I'm sure that this woman has been anticipating this moment since the first time we met.

"Dr. Vidler," Mary says brightly. I hesitate before I meet her gaze. If I see triumph there, I'm not sure how I'll contain myself. I take a deep breath and force myself to look into her eyes.

All I see is sadness, and the air leaves my lungs in a rush.

"Hi," I say, and I feel completely humbled. Mary's smile is kind, and I remember thinking that perhaps I might have liked her, had we met under other circumstances. Looking at her now, I have no doubt her intentions are good.

"Just wanted to visit and see how you're doing. And to check in on beautiful little Daisy, of course," Mary says warmly.

I let her in, and this time there is no opportunity to hide the piles of laundry or clear the tables, and the little stain near the sink is the least of my worries. I make cups of tea, and we sit on the sofa, and Mary holds Daisy and comments at how well she looks and then she asks me a series of questions about our routine and Daisy's health. And when the tea is gone, and Daisy really needs to go down for a nap, Mary stands to leave and finally addresses the elephant in the room.

"I really hoped I was wrong, you know," she says quietly. "About your sister. I sure am sorry that things have gone the way they have."

"Me, too," I say as my throat constricts.

"I just want to say one thing to you, Dr. Vidler. I'm sure that right now this situation feels as dire as can be, but even with your sister in a whole world of trouble, your situation is still one of the easier ones I'll deal with this year." As I gape at her incredulously, she shrugs. "I don't have any other substance-abuse cases on my books where the children have slotted right into a well-established, caring home that can afford to provide for all of their needs. The vast majority of my drug cases end with the momma in prison and the babies in foster care, and I don't need to tell you that arrangement rarely leads to positive outcomes for anyone."

"So why prosecute them?" I ask her unevenly. "Why do they

think that sending a woman to jail under these circumstances is going to help anyone?"

"Well, if I can say something just between you and me for just a moment..."

I'm surprised, but I nod.

"Of course."

"We hold our pregnant woman on a pedestal in this society. We say we want the best thing for babies, so we want to tell their mommas what to eat, what they can drink, what drugs they can use...and there's good intentions there, and maybe it's the kind of thing that's too nuanced to draw lines across but... for *sure* there's a vein of misogyny here, too. Women who use drugs in pregnancy have fallen off the pedestal, and don't we all just love to punish them for that?"

Mary glances at Daisy, and then back to me, and she adds quietly, "In the last few years I've heard all sorts of politicians talking about compassion for people with addiction, but you know what I've never heard? No one *ever* talks about compassion for women who are pregnant *and* have addictions. Maybe we're progressing to the point that we realize that a raging addiction isn't exactly a lifestyle choice, but we're worlds away from applying that same logic to women who happen to be pregnant. We want our mommas to be perfect, and when they stumble and fall, we punish them instead of offer a helping hand, and then we call it *deterrence*."

Mary slips her handbag onto her shoulder and she straightens her suit jacket as I digest this, and then she adds very quietly, "If you ask me, if the state really wanted to help women like your sister, wouldn't they put the thousands of dollars they'll spend on her trial and incarcerating her into early intervention programs, or research into addiction? Or Lord, if it's really *all* about the baby—wouldn't you funnel the funds into setting up a better foster care system or maybe some parenting classes that actually *help*?"

"So why don't they?" I ask, and Mary sighs and shakes her head.

"Well, it's a little bit like this. Half the town is on fire, and the townspeople are all so busy hollering for the fire brigade that no one thinks to find out why people are still playing with matches."

I'm still untangling that analogy hours after Mary is gone. One thing I know for sure, though, is that although she's played a part in the process that's led to Annie's current situation, Mary Walters is not the enemy. She is a well-intentioned cog in the wheel of a system that is just not up to its task.

A few days later, Bernie tells me that the arrest warrant has been issued.

"If you hear from her now," she warns me, "you need to call it in. Immediately. And if she comes to your house, turn her away—or at least, take her straight to a police station. Harboring a fugitive is a felony in Alabama—so if you are in *any* way seen to be protecting her, you can be charged, too. The last thing little Daisy needs is for the both of you to wind up behind bars."

My role has changed now that Annie is officially on the run. Until now, I've been an important player in this scenario—as a support person to Annie and as stand-in mother to Daisy. But that was when Annie's chemical endangerment charge was theoretical, and now it's a cold, hard fact that we need to deal with. Annie is a fugitive, and my obligations shift from the moral realm to the legal one.

If she dares to contact me, I have no choice but to turn her in. Because if I don't—if I help her to hide—then I'll fail at those other, more important roles as her supporter and as Daisy's care-taker. When I first hang up with Bernie, I'm certain that even if Annie walked through my front door *right now*, I'd struggle to call the police or take her to the station. But once I grapple with it, I realize that it's all out of my hands now. I have to prioritize Daisy's welfare.

So I stop hoping and praying that Annie will contact me, and start hoping and praying that she won't—because our relationship has somehow survived a million ups and downs and twists and turns, but I'm pretty sure *this* would be the thing that shatters it.

More days pass and the stable routine Daisy and I have starts to wobble a little. I worry that she's feeding off my anxiety. Her mild irritability builds slowly, until one night, she simply won't be settled. I take her downstairs so that Sam can get some sleep, and then I pace the halls for hours. I sing, I rock, I swaddle—but nothing works. I can get her to sleep in my arms, but as soon as I try to put her down, the crying starts all over again.

When the morning finally comes, I'm so tired I feel sick. My limbs are heavy, and I can barely keep my eyes open through my thumping headache.

When Sam comes downstairs, he takes one look at me on the couch with Daisy and he heads straight to the coffee machine. He returns with two steaming mugs, which he sets on the coffee table, then gently gestures that he wants to take Daisy from my arms.

"You should have woken me up. I could have helped."

"You have to work today. I can sit around the house and be a cranky, tired mess," I say, but I gratefully pass the baby to him and reach for the coffee. "I think she's upset because I am. I just couldn't calm her."

Sam frowns as he adjusts her in his arms, then he gently touches his palm to her forehead and looks at me hesitantly.

"You know she has a fever, right?"

"You're joking." I touch her forehead and groan. Suddenly I notice everything else that I've missed over these hours—the sniffly nose and the slight hoarseness to her cry—both of which I had blamed on the endless hours of crying. "She has a cold."

Sam chuckles and nods.

I shut my eyes and groan. "How did I miss that?"

"Sleep deprivation and stress, honey," Sam says. "She just needs some acetaminophen and she'll be fine."

I make a quick trip to the drugstore while Sam stays home with Daisy. It occurs to me as I'm driving away that this is actually the first time I've left them alone together, and it doesn't seem like a big deal at all—not given everything else that's going on in our lives. Sam *is* such a natural at this—so much more than I am. I really need to let him be more involved with Daisy. It will do her so much good.

After administering a dose of medicine, I cuddle Daisy back to sleep while Sam dresses for work. When he returns to the living room, he sits beside me again and slides his arm around my shoulders. We stare down at the baby—already she's more settled, and now I feel guilty that it took me so long to pick up on something so obvious.

"This suits you," Sam says suddenly.

I scoff at him.

"It suits me? She had a fever this morning and I didn't *notice*."

Sam shrugs.

"You know what sleep deprivation can do. I just mean in general, you're doing such a great job. I didn't think I could love you any more than I already did, but...there's something about the way you are with her...it's a side to you I didn't know was there. I feel lucky I've had this chance to see you playing mommy."

He rests his head against mine, and my tiredness fades, and just for a moment all I feel is the love I have for Sam. It is the biggest and best part of me. It surges in moments like this, until it seems bigger than both of us. I glance down at Daisy—and I know that somehow, even if she sleeps fitfully in my arms, she benefits from being around people who love each other like Sam and I do. I sigh, and I'm somehow simultaneously content and exhausted, ignoring entirely all of the external craziness that Annie has brought into our lives. I'm still not brave enough to ask Sam what his thoughts are on Daisy's future, but just for the moment, we feel like a real family.

Sam kisses the side of my head and moves to release me.

"I have to go to work," he murmurs, but I turn to him and whisper, "Just a moment longer?"

He smiles and pulls me against his chest, and I close my eyes and sink back into the moment. We are safe and all of my problems are a million miles away. Everything else will be fine, eventually—as long as I have Sam.

When several minutes pass and Sam gently moves away, I open my eyes just in time to see the shadow of movement at the living room window. It startles me enough that I let out an involuntary squeal.

"What's wrong?" Sam frowns.

"There's someone at the window."

Sam runs to throw the front door open, and he peers out into the street before he turns back to me and shrugs.

"There's no one there, Lex."

I carefully rest Daisy on the bouncer and run out into the yard.

"There was," I throw over my shoulder. "It must have been Annie." I'm standing on the front lawn now, looking this way and that, and I can't see a thing—so I shout, "Annie!"

"Lexie, keep your voice down, it's eight in the morning—" Sam protests, but I shush him and run to look behind the bushes in our yard, and then out onto the road. She's gone, but somehow, I *know* it was her.

"Are you sure?" Sam asks, and he runs out after me, but I point back to the door.

"Stay with Daisy, just for a minute?"

I run to the end of our street, then back past the house and to the other end. I try to remember exactly what it was I saw in the window, but it was just a shadow. I shouldn't be so sure it belonged to my sister—but somehow, I am. Now, though, she is long gone, and I return to our house, dragging my feet, confused and disappointed and simultaneously a little relieved. I wonder if Annie even knows that if she visits, I'll have to turn her in.

Sam is sitting on the couch close to Daisy, and he looks up at me expectantly. I shake my head and sit beside him.

"It's probably for the best," Sam says carefully. "If she comes here..."

"I know." I sigh. "I'll call the police."

"Do you want me to call in sick or something?" he asks, but he's reluctant, and I shake my head.

"I'll be okay."

I decide to take Daisy to the pediatrician just to be sure that her fever isn't a sign of something more serious. I dress her and strap her into the car seat, but I'm still not great at estimating how long it takes us to get ready, and we are already running a few minutes late by the time I get to the front door.

Inevitably, I hear the shrill ring of the landline right at that moment.

The landline. Only one person calls that number.

I consider ignoring it. It's Annie for sure, but the pediatrician has squeezed us into a slot between appointments and it's a half-hour drive to get to his office—there's really only enough time for me to get in the car and go if we're going to make the booking. I try to figure out what should be my priority—my sick sister, or my sick niece.

I answer the phone.

"I wasn't going to bother you, but I have to see her," Annie says without identifying herself.

"I can't see you. Bernie told me not to—she said to tell you to go straight to the police department. You *have* to turn yourself in."

"I don't know what to do, Lexie. I'm so scared."

I can hear the terror and confusion in her voice. She's alone, and she's frightened, and there is *nothing* I can do to help her.

"Honey, you have to go to the police," I whisper, my throat tightening. "I have to take Daisy to her doctor's appointment now, and I have to hang up the phone. I can't talk to you—if I'm in contact with you while that arrest warrant is out, *I* can get in trouble, too."

"Lexie, this is one last favor—then I promise you I'll stay out of your hair until I have my shit sorted out. I just need to say goodbye to her." Her voice breaks, and then she's pleading, her dignity gone. "I need to h-hold her *one last time*. I'm begging you, Lexie. Please don't let me down."

Annie is distraught and it tears at me, but I'm worn down by the drama and the endless take-take-*take* of my sister and her addiction. As hard as it is, I know I simply have to hang up on her and I have to do it again, and again—for as long as she keeps calling me, until she's ready to accept responsibility for her situation and take herself to the police.

"No," I say quietly, and then I lift the phone away from my ear and move to hang it up.

"Lexie!" she screams my name between sobs. And I choke back tears of my own. I hesitate one last moment, just long enough to hear her choke, "Please, Lexie. Please, I need this so much—"

And then I hang up and I take Daisy for her checkup.

I miss the appointment, and Daisy and I sit in the waiting room for over an hour until her doctor finds another window to squeeze us in. This gives me plenty of time to reflect on the fact that Annie actually contacted me at last, and I hung up on her.

I've done exactly what I was supposed to do, so why do I feel so sick about it? I relive the conversation in my mind, and I'm sure that I missed something. Was there some opportunity that I didn't take, some magic phrase I could have said to convince her to go to the police? Not that I'm convinced *that* would make her situation any better, but surely the sooner she accepts her fate, the more leniency the judge will give her at sentencing.

I think back again—what else did I say? What else did she say? Were there clues about her location, hints of her state of mind? She was clearly desperate; did I offer her any comfort at all? Then it hits me, and there's sudden ice in my veins.

Did I tell her I love her? There wasn't time. I was in a panic, adrenaline was surging through me and I was *so* conscious of Daisy's appointment. I said a lot of words to her, but I missed the only ones that really mattered.

I love you, Annie.

Why didn't I tell her? That no matter what mistakes she makes, she's still *my* Annie—*my* baby sister, and all of my other thoughts and feelings about our present situations are only noise around that fact. I could have said it so easily. I could have said it casually, a rushed *love you, Annie* before I hung up on her, or I could have cut off some of her ramblings and said it slowly, carefully. *I hope you know that I love you, Annie, and I always will.*

Instead, I shut her down, and I hung up the phone.

By the time Daisy's pediatrician calls us in, I've worked myself up into knots. When he asks me what happened, I stare at him blankly and he prompts me, "With Daisy, Alexis. Are you okay?"

"Fine," I say, and I shake myself and explain Daisy's irritability and the fever and my cluelessness. When I'm done, her doctor confirms Sam's diagnosis.

Daisy simply has her first cold, and we just need to ride it out.

"You'd think that I'd have noticed it a bit quicker," I mutter, and her doctor laughs at me.

"Playing mom requires a whole other skill set than playing doctor. You'll figure it out."

Once we're back in the car, I sit behind the steering wheel and I make a plan for the afternoon. We'll go back home, I'll keep giving Daisy her medication, put a vaporizer on in her room and try to take a nap in the rocking chair beside her cot.

I start the car and drive to the parking lot exit, and then I ignore every single decision I just made and turn toward Annie's trailer.

Daisy is in the car seat, hooked under my arm as I walk toward the door of the trailer. I'm well aware that the *right* thing to do is to go home. I should call Bernie, and ask her if I should call the police.

But I'm not going to do either one of those things. Instead, I'm going to let Annie see Daisy, and then I'm going to beg her to willingly go to the police; but even if she refuses, I'll leave the decision in her hands. Any alternative course of action would be a betrayal of her trust, and a message that I have given up on her.

Perhaps her life is already completely out of control, but I need to show her that I still believe in her. I *have* to believe she is still capable of doing the right thing, even now, when the right thing is accepting the extent of her mess and turning herself in. For all of the complexities of our relationship and my frustration with her, even for all of the times when I have resented her and despaired for her, I could never give up on Annie. Until my last breath, I'll be waiting for her to turn things around.

Now, I approach the door of her trailer and my palms are sweaty because this is one of those pivotal moments in our relationship. It's me reaching out, and I'm doing it because I need to, and maybe because she needs me to, as well. I just want to see Annie, and I want her to see Daisy. I don't even know if she will be here, but I know that I had to try. I'm out of solutions. I'm out of ideas. My mind keeps flashing back to that night just two months earlier when I made this trip with Sam in the small hours. It's funny how so much has happened, but nothing has really changed.

At the door, I lift my fist to knock and then I see that it's slightly ajar. I knock anyway, but there is no answer.

"Annie?" I call, and I wait. There is no sound from inside the trailer, so I call again, and my heart sinks a little. Maybe she was here, but she's already left. Maybe if I'd just been more supportive a few hours ago, she would have stuck around. I push the door open and stick my head inside, and then I see her.

She's on the bed, in nearly the same position she was resting in two months ago when we were here the first time. She's lying on her back, but her head is limp against the pillow. There's a tourniquet on her arm, and a needle in her vein. There is something all around her mouth—vomit?

She's still and she's gray.

Everything happens in slow motion from that moment. I fling the door open all the way and I move inside, but I pause to very carefully set Daisy's car seat on the dining room table as if everything in the world is just fine—but it's not, it's just not, and somehow I already know that it's never going to be fine again.

I'm shaking violently as I reach for Annie—but her skin is too cool to my touch and I know that it's too late but it can't be—*it just can't be*—so I untie the tourniquet and I throw the syringe against the wall with violent force and fury. I take her shoulders and I shake her again and again and she's limp—*why is she so limp?* I'm screaming at her, and now Daisy is crying, too.

I lay Annie back onto the bed then fumble in my bag for Narcan—but I stopped carrying it last year. I thought I didn't need it anymore. *Why couldn't I just keep it in there, just in case?* I call 911 and as I press the phone to my ear, I start compressions on Annie's frail chest.

"My sister." I'm sobbing, hysterical—spewing indecipherable words into the phone. It can't end like this. I can't lose her like this. *Why didn't I tell her I loved her? Did she do this on purpose? Is this my fault? I've failed her. I've failed my baby sister.*

"Fire, ambulance or police, ma'am?"

"Paramedics. *Paramedics!*"

Someone else is on the phone now—the paramedic dispatcher. She is asking for the address and I can't remember it. I only know how to get here—so I'm stammering the cross streets and her trailer number and I'm still doing chest compressions and trying to force air into her lifeless lungs between nonsensical sentences. Her chest isn't rising. It isn't working.

"Help me, please help me."

"Is someone else there?" the operator asks, and I'm blabbering like a baby and my tears are all over Annie's face. I brush them away with my wrist as I try again to breathe air and warmth and life into my sister. Then, as I'm compressing her chest again, the sound of Daisy's screaming registers and I whisper, "The baby is here. Oh God, she's here and Annie is…"

"Ma'am, is the baby okay?" the operator asks me urgently. "Try to stay calm. The paramedics are only six minutes away."

"That's too long!" I shake Annie again. "Please don't leave me, Annie, please—I'm so sorry—"

I try more compressions, but then I hear her rib crack and I pull my hands violently back from her chest and drop the phone onto the floor as I do. But I can't actually *stop* the compressions— she needs oxygen to her brain, and every second that I delay will mean more brain damage. So I keep right on with the CPR. I tell myself that I have to stop crying now and save my breath for Annie. Two breaths, fifteen compressions, two breaths, fifteen compressions. It's too late—on some level I know this, but I keep going because I can't and I *won't* be the one to give up on her. Daisy's cries echo all around us in the filthy, freezing trailer. She should be home in the warmth. She should be anywhere but here.

I'm vaguely aware of the flashing lights and siren of the ambulance outside, but I keep going until someone pulls me gently aside. Feeling helpless, I go to Daisy and I pick her up to console her—she's purple-faced from the bellowing—and I press my face into her neck, as if *she* could comfort *me*.

But then…the frantic activity I'm waiting for never starts. The male paramedic is dialing on a cell phone; the woman is sorting through a medical bag.

"Is she okay?" I ask, and I'm bewildered. I look at Annie, and her lips are purple, and her skin is still that waxy-gray color. She is gone. I know that she is gone. But I won't believe it. Someone has to fix this. *I* have to fix this. What can I do? I have to convince them. I can't let them stop.

"I'm so sorry, ma'am," the woman says softly.

"Why aren't you working on her?" I demand, and they exchange a glance.

"We're not going to commence CPR. It's just too late."

"Narcan—adrenaline—you have a defibrillator—" I start to sob, but the female paramedic shakes her head.

"Ma'am, she's clearly been gone for some time. There's nothing we can do."

"No..."

"Perhaps we should take your baby outside?" the male paramedic suggests carefully, and I'm wild-eyed and frantic—*my* baby? I look at Daisy, and I start to sob again, because oh *God*, she has just lost everything and she's not even old enough to understand. The female paramedic stands and gently steers me toward the door as I hear the male paramedic on his phone. He is speaking in a whisper, but even over my sobs, I hear him.

"Yeah, we've got a DOA here—another fucking junkie. I hate these cases—"

I stop so abruptly that the female paramedic collides with my back. I turn stiffly to face the inside of the trailer and a raw, primal scream bursts from my mouth.

"No!"

He turns to me, shocked, and the female paramedic takes a step back as if I'm a physical threat. I know they are only human, and addiction wears medical professionals down, and I've probably thought the same thing myself—but this is not a faceless patient—this is the little girl who used to fall asleep in the bed next to mine. The girl who used to keep her journal tucked in beside her face like a teddy bear. She had hopes and dreams and she had talents and flaws and she is—*was*—everything to me.

This is Annie; *my* Annie. Anne Elizabeth Vidler. How can they reduce this life that mattered to me to a single *label*?

I look between the paramedics and then I stare the man down.

"She is *not* a junkie," I choke. "She is my *sister.*"

They stare right back at me. They don't know that I understand their disgust, but they *need* to know that she was a person, with history and potential and worth, and despite all of the bad decisions and all of the mess and pain of her life, *she deserved a better end to her story than this.*

I step out into the cold and I walk away from the trailer. I'm wailing, and people are coming out from the other trailers, and a stranger asks if she can help me and I can't form the words to answer her. For a moment or two, I pace around the filth outside Annie's trailer, but then Daisy's screaming penetrates the fog of my shock and I remember that she's actually sick.

It is just too cold for Daisy out here, but we can't go back inside the trailer, and even if we did, it's not much warmer. So I take the baby into my car, and I sit behind the wheel. I run the heater to warm her up and I hold her so tightly against me as I sob.

I have to ring Mom.

I have to ring Sam.

My phone is inside the trailer, on the floor. I can't go back inside.

Time loses all meaning. A police car comes, and the coroner, and I watch all of these people crowd into Annie's pitiful trailer and I just can't bear it. I almost convince myself this isn't happening; this whole morning just can't be real. This must be a nightmare—have I fallen asleep on the couch?

I start performing an autopsy on this moment—a postmortem of my failure. Did Annie do this on purpose? How did it even come to this? Where did I go wrong? Why couldn't I help her? Why didn't I just agree to visit her with Daisy? How could beautiful, clever little Annie come to this end—dying alone in this pathetic trailer park—all of that beauty and creativity lost to the world forever…lost to me…lost to Daisy?

Why didn't I tell her I loved her? That would have made the difference, I'm sure of it. How am I going to live with myself? How can I contact Sam? How can I tell Mom? I can't stop crying. This feels worse than when Dad died, because when Dad died, I had to be strong for Annie and Mom. There is Daisy this time, but it feels different—maybe I'm Daisy's, but she's not yet *mine* in the way that Mom and Annie were. But what will happen to her? Am I really all she has now?

I'll fail her, too. No one should trust me to care for this baby. A police officer approaches me, and I want him to handcuff me and throw me in prison—*for failing your sister, when the only thing you ever needed to do was take care of her.* Instead, he gently opens the car door and asks me sadly, "Ma'am? Is there someone we can call for you?"

I asked Annie that question once, and there was no one. I was all she had in the world, and I let her down.

I nod frantically and look toward the trailer. More people are crowding in. There's police tape going up around it.

"My phone is on the floor of the trailer. His name is Sam." My voice sounds artificial, high-pitched and feeble, and now my teeth are chattering. Annie's teeth did that, just seven weeks ago, in the C-section, and I told her it was going to be okay.

I was wrong. I was wrong about everything. It's not okay. It's never going to be okay.

Forgive me, Annie. I love you.

The officer is still staring at me and I'm not sure he understood me, so I focus as hard as I can and I clear my throat and I say, "Please call Sam Hawke. His number is on speed dial on my phone, which is on the trailer floor."

"Okay, ma'am," the officer says, and I watch him walk away. I take an inventory of my physical situation. Daisy is in my arms, gradually calming at last. She is warm against my body, but not too warm. She is okay.

Annie is dead, but Daisy is okay. I repeat this as a mantra for several minutes, thinking I can force myself to accept it. This doesn't work. I still feel like I'm dreaming, and in the moments after I acknowledge this, I almost convince myself that I am.

But my heart is still racing and I'm still panting even now that I'm completely still, and my hands are numb, and as I catalog these things I diagnose myself with physiological shock and I force my best physician's voice into my internal monologue and I assure myself that with a bit of time, the sense of dissociation will pass and I'll be okay.

Then I remember again that Annie is dead and I'm off again on the roller coaster of early grief; this time all I can think of is about how many times I've considered this moment inevitable, and how that *doesn't* make it any easier, but it should. I have had years to prepare for this. I should have had a mental coping kit all packed and ready to go.

But I don't, and it's unbearable, and just when I start to feel so alone that I could almost panic just because *my sister is dead*, I see Sam burst through the crowd. He throws the car door open and he kneels on the ground beside me, and his face is blanched with shock and pain.

"Lexie," he whispers. "Oh, baby. I'm so sorry."

I work my jaw, and I can't make any words come out—but I have just enough sense to gently pass him Daisy and to step out of the car and away from them before I throw up.

I give a statement to the police officer and then we wait for the coroner to finish. Sam wants to take Daisy straight home once the police say I'm free to go, but I can't leave—not while Annie is still inside. So we wait, and they do whatever it is they need to do, and then I watch the coronial staff carry the body board down the stairs. I am sobbing again, but even in my grief I notice how easy it is for them to lift her. It is as if she was nothing at all.

Then Sam asks again if we can go, more insistently this time, and I finally agree. He drives my car—we leave his at the trailer park. At some point, we will need to go back and get it, if it's not stolen in the meantime. I sit beside him in the passenger seat, and my knees feel stiff, because I've been sitting in the same position for hours. I keep thinking about Annie's shoulders and how limp they were but rigor mortis would have set in by now, and now I'm stiff, and I wish for just a passing, fleeting moment that I could be dead, too, with Annie and with Dad, away from all of this pain.

"Lexie?" Sam speaks gently, and I turn to look at him. The sky has darkened and heavy rain is falling. I look toward the windshield and watch as the water runs down onto the hood, rivulets of ice-cold water. I think about the coldness in Annie's body. She must be in the refrigerated morgue by now. What would happen if I went and held her hand? Maybe if I held it long enough, I could warm it back up again.

"Lexie," Sam says again.

This time, I manage to croak out an answer, "Yes?"

"I just wanted to say again—I'm so, so sorry."

"Thank you. And…I know," I say, and I go back to watching the water run down the window. When we finally get back to the house, Sam parks the car in the garage and undoes his seat belt, but I don't move.

"Sweetheart," Sam says gently. "We need to get Daisy inside."

I turn to look at him slowly. I've been vaguely aware of Sam tending to Daisy since he arrived, but I haven't really spared her a thought for hours, other than to obsess over what might happen for her next…what might happen for *me* next. What kind of aunt does that make me?

Am I just her aunt now? Daisy doesn't have a mother anymore.

I'm all she has left. I'm the only mother she's ever known other than those disrupted days with Annie in the hospital.

I didn't even tell Annie I loved her. She rang me and I had the chance and I didn't even think of it.

"Come on," Sam prompts again, and he unbuckles my seat belt for me. I reach for the door handle, but I can't focus long enough to open it. Sam removes Daisy from the car and takes her inside, and then he comes back for me. He opens the door and he gently hooks my arm over his shoulder and he leads me out of the garage and to the couch. I lie still like Annie. I close my eyes and I see her purple lips and her gray face, so I open them again and I stare up at the stucco ceiling while Sam prepares a bottle for Daisy and tops up her acetaminophen, and then he bathes and dresses her and brings her back to me, clean and swaddled and happy.

Annie has robbed me. She has taken my happy ending, and I know that this makes me selfish, because it was never *my* happy ending at all. But I deserved to see her okay again. I deserved another Christmas when we sat beside one another, and we ate spaghetti or turkey or whatever else we wanted and we laughed, and we were both healthy and fully present. I haven't had one of those for years, and goddamn it, I *deserved* it. I deserved for Daisy to watch us interact at that dinner. I deserved for Daisy to be my niece—I deserved to be an aunt who could spoil her silly and then pass her back to her mother to handle all the discipline and hard work.

I deserved Annie to be beside me at the altar at my wedding. I deserved to glance at her in her bridesmaid's gown and I deserved to be jealous of how she outshone me.

And now, she will not be there. She will not be at any of the big events in my life, or her daughter's life. If Daisy had any chance of surviving her rocky entry into the world unscathed, I'm sure that this is lost now. She will forever be the daughter of a dead woman, a woman who died of a drug overdose—a deliberate drug overdose?

Sam has Daisy tucked in his elbow, but he slides his other arm around me, just as he did this morning. It feels like a million years ago now. I remember the moment I saw a shadow at the window. Was that really Annie, or did I imagine it?

Was that my chance to save her, or was it the phone call?

How hard would it have been for me to just agree to meet with her in the first place, instead of rejecting her and leaving her alone? How hard would those three little words have been to squeeze into our last conversation? *Love you, Annie.*

Oh God. What if she did it on purpose?

"Lexie," Sam whispers, and my tears surge again.

"I should have saved her."

"This isn't your fault."

"I was supposed to look after her. I should have let her see Daisy today. I should have promised her I'd find a way to help her."

I press my face into his chest, and I breathe in his scent. He is the warm blanket around my cold heart, but it is not enough— nothing will ever be enough to take away the ache in my chest.

I share awful phone calls with my mother over the days that follow. Our relationship is just close enough that I'm calling her to make sure she's okay, but distant enough that I'm wary when she picks up the phone. All it will take for me to lose my mind completely will be one thoughtless platitude, and surely she is building up a database of them. Robert would have reacted to the news of Annie's death with some condescending, self-righteous commentary, littered with Bible verses and scorn—and Mom is virtually his sidekick. If I hear her say those things, it will be the end of what's left of our relationship.

And then my family will be gone. Not just broken, not just

chaotic: *gone*. I'm more scared of this than I should be, given how dysfunctional we've been for the last twenty years.

But my fears go unfounded. Mostly, we discuss details for the funeral; those little things that really seem to matter in the hollow space between a death and the final farewell. I can't bring myself to ask Mom if she's coming, but she seems to want to know the plans, and eventually I realize that I have to assume Robert has agreed to let her come.

It's important to Mom that the service is in a church, but I know Annie would have hated that, so I insist we hold it at the funeral home. Mom argues initially, but then just as I decide to give in and give her what she wants, she suddenly acquiesces to my wishes and focuses her attention on the wake. Who will be there? Where will we hold it? Who will bring food? We discuss all of this in far too much depth, and it becomes blatantly obvious that it's simply an unspoken plea from each of us to stay on the line—something to connect over, after all of these years of polite, infrequent, surface-level chats.

Mom eventually tells me that she's flying in the day before the funeral, but the request to pick her up remains unspoken until I offer to send Sam. He's more than happy to oblige—he's been hovering around me looking for ways to support me, and I love him for it, but I can't open up to him about how I'm feeling just yet. He keeps telling me this isn't my fault, and I know he's wrong—but I'm not exactly going to argue the point.

As I watch his car leave the driveway to go get Mom, I exhale for the first time in days, grateful for both his assistance and the space.

I have prepared Sam for his first meeting with my mother. I've given him a crash course in the customs of the sect; from the long skirt she'll be wearing to her hairstyle and head covering, and the oddly formal way she speaks sometimes, as if twenty-first-century slang has bypassed her village. I've even warned him to turn the radio off before she gets in the car, to avoid an awkward request from Mom to do so.

"And don't offer her food," I add just as he's walking out the door. He looks at me blankly.

"But...why not?"

"She can't eat with us."

Sam blinks at me.

"Members of the sect can't eat in the presence of nonbelievers. I'm not exactly sure how that will work yet. She'll probably eat before or after us."

Sam rubs his jaw wearily.

"Right. No radio, no food, no profanity, no haircuts. Got it."

I waste the hours while I wait for Mom. I bring Daisy into my bed and I lie beside her and stare at her. I've always seen Dad in Annie's daughter, but now I just see Annie. I run my forefinger over Daisy's eyes and her little lips, and her cheeks and into her fine hair.

"I don't know how, Daisy," I whisper. "But I'm going to do better for you."

When I hear Sam parking the car, I walk down the stairs with Daisy in my arms. Sam leads Mom into the living room, and she pauses when she sees me with the baby. I haven't seen my mother face-to-face in almost twenty years, and she has aged terribly in that time. Her hair is now white, still straight and long down her back, tucked beneath a dark gray scarf. Her eyes are as red as mine must be.

Mom drops her luggage onto the floor and walks stiffly across the room toward me. Her hands shake as she reaches for Daisy, but I pull the baby away from her. She doesn't deserve to hold Annie's child.

My nostrils flare as I stare at Mom, but her focus is entirely on Daisy. She reaches to touch Daisy's cheek, and the baby turns her head toward Mom's finger and tries to gum it.

Don't waste your energy, Daisy. Mom will never provide sustenance.

"She is beautiful," Mom chokes, and I let my gaze linger on my mother's face. She wears so many new lines and so many shadows of sadness. How old is she? Sixty-four, I calculate, but she looks so much older.

I soften suddenly. I don't know why. Maybe it's the tears that roll down over the lines on Mom's face, maybe it's the reality that I just can't stay angry with her—we have an awful few days to get through, and besides, she is *here* now. I pass her Daisy, and she sobs noisily as she helps herself to a seat on my couch with the baby in her arms. I watch silently for a while, but then I notice I'm tapping my foot frantically against the floor and I realize how much nervous energy I'm sitting on. Now that my anger is gone, I'm only hurt and deeply saddened that Annie isn't here. If only Mom had come earlier, she could have been.

Anger starts to rise again at that thought, and I decide that I need to distract myself. I stand, then walk to the kitchen, and I carefully make tea for all of us, focusing hard on each step. When I'm finally before Mom with the tea, she looks up and I see the shadow cross her face. I feel like a complete idiot. Didn't I warn Sam about this before he left? Mom *can't* drink it in the same room as us. It's one of the community's basic tenets; the principle of separation.

"Sorry," I say, and she shakes her head and draws in a deep breath.

"No, no…it's okay. Thank you. I really could do with some tea."

I look up at Sam.

"We can leave the room?" he suggests.

Mom shakes her head again, and hesitates for a long moment before she says, "Obviously, in coming here, I've relaxed some rules. I think this should be one of them, too."

"Really?" I'm stunned, but Mom looks at me helplessly.

"Please don't…just, don't mention it to Robert."

So we drink the tea together, and it shouldn't be a momentous ritual—but for *us*, it is. Mom wouldn't have shared food with someone from outside the community in decades, and even as she sips at her tea, she looks slightly nervous—as if the elders might burst in any second and catch her. So to try to ease the awkward atmosphere, I make small talk.

"How was the flight?" I ask her.

"Good, good…"

More awkward silence, then Mom makes an attempt to break it.

"This house is wonderful."

"Thank you."

And after several rounds of this, the conversation begins to flow a little. But we don't talk about Annie, and it occurs to me that we haven't discussed her much at all since she died. We've discussed the funeral, but the subject of the beloved sister and daughter we're burying remains somehow still too difficult to address.

Sam lingers in the background for a while, occasionally moving into my field of vision. When I meet his eye, he only offers me a reassuring smile. I'm so glad he is here. I smile back, sadly, gratefully. When Daisy starts to fuss, he gently takes her from Mom's arms to put her down for a nap. After he leaves the room, Mom asks hesitantly, "So everything ready for tomorrow?"

"Of course it is." I say the words too sharply, and Mom winces. She knew the answer to that question before she asked it. Besides, of course I've organized the funeral—I've organized everything for the last twenty years. Mom tries now to offer me a sad smile.

"At least Daisy is okay?'

"Daisy is fine for now. There are a lot of decisions to be made in the next few days."

Mom's eyebrows knit together, and then she gives me a critical frown.

"Are you and Sam going to…"

I rise, and my stomach is churning.

"We haven't talked about it."

"Well, you look like you're pretty well set up. I'm sure Daisy will be very happy here."

Now the urge to snap at her is so strong that I have to wrap my arms around my chest to hold it in. I try to stare her down, just like Annie might have done. I'm incredulous—does Mom not realize that the obvious alternative to Sam and me raising Daisy would be Daisy's *grandmother* caring for her? Apparently not, and even if she wanted to, I'd never allow it. Surely she must have considered it. Maybe she even raised the possibility with Robert and he said no. He probably thinks that Daisy is tainted—the dirty, sinful daughter of a filthy, sinful drug addict.

"I have things to do," I say, my tone short. "Make yourself at home."

I head straight for Sam and Daisy. I find them in the rocking chair in the nursery, Sam completely at home with the baby in his arms. I smile at him sadly from the doorway, and I think about all the dreams that we had. I've imagined him here in this very room, settling a child off to sleep. I just assumed it would be our own.

"Everything okay?"

He asks me the question in a soft whisper. I sigh and shrug.

"You know how when someone has hurt you, it takes so little to reopen the wound?"

Sam tilts his head toward me, indicating that I should join him. I move toward the rocking chair slowly then sink down onto the armrest. He slides his arm around my waist, and I lean into him.

"I know your mom has let you down, and there is a lot of history there. But try to keep in mind that she is *here*. You weren't even sure that she would come, and yet she has. She said in the car that it was very difficult to get away, and I wondered if that meant that her husband didn't want her to come. Maybe it cost your mother to be here—and she *has* just lost her daughter. This is difficult for all of you—for all of us. But Deborah was Annie's mother. She might not show it, but she must be suffering."

"She probably thinks that Annie deserved what happened to her."

"Maybe. Maybe not. But she's here, and that counts for something, right?"

On the day of my sister's funeral, I wake at dawn to feed her baby, then I dress in black from head to toe, a black dress, black tights and black shoes. I pair it all with a heavy gray overcoat, and then at the last minute, I add a bright pink scarf. Annie always loved bright colors, and it doesn't seem right to forget about that now. I put my hair in a bun and coat it with hairspray so that it is absolutely still and fixed in place. I don't wear makeup. There is no point. I know that I'll cry it off.

I survey myself in the mirror and note the puffiness around my eyes, and the awful gray bags that now linger beneath them. When Sam wakes, he joins me in the bathroom, and he wraps his arms around me and he says, "I love you, Lexie."

"I love you, too."

Daisy, who had been resting in the bouncer on the floor beside my feet, lets out a strange gurgling sound, and I look down at her in alarm. Then I realize—the sound could almost have been a laugh. She is staring at the swishing movement of my skirt around my knees and, for some reason, this has her amused. I turn a little, testing the theory, and she makes the sound again—this time achieving something even closer to a giggle.

Sam and I crouch simultaneously to stare at her.

"You picked a weird day to let out your first laugh, kid," I say to her, and I look at Sam. "Can you believe that just happened?"

"Maybe she's giving you a message, Lex," he offers. I raise my eyebrows even higher.

"Seriously?"

"We have to take joy where we find it, even on the worst days.

Daisy laughed, which is a perfectly normal thing for an eight-week-old to do. She's hit a milestone—her first milestone—probably right on target. We can celebrate it later, but we need to notice it now. Daisy deserves that, doesn't she?"

I swallow, and my eyes fill with the first of the day's tears. I rise, and I think about Annie. I would love to be able to call her and say, "Hey, how is rehab going? Fantastic, well, you're past halfway done now and guess what, by the time you come out, Daisy is going to be giggling—she's already trying!"

And then Annie would say back to me. "That's great! That makes all of this worthwhile. I'll keep at it, okay?"

I bite my lip to try to contain my tears, but I can't catch them. Sam embraces me, and I fight against the urge to give over to helpless sobs; God, if I start now, how am I going to get through the day? It's just so unfair. It's just all so unfair and it hurts so much that I can't bear it.

"You okay?"

I nod and straighten away from him, then I reach for a Kleenex and dry my cheeks. Sam watches me closely as I pick up Daisy and cuddle her close to my face. I breathe in, then out, and then I turn toward the door.

"I'm here for you, Lex," Sam says, and I stop and turn back to him with as much of a smile as I can muster.

"I know."

"Don't forget it, okay?"

More tears try to surface, and I nod and hastily leave the room. I walk down the stairs and greet both my mother and my future mother-in-law, Anita, who are in the kitchen working in silence to organize food for the wake. Anita has flown into town to help with Daisy during the service and will stay to assist with the logistics of the wake.

Sam has organized all of this directly with his mother, and I'm grateful for that. It means I have completely avoided discussing Annie with Anita so far. I do like my future mother-in-law—she's an elegant, well-mannered woman—but I don't really know her all that well yet, having spent only a handful of weekends and holidays with her over the course of my relationship with Sam. I'm sure that beneath the polite veneer she must at least be shocked at the chaotic family Sam is choosing to marry into. Now, though, she passes me a piece of toast and offers a sympathetic smile. I murmur my thanks and sit at the table to try to force myself to eat.

This day reminds me so much of my father's passing that I have to steel myself against the pain of it. I remember standing on the front lawn, and Annie looking so utterly broken that morning, and racking my brain to think of a way to bring some magic back into the day. Was it right that I insisted she find some happiness that day? Did that set her on a path of seeking happiness in all of the wrong places forever? Now Sam is trying to do the same for me, but life has bruised me so much in the decades since. The last time I wanted to curl up and stop moving forward, Annie was my reason to keep moving. Now that she's gone, do I just stop? Is this the end of me? Or do I transfer that sense of responsibility to her daughter, and repeat this godforsaken cycle all over again?

There are so few people at Annie's service. Eliza is there, and other staff from the hospital. This is so depressing. Nobody is here for Annie. They are all here for Sam and me.

We make our way to the cemetery and I watch as they lower my sister's coffin into the ground. The finality of this strikes me, and the crush of grief starts all over again—this time, so intense that I shake from it. Sam's arm is around my shoulders where it's been pretty much all day, but then Mom starts to wail and he pulls her close, too. I would be lost without Sam today. I see the way Mom leans into him just as I do, and I think about Robert. It is utterly evil that he didn't come. He was a cruel man, but he was still effectively Annie's father for many years—and he *is* Mom's husband. What kind of person is he to be so judgmental, that he would even boycott his stepdaughter's funeral?

We leave Annie's graveside and drive home in silence to the wake. We eat the food Anita arranged, and people try to find ways to reminisce about Annie, but given how little of her they actually knew, it's pointless. They didn't know her, but I did. She was here, and she mattered, and I loved her, and now she is gone—and maybe I failed her, and maybe the system did, too. Maybe if that judge had offered Annie compassion instead of judgment, things might have been different. Maybe if she'd been able to take Daisy to rehab with her, she could have made more progress. Maybe if they'd given her support instead of an arrest warrant, or maybe if she'd been able to go onto a maintenance program instead of into inpatient rehab, or maybe...

If she only knew how I loved her.

All that I'm left with is memories and maybes. How can I build a better life for Daisy when I don't even understand what went wrong with her mother?

I slip out of the stilted conversations and resort to sitting by myself in the corner of my living room. Sam sits beside me, and I turn to him and suddenly I'm in shock all over again.

"This is my fault."

"*Stop*, Lexie. Annie was tortured. I don't know why this happened. Who can understand these things? I know one thing for sure—you tried to help her. You did everything you could have done—you were as patient you could have been—you gave her every opportunity to find her feet. And it didn't work, and it's unfair, and it's brutal, but it is also not your fault. I don't ever want to hear you say that again, okay?"

I try to take what he says to heart, and sit there silently as the crowd begins to thin out.

Finally, I'm left alone in my living room with the small circle of my family—Anita, Mom, Sam and Daisy. The moms clean, while Sam and I sit with Daisy. The table is full of half-eaten trays of food, there are prints on my floor from a dozen muddy feet, and outside the sky is as gray as the feeling in my heart.

Annie is really gone. And somehow, I have to move on.

I decide that afternoon that I'm going to keep Daisy. I'm already her legal guardian, I have bonded with her and I have effectively been her mother anyway—besides which, there is no alternative. Mom is not offering, and even if she did, I wouldn't take her up on it. The last thing in the world I want is Annie's daughter to live in that same stifling environment that damaged her so badly. I promised Annie that I would never let her daughter near Robert, and I'll honor that promise. But I also decide to keep this decision to myself until I can talk to Sam after Mom is gone. A day passes, and another, and I wait for Mom to announce that she is leaving.

But Mom lingers in my life as if she can't tear herself away— and I wish that she and I were close enough for me to ask her what her plans are. Although we're together all day, we don't talk much. Mom changes diapers, she joins me at doctor's appointments—she even gets up for Daisy in the middle of the night a few times. I have no idea how to interpret her actions, but soon my mom has been in our home for a week. The only concession she makes to her real life back in Winterton is a quick phone call back to Robert each night. She cooks a lot—baked goods, elaborate dinners, even hot breakfasts some days before Sam leaves for work. It's an odd thing, because I know what a big deal it is for Mom to eat with us, but since that first cup of tea she hasn't even hesitated about it. Like so many things in my house that week, my curiosity about Mom's relaxed approach to the rules remains unspoken.

I want to ask her if things have changed in Winterton since I left, or if she's just adopted a more moderate interpretation of the rules. I can't imagine Robert allowing either possibility. We have never talked my decision to leave Winterton. I wonder if she understands why I did. Would we get into an argument if I brought it up?

I'm still too tender—still looking for places to allocate blame and guilt and too frightened to dig deeply into anything with Mom in case I shatter our fragile truce. So I don't ask, and she doesn't offer, and instead we share hours of small talk and mutually fuss over the baby.

On the one-week anniversary of Annie's funeral, Sam, Mom and I are sitting around eating lasagna Mom prepared, when she asks without warning, "Will you legally adopt her?"

I feel Sam's eyes on my face, and I know that I should say that he and I need to talk about it—but I'm also suddenly terrified that Mom has decided she wants to take Daisy after all. So I clear my throat, and I say, "She'll stay with me—I'm already her guardian. Down the road, I'll organize something more formal—an adoption, I guess."

Mom nods curtly, then she leans back in her chair and says, "I'm going to go tomorrow. Robert has booked my flight. I'm needed back at school."

"Fine," I say.

Mom rises to clear the dishes from the table. Ordinarily, Sam or I would offer to help—but not tonight. Sam stares at me, apparently completely speechless.

I open my mouth to defend myself, but he rises abruptly and he raises his hands in disgust, and then leaves the room.

I take Mom to the airport. Sam is back at work and I haven't spoken to him since dinner. He slept in the study again, and I know I'm going to have to talk with him as soon as I get home, and I'm dreading it. Mom picks up on the tension, and as soon as we're in the car, she asks, "Is everything okay with Sam?"

"Everything is fine," I lie.

"And are you okay?"

No, I'm definitely not okay. My sister is dead, my fiancé is pissed at me and I'm suddenly a mom.

"I'm fine, Mom. Things will go back to normal now, but I'm so glad you could come."

Mom offers me a slightly hesitant smile.

"It...it was good of Robert to allow me to come."

I groan impatiently.

"Mom."

"You know I chose to submit to him, Lexie. It's not always easy walking the path of righteousness."

There is no point arguing with her, but now it's awkward again between us. We drive in silence the rest of the way to the airport, but when the time comes for us to say goodbye and she cries as she gives Daisy one last kiss, I actually battle the urge to ask her to stay. I impulsively pull her close for a tense hug, and I struggle to hold back my tears.

"Will you come back and see us?" I whisper hoarsely.

"I don't know," Mom admits. "I'll ask Robert to pray about it."

My arms loosen around her, and I watch as she walks through the gate.

"I can't tell if you're trying to push me away, or if it's just happening automatically and you can't stop yourself," Sam says quietly.

I'm sitting on the floor of the nursery, with paint samples and my iPad on the floor in front of me. I look up at Sam, and I swallow hard. I heard him come up the stairs when he walked back in the door from work, and I pretty much froze. I knew a conversation was coming that was going to hurt.

"I was scared that Mom was going to ask if she and Robert could take Daisy. I just said what I had to, to make sure she didn't get any ideas." I'm making excuses, and we both know it. Sam exhales.

"Lexie, *I* want to keep Daisy here, too. It didn't even cross my mind that we wouldn't. I was going to talk to you about it once the dust settled after the funeral. But can you imagine if I had just announced that I'd decided we were going to do it? Without *consulting* you?"

I should be relieved that we're on the same page, but I'm not. Instead, I'm overcome by guilt.

"We had this whole life planned out for us," I whisper, and I shrug at him helplessly. "How does Daisy fit into that?"

"It's pretty simple, actually. The position in our lives that our first child was going to fill is now already taken. Done. Plan updated," Sam says wryly. "You love that baby, and I love her, too. It's a no-brainer. My only bone of contention is my fiancée's nasty habit of making major life decisions without consulting me. There's a serious pattern forming here, and it's making me nervous."

"I *was* going to talk to you about it," I say defensively. "There just wasn't time."

"We have to *make* time for that kind of discussion, Lexie," Sam says impatiently. "I'm so sick of hearing you say that. Yes, I work long hours—well, so do you, normally. We've never had communication problems before. As soon as Annie came back into our lives, you started shutting me out, and I just don't understand why."

"I haven't *shut you out*," I say abruptly. "I—"

"That's exactly what you've been doing," Sam says with a slightly incredulous laugh. "I can't think of a better term to describe it. You've been through hell, and all along, I've been tagging behind trying to support you. Not *once* in all of this have you asked me for help, or even accepted it without a battle when I offered."

"I've accepted your help—"

"When I've insisted. Or you've had no choice."

"But I—"

"Lexie, can you think of *one* time in the last two months when you've reached out to me voluntarily and asked me for advice, or a hug or practical assistance? Just one time."

I think back over the weeks that have passed, and in each of the memories that flit past me, Sam is hovering, offering, waiting, agreeing to help when I asked, but he's right—I *have* asked only when I had no alternative.

"I didn't mean to," I whisper.

"I know, Lex. I know it's habit, and I kind of understand why. But it has to stop now. We're *parents* now. We need to be a team, right?"

He stares at me, waiting for my response, and I'm swamped by a sudden realization of how lucky I am to have a man like Sam in my life. I love him in a way that I never expected—with gratitude and with admiration and with a passion that I feel so sure we can cling to even as the years turn into decades. I don't want to undermine any of that at this early stage just out of a stubborn habit for independence.

"Right."

His serious expression lightens just a little, and he murmurs, "You know, with two doctors for parents—that kid is going to be so smart. We're going to need to work together to stay ahead of her."

The joke shatters the last of the tense atmosphere between us, and I laugh weakly. Sam points to the paint swatches.

"We're officially making this a nursery, then?"

"Well, Daisy obviously doesn't want gray walls in her room. I thought maybe a nice crisp yellow would work well."

"And by that do you mean, 'Sam, cancel golf on the weekend, we have painting to do'?" he asks. There's a hint of a smile in his voice. Sam wants to help. Sam is pleased when I ask him to. I'm already learning. I can do this.

"There are so many things we have to figure out. I only have a few weeks of leave left, so we need to look into a nanny, and

I need to talk to someone to see how we go about making this permanent and we should get Daisy added to our insurance and…" I trail off and groan, suddenly overwhelmed. "And we need to paint this room."

"Make a list, honey. We'll talk about it over dinner."

Sam's calm patience is exactly what I need. I tilt my head at him and I smile.

"Thanks, Sam."

"See how awesome I am?" he says pointedly. "And this is precisely why you should talk to me about this stuff."

"Got it," I assure him, and this time, I really think I have.

A few days later, a police officer comes to my front door. He's holding a small box.

"Alexis? You probably don't remember me. I came to the trailer when your sister…" He trails off, and I nod.

"Can I help you?"

"We found this in the trailer and I thought you might want to have it."

"What is it?" I frown as I take the box.

"It's a journal. It was open on the desk when she… We had to take it as evidence, in case there was a note. The coroner has closed her case as an accidental death, so we're finished with it now and I took a look at it and I figured… Well, seems like the kind of thing a family member would want."

"Accidental?" I repeat, and my heart starts to race. "How could they know that?"

"Are you sure you want to know this, ma'am?" the officer asks me hesitantly, but I nod desperately, and he says, "Well, there were no narcotics in her urine, so the coroner figured she'd been clean for a while and just miscalculated her dose when she relapsed. They subpoenaed her medical records from the hospital and he said she needed a significant dose of methadone, so most likely she was using a lot of heroin back before she detoxed. His

339

best guess was that she just didn't realize her tolerance would be gone—what was once an ordinary dose to her was this time unfortunately lethal. No way to be sure, but it really did look like a mistake. I'm so sorry for your loss, ma'am."

"Thank you," I whisper, and the officer tips his hat toward me and he leaves.

I sit by the fire to open the box. When I see the journal, I see the first page filled with Annie's familiar, flowery script and I start to cry. I touch the page with my fingertip and I trace the words of the first line.

Oh, Annie.

I start to read, and the tears turn to a smile. As my gaze flies over the words, I hear her voice in my mind, reading it to me— telling me things that she *should* have told me over all of those years. I read only the first entry before Daisy wakes up, but I'm glad for the break—because I want to prolong this.

I feel like this is the last conversation I'll ever have with my sister and maybe, if I experience this word by word, I can stretch it out until I'm ready to let her go.

And despite the officer's assurances that Annie's death was a mistake, I'm still not sure what I'll find on that last page. Perhaps she did make a dosage mistake—but she also *relapsed*, and she did so right after I hung up on her.

Whatever she was looking for in that phone call the day she died, she didn't get it. And perhaps I'll live with that guilt for the rest of my life, but there's a slim chance that some clue to Annie's state of mind is waiting for me in those last few pages. That might not bring me peace—in fact, it might mean even more torment.

But if I can just understand her even a little, then maybe I can let her go.

Sam decides to take on the task of finding a nanny, and within a few days he tells me he's found the most overqualified, nurturing woman on earth. She is thirty-three, she has a degree in children's psychology and she is looking for full-time work.

She is happy to live with us, but she is also happy to live separately. If I had drawn up a description of the perfect nanny—à la Mary Poppins—Jayne is what I would have described. From the first moment I meet her, I know that we have the right person.

I've noticed that some people hold Daisy, and other people *cuddle* her. Jayne is definitely a cuddler. She scoops the baby up into her arms with obvious delight, and she immediately launches into a one-sided conversation with Daisy as if this is a completely natural thing for her to be doing. I still struggle to remember to talk to Daisy, so I marvel at Jayne's ease. Sam asks her about infant nutrition, and Jayne teaches us a thing or two about baby-led weaning and the psychology of offering a broad variety of foods once Daisy starts on solids.

"And don't get me started on reading," she says with a laugh. "This is the age to start, believe me. The last family I worked with thought I was insane when I started reading to their newborn twins, but they were eating their words once those kids started school."

Jayne has a trial morning with Daisy, and I take the opportunity to lock myself away in the study and call Mary Walters. It's a task I've been putting off, but now that Sam and I have agreed that we will adopt Daisy, it needs to be done.

"Oh, Dr. Vidler," Mary says softly when she takes my call. "I'm so sorry to hear about Annie."

It strikes me that Mary has never used Annie's name like that before. She speaks it with solemnity and care, and I'm actually quite touched.

"I'm calling because we want to adopt Daisy, and I don't know how to go about it."

"Well, that's just wonderful to hear," Mary murmurs before she launches into an explanation about the process. We'll need a new lawyer—one who specializes in adoptions, but since we're already caring for Daisy and we've undergone the relevant checks, Mary tells me that the process should be smooth enough.

"I wish you all the best, Dr. Vidler. I really do," she says when it's time to hang up—and I believe she means it.

Jayne and Daisy get along just fine during that trial morning. I discuss it with Sam, and we agree that she's perfect, so we offer her the job. Jayne moves into the guesthouse the day before I'm due to go back to work.

Everything is in place, and before I know it, I'm dressing in my work clothes, and I'm kissing Daisy as I head out the door.

I fight a battle against myself as I drive into the clinic. It doesn't seem right that my sister is dead, but that life can still go on as if nothing ever happened. That battle grows fiercer as I force myself to walk through the doors at the clinic. The receptionists greet me with an awkward welcome, careful not to reference what happened, but the sympathy and apology is in their eyes. Even Oliver is gentle with me, offering only a gruff, "It's good to have you back."

When I'm alone in my office, tears loom and I know I'm being ridiculous. This is the job I loved and that I've worked damned hard to get. But I don't want to be back at work. I want to be at home with Daisy. I want to focus on making sure she is okay.

I have patients coming, and once the tide of them starts, it doesn't stop. I eat lunch between appointments, in the downtime between Mr. Williams's sore elbow joint and Mrs. Thomas's eczema. Sam texts me several times during the day. I tell him I'm fine. I don't want him to worry, and I don't know how to explain why I'm not. Just how much time do I think I'm entitled to for grieving here?

When five o'clock arrives I'm exhausted—emotionally and physically—and I cry all the way home. Sam has let me know that he will be late; he is still dealing with a huge backlog of patients and surgeries after these disrupted months, too. I walk through the front door to find Jayne sitting on the lounge while

Daisy kicks in the bouncer, cooing happily, and an exhausted kind of anger comes down over me.

"What is she doing?"

Jayne gives me a confused smile.

"She's had a great day—"

"The television, Jayne," I say sharply. "You can't put a baby that age in front of the television."

Jayne rises and snatches up the remote, then flicks the television off.

"I'm so sorry. The house was so quiet—"

The turmoil inside me bursts, but the energy shoots in the wrong direction. I walk briskly toward Daisy and I scoop her up from the bouncer and I say, "Look, I don't think this is going to work—if you don't have good enough judgment to realize that a newborn shouldn't be watching television, how can I possibly leave you alone with her?"

"But—Dr. Vidler—"

"I'm sorry, Jayne. You should go."

She is staring at me in disbelief, and no wonder—this is coming out of nowhere and I'm being completely unreasonable. I know it, but I also know that I *cannot* go back to the office tomorrow. I can't pretend to care about my patients when my entire mind is full of grief and loss.

Jayne tries to convince me to change my mind, then her pleading turns to irritation and after she packs up her things I hear the squeal of her tires as she drives away. I feel so guilty about how I've treated her that I cry again.

When Sam comes home, I'm too embarrassed and ashamed to tell him what I did. Jayne was perfect and I'm an idiot. He notices that I'm upset, though. "First day back was tough?"

I could tell him that I can't handle this. I could tell him that I need to take some time out from my career to heal and to focus on Daisy, but I can't admit I need to—not even to Sam. I'm strong and I'm independent and I'm not the kind of person who unravels. That's who I've always been, and it's how I understand myself. If I could get through Dad's death and Mom's depression, surely I should be able to cope with this.

"I let Jayne go tonight."

Sam frowns at me, bewildered.

"Let her go?"

"I fired her."

His eyes widen in shock.

"What? Why?"

I shake my head fiercely.

"She had this baby in front of the television all day. She all but admitted it. That was her first day, Sam. That would have been her A game—God, who knows where things would have led from here? She has a snooze on the lounge while Daisy rolls around the floor? What about when Daisy is crawling? She has a little nap and Daisy crawls over to play in the fireplace or the medicine cabinet? *No.* This isn't going to work. I'll find someone myself, and until then I'll take some time off work."

Sam is staring at me incredulously. There's a pause, and I wait expectantly for his response, knowing he's pissed.

"Lexie. This is ridiculous."

"Oh, I'm ridiculous now?" I gasp, and Sam throws his head back and sighs slowly. I stare at him, but my anger and my frustration are running rampant now, and if there was a chance that I was going to be honest with him, it's lost to my defensiveness.

"If you need some more time off, we'll figure it out," Sam says. "But let's *keep* Jayne. We're not going to find anyone else as qualified."

"*No.*"

"Let's ask Oliver if you can work part-time for a while."

"Oh, you're going to go in and do that for me, too, are you?"

"Lexie!" Sam raises his voice and I jump, cringing. He sighs again and rubs his forehead, and then his eyes are pleading with me. "I know you're under a lot of pressure, Lex. I *know* you have a lot to process. But surely you can see that you're being completely irrational about this."

"Now I'm crazy, too, am I? You just keep *pressuring* me. What else do you want from me, Sam? I have to talk to you about everything and go straight back to work and take the nanny you want whether I like her or not and oh—" I laugh bitterly "—and *don't* be crazy, Lexie. Your family is completely batty and that's caused enough problems in our perfect little life here, but *you* can't be crazy, too. Would that be the straw that broke the camel's back, Sam? You can put up with my drug-addict sister and my batty mother, but if *I'm* crazy, too, what happens then, huh? Do you walk out and find someone better?"

"That's enough." Sam stands and leaves the room abruptly, and I'm sitting at the kitchen table alone and all of the nonsense that's just spewed from my mouth circles back through my mind and I want to suck it all back in. The house is suddenly full of my regret, and it feels immense—the distance to go to Sam and apologize is too large for me to cross.

He doesn't sleep in the study this time. He goes all the way out to the guesthouse.

I have a case of confusion-induced insomnia. I pace the halls, thinking about Sam. I reflect on our early days dating, and the giddy heights of our relationship as it progressed—I think about the night he proposed, and how I'd never been so happy or so confident about my future.

Then I think about how wrong it feels that he's not in our house tonight, and how bewildered I am that I have allowed things to get this bad. It's entirely my fault that he's out there. Even I'm not sure why I don't just march across the yard and drag him back to bed.

I am here, living the dream—and apparently somehow, messing it up.

But I don't want to rely on Sam. What if I let him take care of me, and what if I get too used to it, and then he decides he can't deal with this situation and he leaves? What if I grew to really need him, and then something happened to him? Would I sink into a depression like Mom? What would that mean for Daisy?

In the past, whenever things were chaotic, I stepped into a well-worn groove of being the stable one. I'm the person in any situation who keeps a calm head, who copes and who fixes things. Other people need me; *I* don't need other people. Why can't Sam respect that? Isn't that the woman he fell in love with? Sam *thinks* he wants me to rely on him now, but he really doesn't. If I was weak, like Annie…like Mom… God, he'd *hate* it. It's a burden to be around people like that. I know that all too well. I don't *ever* want to be a burden to Sam.

Maybe that's why I couldn't tell him the truth today about why I fired Jayne. I don't want him to know how weak I really feel right now.

I make coffee, and I turn the laptop on and I start to research long-term studies for NAS children. It's better to do something useful than to ruminate on the situation with Sam, even if the studies all say what I already know. There's a slightly increased chance that Daisy will suffer from a hyperactivity disorder, but statistically, the likelihood is that her in utero exposure to narcotics will have little long-term effect on her health, as long as I can provide her with a stable home environment.

Family environment is *everything* to Daisy now. And her only father figure is sleeping in the guesthouse because her mother figure keeps pushing him away. My thoughts circle right on back to Sam. I slam the laptop shut and go back to my pacing.

Daisy wakes for an early-morning feed before I've even gone to bed myself, and I prepare the bottle and sit with her. I stare down at her in the darkness of my room, and she is perfect. She drinks greedily at the formula, and the physician in me notes the strength of her sucking reflex now, and the excellent color in her face, and the increased interaction she has with us—her eyes light up when she sees me. She is becoming well again. Daisy is now thirteen weeks old, and has already undergone a detox from a physiological narcotic dependency.

It's extraordinary to consider the physical suffering she's endured, and how quickly she seems to have left that behind. The worst of her health issues are probably in the past but...then I think about the psychological hurdles ahead of her, and I'm scared again.

Every tear she is going to shed—every time she's going to wonder why she wasn't *enough* for Annie to be well—I'm going to have to walk her through that. Me: the same woman who sobbed all the way home from work today and who can't even admit to her fiancé that she's struggling.

I crumple around my newborn niece, and I breathe in her scent—she smells of innocence, an innocence that will not last long. How will I ever know *what* to tell her about Annie? How will I know when she's ready to hear the truth? What do I ask her to call me? If I ask her to call me Aunt Lexie, as soon as she goes to kindergarten, she's going to ask me why she doesn't call me "Mom." If she calls me "Mom," am I denying my sister's existence? I can't do that. I can't ask that of Daisy. It would be unfair—and I can't ask that of Annie. It would betray her memory.

I try to think of a solution, right here, right now—I can fix this. Perhaps I acknowledge Annie's existence from the very first moments of Daisy's life. Perhaps I put photos of Annie everywhere, *old* photos—before she started to look so tired. Come to think of it, those are the only photos I have of her, except that one where she's holding Daisy in the hospital.

After a while I move her into my bed. I cuddle her in my elbow, and I keep her at my side, and I stare at her as she sleeps. The responsibility—the complexity, the grief—they are all overwhelming, and they bundle together to create a hard lump in my chest. And I'm facing this alone, because Sam is in the guest-house and I pushed him away.

I'm at the kitchen table the next morning when Sam comes in through the door. He offers me a neutral sort of hello before he goes about preparing his breakfast. He arranges his usual morning meal of toast with eggs, and then he sits beside me. Daisy is in her baby seat, sitting on the table while I push my oatmeal around the bowl.

"Lexie," Sam says, and I look at him only momentarily before I lose my courage and I look away.

"Please," I say weakly. "Please let's not do this now. I've had almost no sleep. Please can we talk about it later?"

"Lexie, I just want to help. You're obviously struggling." I close my eyes to hold the tears in. Sam rests his hand on my wrist, offering a gentle warmth. I can't do anything more than nod. "Resign," he whispers.

"I have to work," I whisper back. "We need the money."

"We'll manage, Lexie. It's just for a while. Take this time. Focus on Daisy…focus on our family. I think we *all* need you to be here with her for now."

I open my eyes and stare at him. He's gazing at me patiently, and there's nothing but concern and love in his expression.

"I couldn't have done this without you, Sam," I whisper.

"And there will be plenty of times in our future that I'll need *you* to get through. That's what sharing a life is about, honey."

"I'm sorry," I say softly. "I really am. It's very hard for me to accept help."

"That's become pretty obvious," Sam says wryly.

"And I'm used to dealing with things on my own."

"I know."

"I'm working on it."

"Good. Daisy is a beautiful, precious little girl but…she represents a huge responsibility that we *need* to share. I'm her father now. You have to let me fulfill that role—for her sake and for yours—but also, because I want to. Okay?"

"Okay," I nod, and I exhale.

"So will you take some time out from working?"

Leaving my job feels like a failure—an admission of defeat.

It also feels like a decision that Sam and I are making together, a decision that's right for all of us. Maybe that makes it okay.

"Okay, Sam," I murmur. "Just for a while."

I call Oliver and I resign over the phone. He doesn't sound surprised. I expect that now I can focus all of my energies on Daisy that things will get easier, so I'm confused as days begin to pass and everything still feels so difficult.

I'm at home alone with Daisy all day and there's so much to do. I get frustrated by my bewildering inability to keep on top of things—the laundry piles up and I don't get any cleaning done and we're constantly ordering in because there never seems to be time for groceries. Nights of disjointed sleep leave me feeling permanently exhausted, so it takes little for me to feel frazzled. Sam helps a lot when he's at home, but his work schedule resumes a more regular rhythm and that means he's on call sometimes and there are plenty of days when he's at the hospital from early morning until late at night.

Its late on one of those days when Daisy becomes unusually unsettled. She cries for hours, and at first I tell myself that Sam will be home soon and he'll be able to help, but then he has a ward clerk call to let me know that he's had to go back into surgery and it'll be a few hours.

I try all of the things I know usually calm her—singing, rocking, a bottle…but nothing works. This sudden change in her demeanor frightens me. I check her temperature—definitely no fever this time—and then I run through a mental checklist of all the other things that could be upsetting her.

She's fed, she's having normal bowel movements, she's not

vomiting—but soon she is red-faced from crying. I have been calm up until this point, but now I'm getting frustrated. I'm exhausted and I'm frazzled and Daisy is still crying, and without even deciding to do it, I call my mom. Robert answers the phone and his voice is curt.

"Hello?"

"Robert, it's Alexis. Can I please speak with my mother?"

"It's after midnight, Alexis."

"I'm sorry. I just need to speak to her." It is all I can do to keep my voice level enough that the words are coherent. Everything feels topsy-turvy, even this moment—since when do *I* run to *Mom* for help?

There is a muffled sound at the end of the phone, footsteps and whispers and more footsteps and a door closes. Then I hear Mom's voice, gently asking, "Lexie? What is it? Is it the baby?"

The sound of her voice undoes me. Suddenly, it's not just Daisy I'm scared about—it's everything.

"Mom, Daisy won't stop crying. And I had to quit my job and I thought I'd feel better once I did but I just don't and I can't even settle her down—"

"Hush, Lexie," Mom says gently. "Everything is going to be okay. First things first, love. Tell me about Daisy."

"She's miserable, and I don't know what it could be. I've given her a bottle—I don't think she's constipated—no fever—"

"Love, she's young—sometimes babies are just unhappy. Try cuddling her—holding her close. Lie down with her."

"But—Mom—I *can't* hold her all night."

Mom laughs softly.

"Of course you can. I used to do it all the time with you girls when you were unsettled. Sometimes Dad and I took turns, but you can bet your life that if you needed to be cuddled all night, we found a way to do it. I'd even sleep in the rocking chair with you in my arms. You do *whatever* you have to with a newborn to get enough sleep to get by."

"But—sleeping upright with the baby is a SIDS risk and Sam works such long hours at the hospital and it's just me most of the time—and I just need some sleep—" I'm starting to cry again, and my mother's voice is so gentle, and so consoling.

"Lexie... I think sometimes even you forget that you're human. This stage of life is *always* hard, and you've got a lot of extra things on your plate. Let's think about what else we can do to settle her. Did you swaddle her?"

The swaddle.

"I forgot to do that tonight." I'm embarrassed it has just slipped my mind—my thoughts have just been racing so fast and hard. Daisy always sleeps swaddled—NAS babies tend to have an increased Moro reflex and so they startle more than newborns usually do, and swaddling helps to manage that. But today, all the swaddles were in the wash and without the pile of them on the table to remind me, it was just one step that I forgot to take. I'm suddenly hopelessly mortified by my own inadequacy.

"Can you get her a swaddle, then? Let's try that," Mom asks gently.

My tears had stalled when I realized the problem, but now I start to cry again.

"They're all in the wash. They're all wet. She spit up all over them—what else can I do? Does this mean she's going to be like this all night?"

The problem seems insurmountable, until Mom says gently, "Sweetheart, go and get a cot sheet. It doesn't matter what she is wrapped in, she just wants to feel secure."

I keep the phone to my ear as I go. Almost the second the cot sheet is tucked around her, Daisy shuts her eyes, the exhausted crying stops and she goes straight to sleep. I'm sobbing and laughing and I feel like a complete idiot.

"That's it," Mom whispers gently. "You know what, Lexie? You've *got* this. You have all that you need to be a brilliant mother to Daisy. But there's one thing you've never been good at, sweetheart. I have never once seen you ask for help—not without a struggle first. You can't raise a child without a support network. It's not good for you, and it's not good for her. Promise me you'll think about that."

I rest my forehead against the wall, and I close my eyes and focus on her voice. I don't want to hang up. I love Mom like this—this is the way she was before Dad died—but I haven't seen a hint of it in thirty years. She is comforting me—and it feels amazing.

"Are you going to be okay now?"

I hear Robert in the background—urging Mom to come back to bed, telling her that she's being too noisy, telling her that she needs to leave me to sort this out on my own. I feel a tight, painful contraction in my chest.

"I have to go," Mom says, without waiting for my response. "Call me tomorrow?"

I hang up the phone, and I look at my niece, who is breathing deeply in her sleep.

Mom is right—I need a support network—but I have no idea what that would even look like.

The next morning, I take Daisy to the mall and finally do the long-overdue grocery run. I just need to *see* other people—even if I don't actually speak with them. I feel much calmer by the time we return to the car, and I sing to Daisy while we drive home. As we turn into our street, I see someone on the porch of my house. From a distance, I don't recognize her, but as I get close I'm shocked to realize it is Mom. How long has she been there? I wonder why she didn't call when she arrived— and then I realize that she doesn't own a cell. I park in the garage and get out of the car. As Mom joins me, I blurt, "What are you doing here?"

Mom stares at me. She doesn't seem upset, but something

doesn't seem right. She opens the back seat door and when she sees Daisy, a broad smile transforms her.

"Mom?" I prompted. Mom glances at me, and she shrugs.

"You have always been there for me, Lexie, and I've relied on you far too many times. But *you* need me now, so I'm here to stay—as long as you need me."

This makes no sense. I stare at my mother in bewilderment. She leaves the baby and walks toward me, then pulls me into a surprisingly tight hug.

"I wasn't there for Annie," she whispers. "But I'll be damned if I'm going to make the same mistake twice."

I don't know which of us is more startled when I burst into tears. I feel Mom tense against me.

"Thank you, Mom." I'm dissolving in her arms, and Mom recovers from her shock and starts to rub gently between my shoulder blades. We stand there for a while, and my tears keep coming and coming, as my mother whispers soothing words into my ear.

"Everything is going to be okay. You've been so brave, Lexie. Mom's here now. You just let it all out, sweetheart."

And I do. I cry, and I cry, and my mom fusses over me, and it's funny how it's been so long since she comforted me that I had forgotten that it feels absolutely amazing. Even when the storm of my emotions has passed, she insists that I go for a nap while she unpacks the car, and when I wake up several hours later, the smell of cookies is in the air, and Daisy is tucked in asleep in the bassinet beside me. Downstairs, I hear Mom moving around, and I lie in bed and I actually let myself rest. I can barely believe the way the tables have turned.

When Daisy wakes up, I take her downstairs to Mom.

"You look better already." She surveys my face, and then she gives me a very satisfied smile. "Good."

I drag details out of her over the next few hours. She has—

for the first time in over twenty years—disobeyed Robert. She has left the community against his will.

"But—what about when you go back?" I say blankly. Mom winces, and for the first time, she actually looks a little uncertain.

"I don't know. But I've made the decision to come, and I can deal with the fallout—on my *own*. Got that?" I stare at her blankly, and then I nod because her tone is so authoritative that I'm not even tempted to argue. She stares down at Daisy, and a smile breaks over her face again. "I should have come—so many times. I couldn't live with myself if I made a mistake like that again. Let me be here now."

Mom's arrival doesn't make everything better. What it does is much more complex, and somehow more beautiful even than that. Her presence gives me distance from all that has over-whelmed me. With Daisy close by, she gets straight to work on sorting through the mess that the house has fallen into.

And I just stop. There is no frenetic energy to burn off, and no exhaustion to cloud my thoughts. I still meet almost all of Daisy's care requirements—but now, when I need to go for a walk or to take a nap, I can leave the baby with Mom. This means that for the first time in weeks I get some time to myself—space to hear my own thoughts clearly, and decent stretches of sleep.

I'm like a new person within a few days. I think of all of the newborn mothers who have come to me in tears, struggling to cope with sleep deprivation, and I think about how unsympathetic I've been. "It's just a phase. It will pass." Or, "All new mothers find it difficult. Hang in there. A few months from now and this will all be a memory."

I had no idea what I was talking about. I vow to be much more understanding when I return to work.

Space to think means space to really consider my relationship with Sam. There's no denying he's been endlessly patient and supportive through all of these weeks, but I also start to realize how unfair I've been to him in withholding parts of my history. Sam knows enough about my life to know that my childhood was atypical, but I never really went into any detail.

I never warned him that I have spent most of my life being responsible for things that weren't actually my problem. I just had no idea how much that would impact me. Have I even told Sam about that year when Mom was too grief-stricken to move? Does he understand just how little she participated in all of my efforts to get Annie well over the years?

He knows plenty about the parts of my life I have chosen to share with him. Those parts that I rarely visit myself, though… the darkest days of my history…they are a mystery to Sam, and maybe he won't actually understand me until I completely open up to him. So I start to talk about the times I'd rather forget. We sit up at night while Daisy sleeps in the bassinet beside our bed and we talk—*really* talk, about grief and hope and the past and the future. One day, I surprise him at work with lunch. We sit in his office and talk about Dad's death, the way that Mom struggled to cope and the role that I had to play to keep us all together. It's hard to talk about—hard to even think about—but instead of clamming up, I *tell* him that and Sam listens intently and he says all the right things. When I'm leaving, he thanks me.

"What for?" I ask him blankly, and Sam smiles at me—a proper smile—the unguarded one I haven't seen for weeks. I can't help but smile back, especially when he says, "I said 'thank you' because you trusted me with something that was hard for you to share, and I didn't even have to drag it out of you. That's progress, and I'm happy."

"Me, too," I whisper, and then he kisses me properly—not the polite, public kiss he's been offering me at home in front of Mom.

Sam and I have always had love, but as I open up to him more, an emotional intimacy grows between us that I'd never even thought to hope for. I get a glimpse of what life is going to be like with someone who *truly* knows me…and a taste of parenting with someone who's committed to sharing the load.

After two weeks at our house, Mom tells me that she needs to go home. She says this just as we sit down to enjoy the pie she cooked for dinner, and I'm so startled I drop my fork. She and Sam both stare at me.

"So soon? I didn't realize—I mean—I didn't realize you'd be going so soon. I thought—maybe you'd stay until—" I trail off, because I don't know how to finish the sentence. Mom did say she'd be here as long as I needed her. Things are much better, and I'm feeling much better but—I still *need* her. I feel like I just found her, and I don't want lose her again. Do I have to say it? Is this some kind of test? Mom looks down at her plate.

"I have responsibilities back home. There are lessons to write, exams to mark, and the children at the school really need me. And Robert needs me—he *is* my husband."

"When are you thinking of leaving?" Sam asks.

"In a few days. Robert has booked me a ticket. He said if I come back now, everything is going to be okay."

I can see her reluctance to return, and it's maddening.

"Mom," I say, "why do you let him control you like this? You obviously don't want to go, and I still—" I stumble over my words, then I force myself to say them. "I still need—I still *want* you to stay."

"It's been great being here, Lexie. But this isn't my life. I committed to a life with Robert. I need to go back to it," she says quietly.

"Why do you always put him first?" I snap at her, and I push my plate away from me with force. "You always did this to us. You always chose what *he* wanted over what *we* needed, and—"

"A few days, you say?" Sam's steady, deep voice cuts through my rapidly escalating hysteria, and Mom and I turn to him. He gives me a smile, all tied up in a pointed glance, and I have to take a deep breath. *Let him help. Let him stop the argument. Let him be on your side. He understands.*

"Yes," Mom murmurs. "Robert booked the ticket for Friday."

"Well, then," Sam says lightly, "I think you two should go out for dinner tomorrow night—baby free. Spend some quality time together, before Deborah has to leave. Okay? Daisy will be fine with me."

"I'd like that," Mom says, and she looks at me. "Lexie?"

It suddenly strikes me just how close I came to a screaming match with Mom. We've done this before on the phone in recent years, and had Sam not intervened with his offer of a child-free night, I know that dinner would have quickly escalated to ugliness and we may have lost all our recent progress. Mom has always become very defensive when anyone questioned her loyalty to Robert.

"Thanks, Sam. That would be great."

I pull the pie back toward myself; it's too good to waste. Mom's eyes are on me. I glance up at her and she offers me a smile that's at least part apology. The smile I return is weak, but it strengthens when I catch Sam's steady gaze.

I guess sometimes progress really is two steps forward, one step back. But the important thing is that, overall, we're all moving in the right direction.

As we're getting ready for bed that night, I feel like a chapter of my life is coming to a close. Mom is going, and Sam and I are rebuilding, Annie is gone—and I need to let her go.

"What are you up to?" Sam asks me quietly, and I show him the journal. "What is it?"

"It's Annie's."

"Oh?"

"The police brought it here a few weeks ago. They found it in her trailer. I've been saving it… I didn't want to finish it. But I don't know…it kind of feels like it's time now."

Once we're tucked in bed together, Sam picks up the novel he's reading, and I take a deep breath and I start to read my sister's words. I don't pace myself anymore—I don't make excuses about needing time to process each entry—I just read. These are all stories that I know, but I need to connect with them again. It's the ultimate empathy—I'm seeing our childhood through Annie's eyes, and it is horrifying and magnificent. I see myself through her eyes—and as I read about those early years in the community, I'm no longer the sister who failed her, but the sister who saved her.

"Are you okay?" Sam asks me, again and again as the tears roll down my cheeks.

"Not really," I reply each time. I feel like Annie is sitting on the bed next to me, too, quietly reading her stories into my ear. Every now and again I close my eyes, and I want to reach out and embrace her. One time, I reach across to that side of the bed, and I'm somehow surprised to find empty space there. It is still inconceivable that she is really gone.

It hurts, but I press on because I want to get to the last page—although I'm not quite brave enough to skip forward. Instead, I read faster—I stop savoring every word, and I just want to inhale her spirit through those pages, to see if I can find her secrets. To see if, as she feared, the way to understand her was locked within these pages.

It's not long before I find it, and when I do, I'm not prepared. My silent tears turn to panicked sobs, and when I can't bring myself to explain, I simply point to the page and let Sam read the entry for himself.

"Oh, Lexie…" he whispers. "Shit…"

It makes me feel sick, but I force myself to reread that passage several times before I can really grasp what she's telling me.

"How did I not know?" is all I can think to say.

"How *could* you know?" Sam asks.

I think about the changes in my sister during those years. I think about the vibrant, spirited Annie whom I knew before I left the community—and the fragile, wounded girl who came out three years after me. I think about how every sense of innocence she had about life had been smashed out of her—and how obvious it should have been that something terrible had happened within those walls.

But it wasn't obvious.

And she never told me.

And I never asked. Even when she hinted in the car on the way to rehab, I never pushed—and now I can see that I should have.

Did this secret kill my sister?

Not for a second will I entertain the idea that Annie would have lied about such a thing, not here, not in this book. This journal was such a precious thing to Annie that she carted it around with her for much of her life. She could never hold on to apartments or friends or money in the bank—but she held on to this journal—it was always connected to her memories of Dad. So, even with no way to verify it, and every reason in the world to doubt the very integrity of Annie's word even at the best of times, I'm entirely convinced that this journal is a true account of her life. Her beauty shines through these words, but so does her pain.

Why didn't she *tell* me? Why didn't she contact me? I would have come to get her, I would have found a way to get her out of there—I would have done *something* to make her safe again. But then I think about Annie's time in the community, and I realize that by the time I left and the abuse started, she had already been broken down. She had been "the bad girl" for so many years by that stage. She already believed that she deserved no better.

I close the journal and I press it to the bottom of the top drawer in my bedside table, then I slam the drawer shut.

"I should have been there."

"Would it have made any difference if you were, Lexie?"

"The abuse started after *I* left."

We each ponder that for a moment, and then Sam asks quietly, "So, was this Annie's fault?"

I gasp and twist to glare at him.

"What? Of course not!"

"So whose fault was it?" he presses, and I frown. I'm quickly becoming defensive, because Sam should know better than to ask these questions.

"Robert's," I snap, and he nods and I inhale as I realize the point he's just made.

"Exactly. Robert. Robert's decision, Robert's actions, Robert's *fault*. Not yours."

I sigh again, and the fight drains out of me.

"Yeah. Okay."

I'm imagining Annie, terrified in that bedroom we fought so hard to share. I see her wide-awake and staring at the roof, waiting for those footsteps in the hall, unsafe and alone.

I feel her anxiety now as if it were mine. My breath comes faster, and my pulse starts to race, and Sam lifts me until I'm sitting on his lap and his arms are tightly around my shoulders. I try to focus on the steady beat of his heart against my ear. All I can think is…*at least Sam is here. I couldn't have dealt with this alone.*

"I should have known. She was so broken when she came out. I should have known something had happened."

"Sweetheart, I wish I had some magic phrase to say to you to make all of this better, but I don't."

"I don't need you to make it better. You're doing exactly what I need you to do." I choke the words out, then I turn and press my face into his shoulder. "You're *here* for me."

"Will you tell Deborah?" he asks me, and I groan softly and nod, then shake my head, then nod again.

"I have to, obviously. But…"

"I can be there when you do it. I can help you with that."

"I think I need to read the rest of the journal first," I whisper, but even as I say it, I'm quite terrified of what else I'm going to find.

"Tomorrow," Sam says quietly. "Why don't you take tomorrow to read the rest, and we can talk to her after your dinner?"

"Yeah." I nod, and I take a deep breath. "That's a really good plan."

I tell Mom that I need to take the day to organize paperwork in my office—I mumble something about patient files and catching up on reading journals. I'm relieved when she seems excited to have Daisy to herself for the day.

I try to convince myself that Mom wouldn't have known—*couldn't* have known—but I'm frightened of what it means for our relationship if she did. Mom's loyalty to Robert was always a mystery to me, but now I can't help but wonder how deep it runs. If she knew, if she even suspected—that is the end of our relationship. I'll never speak to her again—I'll never let her see Daisy again.

I spend the day alone in the office. I start back at the very beginning of Annie's journal and I parse every word and phrase looking for clues. By the time I get to the last few pages, I have climbed the highs and lows of her addiction with her, and I have been there for her in a way that I never managed to do during the course of her life.

I've seen the journey with her eyes, instead of mine—and I'm exhausted.

But I stop just before that last page. I'm going to be completely gutted if this journal ends without at least some kind of clue into Annie's state of mind when she reached for the needle that last time. Even if she was angry at me, I want to know. I've had *enough* hiding; now I want to embrace the truth, regardless of how painful it is.

"Lexie?" Mom knocks hesitantly on the study door. "Sam will be home soon—do you still want to go for dinner?"

I close the journal and I leave it on my desk, then I open the door. Mom is a picture of a loving grandmother, with Daisy happy and content in her arms, but she's also a woman reluctant to leave, and powerless to stay.

Mom is looking at me with an expectant, happy look in her eyes and I start to wonder if I *can* actually tell her about what happened with Annie without losing my mind or losing my temper? Maybe I'll wait, and do it with Sam. I'll try to read the mood at dinner, or do it afterward. It might be best to discuss this in private. God only knows how she's going to react.

"Do you still want to go?" I ask her.

"Of course I do, I'm already dressed."

My mother's dress clothes look exactly like day clothes. I give her a smile, and I take Daisy from her arms and kiss her cheek.

"Let me take a shower."

I'm sitting on the edge of our bed, pulling on my shoes, when Sam joins me in the bedroom.

"How are you?" he asks.

"I'm okay."

"Did you read the rest?"

"Most of it."

"Any other shocks?"

"Probably the only other shock was how much she loved me. Because she did, Sam. She *really* did. And she knew that I loved her, even if I didn't say it often enough."

Sam smiles sadly, and he offers his hand, then pulls me to my feet.

"Are we going to talk to Deborah together?"

"I'm going to play it by ear tonight," I say. "If the opportunity arises around dinner, I'll try to bring it up and see how she reacts."

"Okay, Lex," Sam murmurs.

"And *you* are going to stay home with our daughter, and read Dr. Seuss books, even though her only thanks will be to drool and maybe even poop all over you."

He laughs softly. "I know where I'd rather be."

I smile sadly at him. "Me, too."

"If you need to, leave it until you get home, and we'll do it together. Promise?"

"Promise," I say, and I mean it.

I take Mom to a little French restaurant the next suburb over and we have quite a civilized conversation over dinner. We talk about things that are safe. She talks about the schoolhouse at Winterton. I talk to her about my work. She asks if I'll look for a new job.

"I need to talk to Sam about that," I say, because that's the extent of my plan. Mom nods approvingly.

She doesn't mention Robert during the whole conversation, and I'm glad, because I have a feeling that if she speaks his name I might turn the table over in rage. By the end of the meal, I'm wondering if *any* opportunity is going to arise for me to broach the topic of his relationship with Annie. But then Mom makes the decision for me—as we finish eating, she says, "Before we go home—you think we could go visit Annie?"

We drive to the cemetery in silence, and then I curse when we reach the front gates to find they are closed. It hadn't occurred to Mom or me that we wouldn't be able to reach the grave. I park right in front of the gates, and we get out of the car to stare past them.

"I guess it makes sense." Mom sighs heavily.

"What time is your flight?"

"Six. Too early for me to come back."

Suddenly, I know what I have to do, and a frantic kind of madness overtakes me. I go to the trunk of my car and I withdraw a picnic blanket, and I throw it up over the fence. All of the turmoil inside me bursts out as I pull myself up onto the gate.

"What are you doing?" Mom gasps, and I glance back down at her and shake my head.

"Come on, it's easier than it looks."

"But it's probably trespassing—"

"Mom, there's no better way to honor Annie then to go visit her tonight—so climb the damned fence. Let's spend one last moment with her. This is what Annie would have done." Mom is sufficiently moved by my plea, and just as I reach the top I turn around to see my mother close behind. She is surprisingly sprightly climbing up the rails with apparent ease, reaching the top as quickly as I do. As we drop to the other side, we lean into each other and we each start to laugh.

"You're absolutely right. I can imagine her getting to the fence and just looking at it like climbing it was just part of the fun." Mom sighs and smiles at me. "She never really let anyone stop her from doing what she wanted to do, did she? Not for better, not for worse."

We start walking toward the grave, our footsteps a little slow. It is creepy—so many headstones and dark shadows, but I don't feel unsafe—I'm simply aware of the moment. I feel like this is one of those times I'm going to look back on, and I just want to do it right. I need to tell Mom what I have learned about Annie, and I'm going to do it here where Annie can hear me.

When we reach the gravesite, I rest the picnic blanket right beside the new memorial stone. I ordered it when I planned her funeral, but it wasn't ready the day we buried her, so this is the first time I've seen it. I run my fingers over the engraving of her name, and then I sit back beside Mom.

Are you listening, Annie? I'm here, and I've finally heard you.

"Mom," I whisper. "I need to tell you something."

"What is it?"

Mom sits beside me, and she pulls her legs awkwardly toward

her chest. She wraps her arms around them while she waits for me to speak, and I look toward her.

"I lied to you today. I didn't have to work. The police found something in the trailer...it was Annie's journal. Do you remember that little leather journal—that notebook that she used to carry around when she was a kid?"

Mom is frowning, but she nods.

"How on earth did she still have *that*?"

"She left it at my place years ago, but I sent it to her at rehab when she was starting to struggle. I thought that maybe she could journal about the things she couldn't bring herself to say. And she tried, Mom. She left her story on those pages, and I read most of it today."

My voice is breaking. Every time I blink, I see Annie's face. I *left* her. I left her with that man, and he broke her.

Through my tears I see that Mom is looking at me expectantly, and I suddenly feel wary.

"What do *you* think it said, Mom?"

"Well..." Mom crosses her legs beneath her skirt now and smooths the fabric over her knees. After a moment she shrugs her shoulders, and says, "I think your sister was a very troubled young woman. She rejected everything good in her life many times over, so I can't imagine there would have been anything positive in a journal like that. I almost wish you hadn't had to read it, Lexie. I know that I shouldn't speak evil of her...especially so soon after she's gone—but she never took responsibility for her life. It didn't have to go this way."

I start to shake. I'm shaking so hard that I can't sit beside my mother anymore, so I stand, and Mom looks up at me with alarm. Everything within me starts to burn and I snap—the words just burst out of me without care or caution.

"Robert *hurt* her, Mom. He ground her self-esteem into the dust, and then he took advantage of her—and *you* let it happen."

"What?" Mom looks utterly bewildered, clearly clueless about

what I'm suggesting—and that should be a relief. It is, but now…
I can't bring myself to say the words. God, if *I* can't even say
them, no wonder Annie never could. I'm suddenly regretting
this decision—I can't do this next to Annie. I don't *want* her to
hear me say this, in case hearing it makes her hurt even more.

It's a ridiculous thought.

I stare at the grave as Mom pushes herself to her feet and she
takes my hand in hers and she says urgently, "What are you saying? Lexie, whatever Annie suggested—"

"Robert *raped* her."

My words echo around us in the otherwise heavy silence of the
cemetery, and I look down at my sister's grave, and I start to cry.

*Did you hear me, Annie? I told her for you. He can't hurt you any-
more. Mom knows now. You're safe now.*

"No," Mom gasps, and she steps back away from me. "Alexis,
don't you *say* that. It's not true!"

"Annie wouldn't have lied. Not in *that* journal."

"You can't make an accusation like that—it's not fair at all,"
Mom whispers. Her low tone is such a stark contrast to my shouting that I have to strain to hear her. "She was incredibly troubled, Lexie—and Robert would never have done such a thing."

"You know as well I do that he used to hurt Annie in all
kinds of ways. The beatings, the fasting—from the moment we
got to that house, he tortured her—it just got worse and worse
over the years. And he waited until I left to use her for his own
disgusting gratification."

"Lexie, listen to me," Mom says urgently. "Robert was hard
on her, but he cared about her. He just wanted to put her on the
right path, and it seemed to work for a while. After you left, she
changed—she fit in better and—"

"Because she was terrified of him! Because he convinced her
that she was broken beyond repair and too damaged to save.
Mom, can't you see? Didn't you notice *anything*?"

"I noticed how he tried so hard to help her, Lexie—he always gave her such special attention. I know he was hard on her, but that was because she needed it—"

She breaks off. Mom is breathing harder. I watch her pale— even in the moonlight I see the color draining from her face. But my anger is a living thing, and it's not just for Annie that I'm angry. I'm angry for me, too. I'm angry for a childhood that I should have had—a childhood that I never got to experience... because of Mom.

"From the time Dad died, you never put us first—you chose your grief over us, you chose Robert over us. You *let us down*."

"I moved you girls to the community because I thought it would be better for you. And I had to marry Robert, Lexie—I had been withdrawn from, and he was the only way we could get back in. Don't you remember how depressed I was? That was *no* way for you to live. No way for *any of us* to live!"

"Don't try to convince me you did it for us!" I'm shouting again, and now I clench my fists. "We were happy at home. *You* couldn't cope—but Annie and I were coping just fine. You had to hide behind that stupid religion because you didn't have Dad to hide behind anymore!"

"That's not true, Lexie," Mom whispers, and the pain on her face is breathtaking. Am I doing the right thing? Does this all really need to be said, or am I saying it to hurt her? I can't even tell anymore. "I just wanted to be a better mom. Your dad and I went out into the world together and then he was gone, and I just didn't *know* how to navigate it alone."

"So you moved us all into the house of a monster."

"Robert is *not* a monster!" Mom gasps, and I laugh bitterly and turn away from her, back toward my sister's headstone.

"Tell that to Annie, Mom. Face her *grave* and tell her you don't believe her."

Mom approaches, but she stops just behind me. I listen to the sound of her ragged breathing, but my anger is fading—soon all I can feel is remorse. It feels bigger than me, and it's just so big that

I'm not sure how I'm ever going to go on with my life, knowing that Annie was dealing with this pain and I never, ever knew.

Eventually, Mom tentatively touches my shoulders. All of the shouting has faded, and we are both crying very softly. When I don't shake her off, Mom steps closer and rests her arm over my shoulders as she whispers, "This just isn't true, Lexie. How could it be? I would have known. She would have told me."

"She couldn't even tell *me*," I whisper back. "He told her that she deserved it, and she believed him, and then this thing defined her entire life. And it happened in your house—under your roof. How could you not have known? You should have seen it."

"I *would* have seen it," Mom says flatly.

"She had no reason to lie, Mom." I'm pleading with her to look past what she *wants* to be the true, to see just how many questions this god-awful discovery answers. "The journal was for her therapist—she just wanted to be understood."

"They were never even alone together, Lexie. He was at work during the day, and then at night, I was home."

"He went to her room at night after you went to bed."

I feel Mom's arms stiffen over my shoulder, and I turn toward her. Her face is frozen in the moonlight. Uncertainty has crept into her expression.

"What is it?" I prompt, and now I see guilt in Mom's eyes and I shake her hand off my shoulder. "Did you *know*, Mom?"

"No! No. But—" She hesitates, and then I see her start to shake. She steps toward the headstone, away from me.

"Mom."

"He started getting up to pray for her in the middle of the night," Mom whispers. She turns back to me, and presses her hand over her mouth. "He told me that he had to go to her room, to lay hands on her—he had to try to drive the demons out."

Now, Mom's eyes are wild, and by the time she finishes speaking, her voice is high and strained. We are only beginning to understand the immensity of this thing we have missed, but the guilt hits me immediately, and I know it's risen for Mom, too. Annie is *right there* with us—the third member of this triad. She is the missing piece of our family, and we finally understand her...but it's come far too late for us to ever be whole.

"Oh God." Mom dissolves before me, but I will not comfort her. My mother needs this pain—she has avoided it for twenty years. I watch as Mom falls to her knees in front of Annie's headstone, and then she turns and crawls toward it, pressing her face into the cold stone as she wails. I sit behind her on the fresh earth, and we are both sobbing in the darkness for what might have been, and for all the ways that we let our Annie down.

Several hours later, the text comes from Sam.

Are you okay?

Mom and I are sitting on opposite sides of the grave by the time he messages me. We talked quietly for a while, then we ran out of words, and have been sitting in silence. It's so cold that I've been trembling for hours, but whenever I felt the urge to retreat to warmth, I remember that Annie is cold, too. And so we stay.

But after I read Sam's text, I whisper to Mom, "We need to go home."

Mom doesn't say a word as we walk back to the car, and although her sobs have settled, I can hear how tight her chest is from the cold, and how congested her sinuses are from the crying. I feel like I have a nasty case of tonsillitis—my throat is sore from the sobbing, from the yelling, from the tension of it all.

And yet even in all of this, there is something of closure. I didn't expect it, but now that Annie's secret is out in the open, I feel like all that is left are memories of love and regret, and a promise to Annie.

I'll do better for her daughter.

One day, when the time comes for me to tell Daisy about her

mother, I will say in earnest that Annie was a troubled woman who was abused and beaten by life. I can tell Daisy that her mother never got the help that she needed or deserved, and that a system that only wanted to protect Daisy managed to drive her mother to the brink.

I can tell Daisy that it's brutally unfair and wrong, but that at least on some level, the story of Annie's life makes sense.

When we get home, Mom immediately walks to her room. Sam is sitting on the couch, Daisy sound asleep in his arms.

"I guess you talked to her?" he whispers, and I nod, and I release an exhausted sob.

"I feel like I can breathe again," I whisper back, and then I start to cry all over again. I take Daisy into my arms. In her sleeping face, I see all that's left of my sister.

"Come on, sweetheart," Sam says gently. "Let's go to bed."

"There's something we have to do first."

We walk up the stairs, and I crawl onto the bed with Daisy still in my arms. Sam has read my mind somehow—he walks to my side of the bed, withdraws the journal and then passes it to me. I open it to the final pages.

"Will you read her last note with me, Sam?"

"Of course I will," he says.

"Good," I whisper. "Because I really don't think I could do it without you."

40

ANNIE

Dear Lexie,

I have been agonizing over how I could possibly give my daughter the life that she deserves. I have such high hopes for that beautiful girl. I want her to have the life that we would have had if Dad hadn't died, and I just realized today that I can't do that. At least, not right now.

But you and Sam can. I came to your house today—I know you will be mad about that, and I'm really sorry, but I just wanted to see her so badly. At my core, Lexie, I'm a selfish, impulsive person. I wanted her, and I went to her, even though I knew it was the wrong thing to do.

But I'm glad I went, because I saw you two through the window and I saw the love you have for my daughter. It was written all over your faces, plain as day. That's when I knew what I had to do.

At the moment, I'm not a good mother for Daisy—but I want to be, and I think I can be. I'm going to go to the police station this afternoon after I mail this and I'm going to plead guilty when my case goes to court. It's the responsible thing to do—the honest thing. It's hard, and somehow I have to find the courage to silence the voice inside that's trying to convince me to keep running...but I'm going to find a way to do it.

I know that our lives have been one huge mess, Lex. I know that I have brought you so much pain over all these years. You have been a wonderful sister—a wonderful mother to me in so many ways, and I'm only sorry that I haven't been able to repay you by being someone better than I have been.

That's why I'm sending you this journal today. I want you to read this, and I want to talk to you about it—all of it. These truths are my apology to you and a token of my gratitude. You have been so faithful to me—so patient with me. The only thing I can do in return is show you how determined I am to do better. I hope these words are proof of that.

I live my life in the past, in my pain and my rage and my hate. But I have to take responsibility for every aspect of where I am now, and one way I can do that is to take a risk and expose the dark parts of my history. I promise you, Lexie. I'm finally ready to work toward healing and wholeness.

So—this is goodbye, but only for now. Please don't bring Daisy to visit me in prison, and I promise you I won't come to you when I get out—not until I'm standing on my own two feet in a home I can be proud of and with a job that I can use to support myself and to start to pay you back.

You should plan to have Daisy for a long time, Lexie—I'm so sorry for the burden. She is a very lucky girl, and I know you'll take better care of her than I can. She will know you as her mother, and she will probably call you Mom—I'm okay with that, she needs a mom. I have no intention of disrupting the life that you and Sam make for her, not unless the day comes when you and she both want to incorporate me into it.

Please know that I appreciate you. Please know that I love you. Please know that your patient love for me all of these years has been the one thing that has kept me going, and now I know it will nurture my precious baby.

And Lexie—please always tell Daisy that even if I'm not there with her yet, I love her more than anything else in this world.

Love always,

Annie.

41

LEXIE

I roll onto my side and stare at Daisy, and I see Sam mirror my posture. Our gazes lock over the baby. Tears run down my cheeks.

We reach for each other, our hands meeting above Daisy's belly. He wraps his fingers through mine and rests them gently over her—our hands entwined, just as our lives will be. Together, we will be a shield to protect her. Together, we will be a family to nurture her.

We talk in private whispers, and our conversation winds all over the place. I cry a lot as I talk about things that I haven't dared to even think about in decades. I talk because I understand now that secrets can poison a person, and I talk because vulnerability can make a person strong, and I *want* to be strong. I talk about Dad. I talk about Winterton. I talk about Annie, and all of the times I shared with her that were good, and all of the times that she made me proud. And when I finally fall asleep, I'm thinking of those good times, and for the first time since her death, I have found a way to smile when I remember her.

I don't fall asleep until nearly 3:00 a.m., so the movement outside my bedroom door at 4:30 a.m. is exceedingly unwelcome.

I drag myself out of bed and open my door to find my mother and her bags on the other side. Her face is puffy, her eyes are beet red, but her jaw is stubbornly set. I stare at her in disbelief.

"Tell me you're not catching that plane."

"I have to."

I silently lead the way down the stairs into the kitchen. Mom follows me, and when she joins me in the room, I close the door behind her—because I'm going to scream, and I don't want to wake Sam or Daisy.

"How can you even consider—"

"I have to go back." Mom says the words with force, and I laugh hysterically.

"Is there *anything* that he could do that would force you to realize how evil he is?"

Mom looks at me, stricken.

"How could you think I'd go back to *him*? I'm going back to the elders—there are other children there, other teenagers—he needs to be brought to justice. What he did to my Annie—" Mom's voice wavers, and I realize that I've misinterpreted her decision—and now I'm stricken, too. We stare at each other across the table, and Mom leans in to stare right into my eyes.

"He will *not* have any control over my family ever again. I promise you, Lexie. I can't make it right—but I can make sure the whole community knows what he did. I know there's not much we can do to have him charged, but maybe once I tell them, the elders will ask him to leave." I grimace, because we both know the elders in Winterton tend to protect their own. Mom shrugs at me. "But even if they don't, I can make damned sure every woman and child in that town knows that he's a dangerous, evil man."

"And once you've done that?" I ask hesitantly.

Mom swallows heavily, and then she whispers, "I'll figure it out when the time comes."

"Mom, you are always welcome here," I say, and then I raise my chin. "Maybe you're even needed here."

Mom's eyes fill with tears, and she walks briskly around the table and wraps her arms around me. We are almost the same height, but she holds both hands hard against the back of my skull, pressing her cheek against my hair. I feel the jerking movements of her sobs, and I return her embrace.

"I have to go," she chokes. "I already called the cab, and I can't miss that plane."

"Okay, Mom," I say, and we release each other, slowly and reluctantly. I pull my coat on and walk her outside, where we wait in silence. When the cab pulls up to the curb, she turns to embrace me for one last hug.

This embrace is one that Mom and I have not shared since before Dad's death. This hug is different from any of the others. Neither one of us is tense—we are both soft, and open to each other. Something has been righted in our relationship.

Something has healed.

"I'm really proud of you," I whisper into her ear.

"And I have *always* been proud of you. And wherever he is—wherever they are together—your dad and Annie are proud of you, too."

Once Mom has left, I return to my warm bed and to the solace of Sam's arms. As I fall back to sleep, a memory of Annie surfaces. It's the wildly imaginative Annie—the girl who could do anything she set her mind to—the girl who was innocent and undamaged by life. The vision looks a lot like Daisy, and as I drift off to sleep, I make my sister one last promise.

I'll find a way to give her daughter the life that she deserved.

EPILOGUE

Dear Annie,

I missed you today—even more than I miss you every other day. I married Sam today, and it was the happiest day of my life. It's taken us a bit longer to reach this milestone than we'd expected. We've been so focused on Daisy that time just ran away from us.

But the day finally came, and it was almost everything I'd hoped for. Daisy walked down the aisle in front of me in her little purple dress, and she carried a basket of purple-and-white agapanthus petals. What looked so poetic in my head didn't work in practice... Daisy kept laughing and twirling and the petals went everywhere except where they were supposed to. What was left was one hysterically amused not-quite-three-year-old and a crowd of onlookers who laughed right on with her until some of them cried. I was supposed to follow close behind her, but I got so caught up in watching the sheer magic of Daisy Nell Vidler in that moment that I missed my cue and then had to sprint down the aisle to make it to Sam before the song finished.

You should have seen her, Annie, and I really mean that—you should have. There was a gaping hole in that ceremony today where you should have been. I love Daisy, I love my family and I love my life—but I need to tell you that Daisy and I will always, always feel your absence. It is the but at the end of every sentence in our lives...today was a great day, but Annie should have been there. Christmas was wonderful, but Annie should have been there. I feel so happy, but Annie should be here. Daisy is my daughter now, but Annie should be here.

She is so like you, Annie—right from the blond hair to her blue eyes and especially her huge personality. She's full of life and innocence, and every boundary we set for her she questions—not in a mischievous way, but with a sense of magnificent curiosity. Sam and I spend half of our lives explaining "why" to her about every little thing, because until Daisy really understands the reasons why she must or mustn't do something, she never rests.

I want you to know that she is okay. We have photos of you everywhere, and she knows you are her mommy and that you love her and you're watching over her with her granddad. Daisy has just naturally started calling Sam "Daddy" and she calls me "Mom," but you are and will always be Mommy, and we talk to you every night before she goes to sleep. She is meeting all of her milestones, and well... Sam is half-convinced she's some kind of genius and he loves to boast to everyone we meet about how bright she is. Genius or not, time will tell—but one thing is for sure, she is the light of our lives.

She's with Mom tonight because Sam and I are in California for a few days for a short honeymoon. We couldn't bring ourselves to leave her any longer than that, although I do know she would have been just fine—she is Mom's world. Mom lives in our guest-

house and she cares for Daisy while Sam and I are at work, and you know, Annie—these days, Mom is just like I remember she was back before Dad died. Her hands are full because of the way she's thrown herself into caring for us all, but the best part of that is, her heart is full, too.

And things are about to get even better, because in the spring, Daisy is going to be a big sister. It's far too soon to know for sure, but I really think it's a girl. Life has a way of bringing the good things full circle. I think that's why I'm so sure our daughters will be the very best of friends, just as we once were.

Before I go, there is one last thing I need you to know, and it's about Robert. When Mom realized what he did to you, she went right back to Winterton and she told the elders. People wouldn't listen to her at first, but she made such a fuss that soon enough they had to, and eventually several other girls came forward. None of their stories were as awful as yours, Annie...but they were awful enough that he was withdrawn from and then someone actually called the police. From there, things moved as they should have all along.

Robert is in prison now, and in a roundabout way, you did that. It happened too late for you to see it, but your story brought justice to those other girls and even freedom to Mom—who is finally out from under his shadow...she has finally found her own voice.

Those words that you gifted me changed the world for us. I wish with every part of my heart that you were here to see it.
I love you, baby sister. Be at peace, and be free,
Lexie.

★ ★ ★ ★ ★

A Note from the Author

I was blessed to grow up in a large, loud family bursting with aunts and uncles of many different shapes, sizes and personalities. They played an important role in my childhood, each one of them bringing some different, special aspect to my life. My father's brother, my uncle Greg, was much younger than the others—and he was different. He was less a parental figure, more a celebrity to me in some way I couldn't really understand at the time. Uncle Greg told the most amazing stories—his life seemed so full of drama and intrigue and adventure that I was constantly in awe of him.

It took me a very long time to realize that there was a dark side to my uncle. When I was in my early teens, he disappeared from my life when an addiction completely overtook him. Years passed, but then when my grandmother was dying, my father reconciled briefly with Uncle Greg. Less than a week later, before I could have the reunion with him that I'd dreamed of for years, Uncle Greg died of an overdose.

I often get asked if aspects of my books are autobiographical, and the answer is always a firm "no." But I do love to use my research as a way to understand the issues that bewilder me. For this very reason, I've wanted to write about addiction for some time. Annie is not my uncle, but I hope that in reading her story, the love I had for him is evident. Most of all, I hope that her story reminds you that a person with an addiction is not a label or a problem to be solved: the individual is someone's sibling, someone's child, someone's beloved uncle. Addiction is ugly, but its victims each have a story and a life that matters.

When I first read that some US states had made substance abuse in pregnancy a criminal offense, I delved into the issue, simply wanting to understand it. Even after months of research and speaking to advocates in the field, I'm still bewildered by how anyone could think this is an effective way to address any aspect of the issues surrounding substance abuse. The very existence of these laws disregards all advice from medical and women's rights organizations, and when they are enforced, they are incredibly harmful to the health of women and families.

Prosecuting pregnant women who are battling substance abuse issues achieves little more than to further stigmatize and isolate this marginalized pocket of society. When we discourage these women from accessing medical care and support, a situation that is already difficult becomes heartbreaking. And when mothers who need treatment and support to enable them to parent their children are, instead, prosecuted and even incarcerated, the entire community suffers.

It's my hope that Annie and Lexie's situation can raise at least some awareness of the issues around addiction, but also, awareness of what happens to mothers and to children when we deem the *symptom* of an illness—substance abuse—a criminal offense.

In a compassionate society, there *has* to be a better way.

Kelly Rimmer

Questions for Book Club Discussion

1. Which of the two sisters did you relate to most, Lexie or Annie? Were there any characters in the story you didn't like?

2. The story deals extensively with Annie's addiction and the consequences of it for her personally, as well as for her sister and daughter. Did you feel this was a realistic portrayal?

3. Did the story challenge your perspective on addiction in any way? How do you see things differently?

4. Over the lifetime of her relationship with Annie, Lexie makes countless decisions to try to help her sister. Would you have made the same decisions? Where is the line between supporting and enabling?

5. Do you think addicts are entirely responsible for their addiction? What role, if any, does childhood trauma such as Annie's play?

6. How did you feel Luke's role helped or hindered Annie's recovery? Did you see him as a positive or negative influence?

7. The laws referenced through the novel are enforced in a number of US states. How do you feel about the criminalization of substance abuse in pregnancy? Were you aware of these laws before reading *Before I Let You Go*?

8. Do you think the author dealt with such a contentious issue in a balanced way?

9. Which scene in *Before I Let You Go* affected you the most, and why?

10. If you have siblings, did this story make you think about your own relationship with them? What stood out for you in terms of how we deal with family issues?

11. Robert is generally made out to be a violent man, and yet throughout Annie's adult life he helped try to get her well. How do you reconcile the two sides to his character?

12. Were you satisfied with the ending? Did the story end as you expected or did you envision a different resolution for the sisters? Do you think Annie's outcome was inevitable?

13. Who would you recommend *Before I Let You Go* to?